1

HOWARD AIR FORCE BASE, PANAM

March 1997

The UH-1 Huey's blades beat the heavy blanket of humid night air like an old conga drum, shaking the palm trees lining the grassy strip in the rotor wash as the chopper descended.

The lone passenger, Juan Cabrillo, stood braced in the open doorway, taking it all in. His tattered tropical shirt and shoulder-length hair danced in the swirling vortex of air racing through the cabin. His theatrical sense craved Wagner's "The Flight of the Valkyries" blasting over a pair of loudspeakers as the Vietnam-era helicopter swooped into a near-emergency landing. But he wasn't in charge of this rodeo.

As soon as the skids hit the wet tarmac, Cabrillo bolted out the door with a splash of his Birkenstock sandals and bent his tall frame over as the chopper roared away. He dashed toward the nearest Quonset hut, one of three occupied by the local CIA station. There was no time to lose.

Langston Overholt IV, his CIA handler, hovered over a table studying a military map and an open dossier folder. Cigarette smoke clouded the room. He glanced up as his best non-official cover (NOC) bolted into the room.

"Juan, my boy." He extended his hand. "Glad you made it."

Though forty years his senior, Overholt's long patrician fingers still gripped like a bench vise. The elder spook carried the air of a well-mannered English squire. Not a bead of sweat could be found on him despite the suffocating humidity. His moisture-wicking nylon shirt and slacks looked freshly pressed. A Colt .45 in a well-worn leather holster perched on his hip.

Few knew Overholt had been recruited by Allen Dulles personally. Fewer still knew of his wet-work exploits carried out behind the Iron Curtain.

"You said the clock's ticking." Cabrillo nodded at a pallet of tarped gear in the corner. "That my kit?"

"Everything you asked for." Overholt's eyes narrowed. He noticed Cabrillo's brow glistening with sweat. "You feeling okay?"

"Never better. It's a sauna out there." Juan wiped his forehead with the back of his wrist. "Gimme one of those," he said, nodding at the pack of Camels on the table next to the open dossier.

In truth, a bad case of malaria was racking Juan's swimmer's physique. He'd been popping quinine pills like Pez candies for the last forty-eight hours. The worst of the symptoms had passed, but a raging migraine pounded inside his skull.

Overholt tossed him the pack and Juan fished one out as Overholt fired up his Zippo. Cabrillo took a long pull, filling his lungs with as much nicotine as he could—anything to help cut through the headache.

Overholt eyed him again.

"That him?" Juan said as he pushed past his mentor and over to the dossier. A dozen telephoto pictures and a half page of handwritten notes in English and Spanish were all that filled the file marked "Vladimir Suárez, aka Zhukov."

"What's with the Russian general's name?" Cabrillo asked.

"FARC guerrillas love their romantic noms de guerre."

"Must be a real sweetheart. I don't normally associate FARC killers with romance."

Cabrillo studied Suárez's photos. He noted the cunning eyes, haughty smile, and arrogant posture. It was almost as if he knew he was being photographed secretly and was posing for effect.

CLIVE CUSSLER'S
QUANTUM TEMPEST

TITLES BY CLIVE CUSSLER

DIRK PITT ADVENTURES*

Clive Cussler's The Corsican Shadow (by Dirk Cussler)

Clive Cussler's The Devil's Sea (by Dirk Cussler)

Celtic Empire (with Dirk Cussler)

Odessa Sea (with Dirk Cussler)

Havana Storm (with Dirk Cussler)

Poseidon's Arrow (with Dirk Cussler)

Crescent Dawn (with Dirk Cussler)

Arctic Drift (with Dirk Cussler)

Treasure of Khan (with Dirk Cussler)

Black Wind (with Dirk Cussler)

Trojan Odyssey

Valhalla Rising

Atlantis Found

Flood Tide

Shock Wave

Inca Gold

Sahara

Dragon

Treasure

Cyclops

Deep Six

Pacific Vortex!

Night Probe!

Vixen 03

Raise the Titanic!

Iceberg

The Mediterranean Caper

SAM AND REMI FARGO ADVENTURES*

Wrath of Poseidon (with Robin Burcell)

The Oracle (with Robin Burcell)

The Gray Ghost (with Robin Burcell)

The Romanov Ransom (with Robin Burcell)

Pirate (with Robin Burcell)

The Solomon Curse (with Russell Blake)

The Eye of Heaven (with Russell Blake)

The Mayan Secrets (with Thomas Perry)

The Tombs (with Thomas Perry)

The Kingdom (with Grant Blackwood)

Lost Empire (with Grant Blackwood)

Spartan Gold (with Grant Blackwood)

ISAAC BELL ADVENTURES*

Clive Cussler's The Iron Storm (by Jack Du Brul)

Clive Cussler's The Heist (by Jack Du Brul)

Clive Cussler's The Sea Wolves (by Jack Du Brul)

The Saboteurs (with Jack Du Brul)

The Titanic Secret (with Jack Du Brul)

The Cutthroat (with Justin Scott)

The Gangster (with Justin Scott)

The Assassin (with Justin Scott)

The Bootlegger (with Justin Scott)

The Striker (with Justin Scott)

The Thief (with Justin Scott)

The Race (with Justin Scott)

The Spy (with Justin Scott)

The Wrecker (with Justin Scott)

The Chase

KURT AUSTIN ADVENTURES*

NOVELS FROM THE NUMA FILES®

Clive Cussler's Desolation Code (by Graham Brown)

Clive Cussler's Condor's Fury (by Graham Brown)

Clive Cussler's Dark Vector (by Graham Brown)

Fast Ice (with Graham Brown)

Journey of the Pharaohs (with Graham Brown)

Sea of Greed (with Graham Brown)

The Rising Sea (with Graham Brown)

Nighthawk (with Graham Brown)

The Pharaoh's Secret (with Graham Brown)

Ghost Ship (with Graham Brown)

Zero Hour (with Graham Brown)

The Storm (with Graham Brown)

Devil's Gate (with Graham Brown)

Medusa (with Paul Kemprecos)

The Navigator (with Paul Kemprecos)

Polar Shift (with Paul Kemprecos)

Lost City (with Paul Kemprecos)

White Death (with Paul Kemprecos)

Fire Ice (with Paul Kemprecos)

Blue Gold (with Paul Kemprecos)

Serpent (with Paul Kemprecos)

OREGON FILES*

Clive Cussler's Quantum Tempest (by Mike Maden)

Clive Cussler's Ghost Soldier (by Mike Maden)

Clive Cussler's Fire Strike (by Mike Maden)

Clive Cussler's Hellburner (by Mike Maden)

Marauder (with Boyd Morrison)

Final Option (with Boyd Morrison)

Shadow Tyrants (with Boyd Morrison)

Typhoon Fury (with Boyd Morrison)

The Emperor's Revenge (with Boyd Morrison)

Piranha (with Boyd Morrison)

Mirage (with Jack Du Brul)

The Jungle (with Jack Du Brul)

The Silent Sea (with Jack Du Brul)

Corsair (with Jack Du Brul)

Plague Ship (with Jack Du Brul)

Skeleton Coast (with Jack Du Brul)

Dark Watch (with Jack Du Brul)

Sacred Stone (with Craig Dirgo)

Golden Buddha (with Craig Dirgo)

NON-FICTION

Built for Adventure: The Classic Automobiles of Clive Cussler and Dirk Pitt

Built to Thrill: More Classic Automobiles from Clive Cussler and Dirk Pitt

The Sea Hunters (with Craig Dirgo)

The Sea Hunters II (with Craig Dirgo)

Clive Cussler and Dirk Pitt Revealed (with Craig Dirgo)

CHILDREN'S BOOKS

The Adventures of Vin Fiz

The Adventures of Hotsy Totsy

CLIVE CUSSLER'S
QUANTUM TEMPEST

MIKE MADEN

MICHAEL JOSEPH

PENGUIN MICHAEL JOSEPH

UK | USA | Canada | Ireland | Australia
India | New Zealand | South Africa

Penguin Michael Joseph is part of the Penguin Random House group of companies
whose addresses can be found at global.penguinrandomhouse.com

Penguin Random House UK,
One Embassy Gardens, 8 Viaduct Gardens, London SW11 7BW

penguin.co.uk

Penguin
Random House
UK

First published in the United States of America by G. P. Putnam's Sons,
an imprint of Penguin Random House LLC 2025
First published in Great Britain by Penguin Michael Joseph 2025
002

Printed and bound in Great Britain by Clays Ltd, Elcograf S.p.A.

The authorized representative in the EEA is Penguin Random House Ireland,
Morrison Chambers, 32 Nassau Street, Dublin D02 YH68

A CIP catalogue record for this book is available from the British Library

HARDBACK ISBN: 978–0–241–74225–9
TRADE PAPERBACK ISBN: 978–0–241–74227–3

Penguin Random House is committed to a sustainable future
for our business, our readers and our planet. This book is made from
Forest Stewardship Council® certified paper.

CAST OF CHARACTERS

THE CORPORATION

Juan Cabrillo—Chairman, and captain of the *Oregon*. Former CIA, non-official cover.

Max Hanley—President, Juan's second-in-command and the *Oregon*'s chief engineer. Former U.S. Navy swift boat captain.

Linda Ross—Vice President, Operations. Retired U.S. Navy intelligence officer.

Eddie Seng—Director, Shore Operations. Former CIA agent.

Franklin "Linc" Lincoln—Operations. Former U.S. Navy SEAL sniper.

Marion MacDougal "MacD" Lawless—Operations. Former U.S. Army Ranger.

Raven Malloy—Operations. Former U.S. Army Military Police investigator.

Eric Stone—Chief helmsman on the *Oregon*. Former U.S. Navy officer, weapons research and development.

Dr. Mark "Murph" Murphy—Chief weapons officer on the *Oregon*. Former civilian weapons designer.

Russ Kefauver—Intelligence analyst. Former CIA forensic accountant.

Dr. Eric Littleton—Director of the *Oregon*'s biophysical laboratory. Former WMD inspector, U.S. Army 20th CBRNE Command.

George "Gomez" Adams—Helicopter pilot, chief aerial drone operator on the Oregon. Former pilot U.S. Army 160th Special Operations Aviation Regiment (Airborne) "Night Stalkers."

Hali Kasim—Chief communications officer on the *Oregon*.

Dr. Julia Huxley—Chief medical officer on the *Oregon*. Former U.S. Navy veteran.

Kevin Nixon—Chief of the *Oregon*'s Magic Shop.

Maurice—Chief steward on the *Oregon*. Former British Royal Navy.

Arnie Davis—Backup contractor tilt-rotor pilot/copilot. Former pilot U.S. Air Force 20th Special Operations Squadron.

UNITED STATES

Langston Overholt IV—CIA liaison to the *Oregon*.

REPUBLIC OF COLOMBIA

Amador Fierro—Head of La Liga
Rafael Vargas—La Liga
Vladimir Suárez—FARC assassin
Emilio Cabral—Agente Especial Colombian DAS

REPUBLIC OF EL SALVADOR

Rómulo Olmedo—President of El Salvador
Oscar Tamacas—MS-13/La Liga

PEOPLE'S REPUBLIC OF CHINA

Peng De—Ministry of State Security
Linlin Zhang—Ministry of State Security
Colonel Shi Chang—Ministry of State Security

Agent Tu—Ministry of State Security
Senior Captain Zhao Meili—Captain of the *Fuzhou*

PROJECT Q

Reginald Stokes—Captain of the *Baktun*
Dr. Anima Bose—Project Q lead scientist

THE GUARDIANS

Dr. D'Arcy Falconer—the Nexus
Dr. Jagadeesh Gowda
Emily Nighswonger
Aidan Scally

OTHER

Kaarel Varik—Eidolon
Dr. Noam Peretz
Dr. James "Jimmy" Heiskell

All warfare is based on deception.

—SUN TZU, *THE ART OF WAR*

Cabrillo was all too familiar with FARC, the Spanish acronym for the Revolutionary Armed Forces of Colombia. It was the largest and most violent rebel group in the world, spreading Marxist-Leninist ideology throughout Latin America and beyond. Colombia, a nominal American ally, was on the verge of collapse beneath the weight of FARC's ruthless leadership and unrestrained violence. The Colombian Army was mostly busy chasing its tail while taking big casualties trying to subdue a well-trained, highly disciplined, and deadly foe.

"Sweetheart, indeed," Overholt said. "He's FARC's number one assassin and his infamous claim is that he's never failed a mission. The man's more elusive than a jungle jaguar and more venomous than a poison dart frog. Thanks to an anonymous tip, we know where he's currently located—here." Overholt touched a point on the map with his index finger. "But only for the next six hours."

Juan studied the location, paying special attention to the topography.

"At which point he departs for his next mission, according to your message. Any idea what it is?"

"Nothing concrete. But it's somewhat disconcerting that the bigwigs of the Inter-American Drug Abuse Control Commission are meeting the day after tomorrow in Ecuador. That's a perfect target for FARC, since the vast majority of their revenue derives from the drug trade."

"He's smack-dab in the middle of the badlands, where the Colombians can't reach him."

"And the nearest SEAL snatch team is eighteen hours away on another deployment."

"That's why you called me."

"If he gets away, it could prove disastrous. We only have that narrow six-hour window to capture him."

Juan mopped more fevered sweat off his face with his hand. "Why not take him out?"

"His capture would prove superlatively useful in dismantling FARC networks around the region. His corpse wouldn't be nearly as informative."

Juan tossed the cigarette to the ground and crushed it beneath his sandal. "So let's go get him."

Overholt fought back a grin. He'd first met young Juan as a brush-cut, bleached-blond, blue-eyed surfer boy in a polyester ROTC uniform at Caltech just a few years back.

Now look at him. Eager for the hunt.

Born and bred on the beaches of Southern California, Cabrillo had the powerful, broad-shouldered, wide-chested build of an Olympic swimmer and a dancer's natural grace. But it was his artistry on the shortboard and high waves that held everyone in awe. To the casual observer, the young man could've been written off as just another rock-jawed, carefree surf rat with sand between his toes.

Overholt instantly detected a first-rate intellect behind the mischievous smile and recruited him.

Cabrillo eagerly embraced CIA service as the top-tier opportunity to serve his country and deploy his considerable talents. His linguistic skills were off the charts, and his brief flirtation with dramatic theater all proved invaluable as an undercover field agent. His sangfroid courage was second to none, and he handled small weapons as if they were mere extensions of his preternaturally powerful hands.

But it was Cabrillo's innate ability to improvise—what Overholt called his "superpower"—that made the much younger man a prodigy in spycraft. He had proven his gift yet again when he proposed a solution for tonight's mission. It was daring, unconventional, and risky beyond measure.

And the only shot they had.

Cabrillo currently posed as a surf bum and petty drug dealer on the beaches of Tola, Nicaragua—one of the hottest new spots on the world surfing circuit. The Sandinistas found renting longboards to rich German tourists far more profitable than socialism and quite a bit more fun.

Cabrillo's CIA-fake fiancée, Gretchen, taught him how to hand-paint his long golden hair in the balayage technique with dark brown dye in order to camouflage it. It gave the effect of the blond hair mimicking sun-lightened streaks in naturally dark hair and required little maintenance.

Cabrillo was fully Hispanic on his father's side, but inherited his mother's Nordic features. Blond hair and blue eyes were not uncommon in Latin America owing to the extensive European migration of the nineteenth and twentieth centuries. But blond hair still attracted too much attention in this part of the world, a potential buzzkill for an undercover agent seeking anonymity in order to survive.

Cabrillo hated wearing contacts, so he didn't. Besides, his blue eyes were lady-killers and proved useful in that regard on more than one occasion. His physical appearance perfectly fit his cover story, and his faultless *acento mexicano* passed every sniff test by the local criminals and foreign elements he mixed with as he hoovered up intel on international terrorists and gangs.

"Weather?"

"Latest meteorological reports show favorable conditions, including wind speed. Rain moved out an hour ago."

"Check. Do we have eyes on him now?"

"Negative."

"Why not?" Juan glanced at the map one more time.

"Too dangerous. Any other questions?"

"When do we blow this popsicle stand?"

"The C-130 Hercules you requested is fueled and ready to go on the far side of the base."

Overholt checked his watch. "A Jeep will be here momentarily."

Just then, brakes squealed outside and a horn tapped twice.

Juan grinned, unsurprised by Overholt's precision.

"Grab your gear," Overholt said. "I'll be riding shotgun."

"Still don't trust me?"

"Just watching your six, boyo."

"Perfect." Juan crossed over to the pallet and snatched up his gear, including an oil-slicked Uzi submachine gun he slung around his neck and a pair of oversize packs. He slipped the heaviest one over his shoulders.

"If a FARC rebel doesn't shoot you, or an Indigenous warrior doesn't spear you, a jittery Colombian Army patrol may well take aim. And that's assuming Suárez doesn't put a round through your skull at a thousand yards. So keep your head on a swivel down there."

"Just the way you trained me."

A bead of sweat formed on the end of Cabrillo's nose. He wiped it away with a pinch, trying not to think of the migraine crushing his skull.

"Let's roll."

2

SOUTHERN COLOMBIA

Cabrillo leaped out of the Hercules and into the starry void. He plunged through the dark with the rush of a mighty wind in his ears for just over a minute before yanking the rip cord, cracking the ram-air chute open with a violent jerk of his harness. His shadowed form was backlit by a bright half-moon. Normally he would have planned a jump for a moonless night, but the clock was ticking.

There was neither the time nor the inclination to clear the mission with a Colombian government infested by FARC-friendly bureaucrats and security officials. The wrong word in the wrong ear could send Suárez flying the coop, or worse, setting up an ambush that would get Cabrillo captured or killed.

His two-hour flight from Panama gave him plenty of time to pull on a wetsuit and Altama jungle boots, slip into his parachute harness, check his weapons and altimeter. Most important of all, he fitted to his chest the special kit he needed to recover Suárez.

Overholt was right about the weather, mostly. It was clear sailing from Panama. However, the weather reports missed the low-hanging fog just a hundred feet above the landing zone. Cabrillo couldn't see a thing down below. Beneath the fog belt were miles of thick jungle canopy. Hitting one of those trees could snap his neck like a twig.

He wished he had access to one of the new GPS devices that were rolling out into the military services, but they were too big and bulky for a person to carry into close-quarters combat. For now he had to trust a laminated Air Force topographical map and the math skills of the twenty-two-year-old junior navigator, who had given him the green light to jump.

Three and a half minutes later his boots punched through the last of the fog and he got his bearings beneath a gauzy sky, the half-moon now veiled behind the clouds above. He had six seconds before impact. Just enough time to catch a glimpse of his dimly lit target—a large, thatched hut, its stilts half-submerged on the banks of a rushing river. A dozen smaller Indigenous huts were located high and dry in the forest behind, connected by a rutted dirt road. The village, such as it was, had been abandoned by the local Indians after FARC attacks drove them away years before. According to Overholt's anonymous source, Suárez was the sole occupant of the remote village and took up residence in the stilted communal river hut.

Cabrillo tugged on the steering lines of his chute, took a deep breath, and aimed for the center of the wide and coffee-colored Caquetá River.

Splash!

With nearly a hundred pounds of gear weighing him down, Cabrillo was plunged a dozen feet beneath the surface. He wrestled his way out of the tangle of cords and the ripstop nylon canopy now enveloping him thanks to the river's current. He finally broke the surface with a sputtering breath.

The noise of his splash wasn't loud enough to wake the dead, but was the kind of commotion that rang like a dinner bell for the hungry crocodilians dozing on the banks. His wetsuit was only a guard against the high-altitude cold and the vampiric leeches and venomous snakes that infested the river. The thin neoprene wouldn't protect him against the 1,200 psi bite of the speckled caimans patrolling the waters.

So far, the plan to land in the river instead of the forest had proven a good one. What Cabrillo hadn't counted on was the speed of the rain-swollen current. Thanks to the Air Force navigator's apparently superlative math skills, Cabrillo had landed upriver as planned. But the swiftly moving river was proving a challenge. His parachute rig pulled him downriver like a billowing sea anchor. In the few struggling moments it took to free himself, he had already closed the downriver distance to the hut by over a hundred yards. If he didn't act quickly, he'd speed past it with no hope of swimming back.

Cabrillo picked a river landing to avoid crashing into the trees, and Suárez's hideaway hut was located on the bank of the jungle river, at least according to the one aerial photo they had. Unfortunately, that photo had been taken during the dry season. The roiling river now rushed past the crude pylons holding up the ancient thatched structure that was now in the river.

Finally freed from his parachute, Cabrillo threw himself into a furious windmill of swim strokes, clawing at the water with all of his strength, though the malarial effects were taking their toll. Adding to his discomfort was the large and heavy pack that he had transferred from his chest to his back. The graceful California swimmer was now a thrashing humpback gasping for air in a race to cross against the fast-moving current and reach the other side.

And he was losing.

But losing wasn't something Juan Cabrillo had much experience with. He dug into his deepest reserves and his years of training in the water. He closed the gap just in time. As he was about to pass the hut's first stilt, he reached out with his nearest hand and grabbed it.

But his grasping fingers slipped as he lay hold of the moss-slicked timber, and the river tore him away.

Cabrillo kicked furiously to angle himself toward the next stilt. He crashed into it and wrapped himself around it with his arms and legs like a rubberized barnacle against the relentless current. He glanced around to get his bearings.

The original plan was to hit the beach beneath the cover of trees, ditch his kit, and make his way inside. But now he was pinned against the slimy pole, and there was no chance he could swim fast enough against the current to reach the bank. Equally problematic, the stilt was too slick to climb the eight or so feet to reach the floor above him, and even if he could reach it, the only egress from beneath was the "honey hole" cut out of the boards some thirty feet away. Worse, his body began shaking from a malarial fever that suddenly reasserted itself.

He was trapped.

★

Cabrillo's only hope was to try and reach the staircase leading up into the hut. Luckily it was farther downstream, about twenty feet away. He took a deep breath and let go of his stilt, knowing full well his heavy pack would pull him under the dark and turbulent water. He angled himself toward the staircase, but a violent eddy in the current yanked him away and it was only by the grace of God he was able to snag one of the rickety stairsteps before he was swept away for good.

Summoning the last ounces of his strength, Cabrillo reached over with his other hand and hauled himself up onto the stairs just above the rushing water. He pulled his holstered pistol and paused a moment, pointing his weapon at the unlit doorway above, listening for footsteps in the event Suárez had been alerted. But the wily FARC assassin hadn't stirred.

A couple of gasping breaths later, Cabrillo stood on wobbly legs and inched his way forward with a two-handed grip on his pistol. He was grateful the ancient lumber didn't creak beneath each faltering step and the roar of the river proved in his favor. His suppressed pistol was loaded with subsonic ammunition to minimize noise. He preferred a heavier-grained and larger-caliber bullet for man-stopping, but this wasn't an assassination assignment. He always had the Uzi, now tightly strapped in a chest rig, to fall back on if it came to that.

Cabrillo reached the side of the entrance, careful to stay clear of the doorway, where his figure would be framed like a picture. He sliced the pie—a quick peek around the corner—but in the dim moonlight all he saw was a dozen empty hammocks. No sight or sound of anybody, including Suárez.

Had somebody alerted him?

Or was the anonymous tip just a bust?

There was no way of knowing. Cabrillo could only assume danger lurked on the far side of the doorway and his job now was to get inside and find out what he could. He slipped inside in a low crouch with his head on a swivel, gun up, and sped along in short, cat-quiet steps across the rough-hewn boards smoothed by years of bare, calloused feet.

The hut was enormous by local standards, a good forty feet long from end to end and twenty feet across. The size made perfect sense, since it was a communal hut serving an entire tribe. The bulk of the structure was open-spaced with axe-cut poles serving as supports and trusses for a high-pitched roof. A few worn blankets served as room dividers on the far side of the hut.

And behind one of those blankets somebody coughed.

Cabrillo checked the rest of the cavernous space with one quick glance, then raced forward in stealthy silence. He gripped the pistol in one hand and gently pulled back the blanket with the other.

A white woman lay on a cot just a foot from the blanket door. Her eyes fluttered open at just that moment, her brain unable to process the unfolding nightmare of Cabrillo's neoprene form looming over her, pistol in hand. She opened her mouth to scream, but Cabrillo fell on her, clasping his free hand across her mouth.

"*Cállate*," Cabrillo growled, hoping to terrorize her into silence long enough to zip-tie and gag her.

But she was having none of it. Her terrified eyes suddenly narrowed with feral ferocity and she kicked at his groin as she reached up to claw his eyes out. Cabrillo had no choice but to drop his weapon on the cot and grip her neck with his empty gun hand while keeping her mouth shut. Her muffled panic rose as his grip crushed against her carotid artery, her eyes widening with terror as she embraced her last dying moment.

Only, it wasn't.

Cabrillo had simply cut off the blood flow to her brain, depriving it of oxygen until she blacked out and slumped harmlessly into the cot.

Cabrillo didn't want to smack her skull with his pistol. Hitting her hard enough to do that was as likely to kill her as stun her and she wasn't on his target list.

Cabrillo snatched up his pistol and listened for any other movements. He thought he heard a floorboard creak and he headed in that direction, both hands on the pistol grip, the long, suppressed barrel leading the way.

Suddenly, an old electric generator shuddered to life on the far wall. Cabrillo spun on his heel toward the rattling noise of the ancient machine powered by a rusted propane tank standing next to it.

It took Cabrillo a heartbeat to take it all in, but that was just enough time to distract him from the weight of Suárez crashing into him from out of the dark.

★

Suárez hit Cabrillo hard in a flying tackle that would have made Dick Butkus proud.

Cabrillo was tossed off his feet, his back hitting the floorboards with a sickening thud. The pack simultaneously softened the blow, but distended his spine like a plumber's pipe bender. Despite the shock of the bone-rattling hit, Cabrillo never lost his grip on the pistol.

Suárez, the larger man, grabbed the suppressor with one hand while crushing Cabrillo's grip on the pistol with the other, trapping Cabrillo's finger inside the trigger guard as he arced the business end of the barrel toward the bottom of Cabrillo's chin.

Cabrillo countered by bridging his powerful legs upward and twisting his torso, using the leverage of the pack to roll both men over. Cabrillo tried to buck Suárez off in the maneuver, but the Colombian killer was straddling him between his vice-gripped thighs and continued pressing his attack.

As the barrel inched toward Cabrillo's face, the terrible geometry of the curved trigger against Juan's trapped index finger finally collided and the pistol barked. The single shot blistered Juan's cheek before plowing into the propane tank with a metallic *spang*. But rather than ricocheting off the tank, the rusting metal gave way to the hot piece of lead, instantly igniting the propane inside. The resulting explosion knocked Suárez off Juan and set the thatched wall and roof near the tank ablaze.

Suárez's violent departure also tore the gun out of Cabrillo's grip. The two men quickly recovered and both scrambled for the pistol some ten feet away.

Surprisingly nimble for his size, Suárez was on top of the weapon before Cabrillo could reach it. But as the Colombian rolled over on his back to put a round through the American's skull, Cabrillo pulled another weapon from his utility—a direct-contact Taser—and jabbed it into Suárez's crotch.

The Colombian screamed and folded in half like a spring-loaded bear trap, his entire body rigid and contorted in pain. His gnarled hand mashed the gun and a round discharged harmlessly away from Cabrillo, who emptied the last of the electric charge into the killer's body.

Amped up on a new adrenaline load, Cabrillo hadn't noticed the hut had entirely filled with choking smoke and half the walls and roof were now engulfed in flames. The searing heat burned the skin on his face. He suddenly remembered the woman behind the blanket in her cot. He turned to fetch her just as a giant flaming beam smashed into the makeshift bedroom, dragging a roaring heap of burning thatch with it.

He started forward, but the heat was unbearable and there was no chance she survived the crashing timber—and no time to mourn her dismal fate. The hut was going up fast. Cabrillo felt like he was standing inside a tiki torch, but he had a job to do.

He grabbed the paralyzed Colombian and dragged him across the long floor to the entrance, as far away from the flames as he could get. He pulled on his hands-free radio headset as he unzipped his pack.

"Phaeton, Phaeton. Do you read me? This is Torpedo."

"We read you five by five, Torpedo." Overholt's voice rang clear on the headset. "What's your status?"

"Ready when you are. What's your ETA?"

Overholt's garbled answer was swallowed in the roar of burning roof timbers crashing onto the weakening floor as the back wall tore away in a heap of embers.

Cabrillo suddenly saw a fleet of speeding headlights slashing through the dark, the beams weaving and jerking on the muddy road in his direction.

So much for Suárez being out here all alone.

The roaring flames ate away at the remaining roof and walls. Cabrillo ignored the cauldron of unbearable heat as he wrestled the groaning Colombian into the body bag and cinched it up like a madman's straight jacket, immobilizing Suárez's limbs, but keeping his head exposed for air.

The headlights squealed to a braking halt outside in a hail of angry shouts. Cabrillo glanced up to see a dozen men with rifles bolting through the headlight beams and splashing into the water.

He grabbed the bagged Colombian and dragged him down the steps in painful thuds, close enough to the water to toss him in and jump in behind him.

Keeping a grip on the bag and holding Suárez's head above the water, Cabrillo pulled the charging handle on the outside of the Skyhook bag. An attached bottle of helium instantly inflated a heavy black balloon that raced into the sky. Seconds later, the air thundered with the roar of four big Allison turboprops as the Hercules raced in on a low-altitude approach above the rushing water.

Suárez startled, screaming curses and shouting, *"Asesino! Asesino! Te mataré!"*

Cabrillo was about to shut him up when the air split with a horrifying scream behind them.

The woman in the hut was still alive.

Cabrillo wanted to puke. He should've tried to get her.

"Nadia! Nadia!" Suárez was manic with terror.

The wire line connecting the balloon to Suárez's bag snapped taut as the balloon reached full altitude three hundred feet above the river and clear of the tree line.

Shattering AK-47 gunfire echoed from the shoreline. Bullet splashes geysered the water around Cabrillo as he spun with Suárez in the swirling current. Cabrillo called out to Overholt.

"We're good to go, Phaeton."

"ETA in ten seconds, my boy."

Cabrillo glanced back at the shore. Some of the trucks were moving again, tracking their progress downriver. In the moonlight Cabrillo caught a glimpse of the truck-mounted heavy machine guns in their beds.

The original plan was for Cabrillo to get Suárez airborne and then he would hike over to the nearby Peruvian border about ten miles away, where a local would guide him to a waiting airplane. But with the arrival of FARC soldiers now tracking him along the shoreline, that plan was in the crapper. They'd cut him down before he could even get out of the river, or worse, snatch him up.

He needed a plan B, and fast.

The Hercules came in like a thunderclap over the tree line, its Y-shaped nose yoke pointed directly at the Skyhook balloon line.

Cabrillo's instincts took over. He grabbed the restraining straps on Suárez's bag and scissored his legs around the assassin in a death grip just as the yoke snagged the cable. The two men rocketed into the sky with a spine-jolting snap. Red tracers from the truck-bed machine guns zipped through the night sky, alternately streaking for the Hercules or its human cargo suspended in the air as AKs flashed from the riverbanks.

The two men whirligigged as the Hercules gained altitude. Cabrillo's guts dumped into the bottom of his boots at the nearly vertical climb. His eyes fixed on the glowing red sparks pouring up from the still-burning hut with each passing spin, wondering if the woman escaped a fiery death.

"Torpedo, status!" Overholt barked over the radio.

"No time to buy a ticket," Cabrillo shouted as he streaked through the sky at over three hundred miles per hour. "Thought I'd hitch a ride." Cabrillo's grip was wrapped through the straps and cemented with another adrenaline surge, but he wondered if he could hold on long enough for Overholt to reel the two of them in.

"We need to stay low," Overholt said. "That means a lot of turbulence. We're pulling you up now. You good?"

"Just peachy. One question."

"What's that?"

"When does a guy get a cup of coffee and a bag of peanuts on this lousy airline?"

3

Present Day

Juan Cabrillo's eyes popped open. He was tangled up in a twisted heap of sweaty sheets on his luxurious king-size bed. His eyes still bleary from a fitful sleep, he stared at the coffered ceiling for a moment as he sought his bearings. The spinning blades of the ceiling fan provided a whisper of cleansing air that finally cleared his mind. He suddenly remembered he was in his cabin.

Cabrillo normally didn't suffer the nightly terrors haunting men who had spent years in desperate close-quarters combat, reliving each harrowing encounter snatching away an opponent's life. He slept well because his conscience was clear. He hated killing and did it only when necessary—and never out of anger or revenge. He had been taught as a child that even a crazed assassin bore the image of his Maker, even if that image was marred and desecrated by evil. Cabrillo was merely the instrument that made the introductions between them and God sooner than the bad guys had planned.

But the Colombian mission was different. He couldn't shake the regret of having failed. He could still smell the charred timbers and feel the searing heat on his skin. But it was the distant screams of the woman trapped in the burning hut still ringing in his ears.

He hadn't thought of her for many years, and why this nightmare had come back to him now, he didn't know. He willed away her keening cries until they finally faded.

Cabrillo checked the analog clock on the mantle. It was early evening. He had taken the overnight shift to give the scheduled crew a much-needed break from their normal routine. The *Oregon* had been on extended duty for some time now. No one complained, and they all did their jobs. But Cabrillo could see the fatigue in their eyes. They needed a break, and the scheduled trip to their private vacation island was still a few days away.

After Cabrillo's overnight shift was completed, he headed to the Olympic-size pool in the ship's converted ballast tank and put in a solid five miles before heading up to his cabin. He had a mountain of paperwork to sort through before he hit the rack and was glad when he finally crawled into bed. Now it felt like a net. Time to get moving.

Cabrillo untangled himself from his silken sheets and sat up. He had showered after his swim, but now he was slick with sweat and needed to rinse off. He pulled up his prosthetic swim leg from the floor and fitted it on before heading to the shower, a custom affair like the rest of his cabin.

Every member of the *Oregon* crew received an allowance for the design of their private quarters, one of the many perks of working for the Corporation. The hard-charging crew spent months away from shore-bound family and friends. Cabrillo rewarded that sacrifice with Cordon Bleu–trained chefs, world-class workout facilities, and luxury quarters.

Cabrillo had chosen for himself an exact replica of Rick's Café Américain from the movie *Casablanca*, his favorite. Every stick of furniture and artwork, from the ceiling fans down to the handwoven Persian carpets on the floor, were period accurate. And all of that was thanks to Kevin Nixon's Magic Shop.

Cabrillo blasted himself with hot water as he lathered up with his favorite soap, then scrubbed away the briny perspiration that clung to him like his troubled dream. He rinsed off by slamming the lever to icy cold to shock his system, a daily war against the temptations of comfort and complacency.

After a quick toweling, he headed for his dressing room and swapped his swim leg for a dressing leg that not only perfectly matched the color and texture of his skin but even featured a spray of his own fine blond hair carefully placed one shaft at a time. Re-legged, he pulled on a pair of linen shorts, a tropical shirt, and a pair of calfskin loafers. Just as the second loafer slipped over his heel, a message rang in the overhead speakers.

"Chairman, do you read me?" Max Hanley asked. He was the number two in the Corporation. Cabrillo and Max were the ones who originally designed and converted the original *Oregon*, a broken-down lumber hauler, into the world's most advanced combat and intelligence-gathering vessel. In the years since, they had brought her through several iterations, including the current one, the best yet.

Max's natural command abilities as a former swift boat captain played an important role in the smooth operation of the *Oregon* in or out of combat when Cabrillo was otherwise unavailable. But the truth of the matter was that Max's first love was engineering, and in particular, the magnetohydrodynamic engines he designed for the *Oregon*.

"Loud and clear," Juan said. "Is there a problem?" It was unlike Max to call down to Cabrillo's cabin in his off-duty hours.

"I need you to come down to the engine room. We've got a situation."

Cabrillo frowned. There were few problems Max Hanley couldn't handle on his own, especially in the engine compartment. Hanley had also recruited a handpicked, highly experienced engineering crew, all former military like most of the *Oregon* personnel. For Max to call him into the mix meant there was something serious going on. And if the engines were down, the *Oregon* was dead in the water. Powered by stripping free electrons from the ocean with powerful supercooled magnets, the *Oregon*'s revolutionary engines not only drove the boat but powered every other electronic component on the vessel including radar, weapons, sick bay, and the Cray supercomputer. He suddenly realized the absence of the low thrum of the purring engines, a minimal but constant background noise on the ship.

"I'm on my way."

★

The polished brass elevator doors slid open. Cabrillo stepped out into the hallway belowdecks, his perfect gait showing no indication of his reliance upon the artificial leg. That perfect gait was a function of both the prosthetic's custom design and years of dedicated physical training. Juan kept physically fit through a wide regimen of weight lifting, wall climbing, and martial arts, but his primary strength and endurance came from countless hours of swimming. He was as fit as any of the younger special operator Gundogs in his command.

Cabrillo passed into the dimly lit corridor and headed for the engine compartment, which was strangely dark. Juan knew his ship like the back of his hand, and no light was needed for him to make his way forward. But his heart began to race at the thought of a catastrophic event disabling the engines and thus the *Oregon*, leaving his beloved ship and crew at the mercy of the pitiless sea and countless enemies.

He stepped carefully over the elevated threshold of the watertight doorway and into the wide, main compartment. A bank of LED lights suddenly exploded in his eyes, blinding him.

"Surprise! Happy birthday!"

Cabrillo nearly pooped his pantaloons at the cacophony of shouts, laughter, and noisemakers. He rubbed his blinded eyes to clear them. Juan couldn't help but laugh as familiar hands clapped him on his shoulders, and cheerful voices wished him well.

"Okay, you guys got me good," Juan said as his eyes began to clear. When he finally blinked them fully open, he laughed again. He couldn't believe what he was seeing.

The expansive room was crowded with pirates, comic book characters, famous scientists, movie legends, and historical figures variously fitted with togas, crowns, antlers, chaps, and chain mail. Each Oscar-worthy costume was perfectly constructed, historically accurate, and anatomically correct. The 3D printed masks were all custom-fitted and utterly lifelike. Cabrillo imagined he was standing in the middle of a studio cafeteria from the golden age of Hollywood.

The crowd of happy well-wishers parted as Maurice emerged pushing a cart carrying a massive white cake with *Happy Birthday!* emblazoned in dark chocolate script, and a single lit candle.

Maurice, the oldest member of the *Oregon* crew, abandoned his normal attire of crisp white shirt and starched black trousers for an Admiral Nelson costume, including a jaunty black ostrich-feathered bicorne hat—a tribute to the steward's former days in the British Royal Navy.

"Congratulations, Captain," Maurice offered in his cultured British accent. He was the only member of the crew that didn't call Cabrillo "Chairman," a habit Cabrillo could neither break nor condemn in the old sailor and his Old World respect for the rank.

Cabrillo glanced around the room and took in all the smiling faces. He'd personally vetted every one of them. Each had stellar records, impeccable credentials and, most important, sterling characters. They had hired on as employees of the Corporation, which meant they were technically mercenaries. But they were all patriotic to the core, and were glad the *Oregon* never took a job that put American lives or interests at risk even if it cost them money. They had served valiantly and loyally through every imaginable hazard and mission. Cabrillo couldn't believe his good fortune.

Time to make a wish and blow out the candle.

But what is there to wish for? He had it all.

Then Linc and Raven came to mind. The two valued crew members were absent, currently in transit for a mission to Panama. They wouldn't check in for another forty-eight hours, but their implanted trackers indicated they were on schedule. What waited for them on the other side was anybody's guess.

Cabrillo made his wish.

He then took a big, theatrical breath, but gently blew out the single birthday candle to a wild round of applause.

The head chef began cutting the cake as her sous-chefs wheeled in carts of ice cream, fresh-baked Austrian pastries, pots of pour-over Cuban coffee, and a variety of adult libations.

"What kind is it?" Cabrillo asked as the chef handed him the first plate.

"Your favorite. White chocolate macadamia nut cheesecake laced with raspberry sauce."

Juan's eyes rolled with ecstasy at the first bite. "Perfecto."

The head chef flushed with pride. "Enjoy."

"Surprised you made it this far," Max offered with a wide grin and a heavy clap on Cabrillo's back with his meaty hand. Hanley was dressed like Friar Tuck. It wasn't much of a reach. His thinning gray-auburn hair was already ringed like a tonsure, and the heavy wool tunic draped over his high, hard belly. And just like Robin Hood's number two, Max was the man Cabrillo wanted with him in any bar fight or gun battle.

"You look gassed. Didn't you grab any shut-eye?" Max asked.

"Snagged a few winks. Shift change."

Max eyed his friend, one hand clutching his fighting staff. He had his suspicions, but kept them to himself.

Cabrillo took another bite of cheesecake. "Who's minding the store?"

"Linda's in the chair. I'll head topside after I grab a plate of goodies and send her down."

"It must kill her not to be at a costume ball like this." Linda Ross, despite her previous life in the buttoned-down U.S. Navy, had a penchant for wild hair colors—currently cotton candy pink.

"Oh, trust me, she got her Pat Benatar on just fine. You'll see later."

Someone tossed on a Gipsy Kings album over the loudspeakers, one of Cabrillo's favorites.

Juan tugged on Max's elbow and pulled him aside.

"This whole thing wasn't your idea, was it?"

"Me? No way. I know you're not crazy about birthday celebrations, let alone surprise parties."

"Then whose idea was it?"

Max nodded toward a Texas Ranger in the far corner, wearing the traditional buckskins and pistols of an early Western lawman.

"Kevin's idea?" Cabrillo asked.

"Yup."

"Huh. Makes sense."

Kevin Nixon had been a renowned Hollywood special effects artist, winning numerous awards, including an Oscar. His department on the *Oregon*, known as the Magic Shop, created the costumes, makeup, and special effects vitally necessary for the undercover work that Juan and other team members carried out.

In addition, Nixon's department helped transform the *Oregon*'s sleek deck lines from a modern bulk cargo carrier into a rusting, derelict hulk in a moment's notice with phony dead flies in the sills, gut-wrenching stench blown through the HVAC ducts, and a hundred other special effects pioneered by his department. It was all deployed to scare away nosy port authorities and added to the perfect camouflage the *Oregon* needed to sneak into ports around the world undercover.

Max's chest swelled with pride as he fingered his monkish vestments. "Makes me want to go to Hollywood after I retire."

"Not a monastery?"

Max laughed. "And on that note, I'm gonna fetch some cake and relieve Linda. See ya in the funny papers, brother." Max's face suddenly saddened. He raised his palm in a small, priestly gesture and whispered something Cabrillo couldn't hear over the music before he turned away and headed for the snack bar.

Just then, a phlegmy voice growled behind Cabrillo.

"*Qu' buSHa'chugh SuvwI', batlhHa' vanghugh, qoj matlhHa'chugh, pagh ghaH SuvwI''e'.*"

Cabrillo turned around.

A pair of tall, lanky Klingon warriors with pronounced cranial ridges spanning their foreheads sneered at him. They carried traditional *mek'leth* short swords with curved blades and serrated edges, and wore metal and leather armor along with thick-soled combat boots that made them seem larger and more imposing than they really were.

"Nice little suits ya got there, boys."

Dr. Mark Murphy's proud shoulders slumped and Eric Stone blushed beneath his heavy olive-colored makeup. Murph was the *Oregon*'s chief weapons officer and one of the youngest members of the crew. He was doubtless the most brilliant, earning two PhDs before the age of twenty-five. Stoney was his best friend, and the *Oregon*'s chief helmsman.

"Thanks, Chairman." Eric flashed a mouth full of sharpened teeth, his voice altered by one of Nixon's patented voice synthesizers. "We just wanted to wish you a happy birthday."

"Was that how the Klingons say it?"

"Actually, Klingons don't wish each other happy birthday," Murphy said. "So I said, 'If a warrior ignores duty, acts dishonorably, or is disloyal, he is nothing.'"

"That's actually way cooler. Thanks."

Murphy and Stone straightened up and beamed proudly, and wished him happy birthday again before marching off toward the pastry bar.

A few minutes later Cabrillo stood alone fetching a cup of coffee. Kevin Nixon sheepishly meandered over, his spurs clinking with each step. He was one of the few *Oregon* crew members that wasn't former military. After his sister was killed in a terrorist attack, he decided to take a stand and left Tinseltown in search of a more significant life. Technically, it found him—a billet on the *Oregon*, deploying his special talents.

"Happy birthday, Chairman," he said, offering his hand.

"Thanks, Kevin. Nice shindig." He glanced around the room still buzzing with party energy. "You went to a lot of trouble to do all of this."

"Just my way of saying thank you," Nixon responded.

"For what? Getting older is like falling off the back of a turnip truck. It kinda happens all by itself."

"I turned fifty last month," Nixon said.

"Quite a milestone."

"I've been reflecting on my time on the *Oregon*. Without a doubt, these have been the best years of my life."

"Not a lot of starlets and after-party shenanigans around here." Cabrillo held up his empty plate. "Though we've got some pretty mean cheesecake."

Nixon blushed. The brilliant special effects artist had worked with some of Hollywood's most famous actors, directors, and executives. They were the beautiful people with all of the money and power and privileges the industry could afford. But none of them had ever impressed Nixon the way Cabrillo did.

"I don't miss any of it. Besides, it almost killed me." He touched his finger to the side of his nose and sucked air through it like a vacuum cleaner, an embarrassed nod toward a prior affection for illicit drugs. Nixon stood tall and trim in front of Cabrillo. In fact, the two men were about the same size. But when Nixon first came on board he was a physical wreck and weighed over three hundred pounds. Dr. Huxley had put him on a strict diet and exercise regimen, literally saving his life.

Cabrillo smiled. "You're a great addition to the crew. Your services have been invaluable."

"I used to be wrapped up in my own career and my own vanity, but the war on terror woke me up. I just didn't know what to do about it. You gave me a place to use my skills. I've seen and done things I never could have imagined, and all in service to my country." Kevin gestured toward the crowded room. "This little 'shindig' was my way to thank you for the opportunity to serve my country and this crew. You've given me a life with purpose—a life worth living."

Cabrillo was moved by Nixon's heartfelt words and saw the deep emotion in his eyes. He knew it took a lot for Nixon to express himself this way.

"Every time you do your thing, you serve this crew and me. That's thanks enough."

Nixon reached out with an awkward hug and whispered in Juan's ear. "You gave me my life back. I can never repay you for that."

"You don't have to."

Kevin stepped back. "I've seen you risk your life for this crew time and time again. Just know that wherever you lead, we'll all follow—even through the fiery gates of hell."

Cabrillo saw the fierce determination in his eyes.

He believed him.

4

Captain Lanxi sat at his cramped desk in his ship's shabby cabin, working on a secret ledger. A dim lamp barely illuminated his scrawl. His final tabulation was worse than he had feared. He set his pencil down and rubbed his tired eyes.

The holds of his shark-harvesting boat were only half full of illicit cargo. Shark fins were an increasingly rare and expensive delicacy that sold for the price of silver in his country. Chinese people were crazy for shark fin soup, which supposedly had medicinal benefits. In truth, the expensive delicacy was primarily a display of ostentatious wealth. His people reveled in such spectacles, none more so than the government overlords, who secretly supported the illegal trade.

Lanxi's operations, strictly speaking, were prohibited according to Chinese law, which had recently issued a moratorium. The international community had been outraged by China's vast fishing fleet destroying stocks of fish around the globe after having depleted her own in the previous decade. In their ruthless efficiency, Chinese vessels harvested protected species on an industrial scale, including the squid and sharks rapidly disappearing in these waters.

But his employer—one of China's largest criminal gangs—was protected by the government they dutifully served. In fact, it was a Chinese government satellite that had located the heat signature of a large school of sharks migrating in these cold waters.

Lanxi's rusty ship with its ancient engines had only just reached the area a few hours ago. He deployed the longlines after his sonar confirmed the sharks' course, depth, speed, and direction. Miles of steel cable with baited hooks now trailed behind him. With any luck, over the next twenty-four hours, those hooks would be filled with freshly caught sharks and reeled in, and his holds filled to capacity. He might yet keep his head attached to his neck and perhaps even pocket a handsome sum of gold if all went according to plan. And if not? He shuddered to think about it.

A sharp rap of knuckles on his door startled him. It was his sturdy Indonesian first officer.

"Captain, come see. Quickly!"

★

Captain Lanxi stood on the exterior bridge wing, his binoculars pinned to his crow-footed eyes. After thirty years at sea, he had seen inexplicable things. It was impossible to live on the vast ocean and not believe in the supernatural.

But this?

Beneath a blanket of stars, an ancient high-sterned pirate junk ablaze with St. Elmo's fire ran broadside in the far distance, its translucent decks festooned with cannons.

Impossible.

"Radar?" Lanxi barked.

"Nothing, sir. No Doppler reflection at all. No AIS. Nothing."

"Radio?"

"No response."

Lanxi lowered his binoculars and glanced down at the deck. His young crew had gathered along the rail, pointing and shouting at the ghostly vessel. The old captain snorted. The men were mostly rural peasants tricked into indentured service on his boat. They were as superstitious as old women. They complained constantly about the lack of food and sleep and were on the verge of mutiny after so many days

at sea away from home without internet or phone connections. The
apparition in the distance was sending them into a panic.

"What do you make of it, Captain? A patrol vessel of some sort?"

Lanxi was concerned. That boat could mean trouble. He had been
plying the waters of the remote eastern Pacific for months, often crossing illegally into the territorial waters of Ecuador and the other bor-
dering nations in search of his elusive prey. Those nations had become
far more aggressive. An Argentine patrol boat had even sunk a Chinese vessel. In order to save face, the Chinese government would sometimes make examples of criminal fishing boats that were caught in the
act, tossing their captains into prison.

"That's no patrol boat," Lanxi growled.

"Then what is it?"

Lanxi leaned over the railing. "You men down there. Back to work.
Now. Or half rations."

Suddenly an explosion of light erupted in the mast wires.

A giant, eyeless woman shrouded in billowing grave clothes stood
high in the rigging, wielding a flaming sword.

His crew saw her, too, along with a dozen fiery minions who suddenly appeared, laughing and cursing them all.

The howling apparition pointed her sword at Lanxi.

"Captain, turn your ship around—now. Or face my wrath."

The young sailors cried out in terror with one voice. "Captain, turn
around!"

Lanxi turned toward the Indonesian. His stern, unflappable face
was pale with terror.

"What do you make of it?" Lanxi asked.

The Indonesian stammered, unable to form a sentence. He was
raised on tales of demons and ghosts just like the rest of the crew.

His first officer's terror unnerved Lanxi. He'd seen the man still
as an iceberg in the middle of a typhoon that nearly swamped
them. But now the surly Indonesian looked like a child about to soil
himself.

Lanxi spat on the deck. Turning around was out of the question.

"Sir, what should we do?" the helmsman cried out from inside the bridge.

"Steady as she goes. We've got shark to catch."

The eyeless demon raised her flaming sword on high.

"Lanxi, time to die!"

Cannons boomed in the distance. All eyes turned toward the pirate junk.

Seconds later, Lanxi's ship rocked beneath an explosion of cascading water that slammed into the rusting steel. His men toppled over like bowling pins. Lanxi grabbed the rail before he crashed to the deck as well.

They had been hit badly. The old captain knew his ship had suffered a fatal blow. She was already beginning to list.

"Give the orders to abandon ship!"

The radioman hit the alarm and Klaxons wailed. The poorly trained crew scrambled for the lifeboats and whatever jackets they could find. Few of the men could swim, and most wouldn't survive—the lifeboats were in disrepair and nearly worthless.

The Indonesian tugged at Lanxi's arm, his hands welded to the railing. The bridge crew had already abandoned their stations and were racing for the lower decks.

The eyeless ghoul and her demon horde laughed above the cries of the crew.

"Captain, let's go. There's no time!"

Lanxi shook his head. "Go."

The Indonesian didn't argue with him. He turned and fled down the steps.

Lanxi would remain on the bridge and go down with his ship, now listing badly.

Whatever fate awaited him below the frigid waves was far better than the unimaginable cruelties his employers would inflict upon him.

5

EL SALVADOR

The Zodiac's electric motors cut off as the fiberglass hull hissed against the sand and the operators exfilled onto the beach. The crashing waves hid what little sound they had made and the dead light from a new moon blanketed their dash across the beach in a crouching run.

Lieutenant Rivas led the way up the narrow rocky trail, his men hot on his boot heels. A second squad signaled in his headset that they had already reached the front of the gate as Rivas and his squad took up their assigned position. He glanced around at the eager young faces in the dark. Their highly decorated unit had been handpicked for this perilous assignment by the battalion commander.

The risk was high, but the honor higher still.

Their mission was more than an assignment. It was a sacred duty to their people and to El Salvador.

Rivas turned to his corporal studying the LCD display of the drone flying high above the compound. Its infrared sensors illuminated the spectral figures of the guards standing watch inside the walls. So far, no surprises.

That was good. The first rounds of mass arrests across the country had sent a shock wave through El Salvador's criminal underworld. But the coordinated Army and police actions had failed to snag all of the gangsters, especially the top brass. Most of the underbosses had fled the country, but those that remained had chosen to weather the storm inside their armed compounds.

The worst gang, informally known as MS-13, was one of the largest international criminal syndicates in the world, and undoubtedly the most violent. They had dominated El Salvador for decades in a campaign of blood and terror that cowed civilians and government officials alike. It was natural for these last-remaining gangsters to assume President Olmedo's recent efforts would soon fade away, and when they did, the bloody retributions would follow.

Olmedo ordered his commanders to stand down. No new police actions had taken place in the past month. The gangster bosses were wary, but confident. Time was on their side.

Or so they thought, Rivas reminded himself. He and his men would prove the butchers wrong tonight.

He checked his watch. It was 02:44. Across El Salvador, another coordinated wave of mass arrests would begin in just one minute. At this time of the night, most people were in the deepest stages of their sleep cycles. If woken, their cognitive skills and response times were highly degraded. The attacks needed to happen simultaneously so gangsters couldn't warn their compatriots across the country.

Unfortunately, the armed figures on top of the wall were not only fully awake but moving toward the front gate. Rivas's orders had been clear. "Prisoners, not corpses," his commander insisted. President Olmedo couldn't wage a campaign of mass assassinations if he truly wanted to bring law and order to his small nation. Olmedo wasn't a gangster and he wouldn't act like one.

Rivas checked his watch again. The digital readout flipped to 02:45 exactly.

It was go time.

Rivas gave the order. His sniper team took out the two guards patrolling the wall just as plastic explosives tore open the front gates. A sergeant next to Rivas secured the grappling hook on the high wall facing the sea, but Rivas was first on the rope and over the top. If there were any deadly surprises on the other side of the wall, he wanted to be the one that faced them. If he was killed, so be it.

His men knew what to do.

★

Rivas marched down the villa's hallways noting the dozens of gangsters lying on the cold Saltillo tiles, their hands zip-tied behind their backs and clothes stripped down to their underwear. Most had succumbed to the flurry of nonlethal flash-bang grenades his men had deployed, as their bloody ears and pained, migrained faces testified. His men had to shout their orders at the *sicarios*, who were temporarily deafened by the blasts.

Nearly all of them bore the garish tattoos denoting their rank and record of crimes. Several wore the facial tattoos that forever separated them from normal members of any civilized society.

One of his medics was bandaging the leg wound of one of the killers and a second was inserting an IV into the arm of another. His team leaders reported seven gangsters shot, three fatally, including the two guards on the wall. Most of the criminals had escaped serious injury. Rivas wondered if that was a good thing. He'd lost an uncle and two cousins to MS-13. But his opinion didn't matter. Tonight his job was to carry out his orders, and his orders were clear:

Prisoners, not corpses.

His soldiers began yanking the unwounded men to their bare feet and herding them down the corridors to the landing zone outside.

Rivas turned into the doorway of a large bedroom. A huge picture window overlooked the starlit ocean and white-crested waves that crashed against the shoreline. The first of the big transport helicopters approached the island, its huge carbon fiber blades thrumming in the warm night air.

He shuddered at the sight of the life-size Santa Muerte standing in a corner. Skeletal "Saint Death" was the patron saint of killers and cutthroats throughout Latin America. Her gruesome niche was backed by a wall of hammered silver and fronted by a turquoise altar of smoldering incense and dead, guttered candles.

The Saint Death skeleton was undoubtedly human, its smoke-stained bones draped in a blood-red robe. A solid gold crown rested on her skull and a silver pentagram was etched into her forehead. The bones of her left hand clutched a Grim Reaper's scythe edged in dried, black blood. Her other hand held the iron scales of justice balancing what appeared to be a desiccated human heart in one tray and a photo of President Olmedo in the other. Rings bearing expensive stones crowded every finger and thumb. A giant venomous yellow beard snake coiled its taxidermied body around her shoeless feet.

As gruesome as Saint Death was, Oscar Tamacas—tonight's primary target—appeared even more terrifying despite his advancing years. The old man stood between two soldiers with his arms zip-tied behind his back, but his eyes blazed with murderous rage as he glowered at Rivas.

Though in his seventies, Tamacas still had thick, shoulder-length hair and a long mustache streaked with gray. His long face was puckered with acne scars. Stripped to his skivvies like all the others, Rivas could see the slackened bands of muscle now run to fat in Tamacas's thighs and gut. The once fearsome ink on his stretch-marked and crepey skin was faded and indistinct like a child's scrawl.

Physically, Tamacas was a frail shadow of his former self. But the old gangster still radiated pure energy—and evil.

Two of Rivas's soldiers stood by with their M4 carbines at high ready, their hands nervously fingering their weapons, their narrowed eyes fixed on Tamacas.

Rivas approached the fearsome former crime boss.

"Señor Tamacas, by order of the president, you are under arrest."

Tamacas spat on the floor.

"Release me now, *pendejo*. Or I will roast your wife over an open flame as I feed your children to my pigs."

The gravelly voice shot through Rivas like a bolt of frozen lightning. *How did he know about my wife and children?*

The young lieutenant fought the urge to cross himself. He wasn't sure if Tamacas was just a man or a snarling devil. He tried to stare the old man down, but the reptilian black eyes gripped his soul like a vulture's claw. Rivas looked away.

Tamacas grinned.

"Get him out of here!" Rivas finally barked, breaking the spell. Of course Rivas had a wife and kids. Who among his men didn't? The old man had simply guessed.

"Yes, Lieutenant." Two more soldiers with secured weapons each grabbed an elbow and dragged Tamacas away, the two armed soldiers close by. Tamacas cursed vile threats against them all as he was hauled through the door.

The old man's threats weren't entirely idle. His murderous son, Narcisco, was now in charge of the organization and still on the loose, rumored to have fled the country.

Rivas pushed that thought aside as he stood alone in the room. He breathed a sigh of relief. He hadn't lost a single man, and had captured his primary target. It was a good night. He prayed the other operations around the country had gone as well.

He turned to leave, but caught a glance at the grinning, fleshless monster in the corner, and the weighted scales clutched in her lifeless hand.

He whispered a prayer, crossed himself, and left.

6

Lieutenant Rivas rode in the cab of one of the big military trucks rumbling through the gates of the Terrorism Confinement Center (CECOT). The five-hundred-forty-thousand-square-foot building loomed like a medieval castle in the El Salvador countryside. It was as impressive and impregnable as any fortress built with human hands. The facility was ringed by a thirty-three-foot-tall concrete perimeter wall, several interior walls and fences, nineteen guard towers, and a fifteen-thousand-watt electrified fence. Military units patrolled the outside of the complex, and nearly two thousand guards, police, and infantry manned the interior. It was designed to hold forty thousand prisoners, and today's caravan would fill their crowded cells to the limit.

The entire facility had been built with breathtaking speed by President Rómulo Olmedo, determined to turn El Salvador from the murder capital of the world to the safe haven of Latin America. His unrelenting campaign against the criminal gangs that terrorized his nation had succeeded beyond anyone's expectations. The young lieutenant was proud to be part of that effort.

Rivas dismounted from his vehicle after the long line of trucks squealed to a braking halt inside the final perimeter fence. Black-clad police in riot gear barked orders and the prisoners poured out. Within moments, several hundred prisoners—now shackled in chains by their ankles and wrists behind their backs—were herded like cattle into the intake facility, where they would suffer the indignities of whole body scans, cavity searches, cold-water showers, and the like.

The cuffed prisoners ran stooped over, their lines of stripped bodies undulating like a tattooed centipede. Out of that angry herd a head turned, and Oscar Tamacas shot a final, fatal glance straight into Rivas's eyes before disappearing behind a set of large steel doors.

"That him?" the warden asked.

Rivas nodded. "Just an old man now."

The warden shook his head gravely. "He's old-school scary. I've heard stories."

"I know. I've lived with them."

For years, Rivas had held his sobbing mother in his arms as she described the mutilated corpses of her family and the manner of their horrific deaths. Her grief and his family's honor were the main reasons Rivas joined the campaign against the crime lords.

The two men watched the big steel doors slam shut. Shouted orders echoed around the compound. Rivas glanced up at one of the tall towers crowded with vigilant guards armed with machine guns. The prison operation was a well-oiled machine and the men highly trained for their specific mission. Escape was clearly impossible.

"What will happen to him in there?" Rivas asked.

"They'll put him into a separate unit for gang leaders, away from gen pop."

"Is that a good idea, putting the bosses all together like that?"

"You worried they'll come up with some kind of a plan?"

"They're the smart ones, aren't they?"

"Smart? Look at them now. They'll sleep on steel bunks stacked four high with no blankets, eat meals with their hands, and take their water out of troughs like mules. What kind of plans can those smart boys make?"

Rivas shrugged.

Who knew what went through the minds of men like that?

★

The warden was right.

Oscar Tamacas found himself shoved into a communal cell of

eighty other gang leaders, all MS-13. Like the others, his head had been shaved, and he wore the same white cotton shorts and T-shirt. The clothing was meant to mitigate the blue-inked badges of rank and honor swirled onto their flesh—another form of humiliation.

The gangsters in the cell across the wide hallway were Barrio 18, their sworn enemies inside El Salvador. In fact, the entire CECOT facility was segregated that way. The authorities didn't want to turn their prison into a dogfighting slaughterhouse the first day it opened. The Barrio 18 guys began jeering at Tamacas when he was first herded into the unit, but the guards quickly shut them up. The Barrio men lined their cage and stared silent daggers at Tamacas, who had personally killed or wounded many of their number. Any one of them would sacrifice himself for the opportunity to murder Tamacas.

At first, Tamacas was grateful for the setup. As soon as the door swung open he was surrounded by a dozen old comrades, who paid him deferential respect and even affection according to their rank in the alpha hierarchy. The hugs and smiles were genuine enough, but the old fox immediately understood the secondary purpose of the friendly caucus engulfing him.

He was in danger.

Tamacas and the other men in this cage were all MS-13. But not all of them were as pleased to see him, nor as deferential. As a one-time senior boss, he had been a brutal dictator. How else to rule a gang of rabid dogs? Tamacas often had to exercise hard discipline and bloody punishments on his unruly subordinates. A few of the somber faces he recognized; others he didn't. No doubt these glowering eyes or their subordinates had suffered under his disciplinary wrath. Perhaps now they would seek their revenge.

Tamacas knew he could count on the small loyal coterie surrounding him. But for how long?

The old gangster strode over to the nearest steel cot and sat down, careful to hide the weakness in his legs that had plagued him for years. He chatted amiably with his old friends, but something wasn't right. Tamacas had enjoyed a lifetime of privileges that terrorizing others had afforded him—money, wealth, women. But most of all, loyalty. Fear was stronger than love for most men.

But here, now, stripped of his power, his clothes, and even his hair, Tamacas began to feel something he hadn't experienced in seventy years walking the earth.

For the first time in his adult life, he was afraid.

7

THE NETHERLANDS

Captain Liu Yuchen eased back on the yoke of the Boeing 747-8F as it lofted heavily into the sky from the Amsterdam Airport Schiphol.

The massive, nose-loading cargo plane Yuchen piloted was one of the few capable of carrying the vital components of an extreme ultraviolet lithography machine. EUV machines were required to manufacture the highest-quality microchips necessary to build the only computers capable of handling artificial general intelligence (AGI) software. Yuchen's country, China, was hell-bent on acquiring the world's first fully functional AGI computer ahead of any other nation, especially the United States. Acquiring as many EUV units as possible was vital to this effort.

The only company in the world that made these types of photolithography units was ASML, a Dutch firm. It was easier to find a heart donor than to acquire one of their high-demand machines. The United States, unable to fairly compete against Yuchen's homeland in the AGI race, recently pressured the Dutch government to embargo ASML exports to China. The tech company had little choice but to comply with American demands.

No matter, Yuchen reminded himself with a smile. His government had found a willing work-around. A large German firm, with chip-manufacturing plants around the world, was one of ASML's top customers. The Germans were eager to purchase the latest unit for their manufacturing plant in Seoul, South Korea—all in compliance with the Chinese embargo.

But as it turned out, that German firm also manufactured in China. In fact, a controlling share of stock was secretly owned by an organ of the Chinese Communist Party. The Chinese government was more than happy to pay the Germans more than the retail price of the machines, and to put a few well-placed euros into the right pockets of company officers and any export officials connected to the shipment. After all, it was the Americans who were paying for it in the end. Each year China was flush with hundreds of billions of trade surplus dollars with the United States. Not only were the American capitalists willing to sell China the rope to hang them with, they handed them the cash to buy it.

Besides, Europe and China had a long history of trade during the Cold War. Many of China's most advanced military machines that would be deployed in a war against the United States were powered by German and French turbines and electronics. The ASML units were simply another rung in that long and profitable ladder.

Once Yuchen's plane landed in Seoul, the ASML components would be reported as having been unloaded while his plane was refueled. It would then take off again with the precious cargo and the heavily armed security team guarding the shipment. Yuchen's final destination was a restricted airfield near Beijing, where the carefully packaged, climate-controlled modular crates would be loaded into specialized vehicles and transported to the Zhongguancun Science Park, China's own Silicon Valley, for expert assembly.

Captain Yuchen's flight plan from Amsterdam to Seoul tracked north toward Poland, over Scandinavia, and across Siberia and the southern reaches of the Arctic Circle. The "great circle" route was by far the shortest one, saving thousands of kilometers, not to mention time and fuel. The Americans and other Western governments were forbidden to fly over Russian territory, but China was one of the founding members of the BRICS alliance, a loose counterweight to American economic might in the world.

The money and energy spent in acquiring the ASML units were a wise investment. If China acquired AGI before the Americans, the nation would cement its place in history as the most important economic superpower for the rest of the twenty-first century and for many centuries beyond.

★

Captain Yuchen noted his position on the plane's BDS—China's version of GPS—confirming they were on course over the frozen wasteland of Siberia. The starry night's thick cloud cover meant he could see nothing below him, but Yuchen's vivid imagination pictured an icy alien surface racing beneath them where human life was impossible.

He glanced at the small photo taped to his console. The picture of his wife and their ten-year-old daughter was his lucky charm. His daughter's birthday was tomorrow and he had picked up a delicate diamond pendant for her while he was in Amsterdam. He couldn't wait to see the wide-eyed delight in her eyes when he gave it to her.

Yuchen checked the rest of the instruments, including radar. Everything was green and good to go.

"You have control," Yuchen told his first officer.

"I have control," the man said with a smile. "About time."

This would be the man's last flight in the copilot's seat. Next time he'd captain his own plane on Yuchen's strong recommendation. He was a good friend and a great pilot. There's no one Yuchen trusted more on the yoke than him.

Yuchen pulled off his headset and slid down into his seat, shutting his eyes for a short nap before dinner was served.

★

Yuchen dreamed of his daughter running and laughing in the park, pulling a long-tailed kite that flew high in the sky, touching the very clouds.

The air cargo captain had never felt such peace before, not even in a dream. He wanted to stay there forever.

But shrieking alarms slapped him awake.

"Captain!" his first officer shouted.

Yuchen bolted upright and scanned the console. The digital read-outs flashed crazily as if hit by a power surge.

"What happened?"

"I don't know!"

"Calm down. I have the stick," Yuchen said as he took control of the aircraft. But something was wrong. The yoke fought against his powerful hands. "Systems check!"

The first officer's face was bathed in sweat. His eyes and fingers ran over every gauge and switch.

"What have you found?" Yuchen demanded.

"Nothing—I don't understand."

Suddenly, the yoke jerked in Yuchen's hands, the flight controls beneath his feet gave way, and the engines roared into full throttle.

"Help me," Yuchen said. The first officer snatched his yoke, but it was too late. The plane rolled over one hundred eighty degrees, its nose pointed at the ground. Cups, pens, hats, manuals—everything tumbled through the cabin like in a clothes dryer. He heard the muffled cries of the security guards in the holds below.

The seat belt restraints cut into Yuchen's torso as the blood drained from his face. His copilot's fingers punched the radio controls to call in an emergency, but it was dead.

The altimeter was shot, but there was no doubt in Yuchen's mind they were only seconds away from impact. He glanced at the picture of his daughter.

He found no peace.

But he kept his eyes fixed on her until his plane crashed into the ice in a fiery explosion.

8

ABOARD THE *OREGON*

The *Oregon*'s operations center was located far belowdecks and tiered like an ancient Greek theater. The high-tech wonder was all glass, steel, and video displays. Computer stations and monitors were located on each tier. Every function of the ship was controlled from the op center including communications, sensors, weapons, and helm.

Overlooking the op center was the Kirk Chair, so named because it resembled Captain Kirk's command chair in the original *Star Trek* television series. The Kirk Chair provided Juan Cabrillo a commanding view of the op center and, more important, everything he needed for total control of the *Oregon*. It was a leather-cushioned, miniaturized version of the op center itself. Weapons, engines, comms— everything was available at the touch of a virtual toggle switch.

The op center's bulkheads were fitted with floor-to-ceiling LCD panels displaying live images from the 4K cameras distributed around the ship. Though deep inside the *Oregon*, the double-duty panels provided a three-hundred-sixty-degree view of the world surrounding the ship—almost as if standing on the alternate bridge high atop the superstructure.

Max stood at Juan's elbow, his weathered eyes scanning the readouts of speed, direction, and time overlaid on the big view screens, like heads-up displays on a fighter's bubble canopy. He had been more devoted to the *Oregon* than to any of his three ex-wives. As far as he was concerned, she was more reliable and more worthy of his affections.

Cabrillo noted the time. They were still four hours away from the rendezvous spot, where they hoped to intercept a known arms-smuggling vessel heading for the Pacific coast of Mexico. The *Oregon* was pacing at a leisurely twenty-two knots, a fraction of her top end. But the spectacle of a five-hundred-ninety-foot break-bulk carrier rooster-tailing through the water like a speedboat would draw unwanted attention from eyes on or above the water.

Juan surveyed the crew at their stations. This was his A-team. Mark Murphy was at the weapons station, Eric Stone sat at helm, and Hali Kasim—his chief of communications—occupied the comms console. The other stations were crewed by trusted hands as well.

"Chairman, something odd here," Murph said. "My targeting radar indicates multiple small contacts at five miles, bearing oh-eight-nine."

"Birds?"

"Unclear. Intermittent hits. Could be artifacts of some kind."

"Run a diagnostic on your radar."

"Already did. The board's green."

"Put it on the big screen," Cabrillo ordered.

Murph's radar display flashed on one of the giant screens, giving everyone the same view. The radar hits were dozens of fuzzy blips swirling and flowing in synchronized waves like a flock of murmuring starlings.

"Sure looks like birds," Max said.

"Too fast," Stoney said. "Three miles and closing."

The dots suddenly disappeared.

"You sure about that diagnostic?" Max asked.

"No question."

Hali touched his earpiece, a loud squelch pinching his face. "Chairman, I'm getting comms interference."

"The navigational radar is glitching, too," Eric Stone said from his station.

"We've got tangos," Cabrillo said.

"Drones?" Max asked.

"Or very angry pelicans with jammers," Juan said. "Wepps, activate the EMP cannons. Low-divergence beams. Target and prioritize the interference wave sources."

"Aye, Chairman."

Juan took a measured breath. The *Oregon*'s two electromagnetic pulse (EMP) cannons fired high-powered, broad-spectrum bursts of microwave energy, disabling any electronic component in its path. This would be the first test of the EMP cannons since the *Oregon*'s recent overhaul at a Malaysian dry dock.

"Hali, sound battle stations."

Max bolted for his engineering station as the Klaxon began alarming overhead.

Juan glanced at the camera display atop the *Oregon*'s superstructure some sixty feet above the freeboard. Each EMP cannon was stationed inside of a domed turret with three-hundred-sixty-degree radial capacity, one on the port side, one on the starboard. The turrets twisted like R2-D2's head as they sought out targets in the distance. Massive new banks of supercapacitors thrummed belowdecks, pulsing energy to the cannons.

"EMPs firing," Murph reported. "Ten, twenty . . . forty shots fired."

"Nav radar clear," Eric said.

"Comms clear," Kasim echoed.

Cabrillo grinned. "Good shooting, Wepps—"

"New targets!" Murph shouted. Five drones rocketed sky-high in all directions as six others split up in two groups of three. One group sped northeast and the other southwest, seemingly away from the *Oregon*. Both assumed a low-altitude attack formation.

"Wepps, activate the laser-point defense system," Cabrillo commanded. "And stow the EMPs."

"On it," Murph said as he punched toggles. The new fifty-kilowatt fiber-optic laser defense system was mounted in a larger circular turret stationed between the two smaller EMP domes. An improvement on the British DragonFire system, the laser's AI-powered software picked its own targets at will faster and with more precision than any human eye—even Murphy's. Stabilizing algorithms adjusted for wave action at sea, and a camera mounted inside the turret gave the op center a "gun's-eye" view of the action.

The laser dome spun on its gimbals as it began tracking targets.

"There," Max said, pointing at one of the big screens. "You can see them."

Hanley was right. The drones were finally if only barely in sight. They were small, moving fast, and obscured by the sunlight glinting on the water.

"Here they come," Stoney said, pointing at three drones approaching the bow. The drones dropped low—and suddenly beneath the cameras.

Juan glanced up. One of the high-flying drones plummeted directly at them.

"They're astern, too," Hali said, staring at the rearmost wall panel.

"Laser firing," Murph said. Silent flashes of invisible light erupted in staccato three-shot bursts.

Juan's eyes were fixed on the drone above. It suddenly exploded. *Where are the others?*

"Got 'em!" Murph called out just after the drone erupted.

The pinpoint laser spun and shot at the low-flying drones circling over the water a half mile out. One by one, they broke apart and crashed into the sea.

"They're sitting ducks!" Max said, clapping his meaty hands together.

"Not necessarily," Stone said. "Those are probably decoy drones sacrificing themselves to expose the laser's firing pattern and response times."

"Like the Zulus did at Rorke's Drift," Murphy said. *Zulu* was one of his favorite flicks.

"Allowing their AI to devise an attack plan," Cabrillo said as he sat forward in his chair.

Murph called out another hit.

Bang! Oregon steel rang as if struck by a ball-peen hammer.

"Damage report," Cabrillo demanded.

"Starboard bow, just above the waterline," Max called out from his station. "Reactive armor took the brunt. No damage."

"Wepps, how'd they get through?"

Murphy's fingers flew over his virtual keyboard, his mind racing.

"Wave skimming . . . and the cranes are blocking the line of sight."

"Helm, increase speed ten knots, hard to port. Let's give Wepps room to shoot."

"Aye." Stone manipulated his joystick and throttles, powering up the *Oregon*'s big electric engines instantly and launching into a low tuck turn like a hotdogging water-skier at Cypress Gardens.

As soon as the *Oregon* finished the turn, the surviving drones sped away.

"Why'd they stop?" Max asked.

"Analyzing their secondary attack and defense data," Murph said.

Cabrillo nodded. "Their AI is calculating a new attack plan."

Murphy's targeting radar suddenly alarmed.

A massive drone swarm filled the screen. The radar computer counted over two hundred drones.

And rising.

9

The drone swarm overwhelmed the *Oregon*'s targeting screen.

"Must be three hundred of them," Max said.

Cabrillo nodded. "Stay frosty people."

The gun's-eye radar screen suddenly crashed to black. Without it, the laser cannon couldn't acquire targets.

"Nav radar out again," Stoney reported.

"Comms out," Kasim said. "We're blind and deaf."

"More electronic countermeasures." Max grunted. "Feels like we're playing rope-a-dope. Only we ain't got no rope."

"They're learning. Pattern's different this time," Cabrillo said. "Two can play at that game. Wepps, reactivate the EMP cannons. High-divergent beams. And randomize EMP firing patterns. Hose 'em!"

"Roger that." Murph tapped keys. The pulse cannons opened up.

The high-divergent beams unleashed wide, spherical bursts of electromagnetic energy shotgunning across the sky.

"Stoney, evasive maneuvers—flank speed. Everybody else—hold on!"

Eric grinned ear to ear as he shoved the throttles forward and yanked the joystick.

Like a giant Jet Ski, the *Oregon*'s massive, newly upgraded magnetohydrodynamic engines blasted monumental torrents of water through the improved thrust-vectoring venturi tubes beneath her hull. The multidirectional thrusters meant Stoney could turn the five-hundred-ninety-foot vessel on the head of a pin. He executed a well-practiced slalom maneuver he'd used in previous combat. Throughout the ship, crew members clutched whatever they could reach against the turn. The unsecured galley was a maelstrom of breaking plates and crashing pots.

"That'll confuse 'em," Max said with a chuckle as he clung white-knuckled to his console. "Or at least make 'em dizzy."

"Either works." Juan grunted, his body straining against the chair harness.

The targeting radar screen popped back on as more drones dropped from the sky.

"Laser firing," Murphy reported.

"Cannons redlining," Hanley warned, his eyes locked on the temperature gauges maxing out.

"Comms clear."

"Nav clear."

"Shut the cannons down," Cabrillo ordered. They'd done their job.

Bang!

"Hit amidships, port side," Max called out. "Hull breach above the waterline."

"Casualties?" Cabrillo asked.

Bang!

"Crane number one hit," Max said. "Good work, Stoney. That thing was heading for the bridge."

"Wepps?"

"I count fifteen tangos still out there—Check that. Thirteen. They're closing low and fast. Port and starboard."

"Decoys?"

"Kamikazes." Murph checked his console. "Laser down. Capacitors recharging."

"Wepps, Phalanx systems. Now!"

Murph slammed his palms onto a pair of bright red buttons.

Instantly, six metal plates just below the *Oregon*'s main deck dropped like gun ports on a pirate ship revealing six M61 Vulcan Gatling guns, three on each side of the hull. The multibarreled machine guns opened up in a hellish roar. Each weapon unleashed precise bursts of AI-targeted 20-millimeter rounds at the rate of seventy-five per second. Within moments, the last of the kamikaze drones had been splashed.

The op center erupted in wild cheers and applause.

"Comms, hail *Nomad* for me."

"Aye, Chairman."

Juan checked the screens again. No more threats. All clear. He leaned back in the Kirk Chair.

"*Nomad* on the overhead, Chairman."

"Well played, Captain Ross," Juan said.

Linda Ross's high voice giggled in the speakers overhead.

"Almost got you, Chairman. Thought you didn't want to use the kinetics?"

"I didn't. But some traitorous member of my command decided she could run the table on me."

Ross laughed again. "Blame the AI, not me."

Linda Ross was Cabrillo's third in command. She was a former U.S. Navy intelligence officer, a priceless addition to a spy ship like the *Oregon*. She quit the blue-water Navy once she hit her private glass ceiling. Navy brass didn't think anyone would take her seriously in a command position owing to her diminutive elfin stature and helium-squeaky voice, so they never offered Ross her own ship—the only thing she ever wanted.

But Cabrillo instantly recognized the fierce intelligence behind the impish green eyes and offered her the job. She became an outstanding helmsman in her own right, and took command of the *Oregon* when Juan and Max were on mission. She had also acquired superlative sub-driving skills. It was only natural to assign her to one of the *Oregon*'s three submersibles for today's combat-realistic exercise.

"I was hoping the laser and EMP cannons were enough," Juan said. "Glad we added the Vulcans."

Eric and Murph stole a look at each other and fought back a laugh. They were the *Oregon*'s biggest sci-fi nerds.

"Lasers are for rock concerts, not combat," Max said. "I'm an analog guy all the way."

"Next time we'll put a trebuchet on the foredeck," Cabrillo said.

"When do I get to take another run at you?" Ross asked.

"Come on back to the barn. I want to run over today's digital recordings and do an after-action review. We'll come up with a different game plan then."

"Roger that."

Cabrillo nodded at Hali to end the call. Ross would maneuver the *Nomad* underneath the *Oregon* so that it could be lifted up into its place in the boat garage next to the smaller *Gator* and the *Oregon*'s newest vessel, the *Spook Fish*, a deepwater submersible.

Overall, Cabrillo was pleased with the exercise. The *Oregon* had survived the drone attack, and his new drone system had proven frighteningly effective.

The hits to the *Oregon* were real enough, but the drones themselves were unarmed. Max's damage reports were only computer-based estimates. Had Linda's AI-piloted vehicles been carrying real payloads it might have been a very different story.

Still, it was a good learning experience, and all part of the retrofit he and Max had initiated after their mission against the Vendor. Besides acquiring new offensive and defensive systems, significant improvements were made to the power plant, hull design, and several other departments. Everything was still in testing mode.

Cabrillo knew that combat technologies were always changing, but lately they seemed to be accelerating exponentially. He was determined to modify the *Oregon* to make her lighter, better armored, better defended, faster, and more lethal.

He ruefully knew the bad guys would be doing the same.

The *Oregon*'s AI-enhanced defenses had barely survived Ross's AI-commanded drone assault. They were still fumbling in the dark, trying to master this new form of warfare, but the Island of Sorrows incident had made one thing crystal clear: drone technology was the future of combat.

Cabrillo's fingers drummed against his armrest as he studied the after-action data scrolling across his displays. The future wasn't coming—it was here. And they weren't ready. Not yet.

In the distance, thunder rumbled across the Pacific like artillery—a warning of storms to come.

10

COLOMBIA

The pilot's deft control of his ScaleWings SW-51 allowed him to put the wheels softly down on the grassy airstrip. The plane was a near-perfect replica of the famous P-51 Mustang fighter of World War II fame. But like its pilot and owner, Amador Fierro, the carbon fiber aircraft with its cutting-edge avionics was a high-tech wonder and a product of the twenty-first century.

And with its custom-mounted .50-caliber machine gun, it—and he—could also kill.

The four-bladed prop feathered to a stop after Fierro killed the Rotax engine. A Land Rover SUV bounded down the hill as he slid the canopy aft and lifted it on its hinges to egress.

The airstrip was part of Fierro's mountaintop villa nestled on a plateau in the Sierra Nevada de Santa Marta in northern Colombia. The vast estate afforded him breathtaking views of both the mountains and the sea, and was surrounded by a working coffee plantation. He had inherited the property along with the rest of his empire after the murder of his father several years before. His father, Jerónimo Fierro, ran one of the most violent and profitable drug cartels in Latin America. The old man had used his vast wealth to purchase the estate and to fill it with museum-quality objets d'art. He also acquired precious gems, legitimate enterprises, and a healthy stock portfolio.

But Jerónimo's single best investment had been a Stanford MBA for his brilliant young son. Graduating at the top of his class, telenovela-handsome Amador steered clear of the cartel's violent day-to-day operations with his father's blessing. He launched into a successful career as a high-tech venture capitalist in Silicon Valley—laundering family drug money. When his father was murdered, both family honor and boundless potential obligated him to take over the family business.

To avenge his father's murder and eliminate other vermin, Amador relied on the services of the man driving the Land Rover, Rafael Vargas, one of his father's closest advisers and his number one enforcer.

Fierro yanked open the door and climbed into the passenger seat. He was a millennial who shared his generation's values, eschewing the trappings of ostentatious wealth. He avoided the tired clichés of his profession like the plague. Gold-plated AK-47s, diamond-studded crucifixes, and imported African hippos were both poor investments and vulgar. He donated ten percent of his profits into projects for the destitute in his native Colombia and throughout Latin America, but this was a nod to public relations as much as it was to any humanitarian impulse. He had no religious inclinations.

The phone in the dashboard cradle rang. Fierro didn't recognize the number.

"It's Narcisco," Vargas said as he handed Fierro the encrypted sat phone. The stoic cartel hit man betrayed no emotion, ever. Not even when he killed. His demeanor was cold and undemonstrative, like the smooth steel shell of a hand grenade.

"Thank you." Fierro noted the faintest whisper of contempt in Vargas's voice. No one else would have noticed it, but Amador had known the man for decades. Vargas was no fan of the Tamacas family, especially Narcisco. In fact, Vargas cared for seemingly no one except for Amador, whom he protected like a son. No display of affection was possible, certainly, but Vargas would kill for Amador without hesitation.

"Narcisco? How are you?"

"The line is safe?" Narcisco's voice was electronically altered by the poor satellite signal.

Vargas punched the gas and headed back for the villa.

"Totally. What can I do for you?"

"I've been trying to reach you all day. Have you been avoiding me?"

"Not at all. I was flying today. Had to clear my head. What's the problem?"

"You know why I'm calling."

"Yes, your father, I'm sure. It's terrible."

"What do you intend to do about it?" The electronic distortion couldn't veil Narcisco's rising anger.

Fierro bit his tongue. Oscar Tamacas had been warned in advance and told to leave the country, but he refused. The old fool considered himself untouchable and had relied on corrupt government officials still on his payroll for protection. In the past, judges and witnesses could be intimidated or killed, but now their identities were protected, and trials held remotely via Zoom calls inside CECOT. Oscar had completely underestimated President Olmedo's will and determination.

And truth be told, so had he.

Fierro wouldn't make that mistake again.

"CECOT is a fortress. It will take some time."

"So what do you intend to do about it?"

Vargas shot a warning glance at Fierro. *He's a threat.*

Fierro shook his head. *Not to worry.*

"We need to get your father released as soon as possible."

"He's an old man and he's in danger."

"I understand."

The Land Rover raced along the mountain track with ease. Coffee workers smiled and waved as they passed. Fierro treated them well.

"Are you sure?" Narcisco asked. "Every moment my father rots behind bars shows us as weak and Olmedo strong. The other bosses agree with me. La Liga's reputation is on the line."

Fierro sighed. The El Salvadoran had a point. Narcisco looked and acted the part of an old-school drug lord like his father. Alligator cowboy boots, garish jewelry, and the worship of skeletal saints proved Narcisco had no taste. But he was no idiot. And he was an important ally, especially in La Liga affairs.

"You're right. La Liga is at risk. We must free your father and the others as quickly as possible."

"And don't forget, if La Liga fails, so does Project Q."

Fierro and Vargas exchanged a glance. That wasn't a threat.

It was simply a statement of fact. A terrible fact.

Because Project Q was their only lasting hope.

★

"What about the Iranians?" Narcisco asked. "Can't they do something?"

A Quds Force fighting unit had set up a training camp in Panama under La Liga's paid protection. Fierro wanted to scream. He wondered if his El Salvadoran friend was high on coke or merely bipolar— or maybe both. How could he be both cunning and stupid all at the same time?

Three divisions of U.S. Marines couldn't take CECOT. And what did Narcisco think the guards would do if they thought the walls had been breached? Their first order would be to kill all the prisoners. The last thing President Olmedo would want was for forty thousand angry gangsters to be released and set loose upon the country to seek their revenge.

"That's a great idea, Narcisco. But that kind of operation would take a great deal of planning and I'm worried it will take too long. We need something fast."

"So you do have a plan?"

"Of course. We must be subtle. And careful. *Entiendes?*"

"*Sí.*"

"With any luck, your father will be out by the end of the week. Maybe sooner."

"What do you need me to do?"

"Nothing. Just be patient. I'll handle everything. Have I ever let you down before?"

"Never. But if you fail, I'll take matters into my own hands. That's not a threat, *jefe*. It's merely a promise. It's a matter of honor."

"You have my word. I will take care of it."

Vargas pulled to a stop in front of the villa. There was no one at the front door. "Too showy," Fierro had insisted. But armed guards were located in carefully concealed hides around the property. Fierro opened the door for himself. Vargas followed him in. Fierro was still on the phone.

"I need to get on this, so I'll let you go now."

"Thank you, Amador. I'm a patient man. But there is a limit."

Narcisco killed the call.

"He's a dangerous dog," Vargas said, his eyes searching for potential threats beyond the great picture window. "You need to let me put him down."

"He's my friend."

"You have no friends. Only allies who fear you, and enemies who fear you more. Didn't your father teach you that?"

Fierro grinned. "Of course. But you taught *him* that. Even Machiavelli said it is better to be loved *and* feared. Besides, even a dog has his uses."

"Until he rips your throat out. He's willing to risk Project Q to get that careless *viejo* out of jail."

"I know how to handle him. I'll solve his problem and then he'll calm down."

"You are smarter than your father."

"Better looking, too."

"If you change your mind . . ."

★

Fierro poured himself a fine single malt whiskey and took a plush leather chair overlooking his estate. He was lost deep in thought.

La Liga—"the League" in Spanish—was his brainchild.

Fierro had studied history as well as finance at Stanford and had even flirted with the idea of pursuing an academic career in the subject. The primary lesson history taught him was that power was the most important commodity, and that since 1648 the nation-state had the monopoly of raw power.

A few decades ago, it seemed as if non-state entities like terrorist groups and drug cartels had gained the upper hand against the increasingly dysfunctional liberal democracies as they acquired better weapons, communications technology, and access to financial networks.

But the nations of the West began to cooperate, and jointly deployed superior communications technologies and better armed police forces to combat their enemies, including the drug cartels. Pablo Escobar's corpse, the fall of FARC, and a dozen other catastrophes proved state power was still supreme.

The only chance Fierro's cartel had to survive was to acquire more power of its own. Through his towering intellect, force of will, persuasive skills, and the judicious deployment of Vargas against the most recalcitrant, Fierro forged an alliance of Latin America's largest drug cartels.

Narcisco Tamacas had been his first and most reliable convert. As head of MS-13, he brought credibility to Fierro's dream. Other drug lords saw the wisdom of his vision. Ultimately, the nine largest cartels and their subsidiaries in Latin America formed La Liga as a countervailing force to the Americans and their allies. The drug lords pooled their resources, shared intel, and jointly expanded their markets. Latin America seemed on the verge of falling under their complete control and the rise of a super narco-state was at hand.

But the Western nations pushed back yet again and deployed their vast war on terror instruments against La Liga. They froze banking assets, launched targeted satellites, and deployed military forces in devastating counterinsurgency operations. The power of the state seemed as infallible, and the demise of La Liga as inevitable as Caesar's destruction of the Gauls.

Fierro had spent over a decade among the most brilliant minds in Silicon Valley, investing vast sums of his father's money—and reaping enormous profits—in the most promising technologies of the day.

Fierro had acquired a great deal of technological expertise and remained in contact with the brightest scientists and engineers. A plan began to form in his mind.

It was clear that power had always determined the course of history, but the nature of power was changing. Technology itself was becoming the primary source of power. Power that was available to anybody with the will and resources to acquire it.

Fierro had both.

And thus Project Q was launched. Fierro had convinced La Liga to invest tens of billions of dollars for the last few years into the project.

And in just ten days it would be unleashed upon the United States.

La Liga would become a superpower, just like the *norteamericanos*.

Project Q would be a weapon that no nation could resist. Better still, La Liga would dominate the global drug trade, overwhelming its competitors while utterly defeating every prosecutor and police agency around the world.

And all without firing a shot.

But Narcisco Tamacas and his retrograde father could ruin everything. Fierro had to do something now before Narcisco broke his leash.

Fierro threw back the rest of his whiskey, relishing the smooth burn in the back of his throat before heading to his office. He knew just the man who could fix his problem.

11

The dark morning sky rumbled as it unleashed another torrent of rain, drenching the haggard parade of over a thousand migrants winding their way across the first river. They were heading for the line of towering trees demarcating their first steps into the dreaded Darién Gap.

Like hundreds of others, Franklin "Linc" Lincoln and Raven Malloy pulled on their cheap plastic ponchos against the deluge. The thick drops spattered against their hoods like pennies hitting a tin roof. It was so loud no one bothered to speak until the storm passed by.

The two *Oregon* undercover operatives were already drenched from earlier rains and their shabby clothes were salt-stained from the high humidity baking them like stuffed Chinese bao buns between the passing storms. The ponchos hardly mattered, but covering up their faces and forms added to their anonymity among the herd of humanity inching its way forward. In Linc's case, every little bit helped. The African American's muscular frame stood out from the other men, African or otherwise. He looked more like a bodybuilder than the hapless refugee he was posing as.

The poncho helped Raven, too, by dimming her smoldering good looks. Her Native American genetics endowed her with an exotic appearance that could play almost any dark-haired ethnicity, and hours in the weight room shredded her athletic physique. The last thing she or Linc wanted was for her to attract undue attention. A brutal kidnapping—and far worse—was a real danger for every woman on this hazardous trek. The only nod to fashion she allowed herself were the brightly colored woven nylon bracelets she wore.

Linc and Raven had arrived in Colombia's port city Necoclí without incident and on time. A local DEA informant put the two *Oregon* operatives in contact with the Gulf Clan, the brutal gang controlling the passage from Colombia to Panama. Each migrant paid the thugs three hundred dollars, a fee about equal to the annual income for most Venezuelan migrants. The yellow plastic wristband they received proving they had paid also entitled them to the boat trip across the bay to Acandí, as well as armed guides through the Darién Gap inside Panama and protection—at least from their own organization.

God help the poor souls who couldn't afford the fee and tried to hazard the Darién Gap on their own. Called *El Tapón* (the Plug) by locals, the Darién Gap was arguably the world's most dangerous stretch of jungle.

Europeans had been trying to tame it since the Spanish arrived in 1501, but all attempts had failed. Nearly twelve thousand miles of impenetrable jungle, rivers, and mountains made up the Darién Gap, traversable only by foot and occasionally canoe. Even the Pan-American Highway, a continuous band of asphalt stretching all the way from Argentina in the south to Alaska in the north, was interrupted by the single sixty-six-mile stretch at the Plug. The world's best engineers fielding the most advanced earthmoving equipment found it impossible to overcome the Darién's natural boundaries.

Besides the Plug's geographic challenges, there were venomous snakes, poisonous insects, man-eating jaguars, and swollen, flash-flooding rivers that took many lives each year. Another danger was the rival gangs and Indigenous thieves that preyed upon the travelers and, worse, the criminal cutthroats among them who raped, robbed, and killed as they migrated north.

Linc and Raven had learned in their pre-mission brief that a decade ago, two thousand migrants risked their lives annually to get through the Darién. Today that number had exploded to over eight hundred thousand.

Before the march began, the migrants were herded into a fenced area. The crowd's mood was a mixture of excited expectation and terrified apprehension, much like the beginning of a marathon.

Lincoln and Raven circulated through the teeming masses of people, gathering intel. They noted the large number of young combat-aged males in the group, with the youngest and strongest crowding the front. The majority of migrants were Venezuelans and Cubans, both victims of the economic chaos inflicted by their respective socialist governments. Many others were mental defectives, hardened criminals, and the chronically ill. The socialist dictatorships were all too happy to empty their mental wards, prisons, and hospitals and dump their human loads onto the American taxpayer.

The third largest group were Haitians, currently under the murderous sway of men like Jimmy Chérizier, a former police officer turned "revolutionary" whose nickname, "Barbecue," referenced his treatment of his political opponents, not his culinary expertise.

Raven and Linc also passed by clusters of Peruvians, Ecuadorans, and a surprisingly large number of Africans.

The well-heeled Chinese arriving in Necoclí opted to take a shorter "VIP" route in exchange for much higher fees.

Just before dawn, a series of whistles blew, and the gates were opened. The crowds surged through the openings. The young bucks raced ahead like kids rushing into a rock concert arena. The families burdened with children and worldly goods shuffled forward uneasily like cattle negotiating a stock alley on the way to the slaughterhouse.

Linc knew that, in short order, the mass of people would sort themselves out, forming a long line pouring toward the border. The elderly, weak, and young would drift to the back of the ragged line and join the unfortunate who broke their ankles or succumbed to the polluted waters. These stragglers would become like the weakest animals on the savanna, and most likely to fall prey to the predators waiting to snatch them away.

Raven and Linc shared a furtive glance beneath their poncho hoods. The *Oregon* operators had just begun a marathon.

A marathon through hell.

★

Initially, Linc and Raven kept to themselves, staying in the middle of the pack, fully aware of the very real challenges ahead. Despite the hazards they were about to face, neither felt particularly brave. Both were highly trained operators with years of armed combat and field-craft experience under their belts. Linc had been a Navy SEAL sniper and Raven a highly decorated military police officer before joining the *Oregon* crew.

The truly heroic among them were the young families and grand-mothers carrying small children, all risking their lives, bodies, and sanity on a long trek through the Darién Gap in hopes of finding a better life up north.

What broke Lincoln's heart was the realization that most of these people had been sold a false dream of America's golden riches by the very people now putting them in harm's way for a fee. The criminal gang running this operation was a La Liga subsidiary, and earned over eight hundred million dollars each year from this humanitarian nightmare.

But Linc wasn't a social worker, and his mission wasn't to save these people. The mission he and Raven had been assigned was crystal clear: find the Iranian Quds Force base rumored to be operating in the Darién Gap. Once fully trained, the Iranian unit would head north to stab across the soft underbelly of the American southern border to wage war on the Great Satan. Tens of thousands of American lives could be at risk. Maybe more.

Their only responsibility was to find and geolocate the Quds Force base and report back. If possible, they were to determine the nature of the planned attack, and if the Iranian fighters intended to deploy weapons of mass destruction. It was strictly an intelligence-gathering assignment—no combat.

Raven and Linc paid special attention to three separate groups of approximately fifty combat-aged Middle Eastern men, origins unknown. They didn't seem to be in communication with each other, and the few innocuous Arabic conversations Raven managed to catch were inconclusive. The Iranians weren't stupid. Speaking Farsi would have given them away.

There was plenty of time to suss them out in the days and nights ahead. With any luck, one or more of those groups were Iranian and would lead them directly to the Quds Force camp they sought. If not, Linc and Raven would cut their own trail through the unforgiving jungle when the time was right.

Raven was the perfect fit for the mission, being fluent in Farsi, Arabic, and Spanish. Linc volunteered to provide her security. They had to go in unarmed if they wanted to remain undercover. He would need every ounce of his massive wall of muscle to protect his partner. Their DEA contact warned them they would be searched, and if guns, knives, or even radios were discovered they would be turned away, at best, but more likely killed before they could board the boat in Necoclí.

The two operators posed as a couple. Raven's carefully doctored paperwork indicated she was a Tunisian woman and Linc played as Senegalese, generally the tallest men in West Africa. Both nationalities were poorly represented on the migrant trail, which meant the two *Oregon* operators were unlikely to be questioned or challenged by natives.

Linc had considered posing as a Haitian, but he had never been to the country and didn't know the language. He had a passing familiarity with Creole patois after spending countless hours with his fellow *Oregon* Gundog, a Cajun named Marion MacDougal "MacD" Lawless. But Louisiana Creole was vastly different than the Haitian variety.

However, Linc could hold a decent conversation in French. Though he never studied language while in the SEAL teams, one of Dr. Huxley's lectures on the connection between improved brain health and language acquisition drove him into French. He chose the language because of the *Oregon*'s record of operations in Francophone Africa. He wasn't ready for graduate studies at the Sorbonne, but he could hold his own in casual conversation and, better still, listen in on at least some Haitian conversations if needed. Since Raven didn't speak French, Linc took the extra precaution of wearing a neck bandage, feigning a throat injury, and his only verbal communication with her was a low, gravelly whisper in English that only she could hear.

In the last two days, their covers had worked. In order to complete their assignment and to blend in with the other members of the group, Raven and Linc had acquired second- and even thirdhand clothing and shoes, just like all the other refugees. On a hazardous overland route like this one, both operators would have preferred mil-spec equipment, or at the very least, high-end performance gear and Salomon hiking boots. They also couldn't bring proper medical kits. They were posing as desperate, ill-prepared refugees, not yuppie American tourists.

The other challenge they faced was that the trek would take at least ten days, according to the reports they had studied. Many of the migrants had been told by their gangster handlers on social media that the hike was easy and only lasted a few days. Because of these lies, most of the migrants carried only two or three days of water and food. It was clear to the *Oregon* operators that many would run out of supplies long before they reached their destination.

Lincoln and Raven had acquired the same overpriced, low-quality food supplies at the port city as had most of the other refugees. They couldn't pack enough for ten days without revealing they had prior knowledge of what lay before them. They would just have to go hungry like the rest if it came to that.

Two special provisions they had brought along were sewn inside the straps of their packs. These included a string of antibiotic and water-purification tablets, and the micro components of a single-band emergency radio secreted throughout their clothing. The radio parts would be quickly assembled and comms established with the *Oregon* once the Quds Force camp was located.

A third provision was attached to Linc's thick wrist, a scratched-up, raggedy-banded Timex wristwatch—the kind of thing you'd pick up at a thrift store for a couple of bucks. The watch was designed by Kevin Nixon, and besides the fact that it kept pretty good time it was also a GPS device that helped them navigate as well as to record the Quds Force camp location with precision.

Perhaps the brightest light they encountered was the Brazos Abiertos open tent just outside Acandí swarmed by hundreds of chattering migrants. "Open Arms" was a nongovernmental organization, its tent staffed by a few local nurses and aid workers, who handed out liters of water, cheap plastic ponchos, mosquito repellent, and packets of aspirin. They didn't bother trying to dissuade the weakest and most vulnerable from making the trip—nobody was there for a holiday adventure. But few migrants really understood the risks. The Brazos Abiertos people promised legal and financial help once anyone crossed the American border.

What the harried aid workers couldn't promise was that any of them would actually make it there alive.

12

The one-hundred-ten-meter *Baktun* appeared to be a Global-class research vessel with its advanced sonar and radar domes, at-sea laboratories, two moon pools, a one-hundred-fifty-ton crane, and a helipad on the high foredeck. Registered to a nonprofit oceanographic institute, the *Baktun* traveled unmolested under a protective banner of international goodwill.

But in actuality, the hybrid warship had other purposes. The *Baktun*'s high-tech weapons systems were carefully hidden from prying eyes on the sea or in the sky, but easily and quickly deployed. The belowdecks combat information center was bathed in the faint blue glow of LED displays and the low hum of cooling fans.

Captain Reginald Stokes leaned over the shoulder of a senior tech, his clear gray eyes fixed on the live drone camera feed high overhead of the battered South Korean cargo ship *Ocean Queen*. The vessel wasn't broadcasting an AIS signal—a clear sign it was engaged in unlawful activity. Of course, neither did the *Baktun*.

It didn't matter. The Korean could have been a hospital ship on a mission of mercy. The outcome would be the same. The *Ocean Queen*'s luck had run out the moment it crossed into the *Baktun*'s security perimeter. The stubborn Korean captain signed his death warrant by refusing to change direction.

Stokes's orders were clear. His ship was not to be detected by anyone, visually or electronically. A wide variety of technologies kept him hidden from electromagnetic detection. The Koreans couldn't see him on their radar, but they were advancing directly toward his position. Within hours they would draw close enough to be able to lay eyes on his vessel.

Under normal conditions, the ex–Royal Navy surface warfare officer would have exercised the better part of valor, fired up his engines, and raced away. But the fusion reactor powering his vessel was diverted to its highest priority task for the foreseeable future. He had a wide variety of kinetic weapons at his disposal for dispatching the Korean ship, but using them would likely alert authorities.

His other options were decidedly unconventional—even theatrical, as far as he was concerned—but highly effective. The assault was tuned via artificial intelligence programming to the linguistic and cultural forms of the targeted vessel. Korean demons for Koreans, Chinese banshees for Chinese, and the like. Stokes was particularly impressed by the terror inflicted on even the most hardened sea captains when the monsters from their childhood imaginations called them out by name. Such was the quality of his ship's research team.

An emergency radio transmission crackled overhead. The panicked voice was Korean, his English badly broken.

"Affirmative. A sailing vessel. Pirates—demon pirates. I can't explain—"

"That's enough. Jam the transmission," Stokes ordered.

Another tech hit a virtual toggle. The *Baktun*'s high-altitude drone blocked the radio signals. The Korean had baited and set the hook Stokes needed. The few survivors would later confirm what the radio operator had just reported. In this case, white-robed Korean *gwisin* had suddenly appeared in the wires in their spectral forms, their hair-covered faces demanding an immediate course change.

Most ships eagerly complied with the terrifying commands. Sailors were notoriously superstitious. In the past two months, Stokes had only sunk two vessels; five others fled posthaste.

The *Baktun* operated in this location for its remoteness—most commercial vessels chose shorter routes to avoid this costly and

time-consuming expanse of ocean. National governments didn't patrol it, either—not only was there little commercial traffic but it lay
beyond their jurisdictions. What his employer hadn't counted on was
the fact that vessels engaged in illegal activity preferred this patch of
ocean for precisely those reasons.

Captain Stokes turned to his first officer, a swarthy, barrel-chested
Brazilian with a thick mustache.

"Are we still undetected?"

"Yes, sir."

"And no other vessels or aircraft in the perimeter?"

"No, sir."

Stokes turned to one of his weapons officers, a Russian.

"Spartak, do it." He turned his attention back to the live display.

"*Da*, Captain." The Russian manipulated his controllers.

Simultaneously, the holographic pirate ship fired its virtual cannons. Seconds later, the torpedo drone parked against the *Ocean
Queen* erupted, simulating a cannon attack.

The Korean's rusted hull split open like a beer can hit by a blast of
double-aught buckshot. Within moments the ship was half sunk, and
the few survivors swam away as fast as they could to avoid being
sucked down with the hulk.

Stokes had one last calculation. Leaving survivors meant the stories
of demonic pirate ships would spread, and that fear would drive other
vessels far from this location.

On the other hand, who knew what the Koreans actually saw today?
What if one of them had managed to figure out his magic tricks?

Stokes barked an order to one of his drone techs standing in a specialized niche against the bulkhead. She wore a pair of wireless, over-
sized virtual reality goggles that gave the impression of a praying
mantis and held wireless controllers in each hand.

"Amélie, finish the job. And put it on the main display."

The French drone weapons officer mirrored her display onto the
CIC's large LED panel so everyone could watch. She locked red targeting reticles on each of the survivors bobbing in the sea. One by one,
bomb-laden drones swooped onto their victims, each explosion dot-

ting the azure-blue ocean with bloody chum. The CIC team cheered every gruesome death.

Stokes turned to the overhead drone display just as the *Ocean Queen* slipped into the deep, leaving behind a trail of flotsam.

The hollow victory left a bitter taste in Stokes's mouth, the destruction of the hapless vessel akin to a boxing match with a blind man. He hadn't tasted real, peer-to-peer naval combat since his days as a "child" sublieutenant on Her Majesty's frigate *Broadsword* in the Falkland Islands war. His name, indeed, had been "mentioned in dispatches" for his bravery under fire and he wore the jagged shrapnel scar on his cheek as a badge of honor.

But a dishonorable discharge from service had reduced him to decades of illegal but highly paid mercenary work on transport vessels. Years of faultless seamanship finally earned Stokes the command of the *Baktun*, a true if unconventional war-fighting vessel. He craved an opportunity to prove himself against a worthy opponent, not another rust bucket like the *Ocean Queen*.

Deep in his bones he knew he would soon have that opportunity.

13

PANAMA

By the end of the first day the ragged line of migrants had made their way deep into the rugged jungle terrain. The thick roots and sharp rocks poking through the muck took their first victims early, twisting ankles and breaking bones before the journey had even really begun. A few hobbled on. Others turned back in tears.

Heavy rains dogged them through nightfall until they finally encountered a smuggling camp. It was littered with more trash than a city dump. The gangster smugglers served up a hot meal of rice and beans on soggy paper plates, standing under tarps lit with flashlights. The few sheltered spaces—more plastic tarps strung between branches—were flooded with rainwater. Hundreds of cheap tents carried by the best-prepared migrants blossomed like a colorful nylon garden. The foolishly unprepared huddled together under trees, sleeplessly braving the storm. Raven and Linc, like a half dozen others, strung tented hammocks between the trees, suspended comfortably above the water and filth.

Everyone else bedded down as best they could, but few were able to sleep with the drumbeat of rain hammering their gear and the puddling water soaking them to the bone.

★

Just before sunrise the gangster guides woke them with banging pots.

Everyone gathered their things as quickly as they could and they all set off without a meal toward a steep, fog-shrouded summit. The trees and bushes got thicker with each passing step as they made their way up the narrow trail in single file.

Raven and Linc fought to keep their balance on the slippery mud and loose rocks. A steel cable had been haphazardly affixed along the rock wall, but it was broken or rusted away in too many spots to be useful.

A panicked shout behind them meant someone else hadn't been able to negotiate the hazards. The two operators exchanged a glance from beneath their hoods, each reading the other's thoughts. Their instincts told them to race back and render aid to the injured.

But their training told them to stay focused on the mission. There were a thousand other people on the trail that could offer help, including the guides, if they were so inclined. Besides, the two operators would raise suspicions if they started deploying their paramedic skills. While they had witnessed a few small acts of kindness shared between the migrants, in the end it was every man, woman, and child for themselves. A pair of selfless do-gooders would stand out like sore thumbs.

The guides marched ever upward, seemingly undeterred by the near-vertical climb. They must have been born to it. Linc had witnessed aged Afghani men, stick-thin and white-bearded, speed up similar mountain inclines like alpine goats, their young grandchildren hot on their heels. The weaker migrants were already struggling to breathe and their legs burned with lactic acid. The only relief was that the rain had stopped, but the humidity clung to their bodies like steaming blankets.

Thirty minutes into the mountain climb, the guides stopped abruptly—just as the rain began again.

One of the guides pointed at the muddy trail beneath his feet. He had to shout over the rain-swollen river roaring forty feet below them.

"This is Panama now," he said in broken English. "It is against the law for us to go more. We will be arrested. But you will be okay."

"You are abandoning us?" a Venezuelan woman shouted in Spanish.

Another guide pointed his machete to the far distant summit still shrouded by dense morning fog.

"Keep climbing to the top, then head down to the other side. The trail is clearly marked. You will be okay."

"How many days until we reach the refugee camp?" a Haitian asked in cultured English.

"Two days, perhaps three at most."

Raven and Linc knew he was lying. It took at least nine days and often more. The migrants would encounter several rivers that could overflow their banks at any time and prevent an immediate crossing.

And, of course, there were bandits.

More questions were shouted, but the guides ignored them all as they marched back down the mountain toward the morning's camp. One of them muttered, "*Vaya con Dios*"—Go with God—as they passed down the line, ashamed to look at the faces of the terrified mothers and children watching their retreat.

A few young mothers cried out in anguish and several elderly men threw curses as the gangsters disappeared around the first bend.

Raven and Linc saw two dozen young men up front already launching up the trail, determined to cross the mountain with or without the guides. A toothless old Venezuelan standing next to Raven bowed his head and crossed himself.

Raven laid a comforting hand on his narrow shoulder as the migrants behind them inched their way around them and headed up the rocky path.

"It will be all right," she said. "You can stay with us."

The old man shook his head and whispered something that Linc couldn't quite make out before he turned and marched along behind the others.

"What did he say?"

"He doesn't want our help. He wants a priest to pray for him. He's heard rumors that demons inhabit *La Montaña de la Muerte*."

"Does that mean what I think it means?" Linc had enough French that he understood the many Spanish cognates.

Raven flashed a grim smile.

"We're about to ascend the Mountain of Death."

14

THE PEOPLE'S REPUBLIC OF CHINA

Peng De sat at his desk in the top-floor corner office with a two-hundred-seventy-degree view of Shanghai, befitting his rank and prestige in China's Ministry of State Security (MSS). His secret division occupied several floors of the city's newest and most futuristic tower of gleaming glass. China's cities, like its society, were leaving behind the inelegant brutalism of Soviet-era design.

Peng's meteoric rise to the near pinnacle of the infamous organization was based entirely on his merits. The corruption reforms of the past decade had cleared away most of the geriatric dead wood clogging the system. The Party understood that self-serving bureaucrats and crony careerism had warped his country's development for years. Peng was at the forefront of an emergent class of young and dedicated technocrats forging a brighter destiny for China. He was a new breed of Chinese patriot: thoughtful, technical, and incorruptible, all of which made him an exceedingly dangerous opponent.

Peng's primary responsibility for his division within the dreaded MSS was to carry out China's decades-long policy of "unrestricted warfare" against the United States. Unrestricted warfare was a form of asymmetrical combat formulated at a time when America had far superior military and technological resources. The concept was to attack America where it was most defenseless without resorting to actual kinetic combat.

Unrestricted warfare was designed to inflict unbearable social and material costs, divert government resources, demoralize the population, and steal away thousands of lives, all in an effort to delegitimize the capitalist American regime. After all, it was the venerable Sun Tzu who taught the very essence of all strategic thinking: "The supreme art of war is to subdue the enemy without fighting."

Thanks to decades of strategic theft, and especially the efforts of the MSS, China had nearly closed its yawning economic, technological, and military gaps with the Americans. But despite his nation's near parity in military capabilities, the policy of unrestricted warfare continued unabated. And why shouldn't it? It had proven wildly successful.

In his youth, Peng imagined the Americans would have seen through this strategy and done everything they could to combat it. But that was before he had joined the conflict himself and witnessed the workings of both regimes. Corruption wasn't just a Chinese problem— but China had solved it, mostly at the point of a gun or dangling on the end of a hangman's noose.

The Americans hadn't.

Peng was now the tip of the spear in unrestricted warfare, or at least he held the forward end of the shaft. His primary thrust was flooding America with both deadly drugs and millions of illegal immigrants, often at the same time. To do so he had to work with some of the world's most unsavory characters, including drug lords and American politicians. But in so doing he kept his uncalloused hands clean from the actual dirty work involved. "Always kill with a borrowed knife" was one of Peng's most cherished strategies.

Each year now, twice as many Americans died of opioid drug overdoses than died in the twelve years of fighting the Vietnam War. Such was heaven's justice after the Opium Wars and the "century of humiliation" the West imposed upon China. The Americans taught China well. If President FDR's grandfather built his fortune on poisoning Chinese society with opium, wasn't turnabout fair play?

Illegal immigration was equally damaging, overwhelming American social services, the medical and criminal justice systems, employment and housing. And, of course, elections.

Beyond the annual toll of hundreds of billions of dollars on the American economy, China's unrestricted warfare efforts were eroding America's concept of itself. What does it mean to be a so-called "nation of laws" when the nation itself permits such lawlessness? Even a child understood that a nation without borders is no nation at all. What military recruit will pledge allegiance to a borderless entity, let alone fight and die for it? America was demoralized, disoriented, and nearly defeated. Soon it would have neither the ability nor desire to defend itself.

But as promising as these developments were, Peng and his mentors couldn't afford the risk that patriotic American leaders might rise up and turn the tide on these events before it was too late. China had to keep pressing forward in its development. That was why Peng and every other division head in China's intelligence community was additionally tasked with acquiring artificial general intelligence.

The world had already achieved AI. Artificial intelligence was a very powerful computational tool. But it was nothing compared to AGI. AI was like a factory robot, able to efficiently carry out one very specific task assigned to it. But AGI was like the gifted engineer who designed, built, and even repaired all kinds of robots—even the whole factory. It was the difference between a paintbrush and the master painter.

The inescapable verdict of future historians would be this: the nation that first acquired AGI would dominate the planet for the next five hundred years.

Artificial general intelligence would give godlike capabilities to captains of industry as well as of armies. It would exponentially accelerate advances in science, medicine, industrial production, and military capabilities, leaving all other competitors in the dustbin of history.

Peng smiled, his eyes gleaming as he imagined the possibilities. Chinese war planners knew AGI would easily penetrate American military communications networks and launch America's nuclear arsenal into its own atmosphere. The resulting electromagnetic pulse cascade would destroy electrical grids and critical infrastructure, plunging the

U.S. into a stygian darkness, and utterly collapse emergency services, hospitals, transportation networks, and water supplies. Within weeks the Americans would suffer total social collapse. The proverbial Four Horsemen of starvation, disease, death, and civil war would trample across the continent, after which Chinese military forces would sweep in without resistance and harvest America's nearly infinite natural resources.

Peng's normally buoyant mood turned decidedly somber as he viewed the encrypted video his Russian colleague in the FSB had sent him. His anger swelled as the shaky handheld video revealed the gruesome details.

The burnt and broken wreckage of the Chinese 747-8F transport aircraft was scattered for hundreds of meters over the Siberian ice. Peng's Russian was passable, but the attached transcript and washed-out video images indicated that neither the crew nor his security team survived, and the plane's precious cargo of EUV photolithography equipment clearly destroyed.

Peng closed the laptop, his concern rising. He rubbed his closely cropped chin beard thoughtfully. The destruction of the aircraft's cargo was a crushing blow to China's AGI program, the equipment invaluable and irreplaceable, at least for the time being.

This crash was one of several similar catastrophes that occurred in the past year, each seemingly random and entirely accidental. He'd submitted detailed reports suggesting there were too many coincidences to avoid the conclusion some kind of conspiracy was at play. His intelligence work had taught him to infer motives from outcomes. Effects were always produced by causes, and a pattern of coincidences still amounted to a pattern.

Though his conspiracy theory had been rejected by his superiors, this latest event only confirmed Peng's deepest fears.

According to the radar tracking he'd seen, it appeared as if either Captain Yuchen or his first officer committed suicide for some unknown reason by plunging the perfectly operating aircraft into the Siberian wasteland.

But Peng De knew both pilots personally and was deeply familiar with their dossiers. They both had flawless flight records. They nominally worked for one of China's largest civilian air cargo transport companies, but were also on his payroll. Highly respected international pilots like them passed through security gates with frictionless ease, making them perfect couriers for his worldwide operations.

There was no way either man committed suicide. Neither was mentally unbalanced nor given over to alien ideologies. Like him, they were committed Party men and patriotic to the core. They fully understood the vital importance of this delivery.

Peng had also checked the meticulous maintenance logs. They were flawless.

The destruction of the 747 was the final straw for Peng. All his energy and focus would now turn to the conspiracy problem. Who were they? How to find them? How to defeat them? He hardly knew where to begin.

The only thing he was certain of was that if a highly secretive organization truly existed, as he was sure it did, it would possess a high degree of technical knowledge related to the field, as well as the resources to carry out its plans.

Peng had already discounted the work of foreign agents of the Western powers. Certainly the Americans and British were capable of this kind of activity. But his sources within those respective governments had passed along the fact their programs also had suffered seemingly random setbacks.

That led him to only one possible conclusion. There were rumors of a shadowy network of saboteurs known as the Guardians, who carried out such ruthless acts of banditry. But why?

Peng needed a weapon to counter them, and he believed he knew just such a weapon. She was a former agent, the best he'd ever worked with. She possessed a stellar mind with vast expertise in computer science and demonstrated superlative spycraft in overseas work. Unfortunately, she now worked for another division.

But rank had its privileges, and Peng's superiors would support her transfer to his division on the strength of his reputation alone, no matter how disruptive to the other department. She would help him prove the conspiracy was all too real, and that he was fighting on the front lines of China's most important battle.

The Guardians had to be stopped no matter the cost.

15

PANAMA

Linc and Raven had followed the others up Death Mountain. At times they found themselves climbing hand over hand over rain-slicked rocks on narrow, near-vertical paths a Nubian ibex wouldn't have braved.

Against their best operator instincts, Linc and Raven each carried a small child for nearly a mile on the very steepest part of the climb, their young mothers weeping with gratitude. At one particularly perilous gap in the rocks, they lent helping hands to a couple of elderly folk too weak to make the jump by themselves.

The long line of migrants had separated, the strongest surging far ahead and the weakest falling way behind. Both Raven and Linc sensed the danger trailing behind the farthest stragglers. As much as they wanted to help, they knew without weapons it would be impossible to stop an attack by armed thieves. To complete their mission, they had to keep pressing forward, and trust the fates of the poor people behind them to God and the far-less-tender mercies of the predators lying in wait.

Linc and Raven both caught the familiar stench, sulfurous and fecal, hanging in the humid jungle air before they turned the next bend. They saw where the trail had widened and a knot of young families making a wide berth around a decomposing corpse draped against the rocks like seaweed strewn upon the shore. Parents tried to shield their children's eyes from the sack of blackish flesh and bones buzzing with insects, but the sickening smell struck them all. A teenager crossed herself as she vomited, then bolted away.

The families braving the Darién risked everything in search of a new and better life. But the fallen body reminded them all that for some the tragic journey through the Plug ended in an unmarked grave—or worse, no grave at all.

★

Several hours later, the sun stooped behind the mountains, throwing long shadows beneath the towering trees. Raven and Linc had finally topped the mountain and were on the down slope, a tricky path, but not nearly so hazardous as the climb up. The *Oregon* operators now passed knots of exhausted and injured travelers camped on the ground, too tired or battered to continue anytime soon.

Raven avoided the pleading eyes of the young mothers as best she could. Her heart went out to them. A pregnant woman sat forlornly on a rock, her eyes glazed over in numbed terror, an empty Brazos Abiertos plastic water bottle lying at her feet.

"*Espera*," Raven rasped toward Linc's broad back. Wait.

He turned around, his eyes a question mark. Raven nodded at the pregnant woman. He understood immediately.

Raven dropped to one knee, pulled out a half-drunk liter of bottled water from her pack, and handed it to her. The woman's grim face struggled to understand the gesture.

"*Tómalo*," Raven said. Take it.

The woman nodded slightly and began to cry as she grasped the bottle with trembling hands. She struggled to open it. Raven popped the cap and handed it back to her. The woman took a small sip and muttered her thanks, returning it to her.

Raven smiled and shook her head. "*Es para tu bebe*." It's for your baby.

Raven didn't wait for an answer. She stood and marched away with Linc at her side. He didn't say a word.

He only wished he'd done the same.

Twenty minutes later they found themselves all alone on the steeply winding trail until they reached the foot of the next steep climb. They shot each other a quick glance, mustered up their reserves, and sped up the hill just as gunshots rang out on the other side. It was the unmistakable staccato of a short burst from an AK-47.

Screams echoed in the trees.

Both operators instantly dashed into the tree line and found cover just as a dozen panicked migrants scrambled wide-eyed and breathless back over the hill and down the trail. One of the men caught sight of Raven and shouted, "Run for your life! Killers are coming!"

Linc didn't need to speak any Spanish to understand what the man had said. He and Raven exchanged another look and waited in place, listening for more gunfire.

There was none.

But desperate cries and angry shouts filled the air on the far side of the hill.

"I'm gonna take a look," Raven said.

"Right behind ya."

The two operators stayed off the path, stealthily climbing the hill until they crested it, keeping low and out of sight.

A dozen young Hispanic and Haitian girls and women stood whimpering in a small clearing. One masked gunman pointed his AK at them, while another pointed his at a kneeling Venezuelan, likely the husband of one of the women. Two other men were zip-tying the women's wrists, ignoring the corpse bleeding out in the dirt.

The young gunman in front of the kneeling Venezuelan turned to say something. The Venezuelan saw his chance. He leaped at the teenager and nearly had his hands on his throat when one of the other thugs put a bullet through his skull, dropping him into the dirt.

The women screamed in terror as the gunmen all laughed.

"*Apúrate!*" one of them barked at his comrades. Hurry up!

When the last girl was finally secured, the lead gunman turned onto a side trail off the main path, no doubt headed in the direction of their own camp. The other killers jammed their guns into the women's ribs and backs and pushed them along in the same direction, cursing and threatening.

The two *Oregon* operators knew exactly what unspeakable things would happen to those women—and that was before they would be sold into slavery.

Linc glanced at Raven. She was a total professional. She knew the mission and she knew how to do her job, holding her own in the field as well as any other operator.

But he could see the rage welling up in her eyes.

He felt it in his own soul, too.

It didn't matter. They weren't here on a mission of mercy. A base camp of Iranian operators might well be planning a mass casualty event on American soil. It was their job to find that camp as quickly as possible. That was their only job. The job they were paid to do.

But Linc knew that one day he would have to give an account of the life he had lived and the choices he had made, both for what he did—and what he failed to do.

Linc nodded at Raven.

"Any chance you wear a combat leg?"

Raven grinned. "Forgot to pack it."

"I've got the next best thing." Linc yanked on his leather pants belt and unhooked it. Though he had risked their lives doing so, he had successfully smuggled in a hidden belt buckle knife, which he quickly detached. He held up the razor-sharp three-inch blade.

"One knife, four AKs. Sounds about even."

Raven frowned. "You couldn't butter toast with that thing."

"You'd be surprised. Better get a move on. Follow me."

16

Linc got to work with the knife, while Raven unraveled her two colorful wristbands, both made of woven paracord. She and Linc discussed tactical plans as she measured out lengths of the high-strength nylon cord and he cut away a three-inch strip from the bottom of his pant leg before turning his attention to a sturdy stick nearby. They worked quickly. No telling how far away the kidnappers' camp was.

A sudden cloudburst unloaded another deluge of rain. With any luck, that would slow the killers down a bit.

Raven scrambled to the top of the hill while Linc finished up. She was careful to keep her form away from the crest in case one of the killers glanced up and saw her figure silhouetting against the foliage. She stood on the tips of her toes and wiped away the strands of wet hair smearing her face. She saw the tops of the bobbing heads of the kidnappers and their victims snaking down the steep path winding in sharp curves around the hillside. Two kidnappers were up front, two took the rear. The thirteen bound women shuffled and stumbled in between them.

Raven made a quick calculation and scrambled back to Linc, who had finished up his handiwork in just seven minutes flat.

He handed her a club. Linc had found a two-foot stick with three smaller branches at the top. He cut those down and formed a three-fingered prong, then tied a heavy stone into the cleft with the paracord.

She felt the weight of it. Liked the heft.

"Gonna get my Fred Flintstone on. Where'd you learn to do this?"

"There was a Boy Scout troop at my reform school," Linc said as he tested the tensile strength of his own weapon, making sure the pouch was snugly tied to the paracord.

"Seriously?"

Linc gathered up a handful of large rocks.

"Nah. Just watched a lot of *MacGyver*. We clear on the plan?"

"You know what they say about plans."

"Let's go."

The two operators bolted up and dashed forward.

Raven crested the hill, got her bearings, and plunged into the brush, racing down the steepest part of the hill in a headlong rush, desperately trying to keep quiet. Luckily, rain masked most of the noise.

Linc ran in a low crouch as he loaded up his weapon. He was making his own calculations. He had to time his attack with hers.

Without comms.

In the rain.

And the looming shadows growing darker by the minute.

★

The lead kidnapper's lurid mind was focused on the prettiest girl in the line. He marched blithely down the hill, his imagination filling his mind's eye with salacious images, keeping him from seeing the length of nylon filament stretched across the path.

He released his grip on his gun as he fell to catch himself before he hit the rocky ground. Pain shot through both of his palms as the sharp rocks cut into them, his agony temporarily blinding him to the appearance of a pair of women's sneakers suddenly standing by his face.

He glanced up just in time to see the determined face of a black-haired woman swinging her club from high over her head and burying the stone between his eyes, killing him instantly.

The man behind him laughed at first when his commander nearly face-planted in the dirt. But the sudden appearance of the murderous, swift-footed beauty wielding a two-fisted club startled him. He fumbled as he tried to raise his weapon to fire, but he was too slow. Just as he pointed the gun toward her she smashed at it with a baseball swing of her club, breaking his hand before he could pull the trigger.

He screamed in pain as he flinched, his final, fatal mistake. The rock on the end of her club crashed into his jaw with a spray of blood and teeth, knocking him out cold. He crumbled to the muddy ground, never feeling the second blow sinking into the back of his skull and ending his life.

★

Linc had timed his shot perfectly.

He and Raven had worked together enough that they knew each other's capabilities. With nearly clocklike perfection, he had estimated how long it would take for Raven to career down the hill and get ahead of the cruel parade they were determined to stop. He then added the time he thought it would take to run the paracord across the trail, and he had been keeping track of the marching pace of the group.

Just as the first kidnapper was tripping on Raven's paracord booby trap, he swung his own sling like a young David and let fly with all of his might. The paracord sling snapped on release like a mini bullwhip and the fist-size stone rocketed through the air in an unwavering line. It had been a while since Linc had thrown a sling, one of the many primitive weapons he and Eddie Seng, his Gundog boss, liked to build and practice with. But a simple injury wouldn't be enough. Linc had to take the man down, and there was only one strike zone that would do the trick.

His aim proved true.

The hurtling rock hit the man's neck just below the skull with a sickening crunch. The crushing blow split the C2 and C3 vertebrae and severed his spinal cord. He cried out softly as his paralyzed limbs gave way and he tumbled into the dirt.

The kidnapper in front of the man started to turn around at the confusing sounds behind him, but one of his companions up front let out a bloodcurdling scream. He snatched up his weapon as the women began bunching up, shocked by the commotion ahead of them.

"*¡Fuera de mi camino!*" Out of my way, he shouted as he grabbed one of the women and tossed her aside to clear a path. But the few seconds it took to move her away were all that Linc needed to close the gap. Linc was as big as a defensive lineman, but he ran like a wide receiver, and tackled the thug from behind, knocking him down. He pinned the man's face into the mud with his frying pan–size hand and slit the killer's carotid artery with his three-inch blade.

Everything happened so fast the women hardly had time to react. When one of them turned around and saw Linc straddling the corpse, she screamed. The other women gasped in horror, quailing and huddling together, confused and terrified all at the same time, unable to comprehend what they were seeing in either direction.

Linc stood as Raven raced up to him. The rain suddenly stopped as if God himself shut off the spigot.

The women saw her and surged forward, grasping at her, begging to be released, or crying tears of thanks.

"You good?" Raven asked. Linc's muddy clothes were slathered in arterial blood.

"Gonna need a laundromat. You?" He nodded at her blood-spattered club.

"Yeah, all good." She tossed her gory weapon into the mud. "Let's cut these women loose, gather up some weapons, and clear out before their friends start looking for them."

"Roger that."

Linc wiped the blood from the blade before slashing the hard plastic bonds pinning each woman. Raven tried to comfort the younger ones still shuddering with terror and utterly confused. But one of the older women, the first one freed, called out in a loud whisper, "*Mira, allí,*" as she pointed out a shallow cave in the rocks.

The women who had gathered their wits didn't need any instructions and helped Linc drag the four bodies into the hollowed rock. A few of the women spit on the corpses and cursed their souls as they tossed leaves and dirt over them.

Raven gathered up the weapons and found an AK with a folding stock and a 9-millimeter pistol, along with mags. Both guns could be carried concealed. She easily tore down the other AKs and tossed the parts deep into the trees, careful to grab the bolt carriers with their firing pins and hurling them as far down the hill as she could, rendering the weapons utterly inoperable.

Raven then gave instructions to the women to race back up to the main trail, leave behind their dead, and rejoin their friends and family. She urged them to not discuss the rescue nor identify her and Linc. The grateful women pledged eternal silence as Linc scattered the last vestiges of blood and gore on the trail with his shoes. One woman kissed Raven's hands and blessed her before turning away and following the others up the hill.

Linc and Raven waited ten minutes to give them time to escape, half expecting another band of armed thugs to appear from the bottom of the trail. It wouldn't be much of a gunfight if they came up in force. But for once, their luck held. No one came.

The two Gundogs retreated up the hill to resume their journey across the Darién. Another cloudburst opened up, washing away their filth.

17

THE PEOPLE'S REPUBLIC OF CHINA

The diminutive young woman with bright, soft eyes and attractive build flashed her credentials. The chiseled security guard couldn't contain his surprise. He'd never seen that level of clearance possessed by someone so young. He immediately escorted her to the VIP elevator with its uninterrupted ascent to the top floor. Moments later, a secretary pushed open the exquisitely carved dragon door and ushered Linlin Zhang into Peng De's office.

Peng's office, like the man himself, was both futuristic and stylish, a perfect blend of aesthetic form and technological function. Shanghai's steel and glass skyline shimmered with sunlight in the tall corner windows.

Linlin hadn't visited the city in years and had never been to the new headquarters of her organization. Shanghai had been transformed into one of the world's great architectural capitals, just one of dozens of Chinese megacities flourishing like golden blossoms. As China prospered, many American cities decayed into Third World ruins, their streets as filthy and dangerous as the drug addicts littering them. It was hard to believe the United States had ever won any wars, hot or cold.

Peng rose with a smile to greet her. He wore the latest Chinese fashion, a Mandarin collared jacket tailored to his lean build, fitted slacks, and leather loafers. His chin beard and hair were neatly trimmed. Linlin couldn't shake the feeling he had dressed up for the occasion.

She suddenly felt haggard after her long red-eye flight from Germany. She'd managed to freshen up in the airport bathroom, but didn't take the time to stop by her hotel for a proper shower and change of clothes. The last thing she wanted to do was to draw the man's attention to her good looks. But judging by the light in his eyes, she'd already crossed that bridge. An old familiar feeling gurgled in her taut belly, but she flashed a pleasing smile that hid her anxiety.

Peng offered his hand, and they exchanged a comradely handshake.

"So good to see you," Peng said. "It has been, what, five years?"

"That long? Yes, I believe so. Where does the time go?"

"Please." He gestured to one of the two chairs in front of his desk. She took one and he the other.

"Tea? Coffee? Something stronger?"

"That's kind of you to offer, but no, thank you. I think I drank my weight in tea on the flight over."

"I appreciate you coming on such short notice."

"I've only just arrived and came straight from the airport. Your urgent message was cryptic."

Peng gazed paternalistically. "You seem upset, maybe even nervous?"

"Forgive me. I haven't slept in thirty-eight hours. I took the red-eye, but I can't sleep on planes, and caffeine makes me jittery. I must look a mess . . ."

"Not at all. More lovely than I even remember."

Linlin blushed a little, and drew a hank of her chin-length hair behind her ear.

"How do you like your work in Germany?" Peng asked.

"I'm happy to serve wherever the Party needs me."

"I was disappointed when you were transferred away. We worked so well together in the Bright Lantern program. You were my most effective agent."

"You trained me well."

Peng's previous position had been to recruit China's brightest science and engineering students and place them in the most prestigious university programs abroad. Their mission was to ferret out information and technology, and to cultivate compromising relationships with notable colleagues and professors.

Linlin had been the brightest student he'd ever encountered and proved a prodigy in spycraft. But it was her natural, unadorned beauty that disarmed, and in some cases, unhinged the men she encountered. Her time at MIT had been most productive, and her secret reports had proven invaluable. The Bright Lantern program's success had been the fuel that rocketed Peng to the pinnacle of power he now enjoyed.

"It surprised me when you were reassigned to another division." Peng's probing eyes searched her face for clues.

Linlin shifted in her chair. Long hours in coach class—the only seat she could secure—played havoc with her back. But her discomfiture was more than physical. She wondered if he knew she had secretly requested the transfer for several reasons, not the least of which were Peng's paternalistic affections that had taken an altogether different turn.

"We both serve the Party in whatever capacity the Party decides. In your case, the Party has chosen wisely."

Linlin saw the tug at the corner of Peng's mouth. He had a weakness for female flattery.

"Yes, of course. And your time in Germany has been productive. I've read your file. Perhaps it's time to turn the page."

"Your message said it was urgent that we meet in person, but you didn't say why. I assume there is a security concern?"

In fact, she knew he simply wanted her sitting in his presence. As uncomfortable as that was, she saw the opportunity it presented. Close proximity to Peng could be the most advantageous thing for her at the moment—and also the most dangerous.

"I have an extremely important assignment for you if you're interested."

"My work in Germany is important."

"Of course, but not as urgent nor as critical as what I have in mind."

"And that is?"

"Have you heard of the Guardians?"

"Rumors only. A hacker group, perhaps? Nothing specific."

"I believe them to be a highly organized band of dangerous cut-throats murdering our scientists and destroying our valuable equipment."

"For what purpose?"

"To stop our AGI development. Just three days ago, a cargo plane carrying advanced photolithography machinery was destroyed, killing the entire crew and security team."

Linlin's jaw dropped in shock. "I had no idea."

"Given the work you've been doing in Germany, you understand there is no strategic initiative with higher priority. China must acquire AGI first—at any cost—and deny it to all of her competitors."

Linlin nodded. "Agreed. These Guardians must be stopped. I assume they're Western intelligence?"

"My sources tell me the Western powers have suffered losses similar to ours, though they have yet to put the puzzle pieces together as I have. We are dealing with an altogether different animal."

"A crime syndicate? A mercenary outfit?"

"It's unclear. But stopping them is my first and only priority. And you are the sword I need to cut them down."

Linlin's eyes narrowed almost imperceptibly. But Peng caught it.

"I need your help, Linlin. I hope there is nothing in our past that would stand in the way of our collaboration."

That was as close to an apology as Peng would ever give. Linlin accepted it with a gentle lie.

"Of course not. How can I serve you?"

"Before we can destroy them, we must find them. And I believe you might possess our first important clue."

"How so?"

"Six months ago, you filed a field report on a former subject of yours from your MIT days. Dr. Mark Murphy, I believe?"

"He wrote a paper solving a critical interface problem in organoid computing. I reviewed the report and sent it to my superiors. Why?"

"I read your analysis. It was brilliant, if you don't mind my saying."

"You are too kind."

"Not at all. And we both know the central importance of organoid computing for the future of artificial general intelligence. Our very best minds believe that only biohybrid computer processors using lab-grown human brain structures can generate sufficient computational power."

"I strongly agree with that assessment. The human mind is the most powerful computer in the known universe, and at the moment only humans exhibit true intelligence. It's only logical to conclude that building a human brain computer is the surest path to creating machine intelligence."

"No doubt the Guardians understand this as well."

"No doubt."

"And given the importance of organoid computing, I would think Dr. Murphy would be of some interest to the Guardians."

"Agreed."

"Do you think you can reestablish contact with him? Perhaps even rekindle your relationship?"

Linlin bit her lower lip. She and Mark had been intimate. It was one of the unfortunate duties required in the Bright Lantern program.

"I left MIT suddenly, just after graduation from the PhD program. We parted without rancor, though I know he was heartbroken. Knowing Dr. Murphy, I suspect he may still carry a torch for me. I believe I was his first love."

"Have you stayed in touch?"

"No."

"Can you find him?"

Linlin grinned mischievously. In her mind's eye she saw Murphy's parachute pants, skater shoes, and crazy punk rock concert T-shirts. He was both brilliant and juvenile. An Einstein brain trapped in a perpetual teenage mentality.

"It shouldn't be too difficult. I am quite familiar with his peculiar foibles and his obvious weaknesses."

"Then you have your first assignment."

"What resources are at my disposal?"

"Anything you need—a blank check. When can you get started? Of course, you should take a few days off to get settled before you begin."

Linlin stood.

"Time is our enemy. Who knows when these vicious Guardians will strike again? I'll launch out as soon as I make contact with Murphy."

Peng stood as well. "Extract every ounce of intelligence you can get from this Murphy fellow. Find out what you can about the Guardians so we can destroy them."

"And what do you want me to do with Murphy when I'm finished?"

"If you think you can turn him into a working asset, please do so."

"And if I can't?"

"You said yourself he's a brilliant mind and familiar with organoid intelligence. If we can't turn his genius to our benefit, the only logical choice is to kill him."

Linlin smiled impishly.

"Agreed."

18

Dr. Noam Peretz stood on another planet, or so it seemed. Planted on the curve of the steep mountain trail at nearly seven thousand feet, he took in the God's-eye view of the pale granite peaks across the wide horizon, jagged and bleached like broken bones stabbing at the crystalline sky. A pewter-blue lake far below was dusted with dazzlingly white snow glistening beneath the silver disk of the sun.

The cold air clawed at his lungs with each shallowing breath. But Peretz needed this badly. Nothing thrilled his soul more than being on the trail. His daily life in Silicon Valley was crowded with endless demands; a constant bombardment of investor queries, team meetings, and project deadlines. Worse, his colliding worlds of bioinformatics and computational genomics saturated his fevered mind with endless webs of equations and algorithms, even in his troubled sleep. Only out here, in nature's grandeur, and alone on the trail far from people, could he ever find peace and clarity.

Peretz dropped his ultralight pack and yanked out a fleece pullover against the rising chill. It had been six months since he'd been on any trail, and even longer in the high Sierra Nevadas. He'd hiked all his life, and his booted feet had taken him over some of the roughest terrain on the planet. He'd even met his first ex-wife on the Pacific Crest Trail while still in grad school. But these granite spires were still his favorite.

His extreme work schedule had been part of the problem. Pioneering new bioengineering approaches to neural network architectures in the development of organoid intelligence was more than time-consuming. He was practically inventing a new subfield of computer science. A trillion dollars of global venture capital hung on desperate tenterhooks waiting for his next breakthrough.

But what had really kept Peretz off the trail was the sudden and thoroughly maddening onset of EIB—exercise-induced bronchoconstriction. Years of working indoors and sucking in the pollen-infested and chemically saturated air of cities and labs around the world had brought on a series of frightening asthma-like attacks whenever he hit the trail.

On the verge of a nervous breakdown, Peretz engaged the help of both a medical AI program and an exercise researcher at Stanford. Together they developed a workout regimen that had put him tentatively back on the trail. Over time, he'd been able to extend the range, duration, and altitude of his hikes.

Today was his first big test, and so far he'd passed with flying colors. By pacing himself, limiting his gear weight to less than ten pounds, and hydrating at regular intervals, Peretz hadn't needed his inhaler at all to reach this point. His biggest challenge on this or any hike was high altitude. Temperatures dropped an average of three and a half degrees every thousand feet, and oxygen saturation fell about the same. They had estimated that his EIB would likely be triggered at seven thousand feet, a prognosis now confirmed with each stabbing breath coming on faster and shallower.

If the EIB kicked into overdrive, it could kill him.

But a quick hit of albuterol would act as a prophylactic and give him the boost he needed to ascend the next leg of the trail. His plan was to hit eighty-five hundred feet today and set up camp for the night before pushing on to ten thousand tomorrow.

Peretz reached into his pack and pulled out his inhaler. He took another glance around the granite valley, wishing his life were different. He wasn't sure why it wasn't. He had more money than he could ever spend in a dozen lifetimes. Was it the thrill of being the first to cross the line? To build the first AGI machine known to man, and usher in a golden age of human progress?

Those were exactly the kinds of questions he'd come up here to escape.

He popped the cap on his inhaler, put it into his mouth, and drew the deepest lungful of vaporized medicine he could draw.

Peretz held his breath for as long as he could to allow the albuterol vapor to saturate his lungs.

And then he coughed.

And coughed.

And coughed.

Peretz doubled over. Something was wrong. He couldn't catch his breath. He panicked. His shallow breaths turned to panting, and his nose began to run.

He dropped to his knees, wiping away the snot pouring out of his nose and coughing up strings of sticky phlegm gurgling in his throat. His trembling fingers tore at his shirt, trying to free his lungs that felt like they were being crushed inside a hydraulic press.

His quaking body toppled over into the rocky dirt, his diaphragm hard as stone. His oxygen-starved brain blurred his vision until his beloved mountains narrowed to a singular point of mindless black.

★

She approached the body curled up in a fetal position, lying on the trail, an empty inhaler by his hand—and clearly dead. It didn't bother her. She was a doctor and no stranger to corpses. She removed her pack.

Peretz was the only person on the trail she'd seen all day, and he'd been hours ahead of her. She pulled on a glove and checked his carotid. No pulse. His deoxygenated skin was pale as parchment, and his lips blue as India ink. She shuddered as a cold breeze gusted over them.

She actually felt a little sorry for him. She had shadowed Peretz ever since he'd left the trailhead six hours earlier. His speed and endurance were impressive considering his EIB. Fortunately, she was an athlete in prime condition and was able to keep up.

She'd met Peretz at a Stanford alumni dinner a few years ago. He was brilliant and funny and even a little flirty, and between his second and third marriages, as she recalled. An almost comical mop of hair belied the ferocious intellect inside his skull. Her MD/PhD in pharmacology with an emphasis in neuroscience allowed her to almost keep up with him during their intense conversation over cocktails that night. She sensed even then Peretz was throwing open doors into a new and frightening future. What scared her most was his nonchalance about it.

Peretz cut their conversation short because he was late for the keynote speech he was about to give. He left a spare room key on the bar top next to her, but she passed. He had sent a chill down her spine. Peretz was like the civil engineer who made sure the trains ran on time with no concern where those boxcars wound up, even if they might unload their human cargoes at Auschwitz. Surely he understood the social, political, and economic crises AGI was about to unleash on the world if it fell into the wrong hands—but if he did, he didn't seem to care. AGI could be used by dark forces to cripple whole economies, incite civil wars, and establish techno-dictatorships. Such dictatorships would construct an inescapable surveillance state where every action, word, and transaction could be monitored, controlled, or prevented.

And with such a powerful weapon, there could be no "good" hands—that kind of absolute power would absolutely corrupt whoever possessed it.

She didn't balk for a second when she was given Peretz's name as her next target. Acquiring the nerve agent sarin was the primary obstacle in her plan, but the Guardian network readily provided it upon her request in its stable, liquid form. She had easy access to a level 3 chemical safety lab, so aerosolizing it hadn't been a problem and loading it into the emergency inhalers was a simple task. Fortunately, she oversaw the Stanford pharmacy, where Peretz's doctor had put in his albuterol prescription for the climb.

Sarin was the perfect agent. Death was nearly instantaneous, and its effects mimicked an asthma attack. Sarin metabolized rapidly in the body, making postmortem detection highly unlikely even if conducted quickly. In all likelihood, his body wouldn't be discovered for several days and an autopsy conducted many hours after that. She doubted an autopsy would be requested at all. Peretz was a diagnosed asthmatic who obviously died in an asthma-inducing environment hiking a difficult trail with an expended asthma inhaler lying just inches from his cold, dead fingers. Why would any medical examiner call for an autopsy?

She glanced around the valley once again. There was still nobody else in sight in this remote region of the park. Only serious hikers ever came this way, and there were precious few of those this time of year. According to Peretz's intercepted emails, this remoteness was one of the primary reasons he picked this climb. Like many people of his ideological persuasion, he loved the concept of humanity in theory, but actual persons with real names and messy emotions repulsed him or were, at best, tools at his disposal.

She glanced down once more at Peretz's figure. She considered rolling his body down the side of the mountain, making him harder to find and certainly more difficult to recover. An early discovery of his body was now her biggest concern. The park service flew routine air patrols over the area, even if hikers hadn't been reported lost or late by family and friends. Fortunately, the required itineraries all hikers had to file with their permits weren't monitored by the rangers. No park officials checked hikers in or out of the park.

Peretz would eventually be missed after another forty-eight hours, and rangers notified. But what if a routine patrol plane flew over now? They'd see her hovering over his dead body. Police would be called, and she would be identified as a person of interest, especially if she didn't report the incident. And if she did report it? Either way, questions would be asked. Why was she there? Did she know the man? Isn't that quite a coincidence?

Better to leave things alone—and just leave.

Now.

Killing Peretz was the critical mission, but remaining undiscovered was as important both for herself and the Guardians. Her organization possessed considerable weapons to kill and destroy, but anonymity was their best defense.

She shouldered her pack and headed in a different direction, cutting across to a different trail and to an alternate trailhead without security cameras, where a prearranged car had been parked for her use. With any luck, she'd be home by tomorrow afternoon, her bases covered, her alibis intact, and no one the wiser before the body was even discovered.

She wasn't convinced she could save humanity from the impending AGI holocaust, but today she had done her part, fatally tossing one of that speeding train's most dangerous conductors onto the tracks.

19

ABOARD THE *OREGON*
OFF THE PACIFIC COAST OF MEXICO

Eat my plasma bolt!" Murphy screamed as the automaton exploded. The robot's heavy shields had been damaged enough by the grenades tossed by Murphy's squad mates. He was able to take out the mechanical monster with a short burst from his plasma sniper rifle.

Shouts of triumph and "Great job, Scorpio7!" rang out over Dr. Mark Murphy's headset.

"Thanks, guys—couldn't have done it without you."

Murphy was stretched out in a gaming lounge chair, his face covered with a virtual reality mask, his hands gripped on a virtual rifle. His gaming chair was attached to one of several consoles in his private cabin, which was designed to match the hovercraft *Nebuchadnezzar* from his favorite movie, *The Matrix*, steel deck plates included.

He and his best friend, Eric Stone, spent countless off-duty hours destroying all manner of malicious aliens and were world-class masters of the most popular online games. Murph was another of the rare *Oregon* crew members with no former military experience. But his previous career as a cutting-edge weapons designer, his unmatched brilliance and unique skill sets had proven invaluable to Cabrillo.

Murphy had taken every security precaution to protect the *Oregon* from any kind of hacker shenanigans, using multiple aliases, VPNs, and other measures when he played his online games. He shut them all down whenever they went into any kind of threat area to avoid electromagnetic detection. He wasn't due on shift at the weapons station for another twelve hours.

"Let's move out," the squad commander said. She was a twenty-two-year-old Romanian from Bucharest. She wisely used a voice alteration device to mask her youth and gender in the highly competitive, verbally abusive, and testosterone-fueled world of online gaming. He let her lead the squad and pretended to be a newbie on this mission. If the other players had known his most famous gamertag they might not have wanted to play with him for fear of being humiliated by his prowess.

"Roger that," Murphy said as he advanced his mechanical soldier out of the asteroid's long shadows and ran to catch up with the rest of his unit.

Suddenly, an anonymous private text message scrolled across the top of his screen:

U2FsdGVkX19yZGcAuzVxwZ2C+
xodE6TPAGWISx3YV58=

What would have appeared to be gibberish to most people was instantly recognizable to the brilliant MIT graduate.

"Guys, I'll catch up."

"Okay back there?" his squad commander asked.

"All good. Gotta take care of some business."

"Mommy said it's time to go night night?" one of the other fighters asked.

Murphy resisted the temptation to put a plasma bolt in the back of the punk's virtual helmet. The kid needed to learn some manners, but right now Murph had a puzzle to solve.

"You guys stay frosty," Murphy said.

"You too, amigo," the Romanian said as the team pressed forward toward an alien shipwreck on the horizon.

Murph turned his attention to the string of lower- and uppercase letters, numbers, and mathematical symbols. He instantly recognized it as Base64 encoding. He also knew Base64 was commonly used to represent binary data in the ASCII string format.

A code leading to a code.

Murph bailed out of the game window and pulled up an online calculator. He hardly needed it. He often relied on his own split-second mental calculations for firing solutions when he was the weapons officer. Cabrillo compared him to John Glenn performing trajectory calculations faster than Mercury's onboard computer.

Murph opened up a new terminal window and began decoding the encrypted text by entering the command:

```
base64 -d encrypted_file.b64 > decrypted.bin
```

Moments later, the result he came up with was a long binary data sequence of fifty-three digits and characters. The "Salted_" prefix in this new sequence probably meant the data was encrypted using OpenSSL's default method. But now he had a problem. He needed a password to decrypt it—and no idea how to find it.

Suddenly, a second message appeared on his screen:

Find the positive integer solution to the equation:

$7^x \equiv 1 \mod 20$

Murphy tugged on his wispy beard, intrigued. Whoever was sending this stuff was no idiot and didn't think he was one, either. He needed to solve for x in the equation. He popped open his terminal and fired off a quick Python command.

The result was an infinite arithmetic sequence of numbers beginning with 4.

But Murph knew that "infinity" couldn't be the answer. In fact, just the opposite. In cryptographic puzzles, the shortest viable solution was always the most efficient choice. He noticed the numbers all advanced by a factor of 4.

That was the answer.

He then saved the encrypted data to a file, opened a new terminal window, and used the OpenSSL command-line tool. When it prompted him for a password, he entered "4" and crossed his fingers.

Yes.

Murphy flushed with another dopamine hit. The decryption was a success.

The only problem was that it yielded another coded hexadecimal message:

```
45 65 72 6F 20 53 61 61 72 69 6E 65 6E
```

Murphy paused. He was being led down a rabbit hole, exactly the kind of thing a super hacker would do if they wanted to crack into the *Oregon*'s system.

He did a quick gut check and, more important, a mental inventory. There was no way that anything happening in his gaming computer could possibly affect the *Oregon*. Still, it would be smarter to quit this little dance and not take any chances with the intriguing puzzle.

But . . . he was so close to solving it.

He decided to trust his intuition and press on. Besides, converting hexadecimal to ASCII was child's play; a mere matter of consulting a table. He pulled one up, threw it onto a spreadsheet, and then converted each hexadecimal pair to its alphabetical equivalent.

The result surprised him:

EERO SAARINEN

Where did he know that name from? His fingers twitched as they hovered over the keyboard. A few simple strokes in a search engine could pull the name up. But that wasn't any fun.

He rewound his mental computer and could practically hear the high-pitched gibberish of an old audio tape playing backward in his mind. The tumblers finally fell into place.

Eero Saarinen was the Finnish-American architect who designed two famous buildings at MIT. One was a chapel, the other was the Kresge Auditorium.

Murph hadn't thought much about school since he came on board the *Oregon*. He was quite the nerd—a character straight out of *The Big Bang Theory*. But crewing on the *Oregon* had matured his body and his mind. Intense physical workouts, training in tactics and small arms with the Gundogs, and operating the *Oregon*'s advanced weapons systems had changed him for the better.

Those MIT memories were still sweet. The scene of several intellectual triumphs and a few emotional crashes.

Suddenly, a third message appeared:

Find the value of the integral: $\int_0^\pi \sin(x)\, dx$

Another math problem. Murph tore off his virtual headset and dashed over to his steel work desk. He tapped the keyboard and a mirror image of his gaming console pulled up. He grabbed paper and pencil from a drawer and scribbled away. It was the kind of problem he was solving when other kids his age were still watching cartoons. It took just a couple of moments of noodling to calculate the resulting cosine values at the boundaries. He came up with the number: 2.

How did this relate to anything?

As if reading his thoughts, another message appeared:

Decode this Base64 string:

UXVhbnR1bSBMb3ZlICYgdGhlIENoYW9zIEtpd2lz

Once again, Murph opened up a new terminal window, uploaded the text, and deployed the Base64 command. The result shocked him:

QUANTUM LOVE & THE CHAOS KIWIS

That was the name of his favorite punk rock band in grad school. *How crazy is that?*

He was too busy and too broke to follow them around on tour back then. But he owned two bootleg tapes he had listened to until the magnetic oxide layer began flaking and the tape stretched out like an old rubber band.

The only time he ever saw them in concert was when they came to MIT's Kresge Auditorium . . . designed by . . . Eero Saarinen.

That concert was the first time he'd ever taken a girl on a date.

Murph's face suddenly flushed red, a combination of sheer delight and utter dread. He wanted to shout with joy and puke his guts out all at the same time.

Maybe all of this wasn't just a game. He throttled back his emotions and typed a short burst of hexadecimal code into the anonymous text box:

"Linlin?"

She responded in hexadecimal.

"UR the only one that can help me."

"What's wrong?"

"I don't want to die."

Murph's mind raced with endless possibilities. Linlin was the first girlfriend he'd ever had, the only girl he had ever loved. He drove her to the airport when she left Boston years ago. Her parents were sick, and they needed her back in China. But she never came back to Boston. Didn't even reach out to him. All these years, he had no idea where she was or what had happened to her. He assumed it was all about him. She broke his heart, and it had never fully mended.

Murph continued the coded speech with her.

"Why will you die?"

"Can't explain. No time. Can you meet me here?"

Linlin sent a set of coded GPS coordinates.

Murphy pulled up a map. Thailand.

"Ok?" Linlin asked.

"Ok"

"How soon?"

"24hr +/- Are your comms safe?"

"Comms?"

"Communications. Safe?"

"Must go now."

Before he could type a response, her text window disappeared.

Murph's eyes narrowed with confusion.

What had just happened? Was that all a fever dream? He could hardly believe it.

He'd never gotten over Linlin. She was brilliant, beautiful, funny. In his juvenile heart, he had even thought he was going to marry her.

Now she was back in his life. It seemed too good to be true.

Or maybe it was just good. He wasn't sure.

She said she was in trouble.

He had to find her.

20

Murphy made his way into the deepest bowels of the *Oregon*, pushed past the armory, and entered the "air lock," aka the safety room, where pairs of shooting glasses and earmuffs hung from wall pegs. Murph heard the rapid-fire staccato of a semi-auto pistol mag-dumping on the other side of the insulated wall. He geared up and pulled open the interior door to the gun range and stepped through.

The familiar tang of burnt gunpowder teased Murphy's olfactory bulb. He'd come to love the smell after so many hours of training on this very range. As much as he enjoyed a good virtual gunfight in outer space, no game controller haptics could ever match the kick of a real bullet smashing back a heavy steel pistol slide. He made a mental note to visit the Magic Shop and figure out how to incorporate gunpowder smell into a new, full-body virtual reality game he was designing. Kevin Nixon knew all about that stuff.

There was only one shooter on the range, and he stood in lane three. As Murph approached, he watched Juan Cabrillo raise a pistol in his left hand and rip another fifteen-round string of bullets as fast as he could pull the trigger. The red bull's-eye in the center of the paper target twenty-five yards downrange shredded in an instant. That was fifteen rounds in a hole the size of a child's fist.

Cabrillo hit the ambidextrous mag-release button with his thumb, and before the empty mag hit the floor he'd already shoved the pistol into the holster on his right hip—backward. It was only then that Murph noticed Juan's right hand was wrapped in an Ace bandage, and as he got closer, saw that a handball had been taped to his palm.

Murphy instantly understood Cabrillo was practicing one-handed drills with his supporting hand while simulating a wounded and immobilized strong hand. No sooner had Murphy connected the dots, Cabrillo fetched a fresh mag from a pouch with his left hand and slammed it into the butt of his pistol. By the time the pistol was pointed downrange again he had already hit the slide release. The gun was in battery when he put sights on another target in lane seven, angled away some thirty yards downrange. As soon as the sights found their target, Cabrillo cut loose.

Fifteen bullets later, another target was shredded.

Cabrillo set the empty pistol down on the bench, its barrel safely pointed downrange. He removed his noise-cancelling earbuds.

"Nice shooting, Chairman."

"Still a little slow on the left hand, but I'll keep pushing it. How about you?"

"Haven't done one-handers in a couple of weeks. Good reminder."

"We win the gunfight here, not in the field, right?" Cabrillo unwrapped his right hand as he spoke.

"Yes, sir."

"What can I do you for?"

"I'd like to take shore leave early."

"You'll miss the big shindig." Cabrillo was referring to the Corporation's private vacation island they anchored at every year. They'd head out as soon as they recovered Linc and Raven from their mission—assuming everything went well.

The gun range and other training facilities were important, but Juan believed in playtime, too. On the island, the *Oregon* chefs went all out on beachside barbecues, fast-moving toys from the boat garage were broken out, and Hali Kasim filled the night air with thrumming dance tunes. The music buffs on board all agreed that Kasim's mix master skills would've put him at the top of the DJ 100 list if he ever made a go of it. It was all great fun and completely voluntary. It was meant to be a perk, not a punishment.

"Yeah, I know," Murph said. "But it's kinda important."

"What's up? Somebody sick?"

"Not exactly. I just got a message from an old grad school friend. They asked to see me right away."

Juan grinned. He had a paternal affection for the young genius standing in front of him. He'd come a long way over the years, but there was still part of him that was socially awkward, even immature.

The *Oregon* had no standardized uniforms, but Murphy certainly did. He wore his customary black skater pants, Doc Martens combat boots, and a psychedelic concert T-shirt. Cabrillo was never certain if these were actual punk rock bands or just something Murph made up. The one he was wearing today was a doozy.

THE CONUNDRUM TOUR
featuring:
P vs NP
Squaring the Circle
Time's Arrow
Special guests:
The Noise Vandals
Fists of Furry

Cabrillo chuckled. "I noticed you said 'they.' Is that a pronoun preference or an evasion on your part?"

"*She* said she needed to see me."

Cabrillo cocked an eyebrow. Neither Murphy nor Stone were known to be successful with the ladies. Genius could be off-putting, Cabrillo imagined, but not more than Doc Martens for serious young ladies.

"Girlfriend?"

"First." Murph blushed lobster red. "And only."

"Sorry it didn't work out."

"Me too."

"Is she in some kind of trouble? Do you want me to send someone with you?"

Murph hesitated. He'd been running this conversation in his head ever since he stepped into the elevator. He wasn't at all sure what was going on with Linlin. Showing up with extra muscle might scare her off.

But it would be embarrassing for him if Linlin didn't bother showing up at all, or was sitting there with her husband and two kids, maybe playing some kind of a cruel joke on him. He'd never hear the end of it. He also didn't want the Chairman to waste valuable *Oregon* personnel on what could turn out to be a wild-goose chase.

"I seriously doubt she's in trouble. It's probably just a programming glitch she can't figure out. Coding was never her strong suit."

Cabrillo wasn't sure how to assess the situation. Murphy never asked for personal favors. And his specialized skills at the weapons station wouldn't be needed anytime soon. They were next due at the Port of Lázaro Cárdenas to load up a shipment for delivery to El Salvador. To maintain its cover, the *Oregon* operated as a working cargo vessel whenever possible, especially when on a mission.

"When do you leave?"

"That's the problem. I've gotta get there ASAP. I've checked all the commercial flights. Everything's booked up, even first class."

"Then let's have Tiny give you a lift." Chuck "Tiny" Gunderson was the Corporation's six-foot-four, two-hundred-eighty-pound fixed-wing pilot. The former University of Wisconsin tackle was qualified on the half dozen aircraft owned by the organization including the new Gulfstream G400.

"Isn't he on standby for Linc and Raven?"

"In case of emergency only. So is Gomez."

George "Gomez" Adams was the *Oregon*'s primary tilt-rotor pilot. The former Night Stalkers combat veteran would lead the extraction operation if Linc and Raven needed one. Another pilot, Arnie Davis, had just been hired on as a temporary contractor to support Gomez as needed. The former U.S. Air Force aviator had flown Ospreys for the 20th Special Operations Squadron.

Juan checked his watch out of habit. He always had a running clock and calendar in his mind. "It will be at least seven days before Raven and Linc report in. Plenty of time for Tiny to get you there and back."

"Wow. That's awesome of you."

"I'll call the boat garage to get you ashore. You call Tiny with your travel plans so he can get the flight logged, then get your gear packed, and vamoose outta here."

"Thanks, Chairman."

Juan clapped a hand on Murph's shoulder.

"I hope it works out for you."

"Me too."

"But one thing I know from bitter experience. Nothing burns hotter than an old flame on a tender heart."

21

THE PACIFIC OCEAN

Dr. Anima Bose shot a supervisory glance through the thick picture window of her office overlooking the laboratory floor. Her hand-picked team was a well-oiled but highly stressed machine at the moment, feverishly working toward the unbreakable deadline she had set. Speed was of the essence, but mistakes were intolerable at this juncture.

Bose's dark hair was dyed against the encroaching gray and pulled back with precision into a neat bun. Her fierce eyes matched her strong jawline, detracting from her otherwise lovely countenance. She made no attempt to adorn herself beyond the social norms of good grooming. She suffered no fools and believed that both a husband and children would only have been unnecessary distractions from her life's primary purpose.

She had neither the time nor inclination for video calls.

Bose turned back to her computer monitor and her conversation with her employer, Amador Fierro, who was on the screen and transmitting in an encrypted video. He wore a loose, collarless dark blue cotton shirt that appeared more utilitarian than stylish. His roguishly handsome face was framed with his characteristically charming smile, but his probing eyes betrayed his concern.

"Dr. Bose, how are you?"

"Under the gun, so to speak," she replied, "but I am happy to report good news."

"Excellent," Fierro said, visibly relaxing.

"According to our latest benchmarks, we've passed the final milestone. Project Q will be ready to launch in ten days, right on schedule."

"*Gracias a Dios!*" Fierro said. "That's fantastic news." He leaned back in his chair. "My dream will soon be a reality."

My dream? Dr. Bose thought to herself. Surely it was Fierro's vision, Fierro's money, and Fierro's determination to make Project Q a reality. But she was its inventor. She was the agency that enabled this to happen.

Dr. Bose was one of the most brilliant scientists on the planet in a field overwhelmingly dominated by men. Her long family history of glorious scientific achievement peaked when a distant relative, Satyendra Nath Bose, collaborated with Einstein. The subatomic "boson" particle was named after him—such was his contribution to the field of physics. Every Indian scientist lived in his shadow, but every Bose labored beneath it, heavy laden with the burden of unfulfilled expectations. None ever rose to his stature, failing in their attempts to reach a summit that she had been forbidden to climb at all because of her gender.

She was privately ashamed of her affiliation with the Colombian drug lord, but no lab in the world would give her control of a project of this size and scale. Project Q's organoid computer would produce the world's first AGI program, and it would be her genius that would benefit all of humanity, ushering in a golden era of universal knowledge and prosperity.

As soon as Project Q was launched, she would be known as the greatest scientist of the twenty-first century and enter the pantheon of the world's greatest minds of all time.

So what if that invention was born on the back of a crime lord's ambition? A crime lord who would likely be swept away by the very invention he was paying for? A delicious irony, no doubt.

Bose was completely aware she was handing Fierro a weapon that could cause unimaginable harm to his American persecutors. Under his control, her AGI could hack into every U.S. hydroelectric dam and open up the floodgates simultaneously, unleashing billions of gallons of raging water to pulverize cities, wash away precious farmlands, and drown countless thousands of people beneath torrents of concrete, steel, and debris. Fierro could also crash every commercial airliner, killing thousands and wrecking that industry forever. Worse, he could turn every fast-flying, fuel-laden airplane into guided missiles with targets of his own choosing, dwarfing the 9/11 attack by orders of magnitude.

"My apologies for the imprecision of my language," Fierro said. "Judging by your silence, I have no doubt offended you. I have certainly dreamed of this, but you are the primary force behind it."

Bose startled at his words. How long had she been lost in her thoughts? "Will anyone ever know?" Bose asked.

"In due time, of course. You have my word on that. It was part of our agreement. But we have a deadline that must be met first, and I can't allow a premature press release to jeopardize that, no matter how well deserved."

"I understand your concern," Dr. Bose said, swallowing her anger.

"You are standing on the edge of the map of human knowledge, Dr. Bose. A true pioneer, venturing where none has yet traveled."

Bose softened with Fierro's compliment.

"Thank you for appreciating that."

"But a lot can go wrong in ten days," Fierro said, leaning forward, his eyes flashing. "'*Cave! Hic dragones!*'"

"I don't understand."

"Medieval mapmakers could only draw what was known to them. What lay beyond was a mystery. So on the edges of those great navigational charts they scratched a dire warning to those who would dare sail into the great unknown. *Cave! Hic dragones!* is Latin for 'Beware! Here be dragons!'"

"I will not fail you," Bose said.

Fierro's eyes sparkled. "Of that, I am sure." He ended the call.

Bose basked in Fierro's vote of confidence as she stood to leave. But a sudden tingling on the back of her neck stopped her in her tracks. She turned back to the monitor.

Was that a compliment?

Or a threat?

★

Dr. Bose returned to the picture window overlooking the lab floor, monitoring the technicians hard at work. But like a proud mother, her attention returned to the giant containment tank in the center of the unit, the home of the Neural Reef—the pulsing heart of Project Q.

The organoid Neural Reef earned its name because of its appearance. Each "coral" node of the Reef was a cluster of neural organoids, and together they formed a vast, living synaptic "reef" with a unique—and fragile—metabolic cycle. Its flickering bioluminescent nodes indicated the AGI's evolving thought processes. Some clusters pulsated erratically, while others remained in a dormant, low-energy state. The color and intensity of those pulses shifted based on computational load. The closer the Neural Reef came to achieving AGI, the brighter the entire complex became. Once the Reef achieved sentience, it would be lit up like a Christmas tree.

The organoid Reef was housed within a reinforced, cylindrical tank roughly nine feet tall and six feet in diameter. Inside the tank, the Reef was fully immersed in a genetically modified "neuroplasm"—a semitransparent gel designed to sustain and optimize neural organoid function. Like an amniotic sac for a developing fetus, the specialized bio-suspension medium provided structural support, maintained electrochemical balance, and facilitated real-time data transmission between organic and synthetic interfaces.

Oxygen, glucose, amino acids, and neurotransmitter precursors diffused directly from the gel into the organoid structures, eliminating the need for traditional blood vessels. The womb-like gel also contained bio-nano conductors and synthetic neurotransmitter compounds that enhanced signal transmission between organic and digital components.

The tank itself was made from a high-density biopolymer that resisted pressure fluctuations, radiation, and physical impacts, ensuring the delicate system remained stable even in a turbulent environment like a ship at sea.

The Neural Reef was designed to push AGI development beyond

the limitations of traditional silicon-based architecture, which relied on transistor-based logic gates and rigid binary logic. Instead, organoid computing relied on living neurons that mimicked the distributed architecture of a biological brain. Unlike silicon chips, the neural structures within the Neural Reef could adapt, learn, and reorganize themselves in real time. This led to a more fluid and intuitive decision-making process, enabling the system to achieve contextual reasoning and pattern recognition far beyond the capacity of conventional machine-learning models.

The Neural Reef interfaced with the ship's computational infrastructure through a bio-digital neural link, a hybrid of organic tissue and superconducting fiber-optic cables. This link allowed the AGI to interpret raw data streams as sensory inputs. However, it was sensitive to electromagnetic interference and, worse, power fluctuations.

The greatest challenge the Neural Reef faced was its need for an absolutely stable power supply. Even the smallest micro changes in voltage could disrupt and even destroy the highly sensitive system. Powering up the ship's engines risked diverting crucial energy from the Reef, potentially destabilizing the AGI or causing catastrophic neural collapse.

Bose had likened the Reef's rapidly evolving cognition and physical development within the gel-filled containment tank to a human embryo. Though never having been a biological mother, Bose was well aware her organoid creation had triggered her latent maternal instincts. Her pride and future reputation rode on the success of Project Q.

But something far deeper and more primal stirred within her soul. She would defend her creation against any threats—including Fierro—even at the cost of her own life.

22

COLOMBIA

A firestorm raged in Amador Fierro's otherwise highly disciplined mind. If Bose was correct—and he had no doubt she was—he was only ten days away from realizing a plan he had initiated ten years earlier. A decade of preparation, investment, and sacrifice was about to culminate in the Project Q launch.

Few understood the implications. Fierro's possession of AGI would change everything—a massive tectonic shift, rocking the very foundations of the world order.

With AGI, he would first seize control of America's power grid and wage a campaign of confusion and terror, initiating total blackouts, freeze banking systems, crash financial markets, and paralyze commerce. The resulting economic collapse would drive the arrogant *yanquis* to their knees.

Even if he never used it, merely possessing the grid would gain him a blackmailer's advantage. Never again would the Americans demand anything of La Liga or her national allies lest he strangle them to death. The *norteamericanos* would be reduced to cowering dogs shivering in the corner of history, each panting breath a desperate prayer begging Fierro to withhold his wrath.

But that was only if he took things to the ultimate limit. Fierro fantasized about his soon-to-be AGI hacking border patrol drones, satellites, and surveillance cameras to guide *la migra* into fatal ambushes by his gunmen. And he'd treat the *yanqui* special ops teams the same way—drawing them into inescapable kill boxes and targeted assassinations.

Equally important, Project Q could help him decapitate the American judicial system by infiltrating top secret personnel files and doxing the names and locations of unreasonable judges, relentless prosecutors, and incorruptible prison guards—not to mention their families. He would terrorize the law enforcement community as well with targeted assassinations of undercover agents, police detectives, confidential informants, and meddlesome journalists. And he'd use AGI to throw open the cell doors of every prison and mental ward around the world to flood offending countries with armies of raging killers and psychopaths.

Once the Americans were brought to heel, the rest of the world would fall in line as well—or feel his wrath. His AGI would defang and leash all national police and military forces around the globe. La Liga would have free rein.

That prospect alone was worth the billions of dollars invested in the project. But a viable, organoid-based AGI would more than recoup its development costs. La Liga's profits would skyrocket as it designed more powerful and addictive hallucinogenic drugs, streamlined transportation and logistics networks, executed extortion and blackmailing schemes, manipulated stock and currency markets, and stole digital bank accounts.

Nor would Fierro fear a popular uprising. La Liga's AGI would mold minds, condition public opinion, and even remake human culture into its own image. Project Q would seize control of the infosphere through relentless campaigns of hacktivism, misinformation, and faultless deep fake videos. People would come to see his organization as the heroic vanguard of a new world order, crushing the greedy, power-hungry ambitions of the old-guard politicians around the world intent on exploiting the impoverished masses.

In short, Project Q would turn the world's most dangerous collection of drug cartels into an unstoppable criminal superpower.

But that fool Narciso Tamacas could still derail all of it. Fierro had to find a way to get his father, Oscar Tamacas, released from CECOT. President Olmedo was the key. Fierro had to escalate—but something surgical. Nothing too violent, lest he provoke an overwhelming American response. But what?

And Narcisco wasn't the only threat. As Fierro had warned Dr. Bose, an imponderable number of "unknown unknowns" lay in wait over the course of the next ten days. If Project Q failed, all was lost. La Liga would never forgive his ambition, let alone the loss of their billions. They'd baptize him in a vat of acid for that sin.

Fear suddenly gripped him—and fear was the mind killer.

Fierro needed to cleanse his mind, and bring a fresh wind to his soul.

After spending a university semester abroad in Tokyo, Fierro had acquired a love of all things Japanese. But his greatest affection lay with kyūdō, "the way of the bow."

Originating out of the violence of war, Japanese archery had morphed from a combat form to its modern variant—both a ritualized art form and a deeply meditative practice. Kyūdō was still very much a martial art, but the advent of gunpowder ended nearly all forms of samurai combat including archery.

Rooted in the principles of Zen Buddhism, Fierro used kyūdō as a form of meditation, embracing the physical disciplines of the highly ritualized stages of the shahō-hassetsu to drive out the worries of the world and concentrate his mind on the eternal now.

Fierro attributed a great deal of his success in both business and in life to this Zen-like practice. He had converted his father's outdoor shooting range into the kyūdōjō as soon as he had taken possession of the estate. There were ten shooting lanes, but few guests had the patience, stamina, or skill for the art form. Over the years he had brought over several of the very best teachers from Japan—men and women who had achieved the physical and philosophical mastery of the ancient sport.

Fierro wore the traditional wide, pleated trousers, a loose-fitting, long-sleeve shirt, split-toed tabi socks, and a deerskin glove for his shooting hand. Most of all he carried his beloved yumi, a long, asymmetrical bow with a wrapped grip below the center. The yumi's distinctive geometry delivered far more power than the more famous English longbow. All of Fierro's *kyūdō* custom-fit kit was handcrafted by Japanese artisans at great expense.

Fierro approached the *shai*—the shooting lane—with his bow and arrow in hand. He placed his socked feet in the proper stance with the care and intentionality of a calligrapher's first brushstroke on fine paper, grounding himself to both the earth and his destiny. He cast his gaze upon the small circular target some twenty-eight meters downrange.

He then took a deep, cleansing breath and aligned his posture, stacking the bones in his spine like a marbled Corinthian column as he broadened his chest and balanced his weight. His body was now a ladder between earth and sky, his inner spirit aligning with his outward purpose, filling him with a physical sense of stability, centeredness, and serenity.

Fierro next readied his bow, nocking the arrow against the wood's curved embrace with gentle precision in quiet anticipation of the force that would proceed from this moment of tranquility.

He then raised the bow with a solemn grace away from his body and above his head in a slow, ascending arc, the half curve of the bow rising like the sun over a far horizon. With equal control, he lowered the bow in a descending arc, simultaneously extending his left arm even as his gloved hand drew back the string, lowering both until the arrow shaft rested near his upper lip.

Now fully extended, Fierro had finally reached the full draw of the mighty bow. His body was stretched to its maximum effort, the power of the bow testing his physical limits and his acute mental focus. The loss of either would result in catastrophe. Only the harmony of inner calm and unshakable resolve could sustain him now. Stillness of spirit and breath waged war against the explosive power straining to escape the bow's limbs and string.

Every step, every movement, every breath had been the notes of Fierro's unfolding adagio. With his body and mind now perfectly aligned, he was completely focused on the totality of the moment. Everything was in perfect alignment and balance. Time was finally still, and reality reduced to a single point of being. There was neither target nor bow nor distance nor even Fierro. All was one.

Now was the time of crescendo.

The *hanare* was more than the mechanical release of the taut string. Fierro wasn't trying to time the shot to hit the target—just the opposite. It was the letting go of ego, of consciousness itself. The release happened at the moment it was supposed to happen, just as the lapping tide drew away the sand beneath one's feet. The *hanare* was his spirit's exhaled breath, detached from any expectation of outcome. All had been in alignment, all the forces balanced. The pure and perfect release merely let the arrow fly.

And fly it did.

Fierro stood motionless, still at one with the tranquility of the moment. His eyes tracked the arrow's faultless trajectory with dispassionate interest, its destination certain—because *he* was certain. All of his preparation, the intensity of his focus, the precise execution of his movements had already determined the arrow's path.

The razor-sharp tip buried deep into the wooden target with a resonant *thunk*, its shaft quivering with aftershock. President Olmedo's photo was taped to the target, the arrow squarely fixed between his eyes.

Fierro exhaled and lowered his bow, once again utterly confident in the outcome of Project Q. His faultless execution and intensity of focus guaranteed it.

His La Liga would become a superpower, and nothing could stop that reality from happening.

Fierro smiled. He knew exactly what needed to be done.

He would loft an arrow into Olmedo's beating heart.

23

Juan Cabrillo and Max Hanley were in the engineering office poring over a post-action technical analysis following the *Oregon*'s encounter with Linda Ross's drone attack. The two senior officers were drilling down into the performance of the systems, not their crew, who had executed their duties admirably.

Given the outcome of the battle, there was no question Cabrillo and his team needed to figure out how to harden the *Oregon*'s radar and comms systems against electronic countermeasures. Even though they had known Linda's drones would launch an electronic countermeasures attack, her drone systems were able to read and decipher the *Oregon*'s encrypted channels in real time and break through them with relative ease. Those drones were, in effect, flying hacking machines.

But that was a highly technical problem for another day—a problem Murph and Eric would tackle once Murph got back from his vacation.

"The upgraded power plant sure did fine," Max said. "Looks like a thirty-eight percent increase in overall power and an eleven percent increase in top-end speed."

"That's even better than we'd expected," Juan said.

The vast improvement in the *Oregon*'s magnetohydrodynamic propulsion system during the Malaysian refit resulted in radically increased power, performance, and capabilities throughout the ship.

They had begun their propulsion refit by turning back to one of

Juan's favorite subjects at Caltech, computational fluid dynamics. The calculations and resulting design changes wouldn't have been possible without the *Oregon*'s Cray supercomputer.

The first change they made was to alter the geometry of the system's flow channels to minimize turbulence and maximize flow efficiencies. They also added cascading accelerators to optimize thrust.

They also introduced a pulsed power supply, which created rapid high-intensity bursts of power rather than merely a continuous electromagnetic field.

In addition, they significantly upgraded the system's high-frequency electromagnetic coils. This created an even more powerful plasma field that ionized seawater and stripped away free electrons with far greater efficiency and speed resulting in a massively larger electric current than the previous system.

All of the extra electrical energy was either directed to the *Oregon*'s massive Jet Ski–styled impellers to drive the great vessel or stored in the towering new banks of supercapacitors, which powered several systems including—and especially—the new laser-point defense and electromagnetic pulse cannons.

To further help improve speed in the water, changes were made to the *Oregon*'s hull. Frictional drag was reduced by applying dimpled superhydrophobic coatings that reduced energy loss in the wake. The bulbous bow configuration was improved to enhance flow and reduce wave resistance at higher speeds, and the stern was streamlined to minimize wake and drag.

To take advantage of the new higher speeds and power, Max and Juan added movable flaps—like airplane ailerons and elevators—as well as additional interceptors and trim tabs to optimize the hull's angle of attack in the water, while simultaneously reducing resistance and increasing speed.

"Not crazy about those cannons redlining," Max said.

"What do you think happened? Thermal overload in the power supply unit?"

"Could also be the pulse antennas short-circuiting, or feedback loops in the fire-control circuits. Murph and Stoney are better equipped to answer the weapons stuff than me."

"Have Eric nose around to see what he can find."

"I'll get him on that right away."

Hali Kasim's voice boomed through the speakers overhead. "Chairman, Mr. Overholt is on the line for you."

"Put him through on speaker, Hali."

"Aye."

★

"Juan, my boy. Good of you to take my call," Overholt said. His affection was genuine, extending all the way back to the days when he had been Juan's CIA handler. Since leaving the Company, Juan had formed the Corporation with Overholt's blessing. The CIA hired the *Oregon* when the federal government couldn't or wouldn't take on certain missions.

"You're online with Max Hanley," Juan said.

"Mr. Hanley, I trust you are hale and hearty."

"Fit as a fiddle. Yourself?"

"I've been roped into my first pickleball tournament. A charity event. I shall never live it down."

"The pickleball or the charity?"

"Perhaps both. My brother-in-law is a docent for the Rotary Egg Beater Museum in Lick Fork, West Virginia. They've run perilously short of funds."

"I can't imagine why," Hanley said with a chuckle.

"My understanding is that you are still located in the Pacific near the coast of Mexico."

"Just departed Lázaro Cárdenas with a load of consumer packaged goods for a delivery in El Salvador," Cabrillo said. "After we pick up Raven and Linc we're heading out for our annual crew vacation."

"Is there any chance you could alter your plans?"

"I dunno. My crew's pretty worn-out. What's on your mind?"

"There have been a number of disturbing reports recently about a mysterious pirate vessel sinking ships in the eastern Pacific."

"So mysterious I haven't heard a thing about it."

"Survivors claim that specters and poltergeists were involved. It's all nonsensical, but something's going on out there. I was hoping I could get you to take a look around."

"A 'look around' the Pacific Ocean? Might as well ask me to pick out a specific grain of sand on Waikiki Beach."

"There's actually some method in the madness, if you're interested."

"Sounds like a goose chase. Why don't you re-task a satellite or send a Global Hawk for a look-see?"

"Those assets are hard to come by these days with Europe, Asia, and the Middle East boiling over."

"I think we'll pass."

"I'll pay your regular rate."

"And miss out on Max's famous barbecue luau? I don't think so."

"I cook a mean pig," Max said.

"What if I double your rate?"

Juan and Max exchanged a look. The Corporation was a business, after all, and Overholt their most reliable client. He was also a notorious skinflint when it came to government expenditures.

"Must be important."

"Most likely a tale told by idiots full of sound and fury but signifying nothing," Overholt said. "Still, it has caused quite a stir in certain circles. We have no naval surface assets to deploy to the area. I'm hoping you'll prove there's nothing to it."

"How long do I have?"

"As long as you'll give me."

"Seven days, max. We're due to rendezvous with Raven and Linc about then."

"I'll take it. You're approximately twenty hours away from the target area at maximum speed. I'll send you the coordinates of all known encounters. Let me know when you've arrived on station."

"Will do. Thanks for the business."

"And while you're at it, keep an ear to the ground. We're hearing faint rumblings in the darker corners of the infosphere about a new AGI weapon coming to fruition soon."

"Aren't we years away from that?"

"We're not close yet, but the Chinese are throwing everything they have at it. So are others. The whiz kids over at the Directorate of Analysis are getting rather jumpy about it. If you hear anything—no matter how harebrained or half-baked—let me know, pronto," Overholt said.

"Of course."

"Always a pleasure. Ciao." Overholt rang off.

"Guess we're going on a snipe hunt," Max said.

Cabrillo ran his hand through his brush-cut hair.

"At least it's a well-paid one."

"What Overholt said about AGI gives me the heebie-jeebies."

"He's right. There's no end to the possibilities. Targeted genocide via bioengineered viruses. Creating urban firestorms by hacking into gas pipelines and electrical stations. Destroying ports and infrastructure by crashing or sinking oil tankers and freighters at will."

Max shook his head, contemplating the implications.

"Suddenly, a snipe hunt doesn't sound so bad."

24

The brightly colored *songthaew*—a Toyota pickup truck fixed with two bench seats and a roof, like an open-air school bus—squealed to a halt.

Mark Murphy unspooled his long frame from his cramped seat, trying desperately not to step on any toes or bump his head against the metal roof as he made his way to the back of the truck. The ultra-polite locals all smiled and giggled as the gangly American finally exited with an awkward bounce of the shock absorbers. The truck beeped its horn and sputtered away, leaving Murph alone by the side of the sandy road, shouldering a small backpack.

He'd seen the blue waters of the Andaman Sea off and on as he'd made his way down the coast from Bangkok in the back of the *songthaew*. But it was only after the chattering passengers, squawking chickens, and sputtering engine had departed that he could hear the gentle rush of waves brushing up into the fine sand a few hundred yards away. He smelled the salty tang of the sea and even the hint of pine. He wiped the sweat from his forehead with the back of his hand. The temperature wasn't bad at this time of day, but a short downpour a few minutes ago had turned the humidity index up to infinity.

He glanced around and spotted a handwritten sign nailed to a palm tree that read in Thai and English "Sunset Bar" with an arrow pointing toward the beach. He didn't bother to double-check his phone for instructions. He'd read and reread Linlin's follow-up coded text message a hundred times if he'd read it once, searching for an emotional subtext beneath the words, but found none. He knew he was in the right location, at least physically. Emotionally he felt adrift, like a ship without a rudder in a hard wind. He thought he'd gotten over the Asian beauty. But the closer he got to seeing her again, the more he realized he'd only buried his feelings all these years.

He had to play it cool.

He checked his watch. He'd timed his arrival perfectly.

Murph made his way through a patch of coconut palms. Closer to the beach the trees turned to pines. When he finally cleared the tree line he stood on a wide and nearly deserted stretch of golden-white sand. He was greeted by a spattering breeze and the fiery red orb of the sun plunging into the far horizon—real postcard stuff.

The lone structure on the beach was the proverbial thatched-roof surf bar. A couple of empty fishing skiffs were pulled up on the shore some hundred yards away. The setting sun threw long shadows across the sand as the notes of an acoustic guitar wavered in the air. As he plodded forward, he counted nine local patrons and noted the bartender behind the bar.

Murph bounded up the rickety steps. The handsome, well-built bartender smiled and nodded at him as he polished a glass. Murph looked around. There were two dozen tables, but only three were occupied. The best table in the house was wide-open, perched on the corner of the open-air restaurant with an unobstructed view of the sunset. Murph was concerned.

Where was Linlin?

He spun around to face the ocean.

And there she was. Her hair danced around her face, jostled by the wind. The last rays of the setting sun cast an ethereal glow behind her lithe figure, darkening her face.

The bar's automated dusk-to-dawn lights popped on, lighting her up.

She smiled demurely.

Murph's hands quavered as he finally managed a raspy "Linlin."

"Hey, Shaggy."

Murphy smiled. She once told him he looked a little like Scooby-Doo's best friend. Shaggy was her pet name for him. Nobody ever called him that except for her.

Linlin stepped off the beach and onto the stairs. She was barefoot and her toes were caked with fine sand. Her shoes dangled from her overstuffed day pack.

"You made it," she said as she wrapped her arms around him. Murph's heart raced as he pulled her close to his chest and felt her breathe a deep sigh of relief.

She glanced up into his face. "I wasn't sure you'd come."

"Are you kidding? Of course I came."

She stood back a step and studied him, pinching his biceps.

"Wow, you've changed. You're all buff now."

Murph blushed. "Sort of a gym rat these days. You look pretty great yourself." In fact, she looked bone-weary, he thought.

Linlin tucked a length of unwashed hair behind her ear. "I'm hungry. Let's get something to eat and we can talk."

"Yeah, I'm starving."

Linlin headed for the premium table at the corner end of the bar, set her pack down, and grabbed a seat. Murph pulled off his pack and fell into the chair next to her just as the bartender approached with menus.

"Something to drink before you order?"

"A couple of Singhas," Murph said. He turned to Linlin. "Beer still okay with you?"

"Sounds great."

"Be right back."

Murph waited for the bartender to get out of earshot. He leaned in close and whispered, "So what's this 'I don't want to die' stuff all about?"

"It's a long story, and I'm sorry I've pulled you into it."

"No problem."

"Of course it is. You haven't heard from me in years and now suddenly I've dragged you halfway around the world."

"How do you know where I came from?"

"I assume anywhere you came from is at least half a world away from this faraway place."

Murph chuckled. "Yeah, and then some."

"And I never stayed in touch. I'm very sorry about that. I left suddenly, my parents got sick, and I just . . ." Her voice drifted off.

"How are your parents?"

Linlin dropped her gaze to her lap.

"They both passed."

"I'm so sorry."

"It was a bad time. I just, well. I'm just sorry things worked out the way they did."

"I get it."

"And you? How have you been?"

"Great. But we're not here to talk about me. What's going on?"

Before Linlin could answer, the bartender was back with a couple of cold bottles of beer and glasses. He poured them at the table.

"Decide on dinner yet?"

"Couple of the house specials," Mark said. "Extra-spicy."

The bartender grinned. "You sure about that?"

Murph glanced at Linlin. She smiled.

"Yup."

The barkeep finished his pours. "Two specials, extra-spicy. Coming right up."

Murph watched him disappear through the swinging kitchen doors shouting orders in Thai, then swept the room with his peripheral vision the way Eddie Seng had taught him, taking everything in but not being too obvious.

The other tables were occupied by locals. Three men sat together at one table with two women, and two men were at another several feet away. A husband and wife—judging by their whispering intimacy—sat farthest away. All were between thirty and fifty years of age. They were eating, talking, and laughing convivially. None carried weapons.

"Everything okay?" Linlin asked.

"Yeah, sure." He lifted his glass. So did she. They toasted carefully.

"Old times," Murph said.

"Good times." She offered a winsome smile.

Murph's heart skipped a beat. They both took a sip.

"So, what's the story?"

"The Chinese government thinks I'm a traitor, and they've put me on a kill list."

"What? Why?"

"I've been working for Zephyron Dynamics for the last five years. I'm a senior project manager for their AGI program."

"I've heard of them. Impressive."

"Not really. The Germans are lagging badly."

"I take it your government doesn't approve of you working there?"

"Just the opposite. The CCP owns a secret share of the corporation. They mask it through a shell company."

"So what's the problem?"

"The Ministry of State Security has placed several agents in the company, and I've been closely scrutinized. I've even found bugs in my apartment."

"With your credentials, I'm surprised the MSS never recruited you directly."

"They tried, but I resisted until they threatened to pull my passport. So I began feeding them small pieces of worthless information. They finally figured out what I was doing."

"And they called it counterespionage or something, right?"

"Exactly. I—" Linlin's eyes widened. She grabbed Murphy's arm and pointed at the shoreline. "Mark—"

Murphy turned in his seat. The overhead lights beneath the thatched canopy dulled his vision, but he thought he could make out the forms of three men emerging from the surf, running in a low crouch—

Bang!

An ear-crushing explosion and flash of blinding light erupted near the couple at the far table, tossing the two of them aside like rag dolls. A woman's scream and the frantic shouts of men added to the confusion.

Murph's ringing ears and blurred eyesight told him a flash-bang had gone off. He could still make out the blazing rifle barrels storming up from the beach.

He snatched up his backpack and grabbed Linlin's hand and yanked her out of her chair. "Let's go!"

He dragged her toward the rear of the joint just as the chest of the barkeeper flowered bloody red and he toppled to the floor behind the bar.

"There!" Linlin shouted as she pulled on her pack, pointing at a Yamaha motorcycle parked in the rear.

The two of them dashed for the sporty bike as more bodies hit the floor. Murph prayed the driver had left the keys in the ignition or somewhere nearby as automatic gunfire ripped in the air behind them. He had a pistol in his pack, but even if he could draw it in time he stood no chance against a team of commandos armed with automatic rifles.

Keys! Miraculously still in the ignition.

Murph leaped onto the beast and hit the electric starter as Linlin jumped on the seat behind him. Murph cranked the throttle. The rear tire fishtailed in the sand before it finally got purchase and moments later the two of them rocketed away through the trees, Linlin holding on to Murphy's rock-hard torso for dear life.

Murph navigated the bike with ease, his body flush with adrenaline and testosterone. The front wheel finally found the frontage road and he maneuvered onto it. He kicked the bike into high gear, the sound of gunfire fading away.

"What are we going to do?" Linlin shouted from behind.

"No worries," Murph called over his shoulder. "I know a safe place. The safest place on earth."

★

Colonel Shi Chang watched the Yamaha race away through the tree line as he thundered up the stairs, his wetsuit dripping on the restaurant floorboards.

He smiled.

The Chinese special forces operator clicked his molar mic and called out to the rest of his team.

"All clear."

Instantly, the bartender stood up from behind the bar, a wide grin on his handsome face. His shirt was soaked in fake blood and torn apart by the small explosions from the special effects squibs.

The other "wounded" members of the team climbed to their feet with nervous laughter. The married couple had the hardest time. The reduced-power flash-bang that exploded near their table still managed to bloody their noses and ring their heads like dinner bells. Two other members helped them to their feet as a third broke out a medical kit.

Chang's number two, Sergeant Xuanyi, ambled up to him.

"That couldn't have gone any better. I was worried that *guilao* was going to pull his peashooter." A tail reported the tall American had previously entered an English-owned dive shop with known ties to Western agencies, where he was given a black-market pistol.

"I doubt the fool knew how to use it," Chang said.

"Think she'll be okay?"

"We've done our part to sell it. Agent Zhang's fate is in her own hands now."

25

Juan and Max were the only hands in the op center. It was well past midnight, and they were on station for what Cabrillo had officially dubbed "Operation Snipe Hunt."

Overholt sent over the coordinates of the reported sightings of the mysterious demon ship supposedly haunting the vast and desolate eastern Pacific. Eric Stone ran those coordinates through his own variant of the Israeli targeting program Gospel. Stone's AI-powered decision-making software generated a search grid for the *Oregon*, designed for the highest probability of contact given the previous incidence reports. It was still a long-shot, Hail Mary play, but if Overholt was willing to write the check, Cabrillo was more than happy to cash it.

The *Oregon* had been on station and following its preprogrammed course for over three uneventful hours. Max monitored the navigational sonar and radar systems, but nothing had popped up. The *Oregon*'s mil-spec equipment wasn't picking up any mystery ships. They hadn't seen a single fishing trawler or even a vagrant shipping container bobbing in the sea since arriving on station. They were in a literal dead zone, about as far away from civilization as an abandoned satellite circling Mars. Overholt's phantom threat was likely just a phantom and no threat at all.

But Cabrillo had other things on his mind. He wasn't at all happy that neither Linc nor Raven had reported in since their arrival in

Colombia three days earlier. In theory, all that meant was that they hadn't found the Quds Force base yet, which wasn't at all surprising. He preferred regular radio check-ins, but they were undercover and it wasn't possible. He had complete faith in his two Gundogs, but no amount of planning or preparation could prevent unforeseen catastrophes.

Juan's eyes scanned the small monitor on the Kirk Chair console. Raven's and Linc's trackers were still blinking active and on the move. That was a good sign—unless the trackers were located in the bellies of a couple of engorged crocodiles meandering down the river.

"We're like a worm on a hook dangling over my momma's bathtub," Max said. "Not much chance we're gonna get any bites."

"I'm not looking to get bit."

"You know what I mean."

Cabrillo yawned and checked his Doxa Sub 300T wristwatch. "Twenty minutes until we're relieved. After that I'll head on over and hit the pool and turn some laps."

"Knock yourself out. I'll be heading for the galley. There's a tray with a hot meatloaf sandwich and a couple of fingers of Buffalo Trace waiting for me."

"I know there's a biting joke in there somewhere, but I'm too bored to go find it."

"Why don't you head down to the pool now?" Max circled his finger in the air, indicating the op center. "I can cover this shindig from the Chair."

"I'll sit tight, but thanks." Cabrillo never cut corners, especially on shifts. Max knew that. But the hopeful look on Max's hungry face betrayed his true intentions.

Cabrillo grinned. "And don't worry, your meatloaf sandwich will taste just as good cold."

★

BANGALORE, INDIA

A torrential downpour nearly flooded the street where the UberGo pulled to a stop in front of the quiet, out-of-the-way restaurant.

Dr. Jagadeesh Gowda dashed the short distance between the parked cars along the curb and to the front door without bothering to open his umbrella. He arrived beneath the awning dripping wet and watched the Tata Tiago pull away, satisfied he had arrived only a few minutes late. The storm had snarled Bangalore's already tortured traffic to a near standstill. The front door opened with the tinkle of a familiar bell.

The candlelit restaurant was one of Gowda's favorite haunts, its understated elegance heightening its romantic ambience. He was greeted by the manager, who helped him off with his stylish Burberry trench coat. The sweet aromas of jasmine and cardamom perfumed the air.

"She's waiting for you." The manager nodded toward a high-backed booth at the far end of the restaurant before turning to hang up his raincoat. They stood near the restaurant's big plate-glass window overlooking the street.

"Thank you," Gowda said. From the corner of his eye he saw the faint blue glow of a video camera screen inside a dark car parked across the street.

"The usual, sir?"

"Of course," Gowda said with a pleasant smile. "Only, make my whiskey a double."

"A long day at the office, sir?"

"More like a celebration."

"Very good, sir. Your dishes will arrive shortly."

"Excellent."

Gowda worked his way past the tables of couples devouring plates of some of the best-cooked dishes in all of Bangalore, home to India's "Silicon Valley." Not a few female eyes raked over his athletic build as he marched by.

Dr. Gowda slid into the open bench opposite a stunning woman, whose face lit up the moment she saw him. Her natural beauty required no adornment, but the gold-chained pendant around her neck drew Gowda's attention.

"So glad you made it in this storm," Gowda said. They both wore forced smiles.

"Wouldn't miss it for the world." Her eyes darted down to the condiment tray on their table. She discreetly held up a car key fob—in
reality, a miniature radio-frequency detector. It flashed a silent red
light, indicating the table had been bugged.

"Traffic was terrible," Gowda said, lifting his smartphone from his
pocket and setting it carefully next to the condiment station. "I'm famished."

The two of them locked eyes and then nodded slightly in perfect
synchronicity. Anyone watching them would have missed the gesture.
Gowda pushed a button on what appeared to be a cell phone but in
reality was a phase inverter, a higher-tech version of a noise-canceling
device. The phase inverter recorded all ambient noises in the room,
including their conversation, then processed it in real time to invert the
waveform, which created a destructive interference pattern. The software was careful to allow a few innocent words to dribble through.
The overall effect would garble their conversation but not entirely destroy the bug's reception in order to avoid suspicion that it had been
discovered and disabled.

"We don't have much time," Gowda said in a low whisper. "You
saw the two crows across the street?"

"You mean Dumb and Dumber?" The young beauty giggled.
"RAW needs to find better recruits." The Research and Analysis Wing
was India's version of the CIA. Their agents routinely kept tabs on
high-value persons like Dr. Gowda, one of the most prominent computer science researchers at the Indian Institute of Science. He was
currently working on a top secret organoid intelligence project under
contract with the Ministry of Defense.

"With any luck, the RAW boys would chalk up the bug's interference to the weather. If not, they'd do something about it."

"Why the urgency?" she asked.

"Why do you think?"

Gowda reached into his sport coat and gripped the package. He
hesitated. India only used the death penalty in extreme cases—and
this was about as extreme as it got. But it was necessary, and she understood the risks as well as he did.

They were both Guardians.

Originating as a faction of rebel Japanese computer scientists, the Guardians had recruited like-minded scientists and technologists worldwide, united in their belief that the advent of AGI was a human-extinction and potentially planet-killing event. Because the movement began in Japan, they adopted the Japanese mythology of the *tengu*. These were the spiritual protectors of both the natural and cosmic orders, opposing the pride and vanity of arrogant monks and unscrupulous samurais—the corporate CEOs, university academics, and military generals of their day. All were legitimate targets wherever they may be found.

The Guardians' cause was as sacred as it was practical. Humanity was ill-prepared for the godlike powers AGI would confer upon the most ambitious and amoral among them. Nuclear weapons paled in comparison because they could never be used without harming the planet. But AGI could be deployed covertly, collapsing whole societies at the virtual flip of a switch with literally no fallout to the attacker.

Gowda took her hand in his and gently kissed her fingers in what appeared to be a romantic gesture straight out of a Bollywood soap opera. In fact, he was passing off to her a necklace identical to the one she was wearing, the pendant of which contained a miniature hard drive. In a few moments she would excuse herself to the restroom, switch necklaces, and return the other one to him.

They had developed this little ruse of extramarital misbehavior in order to deceive their watchers. Gowda needed a trustworthy and reliable person to pass off the intelligence he gathered from his work at the institute. Meeting someone regularly would have drawn suspicion unless that person was a gorgeous young lady with whom the RAW agents themselves would have liked to become entangled. She was, in fact, married to his brother, a brilliant scientist in his own right, who had recruited the two of them into the Guardian organization.

Their drinks arrived. The waiter set a cosmopolitan in front of her and a double shot of Johnnie Walker Black Label in front of Gowda.

"Your meals will be arriving shortly," he said. "Enjoy."

"Thank you," the woman said with a smile. She watched him step away. "So, quickly, what's this about?"

"Do you remember the woman from Hyderabad whom we saw practicing Bach's fugues a few years ago? I can't remember her name." Gowda was making a cryptic reference to organoid intelligence via the great composer's organ fugues and to Dr. Bose, who had conducted her pioneering research in a lab in Hyderabad, India, several years prior.

"She's no longer with us, as I understand it."

"No. She's very much alive apparently, and still playing. And getting quite good."

"How good?"

"Rumors are she might be ready for her first full concert."

"Where?"

"Not sure. I hope to find out. That's one concert I'd hate to miss."

Another waiter appeared with a condiment tray. He was unfamiliar, and the sleeves of his ill-fitting serving coat were three inches too short.

"Excuse me, sir, madame. I noticed your condiment tray needed to be refreshed. May I?"

Gowda fought back a hearty laugh. *Where does RAW find these clowns?*

"Yes, of course. Thank you for noticing." Gowda picked up his smartphone/interference device and pocketed it as his sister-in-law handed the RAW agent the old condiment tray.

"Thank you both. I'm sorry to have disturbed you," the agent said as he carried the old condiment tray and his bug back to the kitchen.

Gowda thought about activating his phase inverter again so they could continue the conversation, but that would only draw suspicion. He saw the concerned look in his sister-in-law's eyes. She fully understood the gravity of the situation. More important, she now had possession of the scant documentation he was able to download in her pendant. She would hand it off to his brother and he would pass it up through the network.

They exchanged a knowing glance just as another waiter arrived with their mouthwatering dishes. The RAW boys were listening hard now. Time to play the game of lovers once again, and enjoy an incredible meal together. As inept as their watchers could sometimes be, it was possible the two of them had made a mistake somewhere along the line. If so, this could be their last meal together, and his sister-in-law would be swapping out that pretty pendant for a noose around her perfect neck.

26

Deep in the belly of the *Baktun*'s combat information center, Captain Stokes studied the monitor, his bleary eyes fixed on the bright yellow triangle denoting the cargo ship *Agua Linda*. The errant vessel had just crossed into the *Baktun*'s no-go perimeter of drone buoys and needed to be turned aside. It was just past two o'clock in the morning.

Moments earlier, Stokes had been roused from a fitful sleep when the intruder alert had sounded and his first officer appeared at his cabin door. A fresh cup of hot Royal Navy "HMS *Bulwark*" tea helped ease him out of his stupor.

According to the *Baktun*'s available databases, the *Agua Linda* was steaming from the Port of Busan, South Korea, to Ecuador's Guayaquil Port with a load of washing machines and other household appliances. Nothing terribly unusual other than the fact its captain had decided to take an unconventional route for unspecified reasons.

"It's a Panamanian-flagged vessel," Stokes's first officer said, reading from the big display. "Captained by Diogo Neves, a Portuguese." He sniffed. "Hard to believe that pathetic little tourist trap was the world's first global superpower."

Stokes's eyes narrowed as his mind reached back into an ancient memory from his public school days. "'My name is Ozymandias, King of Kings; Look on my Works, ye Mighty, and despair!'"

"Sir?"

"Percy Bysshe Shelley."

The first officer frowned with confusion.

"The poet? Never mind." Stokes turned to his drone tech. "It's probably a contract crew. Program your drones accordingly. Follow your protocols."

"Aye, sir."

With orders to keep the *Baktun* invisible and hampered by his inability to power up his engines to flee, Stokes had to rely on his least-lethal means of persuasion to get the *Agua Linda* to change course. If he had his way, he'd simply blast them out of the water with the deadlier weapons at his disposal.

The *Baktun*'s radar invisibility was assured by its AI-assisted cloaking system. Radar detection worked by sending out radar signals. When those signals struck hard targets, they bounced back to the radar receiver and thus provided target location.

But the *Baktun* had engineered a unique way to defeat conventional radar detection. Every exposed surface of the ship was coated with a variety of metamaterials like split-ring resonators, each of which possessed negative refractive properties. Negative refractive metamaterials didn't reflect radar waves so much as bend and curve them, much the same way rushing water flowed around smooth stones in a river. Of course, not all radar wavelengths were the same nor were they on the same platforms—land, sea, and air systems were all broadcast at different angles relative to their targets.

To compensate for the wide variety of wavelengths and angles, the *Baktun*'s metamaterials were dynamically adjusted by an AI-assisted program to match both the frequency and angle of incoming radar signals. It was therefore virtually impossible for any conventional broadband radar system to fix a location on the *Baktun*.

In order for the *Baktun* to remain entirely invisible beyond radar detection, it needed to keep all intruders at arm's length—or more precisely, beyond visual range. Deploying the *Baktun*'s traditional kinetic weapons would easily destroy commercial vessels that entered into its visual range, but such weapons would also alert naval authorities.

Stokes's orders were clear: draw no undue attention unless absolutely necessary—under penalty of death. Nothing short of the imminent sinking of the *Baktun* and its precious cargo would allow the deployment of his more lethal arsenal. The "spectral drone theater," as Stokes derisively referred to it, had proven quite effective, and thus he would rely upon it yet again. There was no virtue in risking his neck for a load of dishwashers.

★

Twenty minutes later the *Baktun*'s holographic projection drones landed at various points around the *Agua Linda*'s decks.

Stokes retired to his captain's chair with a tablet to review his systems logs, simultaneously bored and disgusted by the spectral charade unfolding on the monitors. His minions were perfectly capable of handling the whole affair. He knew that in moments a giant witchlike creature wielding a flaming broadsword would begin brandishing curses as it called out Captain Neves's name in his native Portuguese. Other drone-borne demoniacs would dance and shriek in the wires. As if on cue, the cacophony of ghastly screams and spine-chilling expletives filled his command center's audio speakers.

A few moments later, his first officer called out.

"Sir . . . there's no response."

Stokes didn't bother looking up from his tablet.

"What do you mean?"

"I mean, there's nobody responding. There's nobody even on deck. No one has come out of the bridge."

"Put it on the big screen."

Stokes finally glanced up from his tablet. His first officer was right. The *Agua Linda*'s deck was devoid of a single crewman. Even at this late hour, that was impossible. At a minimum, there should have been at least a night watch on the bridge.

"Perhaps we've caught someone napping while on duty. Send a scout to check out the bridge."

Moments later, a camera drone hovered near the cracked and dirty bridge windows, feeding a live image of the interior. Clearly nobody was inside.

"Maybe we found a *real* ghost ship?" the first officer asked.

"Don't be ridiculous."

"What are we going to do?"

Captain Stokes darkened, lost in thought.

Strange, indeed.

★

The *Oregon* had spent another fruitless twenty-four hours plying a mind-numbingly boring search grid in the remotest and least traveled patch of the Pacific. Operation Snipe Hunt felt like a bust.

Until things got very interesting.

Juan sat on the edge of the Kirk Chair, surrounded by a full complement of op center crew with Linda Ross occupying the weapons station in Mark Murphy's absence. Most prior demon ship attacks had reportedly occurred at night or in the early-morning hours, which was why Cabrillo's best team was on duty on the overnight watch.

"I don't believe what I'm seeing," Max said. A spectral, three-masted pirate ship sailed in the distance on one of the big wall monitors. But Hanley was referring to the howling twelve-foot-tall witch-monster and her flaming sword on the nearest crane's platform.

"Hali, put our guest on the overheads," Juan ordered.

"Aye, Chairman." The comms officer hit a toggle. The witch's eerie voice bellowed in Portuguese over the speakers.

"Hit the translator, Hali."

Kasim mashed a toggle. "Translating to English."

"—before it's too late, Captain Diogo! Or you will all perish in flames! Turn around now! Turn around!"

"Kill the transmission."

Hali tapped the toggle, cutting off the witch mid-rant.

"Well, looky there," Linda said, pointing at the bridge-eye camera. She zoomed in on the image. A quadcopter camera drone hovered outside the filthy windows.

"Stoney, grab a close-up of our witchy friend. Her demons, too."

"I was just thinking the same thing." Seconds later, Eric Stone grabbed extreme closeup images of a dozen projector drones perched in the rigging and other locations, each ablaze with fine light.

"Holographic drones," Stone said. "Cool."

"Linda, let's hit 'em with an electromagnetic pulse cannon. See what happens."

"I'd rather you and me grab a couple of Benellis and put some double-aught buck in their bellies," Max said. He and Juan busted clay targets off the stern of the *Oregon* once a month in friendly competition. They were equally matched.

"You might still get your chance if the EMP cannons don't work." Cabrillo wasn't worried about an electromagnetic pulse harming the *Oregon*. Once he and Max decided to upgrade to electromagnetic pulse cannons, they had to harden all of the *Oregon*'s electronic systems to protect her gear from their own weapons system. The bonus was they were now protected from everyone else's EMP attacks as well.

"Firing pulse cannon," Linda said. One of the domes on top of the superstructure spun on its axis as the cannon raised and lowered under Linda's direction, fire-hosing the drones in a bath of electromagnetic radiation. One by one, the holographic images snuffed out like blown birthday candles, the witch being the last to go.

"Too bad. I really had a hankerin' to pull out the boom sticks," Max said.

"Chairman," Linda shouted as she pointed at the starboard-forward wall monitor.

In the far distance, the holographic pirate ship had turned broadside, and her banks of spectral guns cut loose in a fiery cannonade.

Boom!

The *Oregon* shuddered with an eruption beneath her waterline.

27

The *Baktun*'s combat crew cheered when their drone torpedo shadowing the *Agua Linda* exploded.

Captain Stokes fixated on the weapons monitor. His eyelids lifted with the rising geyser of water erupting against the *Agua Linda*'s hull spewing up into the night air. It was a glorious sight, but—

"Something's amiss," Stokes murmured as he loomed over the weapons station.

"Sir?" the Russian weapons officer said.

The geyser of water fell back with a crash, and the *Agua Linda* rocked slightly with the blast. The torpedo drone's carbon-fiber body was nearly impossible to detect, which made it quite dangerous. It carried a relatively small warhead, but its charge was ample enough to sink any commercial vessel.

"The *Agua Linda* isn't sinking. Why?" Stokes demanded. His first officer now stood beside him as well.

"She doesn't even appear damaged," the first officer said.

The Russian checked his monitor. "Perfect explosion."

"Two explosions," the sonarman said. He was a former South Korean naval officer.

"Two?" the first officer said. "How?"

"Reactive armor," Stokes said. He grinned broadly. "This is not a commercial vessel. It's a decoy, like an old Q-ship."

The Russian's face broke into a wide smile. "A combat vessel in disguise."

"We should retreat," the first officer said. He turned to the helmsman. "Prepare for evasive maneuvers. Full power."

"Aye, sir," the helmsman responded.

"Stand by," Captain Stokes said, delaying the helm order.

Activating the *Baktun*'s laser-induced plasma detonation wave propulsion (LIPDWP) system would rob power from the *Baktun*'s more important operations and likely disrupt it, if not damage it.

The whole purpose of the *Baktun* was to provide a secret and safe platform for the development of Project Q.

Dr. Bose's organoid computer and associated hardware consumed the vast majority of the electricity generated by the *Baktun*'s internal confinement fusion reactor. She had just briefed him on their progress. They were days away from success. Any disruption of her electricity supply at this crucial juncture could prove catastrophic.

The *Baktun*'s fusion reactor produced ten times the energy of an Ohio-class S8G fission reactor, though it occupied a smaller space. Without an ample supply of electricity, Project Q would crash to a halt.

But Stokes had to rob Peter to pay Paul. The only way the *Baktun* could activate its plasma wave propulsion system was to redirect the energy supply away from Project Q. An enormous amount of electricity was needed to power the high-energy optical-fiber lasers—each thinner than a human hair—that laced the torpedo-shaped pod beneath the *Baktun*'s hull. The resulting rapid expansion of superheated plasma underwater created both a supercavitation bubble and a shock wave.

That supercavitating zone essentially eliminated all friction between the energy pod and the surrounding seawater—and generated incredible speed. The successive plasma shock waves, in turn, produced explosive thrust and drove the *Baktun* in any direction Stokes desired by manipulating the energy flow.

Stokes hardly understood the physics of the thing, but he knew his disguised research vessel could reach unheard-of speeds and all without conventional fuel or propellers.

But the former naval warfare officer wasn't ready to turn tail and run just yet. Stokes had been waiting for years for a combat opportunity like this. The *Agua Linda*, even if it was some kind of a disguised gunboat, couldn't possibly know his location. How could it attack him?

Yes, the *Agua Linda*'s ability to knock out his holographic drones with what appeared to be an electromagnetic pulse weapon was surprising, but hardly concerning. The *Baktun*'s systems were hardened against such a thing. But what other weapons might the *Agua Linda* have up her sleeve?

"Comms? What kind of chatter are you picking up?" Stokes asked.

"*Agua Linda* hasn't broadcast any radio or distress signals. She's quiet."

Further proof she wasn't damaged, Stokes reasoned, nor in need of assistance. She was no sitting duck. It would be a manly fight.

Now was his chance.

"Weapons—fire the nano-torpedoes. Helm—activate laser propulsion. Evasive maneuvers."

"Aye, Captain."

★

"Missile detected!" Linda shouted.

"Course and speed?" Cabrillo asked.

Stoney threw the radar track up onto one of the big monitors as he called out the stats. A bright red orb on the radar screen streaked at over six hundred miles per hour toward the *Oregon*.

"Activate missile defenses." Cabrillo hardly needed to give the order. Linda had already activated it, exactly according to protocol.

"Heading our way," Stoney called out. "No . . . Wait . . . Veering off course . . ."

The missile track drifted several points away, then suddenly dropped off the screen.

"Malfunction?" Cabrillo asked.

"Maybe a wave skimmer," Max said.

"Just splashed," a sonarman said, one hand pressing against his headphones.

"Crashed?" Cabrillo asked.

"Multiple splashes . . ."

"Debris?" Max asked.

The underwater sonar track appeared on a big wall monitor. All eyes turned to it. A cluster of twenty green blips appeared—and moving fast.

"Computer counts twenty . . . heading our way . . . high-speed screws—seven-zero knots!"

"Torps," Juan said. "Sound battle stations."

"Wait . . . Look," Ross said as the Klaxon alarm rang.

The green dots split up into smaller triads, and the triads, in turn, split up. They began moving in strange patterns.

"They're swarming," Juan said.

"AI torpedoes?" Max asked.

"Stoney, get us out of here," Juan said. "Wepps, anti-torps."

Linda Ross punched the firing button for the *Oregon*'s new advanced torpedo defense systems. The miniature torpedoes were fire-and-forget, AI-guided munitions. They would select their own targets and take them out either singly or in groups faster than any human could react.

As Ross launched the torpedoes, Stoney slammed his throttles forward and jerked the joystick. Seconds later, the engines launched into full power. The *Oregon* lunged forward and then staggered into a steep turn like a drunken racehorse. Everyone in the op center strained against their safety harnesses, their buckles fastened when battle stations sounded.

"Wepps, get a fix on that vessel," Cabrillo ordered.

"Trying . . ."

"Not good enough."

"Can't get a radar lock," Linda said. "No radar signature."

"How's that possible?" Hali asked.

"Cloaking," Juan said grimly. It was the only explanation possible.

"How is *that* possible?" Max asked.

"A question for another time."

Cabrillo glanced at the weapons monitor. His cloud of defensive mini torpedoes broke up the same way the incoming attack torpedoes had done. It was an underwater AI chess match now.

"Wepps, get an estimated trajectory of the missile launch location. Load the starboard Melara 76 with high-explosive rounds. Set to air-burst mode. Estimate a bracket for wide-area effect."

"Guess we're shooting shotguns after all," Max said, beaming.

"Yeah, blindfolded and in the dark," Juan said.

"Solution plotted. Firing."

The *Oregon*'s refit had stripped away massive amounts of weight, machinery, and maintenance issues when it eliminated the bow-mounted 120-millimeter smoothbore cannon and the multiton rail gun, both of which required massive hydraulics to lift and operate.

In their stead, Juan had placed four proven naval deck guns hidden inside of what appeared to be standard forty-foot shipping containers permanently located on deck. Two of the containers held long-range OTO Melara 127-millimeter naval guns. The two others housed medium-range versions in 76-millimeter. Both systems were capable of firing a wider variety of munitions at much higher rates than the *Oregon*'s previous guns. When activated, the sides of the shipping containers dropped and the roofs drew back automatically.

The Melara 76 boomed overhead like kettledrums from hell, firing two rounds per second.

"Incoming torps," Stoney shouted. Juan glanced up as alarms shrieked. Five of the green blips had slipped through the *Oregon*'s defenses—

And five explosions erupted beneath the hull.

"Damage report."

"Venturi tube outlet nozzle . . . port-side fin . . . port-side stabilizer—all down," Max said, studying his engineering panel.

"Full stop," Juan ordered as the Melara continued booming overhead.

"Aye," Stoney said, killing the engines.

"Hull damage?" Juan asked.

Max pressed his headset harder against his ear, listening to his engineer's report.

"No breaches reported. All good."

Before Juan could give the order, Max dashed for the engine room. The propulsion system was his baby. He'd run into a fiery building to save it if it came to that.

But Cabrillo's fear was that the invisible hunter might be closing in for the kill.

"Wepps?"

"Nothing on my screens."

"Sonar?"

"No screws in the water, shipborne or otherwise."

Every other station reported "All clear" as well.

"Maybe we hit him," Stoney said.

"'Maybe' can get us killed." Juan scanned the wall monitors. His team was right. No more threats presented on the screens. They seemed out of harm's way—for now.

"Everyone stay alert. Hali, kill the Klaxon, but stay on battle stations."

"Aye."

Juan unbuckled his harness and approached Linda's station.

"Anything pops up—you know what to do."

She nodded. "I guess there really was a demon ghost ship after all. Just not the holographic type."

"That wasn't any ghost. And for whatever reason, he was pulling his punches."

"Why do you say that?"

"Those AI torps he threw at us? Too small to sink us, but clearly designed to select damage points to stop us in the water. If they have that kind of advanced tech, I guarantee you they've got even bigger and nastier arrows in their quiver."

"Then why not use them and send us to Davy Jones's locker?"

"Dunno. Maybe he wanted to avoid satellite detection of a larger launch. He clearly doesn't want to be seen. He's hiding something."

"I wonder what?"

"We'll have to ask him when we find him."

"*If* we find him. What do we do now?"

"We wait for Max to give us our marching orders. Can't finish our snipe hunt until we get our girl fixed up."

Linda stood. "I'll head over to the boat garage and get the ball rolling."

"I want repair crews under the boat in fifteen minutes. Sooner, if we can."

28

I'm here in the room now, sir."

Agent Tu was a square-jawed senior operative in the Ministry of State Security. He stood by the unconscious woman's bedside in a private suite in Taiwan's premier hospital. Her dark red hair had been shaved off of one side of her thickly bandaged skull. IV tubes snaked into her tattooed arms.

The man's boss, Peng De, was on the other end of the encrypted cell phone.

The woman had survived a horrific traffic accident, or so the incident had been reported by a compliant police commissioner. In fact, she and a companion had tried to kill Huang Tzu-ming, a senior executive with one of Taiwan's largest shipping companies, by running his car off a high mountain road. But Agent Tu, Huang's driver, was a world-class expert in advanced tactical driving. He not only avoided getting wrecked but turned the tables on their attackers, forcing the two would-be assassins into the rocky gorge in their stead. The male driver had burned to death, but the female passenger had been tossed from the vehicle, shattering her spine and crushing part of her skull but saving her life.

At least for now.

Mr. Huang, a Taiwanese native, was a primary conduit in China's superchip and graphics processing unit pipeline—the most advanced, integrated, and specialized processors needed for AGI development. Both were banned for sale and export to mainland China by Taiwan, the world's primary source for AGI semiconductors.

But the Taiwanese shipping executive had been secretly arranging for the illegal sale and transshipment of these critical components to Beijing for years. His efforts had provided China with tens of thousands of graphics processing chips and were responsible for sixty percent of China's annual supply. He was a perfect target for the Guardians and was the reason why a half dozen MSS agents like Tu had been secretly assigned to Huang's security detail.

"How is our friend Mr. Huang doing?" Peng asked.

"Broken collarbone, slight concussion. He's already been sent home—under guard, of course."

"And his home?"

"I've doubled security there. Cameras are all fully functional."

"Excellent. And the woman?"

"She's in a medically induced coma. Stable for now, according to the doctors."

"How soon can you transport her?"

"Twenty-four hours at the earliest. I will have one of my people with her in the room at all times, and two more on the floor."

"Is that sufficient?"

"There is a strong police presence throughout the facility. We have the complete support of the local authorities."

Agent Tu was on a first-name basis with several of Taiwan's senior police and intelligence community officials. Despite the patriotic outbursts of pro-independent politicians, many of Taiwan's elite saw the writing on the wall and had already formed discreet alliances with the Chinese Communist Party to secure their futures when the island finally unified with the mainland.

"Last you reported, she had no identity," Peng said. "Any progress on that front?"

"She erased all of her online records—social media, bank accounts, everything. But twenty minutes ago we finally confirmed her identity."

"Excellent. How?"

"Four years ago, she completed an online DNA test for family history. She deleted her account later when she expunged her other records, not realizing we owned that database. It was easy enough to take a DNA sample from her in her current condition."

"And what did you learn? And I don't care if she's six percent Cherokee Indian."

"Emily Nighswonger, age twenty-nine. Former AI bioscience researcher at the Lawrence Livermore National Lab. She left the position eighteen months ago and hasn't been heard of since, not even by her family. Presumed dead."

"And the driver?"

"We were only able to lift partial fingerprints from his remains. But we're certain his name is Aidan Scally, age thirty-seven, an assistant professor of physics at UC Berkeley currently on leave. He's also ex–U.S. Army intelligence."

"Guardians," Peng hissed. "These people are Guardians."

"My conclusion as well, sir."

"Whatever you do, make sure that woman stays alive. Spare no expense. I must have her for questioning."

"I understand," Tu said. This woman was the first Guardian they had ever gotten close to, let alone captured. Under proper interrogation techniques, Peng might finally break open the impenetrable wall of secrecy that had so far protected the global terrorist organization.

"I'm sure you understand the gravity of the situation," Peng said before ending the call.

"Of course."

Tu had been in the MSS long enough to know that *the* situation was *his* situation.

And if the woman died while under his custody, so would he.

29

Captain Stokes glowered at the tall, bearded Sikh standing guard outside of Dr. Bose's office, barring his entrance. The ship was under Stokes's command, but Bose was in charge of Project Q. Under normal circumstances, Stokes would never have allowed the effrontery of an armed man on ship not under his authority, but his employer, Fierro, permitted it.

Stokes bristled at the thought he couldn't breeze through the closed door behind the broad-shouldered Sikh, but he held his temper. The Indian's eyes blazed with contempt, his soul poisoned with the silent, generational fury of a proud warrior people humiliated by their former British colonial masters.

The British captain's simmering rage threatened to boil over and engulf the Sikh, his mood befouled by the *Agua Linda*'s airburst shrapnel. Stokes managed to contain himself only because his two wounded crewmen were stabilized in the hospital and minor repairs had already been effected.

"Enter," Bose said from behind the door.

The Sikh's eyes smiled with contempt. "You may enter." He didn't bother opening the door.

Stokes sniffed as he brushed past the Sikh and entered the office. Bose didn't bother looking up from the reports on her desk, a pair of reading glasses perched on her fine, aquiline nose.

"You wanted to see me?" Stokes demanded.

Bose turned in her seat and removed her glasses.

"You do realize the sudden power surge you stole from the reactor nearly crashed Project Q?"

Even angry, she was quite a handsome woman, Stokes noted. "It was an emergency decision."

"You could have destroyed the organoid computer, you . . . you *foolish* man."

"And you realize if we had been captured or sunk, the result would have been equally catastrophic?"

"Your job is to keep either from happening—while allowing me to continue my work."

"Not getting sunk allows you to continue your work."

"I hope you understand the gravity of our mutual situation. As pleasant as Fierro appears to be, our lives are forfeit if we fail him. Luckily, I believe we can still meet our deadline."

"I've known men like him my whole life. I'm well aware of the danger he poses behind that slithering smile. Trust me, I have no intention of falling into his disfavor. For *both* our sakes."

Bose softened. They weren't really enemies. In fact, the two fiery personalities shared an unspoken yet nearly irresistible attraction. She knew Stokes fully understood that Project Q consumed the vast majority of the ship's energy stores. The whole reason Stokes was forced to rely upon the "demon pirate" games was to minimize power consumption—otherwise, the *Baktun* could simply race away at the first sight of any encroaching vessel. So far, he had waged his stealth campaigns with great success.

"I'm grateful, Captain. In a few days, your superior efforts will bear much fruit. We'll both make history."

"And I will do everything in my power to ensure that happens, Doctor. The world deserves to know your brilliance."

The arrogant pose of the genius computer scientist melted into a blushing schoolgirl's smile.

30

Juan Cabrillo was in the pilot seat of the bubble-canopied *Spook Fish*, the *Oregon*'s latest submarine. The three-passenger deepwater submersible was capable of depths in excess of four thousand feet. It could extend its working reach another five thousand feet via a graphene power cable attached to a drone deploying surgically adept arms and welding torches. Cabrillo had acquired the *Spook* for treasure hunts and wreck recoveries at depths his other two larger submersibles couldn't reach.

Right now, he was in far shallower waters, hovering just beneath the *Oregon*'s hull. Cabrillo deftly deployed the *Spook*'s clawed hands to support the last repaired directional tube Max was now fixing back into place. Four of the ship's propulsion tubes that provided maneuverability had been damaged, as had the single straight-line venturi tube. Max's engineering team was all dive-qualified, which was the primary reason all of the drone-torpedo damage underneath the hull had been repaired in record time.

Hanley was on board the sixty-five-foot *Nomad*, the *Oregon*'s flat-faced, Tic Tac–shaped submarine, manipulating its underwater arms and assisted by a trio of *Oregon* divers working just beyond his three visual portals.

The encounter with the cloaked mystery ship was another wake-up call for the *Oregon*. Just as with the war-gamed encounter with Linda, certain vulnerabilities had been exposed. Fortunately, all of the damage inflicted had been relatively minor, though clearly it could have been far worse, if not fatal. Whether or not the *Oregon* had managed a blind hit on his opponent was unclear, as was the reason for the other ship's retreat. For now, he called it a draw. But Cabrillo and his brain trust needed to make sure the next round went decisively to the *Oregon*.

"Chairman, Mr. Overholt is calling for you. I told him you were busy, but he insists on speaking with you."

Juan raised a curious eyebrow. Overholt knew they were in the midst of repairs following his after-action report. They both agreed continuing to chase the phantom was a waste of effort now that it was alerted to the *Oregon*'s presence, but at least Cabrillo had provided confirmation that something was afoot.

"Patch him through."

A moment later, Overholt's voice crackled on the speakers.

"How are the repairs coming along, dear boy?"

"Depends on how many more phone calls I have to take. Pending no more interruptions, we should be all wrapped up within the next few hours. What's up?"

"You needn't be churlish. I have another opportunity for you."

"Frankly, Langston, you've got my head spinning. I've got two operators undercover in Panama on one mission for you, and I just finished a blind man's brawl on another one."

"You're the best juggler I know."

"Not sure I signed up for this circus."

"Every respectable one needs three rings. Do you remember the briefing I sent along to you about President Olmedo?"

"Of course. I really like that guy."

"There is much to admire, certainly."

Cabrillo had double-majored in engineering and political science at Cal Poly and always kept abreast of geopolitical developments. He had closely followed Olmedo's surprising rise to the presidency of El Salvador against all odds. Decades of the most violent crime in the Western Hemisphere, coupled with banana republic levels of corruption and incompetence, had left the tiny nation an economic and political basket case. To everyone's astonishment, the young president had proven to be a bold and visionary leader with a goal of transforming his nation into the Singapore of Central America.

To do so, the incorruptible reformer waged a relentless but law-abiding campaign against the criminality and corruption that had crippled his country's people and progress. He still faced a number of obstacles. Overholt's briefing had laid out Olmedo's most pressing predicament.

The Chinese government's economic Belt and Road Initiative had stretched its tentacles around the globe for over a decade, offering large loans and trade contracts to nations needing both.

The poorest nations—especially the ones headed by corrupt politicians—had been the most eager to participate. The Chinese targeted critical infrastructure projects like transnational highways and shipping ports, offering to build or refurbish them using Chinese engineering and Chinese bank loans to pay for the effort. It was all done in the name of fostering economic development with the promise of lifting them out of poverty and into prosperity through increased global trade.

Of course, that was mostly a lie. The initiative was simply another stone in China's "unrestricted warfare" sling. The Chinese were loaning money to nations they knew couldn't afford to pay it back. Those pieces of critical infrastructure built by Chinese firms and Chinese labor with other people's borrowed money were all collateralized. If the struggling governments failed to repay their loans, the properties in question would be seized. After a decade of such predatory efforts, the Chinese had acquired some of the most strategically valuable real estate on the planet.

Before Olmedo, El Salvador's previous administration had fallen prey to its own greed and China's strategic plotting and foolishly signed up for the initiative. The nation's Port of Acajutla was now at risk, as the outsize loan repayments were overly burdensome to the small economy. The last thing the United States needed was for China's Navy to find a Pacific Ocean toehold in Latin America or, more likely, another gateway for illegal drugs, people, and guns to flood into the region.

Fortunately, there was a proviso sequestered deep in the volumi- nous folds of the expansive but poorly translated bilateral treaty. That provision allowed El Salvador to terminate the agreement if China was ever found to have violated El Salvador's national laws.

Olmedo also eagerly sought strategic partnership with the United States, but his greedy predecessors and their Chinese benefactors had tied his hands. He quietly turned to the Americans for help. Overholt was tasked with finding a solution and now he had his opportunity.

"Are you still scheduled for that drop off in El Salvador?"

"Delivering tomorrow. Why?"

"My sources report the *Golden Lotus*, a Chinese-flagged vessel with known ties to the MSS, is approaching the Port of Acajutla with a contraband cargo."

"Let me guess. You want us to secretly board the vessel once it's docked, document its illegal consignment, and send that evidence back to you, and all without getting caught to avoid an international in- cident."

"Precisely. I'll hand it off to the State Department and they'll raise a ruckus. With any luck, your mission will break China's stranglehold on El Salvador's economic neck."

"And bring President Olmedo fully into America's orbit."

"Exactamundo."

"Any idea what that ship is carrying?"

"Our source on the other end couldn't get close, and I've been ad- vised that Chinese security is tight at Acajutla. There's a section of the port under their exclusive management—and that's where you'll find your target berthed when it arrives."

The *Spook*'s giant bubble canopy gave Juan a nearly three-hundred- sixty-degree view of the ocean around him. He easily spotted the lead diver signaling to Max the "all clear" signal. Hanley's mechanical grip released on the big directional nozzle and he backed away. Cabrillo manipulated his controls and followed suit.

"I'll let you know when we've arrived and keep you posted as we progress."

"Outstanding."

"For another fee, of course."

"I'm already paying you double for the 'snipe hunt,' which we've now canceled."

"For which we are eternally grateful." Cabrillo twisted the joystick and nosed the *Spook* toward the *Oregon*'s moon pool doors.

"Uncle Sam isn't made of money."

"I don't think our rich uncle will mind adding a few more measly bucks to the thirty-six trillion dollars he's already borrowed from his grandchildren."

"That's legalized piracy, Cabrillo."

"Are you referring to me or Washington, D.C.?"

"You have me over the proverbial barrel. What alternative do I have?"

Cabrillo chuckled. "None. Talk soon."

31

The *Oregon* was anchored a mile offshore from the Port of Acajutla. The *capitán de puerto*—the harbormaster—had denied her entrance. At first, Cabrillo assumed his cover had been blown, but a few quick questions and a consult with a commercial vessel tracking system confirmed that the busy port was, indeed, suffering a logjam. Though highly efficient and flexible, the small port only had three piers and eight berths, and accommodated everything from container ships to cruise ships. President Olmedo's reforms had transformed El Salvador into a minor economic miracle in short order. There were big plans for a significant expansion, but for now Acajutla Port was more crowded than a Costco parking lot on Christmas Eve.

Cabrillo graciously informed the *capitán de puerto* that his schedule was a bit flexible, and the grateful harbormaster promised swift service as soon as a dock became available.

In truth, Cabrillo was grateful for the mix-up. It wasn't actually necessary for the *Oregon* to dock in order to gain access to the port or their target, the *Golden Lotus*.

The other advantage to the change in plan was practical. Since Raven and Linc hadn't called in for an exfil, Juan authorized Gomez to make the short hop in the tilt-rotor to pick up Murphy and his friend Linlin Zhang from the San Salvador airport and ferry them to the *Oregon*.

Juan was deeply conflicted. On the one hand, he was thrilled Murph and his friend had escaped the assassination attempt in Thailand and had made it all the way back to San Salvador in one piece. Murphy had called Juan from the *Oregon*'s Gulfstream on a secure line while still en route over the Pacific and filled him in on the details of the Thailand attack. Murph was no fool—he would never put the *Oregon*'s security at risk. The talented weapons officer made a compelling case that Linlin's life was in danger and she had no other alternatives.

But Cabrillo wasn't accustomed to strangers coming on board the *Oregon* unless they had been thoroughly vetted, and he didn't consider Murph's history of tickling tonsils with his former girlfriend a proper background investigation. Cabrillo believed Murphy, but that didn't change the fact she was an unknown quantity. He offered an awkward compromise Murph readily accepted. Cabrillo also ordered the special effects crew to "dirty up" the *Oregon* just enough to keep Linlin in the dark regarding the ship's true capacities.

Gomez landed the thundering AW tilt-rotor aircraft with feathery grace and cycled down the engines. Murphy and Linlin hopped onto the *Oregon*'s main deck, ducking low beneath the slowing carbon-fiber blades circling overhead, their backpacks in hand.

Murphy led her toward the door of the soaring superstructure perched on the *Oregon*'s aft end. The two of them stepped over loose cables, past dented and rusty oil drums, and through the doorway flaked with peeling paint. Once inside, Linlin's nose curled at the overwhelming smell of Pine-Sol. The potent aromatic embellishment was the finishing touch on the Magic Shop's "trashy *Oregon*" set design.

Murph drew her by the hand down the long, narrow corridor of faded and cracked linoleum and into the galley—a mass of clean but scratched and marred stainless steel benches. The order window's rolling shutter was bolted closed.

Juan greeted the two of them with a welcoming smile, wearing his customary linen slacks, leather loafers, and silky tropical shirt.

Eddie Seng, Juan's director of shore operations and head of the Gundogs, stood next to him. The former CIA undercover had spent years in China. The wiry close-quarters combat specialist wore his hair long and his beard thick.

Murphy stumbled over and Juan bear-hugged him.

"Now you're safe," Cabrillo said. He turned and faced Linlin, thrusting out his hand. "Juan Cabrillo."

Linlin took his hand gratefully. Her slim, unmanicured fingers offered a firm grip.

"I can't thank you enough, Captain."

"Chairman," Murph corrected.

"My apologies—"

"Juan is fine. Welcome aboard the *Agua Linda*." He turned to Eddie. "My navigator, Eddie Seng."

"*Nǐ hǎo*," Eddie said, using his most pronounced American inflection. As an undercover he mastered the Chinese mainland accent and various Mandarin dialects, but he didn't want Linlin to suspect he'd ever been there.

It must have worked. She fought back a grin, no doubt amused by his unusual perversion of her mother tongue.

Seng waited until Linlin offered her hand first, out of courtesy. He was careful not to stare daggers through her lest he be perceived as aggressive or rude, but his trained eye took in every possible detail. He had only survived his years in a low-trust, high-surveillance culture like Communist China by being able to read people instantaneously.

"*Nǐ hǎo*." The brief handshake ended with a slight nod of their heads, a sign of mutual respect. Linlin turned to her faultless English. "Where did you learn to speak Chinese?"

"I was born in New York City. Chinatown, technically."

"I've never been there."

"I think you would enjoy it. If you ever go, I will give you my parents' phone number. They would be happy to host you."

"That's very nice of you to offer."

Eddie's high-alert sensors dropped a few degrees. Linlin was completely charming. Still, he couldn't escape the feeling that he was the one being interrogated.

"You look utterly exhausted," Juan said.

"I didn't sleep much on the plane," Murph said. "Too jacked up on adrenaline and coffee."

Cabrillo nodded. "Long plane flights are the worst."

"I appreciate you letting me take shelter with you," Linlin said. "When Murph said he knew a safe location, I had no idea he was referring to a cargo ship at sea."

"I don't know your situation exactly," Juan said, "but whoever's looking for you will be hard-pressed to find you here. Have you ever been on a working cargo vessel before?"

"No, I haven't. I'm intrigued. I would think it a very romantic life."

"Hardly. It's pretty boring stuff. We're like a giant delivery truck. Having said that, I'm going to restrict you to your private quarters while you're on board. The decks can be very dangerous. Lots of heavy equipment. It's for your safety."

"I understand."

Cabrillo noted Linlin's eyes narrowing slightly.

The rolling shutter suddenly opened with a stuttering racket. One of the *Oregon*'s sous-chefs, dressed down in working utilities rather than the customary Cordon Bleu–styled jacket, stood grimly behind the counter, a smoldering cigarette dangling from her lower lip—fully in character. Juan picked her for this assignment because she'd spent a year acting in Off-Broadway productions before heading to cooking school. She relished the chance to play the role of the grumpy ship's cook while secretly keeping watch over the stranger.

"I'm sure you guys are starving." Juan waved a hand at the counter as he turned toward Linlin. "Cookie there will whip you up anything you want, so long as its eggs, bacon, or hamburger." He leaned in close. "She doesn't have much of a repertoire, but it's still pretty good."

Linlin began to demur, but she suddenly realized Cabrillo wanted to speak with Murph privately.

"Thank you. I am rather famished." She smiled and made a beeline for the stainless steel counter.

As soon as Linlin was out of earshot, Juan pulled Murph aside by the elbow. He kept an eye on her as he spoke with Murphy in whispered tones.

"So what does she know about us?"

"Only that we are a cargo vessel hauling on a contract basis. I told her she'd be safe here."

"And she is. But she's not an idiot, is she?"

"One of the best computer scientists I ever studied with."

"And what does she think you do on this ship being perhaps an even better computer scientist? Clean the bilges?"

"I told her I ran comms and maintained the electronics because I needed a career change, and the only computer stuff I do anymore is gaming."

"And she believed you?"

Murph grinned, and pointed at his wrinkled concert T-shirt. "Do I look like a weapons officer on the world's most advanced espionage ship? Or a goofy gamer?"

Juan shook his head. Hard to argue with that.

"And what's her story?"

"She works at a German computing firm and the MSS thinks she's a traitor, so they tried to kill her—me, too, by the way."

"Why did they think she was a traitor?"

"She was explaining it to me when the bad guys started cutting loose with their gats."

"'Gats'? What are you, Dashiell Hammett now?"

Murph shrugged. "Been watching a lot of noir detective movies lately."

Juan sighed through his nose, thinking. Something wasn't quite right, but he couldn't put his finger on it.

"You trust her?"

"Totally. Question is, do you trust me?"

"Of course I do. But the truth of the matter is she doesn't have security clearance. Neither does my sweet ninety-two-year-old *abuela*, and I wouldn't grant her access to the lower decks, either. So just like we agreed, she can stay on board, but only up here. By the way, did you confiscate her phone?"

"Soon as we got on the plane. I told her it was for her own protection. She didn't have a problem with it. I already ran a diagnostic on it while she slept. It's clean." Murphy pulled her phone from his pocket and handed it to Cabrillo.

"I'll hold on to this for the duration. Go grab some grub, and take her to the guest cabin. It's already been made up. Does she need anything else?"

"She hardly packed anything. Maybe some clothes?"

"If some of our ladies can't find a wardrobe for her, I'll have Nixon put something together."

"That's more than I could ask for."

"She'll be confined to her cabin, even her meals. Understood?"

"Perfectly."

"How long do you think she'll be with us?"

"Depends on how soon she can find a place to hide. She has to be careful how she reaches out. The MSS will be monitoring all of her known contacts. It will be a few days at least. Is that a problem?"

"I briefed you on the *Golden Lotus*—and you know about Linc and Raven. I'm not expecting any serious problems, but if things get kinetic, she's exposed up here. She can't know what we're doing, but her life is technically at risk. Are you willing to take responsibility for that?"

"She's safer here than anywhere else. So yeah, I'm comfortable with that."

"Then she can stay however long it takes—but the sooner she's off this ship, the better. She's already seen the tilt-rotor. She doesn't need to know about the rest of our toys."

"Agreed."

"In the meantime, I need you to get back to work. You read the two after-action reports I sent you?"

"Yeah. Crazy stuff. I've got a few ideas about that cloaking device I want to check out."

"Good. After you get your girlfriend squared away, come find me in the conference room. We've got a mission to plan." Juan sniffed the air. "After you take a shower."

Murph smiled. "Aye." He headed for the serving window.

Juan turned to Eddie, lowering his voice.

"Thoughts?"

"Cute girl."

"Besides the obvious."

"Not sure. I usually read people as friend or foe."

"And?"

Eddie glanced at Murph and Linlin laughing and chatting like they were still lovers in university together.

"I don't know yet."

"When you have some time, see what you can find out about Murph's pretty little birdie—but don't let Murph know. I'll send you what I have."

"You got it, boss."

32

Juan and his team had put together a simple plan for tonight's mission. Simple, but not easy.

The *Oregon* team never got the chance to board the *Golden Lotus*. The Chinese vessel had docked and unloaded in record time, its container cargo warehoused under padlock.

The first part of the *Oregon*'s mission now was to find the contraband container—a needle in a haystack if there ever was one. The container storage area for the Port of Acajutla currently covered over fifty-seven thousand square yards with a capacity for over thirty-four hundred containers. The storage yard was bursting to capacity in both the open areas and nearly spilling out of several warehouses.

The good news was that one of those warehouses was owned, operated, and secured by a Chinese firm fronting an MSS operation—with civilian-garbed MSS guards patrolling the place. Since the *Golden Lotus* was known to be owned by an MSS cutout company, it was highly likely the container would be stored inside the Chinese warehouse.

The better news was the container's identification number had been provided by Overholt's contact. Unfortunately, it was still unclear what was inside the container. The suspicion was either guns or drugs. The extremely high-value contraband shipment was handled at the Chinese docks by a third-party intermediary, a notorious triad organization with long association with the Chinese Communist Party.

This was nothing new. Mao had partnered with criminal gangs

even before the 1949 Revolution; in fact, those gangs had helped facil-
itate the Communists' victory over the Chinese Nationalist forces.
Lacking the necessary resources for international operations during
the early part of their regime, China's security services relied heavily
on the triads to carry out various global operations including money
laundering and even primitive wet work.

Juan had heard firsthand from some of the old-timers the CIA had
similar associations with American criminal gangs, though for what
reasons was never made clear.

The other challenges Juan and his team faced were getting inside of
that container, determining what was inside, and documenting it.
With that documentation, Overholt could supply the U.S. State Department with the necessary evidence to sever China's predatory trade
treaty with El Salvador.

Of course, all of this had to be done without a direct confrontation
with Chinese nationals nor could the *Oregon* or its personnel be identified with the operation. The last thing the United States needed was
an international incident given the current state of high tensions over
the Taiwan situation. Overholt didn't want an obscure operation in El
Salvador to become the Sarajevo event igniting World War III.

Local port authorities and law enforcement provided minimal but
decent security around the port facility. The container storage areas
were fenced, well-lit, and covered by security cameras.

The *Oregon*'s long-range optical sensors along with a few discreet
drone flybys revealed six armed MSS guards at the Chinese warehouse: two patrolling outside and four inside. The Chinese warehouse
itself was a newly refurbished building with concrete walls and a roof
that was peppered with vents, but had stairwell access as well. It stood
some distance from the other warehouses, giving the patrolling guards
clear lines of sight. Though the port was a twenty-four/seven operation, the Chinese warehouse had shut and padlocked its doors for
added security.

It was a tough nut to crack, but Cabrillo had shelled quite a few in
his day. This one hopefully would be no different.

★

The operation began just three minutes after 02:00 as the first tendrils of lightning cracked overhead. A series of squalls had begun rolling in. Weather reports indicated they would grow in intensity over the next twenty-four hours. Juan and his crew would be in and out before things got crazy.

The operation's opening salvo was a narrowly directed energy beam fired from one of the *Oregon*'s EMP cannons. Murph carefully swept one side of the container yard, knocking out lights and cameras with each burst. He continued that process until the Chinese warehouse was similarly darkened, as was the next one over. They hoped people on the ground would assume the storm was responsible for the temporary shutdown across the yard. By hitting a large portion of the yard, the Chinese wouldn't think they had been singled out and targeted.

With the lights and cameras knocked out, the *Oregon*'s newly acquired Joby S4 eVTOL leaped off the *Oregon*'s deck. The four-passenger, electric-powered tilt-rotor flew in near silence through the thundering, windswept night.

Gomez carefully followed the Joby's AI-chosen path, its sensors and algorithms assiduously avoiding visual and radar detection until it hovered just inches above the warehouse roof.

Juan and Eddie Seng slipped off the skids and padded over to the nearest transom as the stealthy Joby slipped back into the dark. If anything went sideways tonight with the Chinese guards, Cabrillo wanted both Eddie's sangfroid bravado and linguistic expertise deployed.

Seng opened his pack, pulled out his surveillance gear, and quickly deployed a tiny quadcopter equipped with a night vision camera and audio. Thanks to his first-person view goggles and handheld controller, Eddie was able to deftly maneuver the whisper-quiet surveillance drone through the crowded warehouse stacked with containers. Within moments he located the four interior guards, each highly alert and attentive to their duty, deploying flashlights against the dark.

Clearly, they were concerned about whatever it was they were guarding—yet another confirmation the *Oregon* team was in the right place at the right time.

With the guards located, Seng turned to finding the container. Their plan A hinged on a quick ingress and departure; no telling when shift changes or other potential disasters could upend the applecart. The prevailing thought was that the target container had only just been unloaded and therefore would be near the front entrance and not stacked somewhere in the back. It took all of two minutes for Eddie to find the correct alphanumeric-sequenced ISO code and signal a thumbs-up. "Got it."

With all six positions of the guards confirmed and the container location secured, Cabrillo radioed back to Hali Kasim. "We're good to go. Let her rip."

Moments later, Kasim engaged the *Oregon*'s supremely powerful electronic surveillance suite affectionately known as the Sniffer, a primary means of carrying out the *Oregon*'s intelligence-gathering missions. The Sniffer was designed not only to hoover up all manner of electromagnetic signals but also to intercept and decode virtually any form of encrypted signals.

The Sniffer was equally capable of breaking into and manipulating those signals. Tonight's plan A avoided direct confrontation with the guards, but still disabled them by hacking into the encrypted Chinese security comms.

The Cray-powered Sniffer then manipulated the comms signals in the guards' earpieces, broadcasting a series of subtle binaural beats and other sonic wavelengths synced with theta and delta brain wave frequencies. The theory was this would induce a form of audio hypnosis that would immediately paralyze the guards in an eyes-open but mindless stupor, rendering them oblivious to the world around them. Once awakened, they would remember nothing.

"Wow, looks like it's working," Seng said. "I thought it was a load of sci-fi nonsense."

"I was afraid Murph might have fried their comms with the EMP cannon," Cabrillo said. "I never should have doubted the lad." Both men carried holstered tranq pistols on their hips in case Hali's audio hypnosis trick didn't work.

"Okay, let's go." Juan had already picked the lock of the roof's access door. The two men sped noiselessly down the steel staircase and onto the floor. The two operators moved in perfect sync. Thousands of hours of training together had given the entire Gundog team a near-telepathic connection. They always carried comms, but hardly needed them. They knew each other's rhythms, strengths, preferences. As the head of shore operations, Seng knew each of his operators intimately, including his boss, Juan Cabrillo, who was as good as any of the decorated former combat operators on the team.

Within moments, they arrived at the target container. It was on top of a three-high stack, some seventeen feet off the ground.

"How much time do we have, Hali?" Cabrillo asked in his comms.

"Hypno-signal is still strong, so as long as you need."

But who knows how long the effect will last? Juan asked himself.

"Let's get after it."

The two men scrambled up the container stack without climbing ropes, utilizing the forklift pockets, vertical locking bar brackets, and horizontal catches. They had practiced this maneuver a few times in the holds of the *Oregon* for just this eventuality. The practice exercise also taught them to bring carabiners and straps so they could easily secure themselves at their lofty height. They attached themselves to the left door, since the right door had to open first.

Eddie pulled out a pair of bolt cutters and snapped the bright blue bolt seal. The bullet-shaped steel pin with bar-coded numbers was an important security measure for any shipping container. The only way for thieves to open the bolt was to destroy it, signaling to the rightful owners that the contents had been either stolen or tampered with. With the bolt cut and its two parts pocketed, Eddie grabbed the handle for the right-door locking rod and rotated it, unlocking the cams from their slots in the doorframe. He nudged the door farther open with the toe of his boot and looked inside.

"Didn't expect that," he whispered.

Juan craned his neck over the smaller man's shoulder. Inside was a large steel tank approximately eight feet long, and three and a half feet wide and tall. It was well secured to the deck with bolts and heavy-duty straps. Chinese ideographs were stenciled on the facing side:

两千五百升

"What does it say?" Cabrillo asked.

"Twenty-five hundred liters."

No smell emanated from the enclosed space, but the hairs on the back of Cabrillo's neck stood on end, his worst fears crystallizing in his mind. He and Eddie unhooked themselves and swung inside.

Cabrillo pulled out a respirator from his pack and slipped it over his face and donned a set of heavy rubber gloves. Eddie did the same. Not knowing what they would be facing on this trip, the two men had packed plenty of protective gear.

Eddie handed Juan a sturdy glass test tube with an absorbent test strip parked inside of it. Cabrillo stepped over to the small sealed opening at the top of the tank, twisted it open, and glanced inside.

"What is it?" Eddie asked through his mask.

"Clear liquid. No telling." Cabrillo dipped the test strip into the fluid, careful not to get any on his gloved fingers. He was even more careful to drop the saturated strip into the tube and seal it up quickly. He handed the sealed tube gingerly to Eddie.

Seng studied the strip as Cabrillo resealed the tank.

Eddie pulled off his respirator, wanting to make sure the mask's view screen hadn't affected his perception of the color of the strip. His frown said it all.

"That bad?" Cabrillo asked.

"Yeah." Seng nodded at the tank. "You're staring at twenty-five hundred liters of pure fentanyl."

★

Juan darkened. That much liquid fentanyl wasn't just a problem.

It was pure evil.

Fentanyl was fifty times more potent than heroin. Just two milligrams of the liquid opioid could kill an average adult. If evenly distributed around the planet, the contents of that tank would theoretically kill one and a quarter billion people.

Equally bad, that same drug—ironically used as a highly effective anesthetic and painkiller—was designed to make other illegal opioids more powerful and therefore more addictive. Fentanyl had already killed hundreds of thousands of Americans in recent years, and turned many of America's inner cities into violent and filthy zones of zombie-like addicts.

"We've got our evidence now. But we can't just leave that crap behind," Juan said.

"And we can't blow it up or burn it or drain it out—it would trash the environment, and who knows how many innocent civilians would die."

"We need to get back to the *Oregon* and come up with a plan," Juan said as he fished around in his pack. "Hand me that busted bolt seal."

"Aye." Eddie pulled the two broken pieces from his pocket and handed them to Juan, who now held a tablet in his hand. He scanned the barcodes on the bolt halves. Seconds later, a miniature thermal printer spit out an identical pair of barcode labels.

Eddie handed him a brand-new, bright blue bolt seal, identical in size, style, and color to the one they had destroyed. Every shipping line used its own preferred color and style of bolt seals and it was easy enough to pull one from the *Oregon*'s stores. They used bolt seals in their own containerized operations, but they also kept a stock of nearly every kind of seal currently in use worldwide for just this kind of work.

Juan fixed one transparent label to the long, bullet-shaped male side of the seal and then the other to the short female receptor as Eddie bagged up the gear for both their packs. Unless inspected under a microscope, no human eye would be able to detect the deception.

Six minutes later, the two men had shut the container door, snapped the new bolt seal in place, and planted a tracker. They then scrambled back up to the warehouse roof and climbed into the Joby S4 hovering just above the deck for the short flight back to the *Oregon*.

33

ABOARD THE *OREGON*

Juan and Eddie made a beeline straight from the *Oregon*'s landing pad to the biophysical lab belowdecks. Dr. Eric Littleton, the lab's director, was primed and ready like an eager prizefighter waiting for the first bell. Juan had called ahead with his suspected fentanyl discovery and Littleton was ready to receive it for testing confirmation. He began his investigation immediately.

Like Juan, Dr. Littleton was a Caltech grad. He earned his doctorate in biochemistry with secondary specialities and certifications in nuclear physics, biophysics, and weapons design. The former weapons inspector had performed site inspections and forensic analyses of weapons of mass destruction sites as an officer in the U.S. Army before transferring to the civilian side of the house. He'd overseen numerous overseas missions involving chemical, biological, radiological, nuclear, and explosive weapons. His education and experience were impeccable.

Cabrillo knew in the current environment of asymmetrical warfare there was no telling what they would come up against. Today's fentanyl discovery proved his wisdom in bringing the dapper southern gentleman on board and creating his department.

"How long, Doc?" Cabrillo asked.

"If you want a definitive confirmation of fentanyl, a liquid chromatography-mass spectrometry analysis is the gold standard."

"So . . . how long?"

"If it's a pure, unmixed sample, should be fairly quick. Thirty minutes max."

"Make it fifteen, if you can."

"Go grab a cup of joe in the canteen. Should be done by the time you bring me back one."

"You got it."

Twenty-one minutes later, Cabrillo reappeared with two steaming cups of fresh-brewed Cuban pour-over with Linda Ross and Max Hanley in tow. He handed one to Littleton.

Despite the early-morning hour, with an operation underway, the entire crew was wide-awake and alert, and ready to contribute any way they could. The galley was fired up and serving hot coffee and breakfast burritos to fuel the crew for the long day already unfolding.

Littleton popped the lid on his coffee, and pointed at the computer screen on his desk.

"You were right, Chairman. This sample is a saturated solution of fentanyl base, the most potent form of all. You said you found twenty-five hundred liters?"

"Yup."

Littleton whistled. "It's worth millions. Could kill millions and millions more." He blew on his coffee and then took a noisy sip.

"The question is, what do we do about it?" Cabrillo asked.

"We've discussed some options but none of them good," Linda said. "We need to knock this thing out, and do it without the Chinese knowing about it. We can't destroy the container or the warehouse. Can't drain it away—"

"Heavens no. You'd have a mass-casualty event on your hands."

"Then what can we do?" Hanley asked.

Littleton took another thoughtful slurp of his hot coffee.

"We'll need some kind of enzyme or catalyst to neutralize it . . . and in sufficient quantities."

Max frowned. "What kind of enzymes or catalysts?"

"We could possibly neutralize it with certain chemicals we might have on board."

"Such as?"

"Ethanol could partially denature it. Hydrogen peroxide could oxidize it, rendering it inactive. Sodium hydroxide might neutralize it through a base-induced hydrolysis reaction . . ."

"Everybody knows that," Max said, trying to cut the tension with his snide sense of humor.

Littleton was still lost in thought.

"Calcium chloride, maybe? Some ships use it for moisture control and deicing. Mixing it with the fentanyl might form a less soluble complex, which might precipitate out of the solution. Even a sufficient amount of bleach—"

Linda Ross shook her head. "We're not carrying hazardous chemicals these days."

"Not even as cleaning supplies?"

"Afraid not. We've rid ourselves of as many combustibles as we can given our combat operations."

"Any other possibilities, Doc?" Cabrillo asked.

Littleton's laughing eyes narrowed, his mind running through countless chemical formulas. He snapped his fingers. "You know, if we had enough styrene monomer . . . even acrylic acid . . ."

Linda shook her head again. "Nope."

"You're sure? Not even as cargo?"

"As director of operations, I promise you, we don't have it."

"May I see the cargo manifest?"

Linda shrugged. She wasn't used to being challenged, but she was humble enough to know that Littleton was the expert on this one.

"Sure."

She pulled it up on his computer screen, then stepped back.

Littleton set his coffee down and scrolled through the list. A wide grin brightened his face.

"I know how we can do it."

"Do what?" Max asked.

"Polymerize the fentanyl."

"How long will it take?" Cabrillo asked.

"It . . . depends." Littleton stifled a laugh.

Cabrillo wasn't sure what was so funny. "Depends on what?"

"How many box cutters do you have?"

★

Linda Ross sounded the ship-wide call. Thirteen minutes later, every available *Oregon* crew member assembled in the hold, where Dr. Littleton and Juan stood next to a shipping container, both of its doors flung wide open.

"When you answered, 'It depends,' you weren't kidding, were you?" Juan said.

Littleton's eyes sparkled with mischief. "Pun intended."

The head of the *Oregon*'s biophysical laboratory worked his calculations and determined he needed one hundred eighty-five pounds of SAPs—superabsorbent polymers—to neutralize two thousand five hundred liters of liquid fentanyl. But rather than try to manufacture a time-consuming batch in his lab, he discovered a hidden treasure trove supplying more than he needed.

To get the final amount of absorbant required tearing open and stripping out two thousand eight hundred XXL Depend-branded adult-size overnight diapers and extracting the dry, granular powder from them.

In fact, the *Oregon* had picked up an entire forty-foot shipping container filled with several thousand boxes of adult diapers, and in particular, the double-extra-large, overnight variety. An enterprising retailer discovered there was a large American retired expat community in El Salvador, and apparently a quite incontinent one. The *Oregon* had been hired to deliver it.

Ross organized the team into two highly efficient production lines. She had rounded up fourteen box cutters, which wasn't enough but hardly a problem. Nearly every member of the crew carried their own personal pocketknives—razor-sharp Benchmades, Kershaws, and Spydercos. The former Marines invariably wielded their venerable Ka-Bars. Thanks to Linda's organizational skills, the task was completed in just over eighteen minutes.

The first members of the team stripped the cases off the pallets.

The second passed along the cases.

The third cut the cases open.

The fourth yanked boxes out of the cases.

The fifth cut those boxes open.

The sixth pulled out the items from inside each box.

And the seventh group, all masked, harvested the absorbant from each diaper.

The final group in the chain gang stood nearby stacking and bagging the trashed remains and disposing of them in designated containers.

The *Oregon* crew had broken open the shipping container and pillaged the contents of a retail product designed to absorb urine and turn it into a jellylike substance. And that's exactly what the absorbants would do to the fentanyl shipment—transform twenty-five hundred liters of the clear liquid poison into a thick, gelatinous mass unyielding and dense within the tank, rendering the drug useless, its fatal potential neutralized.

Eddie and Cabrillo planned on heading back to the warehouse with the absorbant load, but the weight of the material and the fact it would be getting light within three hours required at least three more pairs of hands. Littleton insisted on being the point man to deliver the contents into the tank, since it was the most dangerous job, but also the most technical. Cabrillo suspected the latter argument was specious, but obliged him anyway. He knew the man would take the appropriate precautions.

Eddie checked his watch as the last bag was being cinched up. "I sure hope that audio hypnosis trick works again."

"Lightning never strikes twice," Max said. "Maybe we need an alternative."

"Of course it'll work," Eric Stone said, his pride stung. He had worked with Hali to design the audio hypnosis program. "Roy Sullivan proves it."

"Who's Roy Sullivan?"

"Roy Sullivan was a U.S. park ranger in Virginia. He holds the

Guinness World Record for being struck by lightning seven times over the course of his life. Heck, all we need is for this to work twice. Piece of cake."

"Sometimes you worry me, son."

Suddenly, Hali Kasim's voice echoed throughout the cargo hold. "Chairman, we have a problem."

"What is it?"

"That Chinese container is on the move."

34

Juan and his senior team assembled in *Oregon*'s op center moments later. Cabrillo fell into the Kirk Chair and everyone else took up their various duty stations, including Murph. His friend Linlin was still confined to quarters, and the *Oregon*'s security team had kept a distant but careful eye on her.

So far she'd been compliant, but Cabrillo was concerned. She surely had noted the hustle and bustle of activity over the last few hours and he didn't want her wandering around in the middle of this operation. She was becoming a splinter in Cabrillo's mind—but that was a problem for another day.

Hali had alerted Cabrillo as soon as the tracker began moving. Moments later, one of the *Oregon*'s surveillance drones began broadcasting the infrared image of the container as it was being loaded onto a flatbed truck.

A second drone piloted by Murphy took over from the first and was now tracking the container truck from overhead as it rumbled away from the port, the image displayed on one of the big wall monitors. The imagery was sketchy. A heavy squall had slid over the region and the thick raindrops falling in sheets played havoc with the drone's camera transmission.

More disturbing than the container truck's sudden departure was the two escort vehicles. One was a black Chevy Suburban with four armed guards leading the mini convoy about a half mile farther up, and a trailing SUV with four more armed guards following in the rear.

It wasn't enough security to draw a lot of notice from officials, but enough to deter any would-be attackers.

And with a cargo this valuable, the Chinese were no doubt keeping at least one rapid-response team on standby somewhere in the vicinity.

"This is not good, people," Max said. "We gotta stop this thing pronto and without confronting the Chicoms directly."

Eddie Seng grunted in agreement. "Not unless we want to start a shooting war."

"And Overholt warned us that neither the *Oregon* nor the U.S. can be implicated in any kind of operation," Juan reminded them.

"Where the heck is this little parade even headed?" Linda asked.

"Most likely a lab," Hali said. "But that could be anywhere."

"Then why don't we just track it to its destination? Report it back to the Salvadorans?"

Juan shook his head. "If it's a Chinese lab, they won't touch it. They're even more skittish about a confrontation with the Chicoms than we are. And Chinese lab or not, there's going to be some serious security there. So we have the same problem as before. We can't have any direct confrontation with Chinese nationals and we can't draw attention to ourselves, which a gun battle will most assuredly do."

"What if we swap out the container?" Eric Stone asked. "Then we can neutralize the fentanyl back here on the ship."

"We have plenty of empty twenties," Linda said. "Full ones, too, for that matter, if we need to spoof the weight."

"There's still the matter of 'how'?" Max said.

Gomez had been standing toward the back, still kitted out in his flight suit. "What's the weight we're talking about here?"

"The container's about five thousand pounds, empty. The fentanyl adds another seven thousand pounds, and that tank probably a thousand."

"The AW can sling up to fifteen thousand pounds," Gomez said. "But in this weather I wouldn't risk that heavy of a payload. It'd be like flying a kite in a hurricane. And forget any kind of range."

"Well, there goes plan B," Eric said. The *Oregon*'s tilt-rotor was the ship's heaviest lift airframe.

"We still need to break into that container, and we need to find a way to do it without the Chinese knowing about it," Linda said. "And do it without kinetics . . . while it's still on the move . . . to God knows where."

Max rubbed his tired eyes with his meaty paws. "C'mon, people, think!"

Hanley's angry outburst cut through the room like a trumpet blast. The op center quieted as everyone puzzled over the problem.

"Maps," Stoney finally blurted out.

"Maps? What about them?" Ross asked.

Stoney turned toward Kasim. "Hey, Hali. Question."

"Shoot."

"We used the Sniffer to break into the comms of the warehouse guards, right? Changed the signal output for the audio hypnosis trick?"

"Exactly."

Stoney pointed at the convoy on the screen.

"GPS maps. Everybody uses them now. Especially when they're in a foreign country. Why can't we use the Sniffer to break into their GPS? Reroute them?"

"Spoofing them." Max grinned ear to ear. "I like where this is going."

"I'm sure we could. We have to break into their system . . . put up a stronger signal than they're currently receiving. I'll need to put a drone on top of that trailer to do that. And pronto."

"We don't want them to smell something fishy going on with their maps," Juan said. "Find out what final destination they plugged in, and then we can send them on a slightly different route without raising their suspicions."

"And then?"

Juan stood. "There's only one option. The thing we always do. The one move that never fails us."

Max clapped his hands together.

"We're gonna do a plan C."

35

The thundering storm made for a harrowing trip, but provided excellent noise and visual cover for the *Oregon*'s AW tilt-rotor.

True to his word, Hali deployed the Cray supercomputer and the Sniffer to piece together a spoofed GPS map that fed into each of the three vehicles of the fentanyl convoy. The final destination the Chinese had chosen was a village near the San Vicente volcano, a region of hidden valleys, remote farms, and isolated villages.

Hali and Stone fed the AI program a series of prompts, explaining exactly what they wanted it to accomplish. The AI program quickly determined a route that took the convoy off the main road and into the mountains, convincing the Chinese the longer, more remote, and tedious route was still the fastest by peppering their maps with fake warnings of road constructions, lane closures, and traffic accidents. The Chinese bought it—hook, line, and sinker.

Based on the available terrain, Juan and the other four operatives carefully selected their ambush points, kitted up, and piled into the AW with Gomez on the stick. He set the AW down in a cyclone of rotor wash on a rain-soaked field a half mile from their destination some thirty minutes before the convoy would pass by. The half-mile march over steep mountainous terrain in the pouring rain would eat up at least fifteen more minutes.

The powdery fentanyl-neutralizing absorbing agent was packed into three sacks of fifty pounds each on the backs of three men. Waterproof covers protected the liquid-absorbing materials from the deluge of rain.

Linda Ross carried a fourth sack with the remaining thirty-five pounds under protest that she wasn't being treated equally. But her verbal complaint turned into silent gratitude as she ascended the first steep, rocky embankment. Her pack straps dug into her shoulders and lactic acid fried her thighs on the forced quick march up the slippery mountain path.

Cabrillo led the way with Eddie hot on his heels. Dr. Littleton, the *Oregon*'s best mountain-wall climber and former high school all-American wide receiver, easily kept pace with the trained operators despite the extra fifty-pound burden on his heavily laden back. Linda was right behind him acting as sweep. MacD, the former Army Ranger and *Oregon* Gundog with the honey-sweet Cajun drawl, cut a separate trail heading for a different location.

The team badly needed their comms beneath the roar of rain pelting their headgear. The mission required the utmost speed, stealth, and timing—and they only had one chance to pull it off.

★

The driver of the rear guard vehicle in the convoy swore violently as the thick rain nearly blinded him. The Suburban's wipers slapped furiously across the windshield, but were unable to keep up with the deluge. Yet the driver's orders were clear and the security protocols set. He had to keep pace with the container truck no matter what. The three other guards sat in stoic silence, their hands clenching whatever secure holds they could find.

The thunderous cracks of lightning overhead were nearly deafening, but the gut-wrenching sound of an erupting tire was unmistakable. The red-faced driver cursed furiously as the wheel jerked in his hands. He pumped the brakes and pointed the nose of the big SUV toward the side of the narrow one-lane road, finally bringing it to a shuddering stop.

The man riding shotgun, the unit supervisor, snatched up his cell phone and called to the other two vehicles, informing them they had blown a tire.

A voice from the lead guard vehicle crackled on his radio. "Do you want us to stop? Come back and lend you a hand?"

"Negative! We can handle a flat tire." The supervisor had to shout over the din of rain pummeling the Chevy's roof. "Proceed to the final destination. We'll be back on the road in fifteen minutes and catch up."

"Affirmative."

The two men in the front seat exchanged a glance. Neither wanted to get out in this storm. The supervisor turned around toward the two junior gunmen in the back seat.

"Well? What are you waiting for? Get out there and fix that tire."

★

The Chinese MSS officer in the lead SUV dropped his radio back into the tray. If his boss said to keep going, they'd keep going, but he didn't like it. He preferred the team to stay together, but this was an unusual mission, and it was very high priority. He wasn't going to make any decisions that could put it at risk. If something went wrong, it would be on the team leader, not him.

Just as with the vehicle in the rear, the SUV driver struggled to see through the windshield in the sheeting downpour. But maintaining speed was essential. Their orders were clear—they had to arrive at a specified time. Arrangements had been made. No alteration to the time schedule was permitted.

The incredibly bad traffic and road problems on the planned route were unanticipated. The new route provided by their excellent GPS service helped avoid those difficulties but extended their travel time beyond acceptable limits if they didn't maintain speed.

As lead vehicle, their primary responsibility was to scout ahead of

the container truck for poor road conditions or, worse, armed resistance, such as thieves or foreign agents, that might be foolish enough
to attempt to steal the invaluable contents of the truck. Other than the
circuitous rerouting over small, rural mountain roads and the poor
weather, the mission was proceeding as planned.

The GPS map pointed them up the narrow mountain road, indicating a sharp hairpin turn just ahead. The nervous driver followed the
little blue arrow on the screen, leaning forward and squinting through
the water cascading across his windshield, careful not to slow down,
as per his orders.

He could barely see the climbing road as it disappeared around the
sharp bend of rock up ahead. For an instant, he thought a patch of fog
had suddenly risen to hide the thin ribbon of asphalt in front of him.
But the sickening feeling of free fall in his gut and the sudden lifting
of his body up out of his seat and against his restraints told him the
vehicle had gone airborne.

The four men screamed as the Chevy tumbled down the side of the
mountain, unaware the *Oregon*'s AI program had erased the "Road
Closed" sign from their digital map.

★

Unaware of the events in front of and behind him, the container truck
driver kept his foot on the gas and rumbled forward despite the slashing rain and poor visibility.

The young guard next to him sat unflinchingly in his seat, the only
other passenger in the vehicle. This was his first foreign field assignment.

The driver flinched as the engine lights suddenly all winked on and
the truck shuddered to a halt. "Call ahead," the driver told the guard.
"Tell them what happened. I'll check the engine."

The guard nodded curtly and grabbed his radio.

The driver muttered a curse under his breath as he pulled on his
raincoat and jumped out of the cab into a puddle, then slammed the
door shut behind him.

The rain-soaked driver unhooked the rubber latches on the fiberglass hood, lifted it up, and planted his feet on the catwalk step. Gripping the edge of the frame for balance, he leaned over to peer into the engine compartment. The massive diesel engine ticked with heat, its intricate web of belts and hoses still as the grave. He jerked and pulled at various wires and connections but couldn't figure out what was wrong.

Something stung his face like hot grease. He lifted one filthy hand to wipe it away, but his world was shrouded in unfathomable darkness.

Utterly unconscious, he fell backward into a puddle with a muddy splash.

★

Still inside the cab, the young guard riding shotgun became increasingly nervous. He attempted to radio his supervisor, but there was no response. He could hear the driver lifting the hood and feel the cab shifting under the man's weight as he climbed up to inspect the engine compartment. But without the windshield wipers working and with the windows fogging up, he couldn't see a thing.

The guard then changed radio channels and tried to reach the rear vehicle, but his unit only squelched and squawked, no doubt affected by the storm. He slapped it a few times, but to no avail. The other SUV wasn't responding, either. The inexperienced guard didn't realize the area was now blanketed with a jammer.

The sudden lurch of the cab and the heavy thudding sound of a body hitting wet ground raised an alarm in the young man.

He called out to the driver, but he could hardly hear his own voice over the roar of the rain pelting the cab's steel roof. There were no more sounds of the driver tinkering with the engine.

Something was definitely wrong.

He pulled his pistol and pushed the passenger door open, his gun at high ready. No sooner had he opened the door than a couple of pellets struck him in the neck and face, and within seconds, he, too, lay in the middle of a muddy puddle—face down.

★

The four *Oregon* operatives broke out from their concealed positions and raced toward the back of the container truck.

"We're burning daylight, kids," Juan whispered in his comms as he flipped over the guard he'd dropped with his tranq pistol.

No point in letting the man drown, Cabrillo thought. He had killed plenty of men in fair fights over the years, but never relished it—he cherished life. Letting this guard drown in a puddle of mud would be no less an act of needless killing.

"I've still got eyes on," MacD said in his comms. His sniper rifle had shredded the front tire of the trailing SUV. "These boys back here will be on the road in six mikes, and they're about two mikes behind you at full speed."

"Copy that," Juan said. "Keep us posted if anything changes."

Eddie Seng broke out his trusty bolt cutters and broke the bolt seal. He and Cabrillo flung the doors open.

Dr. Littleton was first into the truck, respirator and gloves pulled on. He quickly unsealed the steel fentanyl tank and emptied the contents of his bag into it. The Gundogs brought up their respective rucksacks.

"Last lug nut affixed," MacD reported over their comms. "You guys need to hoof it."

After Littleton emptied the last bag of absorbant, he took a handheld electric drill with a paint-mixing paddle attachment previously wiped for DNA and fingerprints, submerged it into the tank, and pulled the trigger. The absorbant would do the job without his help, but he wanted to accelerate the process.

"You hear that, Doc?" Juan said.

"Just give me a second." Littleton stirred the paddle as it spun around. The granules swirled and dissolved, thickening almost immediately. Within minutes the fatal liquid would be polymerized into an unyielding gel.

"Okay, second's up. We go—now."

Littleton detached the mixing wand and let it fall to the bottom of the tank rather than fish it out and risk splashing the poison on himself or, worse, one of the others. Leaving it behind didn't matter. The Chinese would figure out soon enough their priceless shipment of fentanyl had been sabotaged.

Littleton scrambled out of the truck and the doors were slammed shut. Another fake set of barcodes was placed on the replacement bolt seal and the team melted back into the forest, heading for the AW. They made good time, their backs no longer burdened by the weight of the absorbant.

As the team plunged back into the tree line and headed for the tilt-rotor waiting for them, Eddie called out, "Hope that ketamine does the trick."

"Might not matter," Linda said. "We were in and out of there before they knew what hit them."

Seng was referring to the tranq gun pellets, which were a brand-new combination of tranquilizers. The original formulation had a proven record of knocking people out almost instantaneously. But the addition of ketamine was a new twist. Ketamine was a drug long used by anesthesiologists during surgery, and had the beneficial side effect of completely wiping out the patient's memory of the surgery, along with the pain.

The hope was the new tranq gun formulation would have the same effect on their targets as with the audio hypnosis. The guards would wake up as muddy, wet messes, but with absolutely no idea of what had just happened. That would hardly exonerate them, though, and they would no doubt be blamed for the ruined fentanyl, their fates dangling perilously in the hands of their ruthless superiors.

But the new pellet formulation was only part of today's plan C. The container truck had been stopped with a temporary disabling device, a variant of the *Oregon*'s electromagnetic pulse technology. Littleton assured the team the absorbant would do the trick within minutes, and MacD was almost as good behind a rifle scope as Linc.

The lead vehicle had been both spoofed onto the new route and then separately re-spoofed over the edge of the washed-away mountain road. Whether or not their tumbling encounter was fatal was up to God.

MacD was already in the tilt-rotor when the rest of the team arrived.

Gomez lofted them into the air in a low, sweeping arc, out of eyesight from the rear guards now scouring the crime scene.

36

Linlin perched uncomfortably in the steel chair, eagerly waiting for her breakfast. She was reading a book on her e-reader, which she'd fished out of her backpack slumped in the corner.

The only other reading materials in the cabin were two dog-eared and coffee-stained copies of *Seatrade Maritime Review*, which she had read cover to cover, twice. She was now thoroughly up-to-date on the latest shipping news regarding regulatory compliance, logistics, and industry best practices for 1997.

She also did a lot of pushups.

Her boss, Peng De, wouldn't call this a successful mission so far. Neither would she.

The MSS operative began to wonder if the kindly ship's captain in the tropical shirt had pulled a fast one on her. Locked away in the small, windowless cabin, she felt more like a prisoner than a protected guest. She also noted at least one crew member was always nearby, as if guarding her.

Linlin had just showered and dressed, and her hair was still slightly damp. The day before, a diminutive woman introduced herself as the ship's doctor and delivered several changes of clean but ill-fitting women's clothes. Dr. Julia Huxley also inquired about her health. Both were kind gestures, but the visit was short and professional, and not a social call. She'd had no other visitors.

Linlin's meals always arrived promptly on the designated hour. The shy hand that suddenly tapped on her door came as no surprise. She set her reading tablet down.

"Come in."

A smiling Murph pushed through carrying a food tray with a covered dish, a silver pot of hot water for tea, and a frosty-cold glass of fresh-squeezed orange juice. The lanky lover boy also wore a serving towel draped over his arm the way he'd seen Maurice do it hundreds of times before.

Linlin's eyes brightened as she stood. "Murph! So glad you came."

Murph lifted the cover off the plate with a flourish, releasing a puff of steam.

Linlin's eyes widened.

"Chicken and waffles! My favorite! You remembered."

"Of course I remembered. How could I ever forget?"

Murph suddenly blushed, regretting the emotional outburst. He promised himself to control his feelings, which, like his racing heart, were galloping away at a thousand miles an hour. He tried to cover his tracks by describing the specially prepared breakfast.

"Cookie whipped you up a batch of buttermilk fried chicken with cheddar and chive waffles, drizzled with spicy honey, along with a rasher of pork belly bacon on the side."

He set the breakfast tray down on her desk.

"Wow. Sounds more like a meal on a cruise ship than a cargo ship."

"The Chairman was pulling your leg before. Cookie obsesses about food." Murph gently pushed aside her e-reader and set her place with a single service of silverware, a cloth napkin, and a thick ceramic mug for her tea.

"Aren't you joining me?" she asked.

"I'll eat later. I'm kind of in the middle of something right now. I just wanted to grab your breakfast for you and see how you're doing."

"Well, to be honest, I'm pretty bored. Not much going on in here. Just glad I brought my e-reader."

She waved her hand around the cabin. The small ten-by-ten room was gray-painted steel, with a narrow cot, a small desk and chair, and an old, battered AM/FM radio that only picked up staticky Spanish-language stations. "Not that I'm not grateful, of course."

"No, no, I get it." Murph nodded at the e-reader. "Whatchya reading?"

"I'm rereading *Neuromancer*."

"Classic. One of my favorites, ever."

"I know." She smiled. "It's great. But I can only read so many books. Wish I had a gaming computer in here."

"I've got a monster gaming machine back in my cabin, but well, you know. You're kinda stuck here for a while."

"Yes, of course." She smiled again, trying to prompt him to the next obvious thought. It worked.

"I asked about bringing you a laptop but, um, we don't seem to have a free one available right now. Sorry about that."

"I understand. I just threw everything into a pack when I heard they were coming . . ." Linlin's eyes teared up as her voice trailed off.

Murph laid a hand on her shoulder. "I'm sorry that happened to you. It must have been scary."

She sniffed, but didn't say a word.

"What's wrong?"

"I don't know what the future holds."

"We'll figure something out."

"I'm scared, Murph. And I'm tired of being alone. Can't you stay here with me?"

"I wish I could. It's just that I'm really slammed right now. We'll talk soon, I promise."

Linlin nodded hopefully. "Of course. It's a busy ship." She forced another smile. "You still play *Slayers*?"

"Heck, yeah. Old-school."

"Maybe we can play it together sometime in your cabin when things settle down?"

"Yeah, that'd be cool, for sure."

"I'd really like to spend time with you. And really, thanks for everything. You saved my life."

"It was a no-brainer."

"Are you sure you can't stay for a little while?"

"Sorry. There's just a lot going on."

"I've been hearing lots of sounds. Almost like a military operation
or something."

Murph frowned. He wondered if Cabrillo was right. Maybe it had
been too risky to bring her on board. Even stuck in her cabin she was
noticing things, and drawing conclusions.

He pushed the thought away.

"Nah, it's nothing like that. We're not military. We just have a lot
of cargo we need to unload, and the port can't let us in yet, and we're
far from shore. Some of it is time-sensitive . . . medical supplies. And
the tilt-rotor can't carry a whole lot, so we've had to make multiple
flights. Really, it's no big deal."

"That makes sense."

Murph swallowed hard, hoping she bought it. He wasn't very good
at either poker or lying. He nodded at the breakfast tray.

"You better eat while it's still hot."

"For sure." She dropped into her chair, snatched up her fork and
knife, and dug in. She forked a big chunk of honey-soaked waffle and
chicken into her petite mouth. Her eyes rolled with delight.

"Good, eh?"

"Incredible."

"Cool."

She swallowed her bite. "Seriously, thanks for the chicken and waffles. It's very thoughtful of you."

Murph shrugged. "I'll stop back as soon as I can, for sure."

"Yes, please do, Murph. I'd love to catch up. Really, I would."

Murph blushed again. "Well, okay, I guess I gotta go. Bye."

"Bye."

Murph backed awkwardly out of the cabin and shut the door behind him.

Linlin took a bite of the perfectly cooked bacon, savoring the smoky sweet flavor. She smiled to herself. She had played her hand well.

Now Murphy and the others would believe she was merely a compliant guest gratefully resigned to her quarters, killing time on her e-reader. No threat at all.

Now she could get to work.

37

Colonel Shi Chang and his squad of MSS operatives set up shop in a luxury boutique hotel near the Acajutla Port posing as wealthy Chinese investors.

Chang and his team had followed Murph and Linlin all the way from Thailand. By pretending to try and kill her at the beach bar, they had convinced the gullible young American that she was on their hit list. This not only added to her credibility as a traitor to China but also invited her deeper into his circle of trust. So far, the plan had worked brilliantly.

Chang and his men were dressed in designer linen shirts, tailored trousers, and sunglasses. His three female operatives were similarly styled and carried themselves with the same athletic poise as their male counterparts.

The Chinese swept into the lobby past cascading bougainvillea, their true intentions concealed beneath a feigned indifference to the resort's opulence and its scantily clad clientele lounging by the infinity pool. To the resort staff, they seemed like just another group of affluent visitors who, strangely, insisted on carrying their own heavy bags.

The colonel was somewhat surprised the poorly dressed American had access to a private Gulfstream jet that by all accounts had been chartered by him for the Thailand trip—a very expensive proposition.

It was easy enough to track the plane's tail number as it routed out of Phuket International Airport on its circuitous journey to San Salvador.

Chang notified Chinese agents already on the ground in San Salvador when the American's destination was finally determined. They observed Murph and Linlin as they deplaned at a privately owned FBO at the main international airport and immediately transferred to a waiting tilt-rotor aircraft. His own assault team arrived just fourteen hours later.

A reliable contact within the airport's tower forwarded the tilt-rotor's radar track along with its final landing destination—a ship anchored a mile offshore from Port Acajutla.

The young American was nothing if not surprising in his access to resources, Chang thought. He reached out to Peng De and reported his findings.

"Do you want me to organize a boarding assault?" the colonel asked. Chang was the youngest man to hold that rank in the infamous organization having earned his stripes by his aggressive attitude and tactical skills.

"Not yet," Peng said. "If she were in trouble, she would have reached out to me by now. I suspect she's burrowing deeper into the rat's nest. But have your team ready. At some point she will need your assistance."

"We stand ready now, sir, awaiting your command."

"Very good. And, Colonel, might I suggest you get some rest while you wait?"

"My team is rested and ready, sir."

"Then at least try the coffee while you're there. I understand it's the best in the world."

"Is that an order, sir?" Chang leered beneath his sunglasses at a particularly attractive young woman diving into the pool not far from his balcony.

"Merely a suggestion. But avoid all other distractions."

It seemed as if Peng De could read his mind. Always.

"Understood, sir."

38

"There they go," Raven whispered. She and Linc were hidden in the trees in the evening gloom. The two *Oregon* operators watched a dozen LED headlamps bounce in the dark as the Iranians broke camp from the main body of migrants and threaded their way into the jungle.

It had been four arduous days since the rescue of the girls farther back on the trail. Fording perilous rivers, slogging through mud, scrambling over boulders, and sometimes surrendering their meager belongings to armed thieves had taken a ragged toll on the civilians making the hazardous trek. Several had disappeared altogether.

Every instinct in Raven and Linc had been to stay back with the stragglers and protect the weakest members of the herd from the predators. But their mission was too important and too many other lives were possibly at stake. They made the heart-wrenching decision to speed forward, and as the days progressed they finally caught up with the lead groups of younger men at the head of the column.

Raven had edged close to one cluster of young Arabic speakers she had observed early in the trip. The men had set up camp just off the main trail, and built small fires to boil water for tea. In the gloaming light of early evening, two of the men fell into their native Farsi tongue, reminiscing about one particularly striking green-eyed girl from their village when an older man barked harshly at them in Arabic to shut up.

"Boys will be boys," Raven whispered to herself.

"Who's there?" another Arabic voice shouted in her direction.

The other men suddenly quieted. Several stood, and two began heading her way, searching the ground with flashlights.

Raven bolted in a noiseless crouch through the trees and back to Linc, who'd set up camp near a young family on the main trail. A toddler was wearing out a candy bar Linc had given him.

Raven told Linc what she had seen and heard. This was the break they had been waiting for. Their mission was to find a hidden Quds Force base camp somewhere out here in the Darién Gap. They hadn't picked up a single clue so far until now. A group of Iranian-speaking fighting-age males might well be headed for their mission target.

The two operators gathered up their gear and made their way back just in time to observe the Iranians breaking camp in the dark and leaving. Whether or not Raven had spooked them didn't matter. They were leaving the main body and heading for another destination—it had to be the Quds base.

Linc and Raven were clearly outnumbered and carried only two guns between them. But their mission wasn't to engage the enemy, only to discover their location. They gave the Iranians plenty of space before setting out after them, careful to keep themselves hidden. It was rough going. By not using their headlamps or flashlights, the two stealthy operators managed to stumble over nearly every tree root and sharp rock on the path the Iranians were taking. They trudged for hours, keeping count of the Iranian headlamps ahead of them, making sure one or more of them hadn't snapped off their light and circled back.

By the time the sun rose, the jungle path had turned into a steep mountain trail, where the trees were thinner and the sight lines much longer. The Iranians doused their lights, which made it more difficult to track them, especially as the trail curved and dipped on the snaking route up the mountain.

With light and elevation on their side, the Iranians finally decided to follow security protocols, whether out of training or skittishness was unclear. Raven and Linc were losing ground to the advancing party. Every time a rear-guard sentry turned around or halted, the two operators had to scramble for cover by ducking behind trees, hiding behind boulders, or even retreating back down the trail.

Despite their burning thighs, throbbing heads, and parched throats, the two Gundogs continued noiselessly up the trail. The Iranians had traveled for several hours and covered at least twenty klicks. Was it possible their base camp was at the top of this mountain?

A young Iranian stood at the apex of a steep hairpin turn, his eyes sweeping back and forth down the mountain and across the forested valley below him. He took a long pull of water from a canteen, then lit a cigarette, his eyes never ceasing their search. Ten minutes passed. He rubbed his cigarette out and pocketed the butt before turning on his heel and scrambling up the trail until he disappeared around the bend.

The two Gundogs exchanged a glance. No doubt the rest of the group had moved on quite a distance and the young Iranian was racing to catch up. They would all be out of earshot by now.

Linc and Raven carefully broke out their water bottles and a couple of power bars, slaking their thirst and hunger quickly, always with their eyes on the trail.

Raven was press-checking her weapon as Linc pulled the cheap AK rifle from his pack.

"Not a Barrett, but it'll do," Linc said.

Raven smiled. "It's the samurai, not the sword."

"Let's see what's what."

The two operators sped to the top of the trail bend and peeked around the corner. The rocky path led into the black mouth of a yawning cave.

"Bingo," Raven said.

The two Gundogs crouched behind a boulder, staying out of sight, their ears on high alert, their heads on swivels, hoping they hadn't missed any Iranians who might have dropped off the main trail and circled back around behind them. None had.

They waited in that posture for another ten minutes. Dead silence. Lincoln checked his watch. He signaled "ten more" with his hands.

Another ten minutes passed. Nothing.

"I'm tired of this," Raven said as she bolted for the cave entrance.

Linc raised his weapon to cover her advance.

Raven leaned against the rock just beyond the cave's mouth. She waited, listening, then did a quick peek around the edge, and pulled her head back.

She turned to Linc and signaled "All clear."

But even from this distance Linc could see the look in her eye.

Not just all clear.

They were gone.

39

Juan Cabrillo was deep in the bowels of the *Oregon*'s engine room with Max Hanley when he took another call from his primary client, Langston Overholt IV.

"Kinda in the middle of an inspection, Lang. What's up?"

"Just wanted you to know the fentanyl sample and evidentiary materials you passed along have been received. The secretary of state is beyond thrilled. Well done."

"It's why you pay us the big bucks—speaking of which, when can I expect your deposit?"

"Any day now. But I have even better news. President Olmedo has expressed his extreme gratitude and has requested a personal meeting with the *soldados asombrosos* who pulled off the mission."

"Yeah, sure. Someday. Maybe."

"He was hoping tomorrow."

"We've got a lot on our plate right now. Still getting squared away from our last two missions. I'll pass."

"Consider it a diplomatic mission."

"I'm expecting a call from Linc and Raven any minute now. I've got to be ready for the exfil."

"President Olmedo will soon be an important strategic partner. He's also a true visionary—the future of Latin America. Perhaps even a George Washington for his people."

"Bad teeth, eh? That's too bad."

"I thought you were a fan."

"I am, very much so. But I'm not much of a schmoozer."

"Neither is he. I've only had one conversation with him. He's no ordinary politician. Something of a philosopher king. I think you two will hit it off famously."

"You sure I can't take a rain check?"

"You've thrown a Hail Mary on this one, and now we're just inches from the goal line with Olmedo. I need you to punch it through with a quarterback sneak and score the winning touchdown."

"A football analogy? I thought you were into the pickleball thing."

"A presidential escort will pick you and your team up at the airport at precisely ten a.m. tomorrow. You'll be taken to Olmedo's personal residence for brunch. It's quite an honor."

"It's more like a pain in my keister. But you're right, I actually would like to meet him."

"Wonderful. I'll confirm with his people."

Overholt rang off.

"Champagne and pupusas with a president? Yeah, I can see why you're dragging your feet," Max said in a mocking tone. "What's wrong with you?"

"I've got a lot on my mind."

Max nodded. "Linc and Raven. Yeah, me too. You know if there was a problem, they'd reach out."

"If they can."

★

Murphy's first mistake was to assume Linlin was not a threat to the *Oregon*. The puppy dog devotion that flashed in his lovelorn eyes the moment he saw her destroyed any suspicions he may have entertained.

His second mistake was to assume she was as naive as he was. His childish emotions betrayed his brilliant mind. He should have known his lame explanation for why a man with his training and expertise was working on a civilian cargo ship wouldn't hold up under modest scrutiny.

Murphy's third mistake was failing to realize that hiding his true work on board the vessel was telling her the vessel itself must be hiding some larger secret. What could it be?

Murphy blocked her access to the ship's computer. Why? Who in the world would want to steal the manifest of an insignificant cargo ship? Preventing her from accessing the vessel's mainframe meant there was something valuable on it.

Mark Murphy had his many faults, but he was no criminal. She was certain he wouldn't be involved in illegal activities. Whatever was valuable on that mainframe was something Murph wanted to protect, and despite his childish prevarications, nothing was more important to him than computer science. His brilliant paper on organoid computing alone proved that.

Could it be something as valuable as an organoid computer?

Linlin's pulse quickened. *Of course!*

What better place to hide such a monumental project than a completely anonymous cargo ship?

Linlin gleamed with satisfaction.

Thanks to Murphy's series of ham-handed mistakes, her mission to find an operational organoid computer seemed tantalizingly close.

And Cabrillo was clearly no ordinary ship's captain. Linlin had trained with some of China's finest special warfare operators and she knew the type well. Despite his roguish charm, the "Chairman" carried himself with the self-possessed confidence of a sheathed blade, just like the one hidden beneath his tropical shirt. His navigator, Seng, was cut from the same cloth.

What more proof did she need?

She'd laid low long enough, and had taken the proper security precautions. It was finally time to take the next step.

★

Linlin had placed her empty breakfast tray and dishes out in the corridor to be retrieved by a member of the ship's crew. Now she sat at her desk with her e-reader on the table and her backpack at her feet. She appeared to be scrolling through a booklist on her reader. But she wasn't.

Linlin had already performed several clandestine visual inspections of her small cabin and was utterly confident she was not under optical or electronic surveillance, though an *Oregon* crew member was lurking in the passageway outside of her room even now.

She carefully opened up her backpack and pulled out her espionage gear. She'd packed her bag as if she had just thrown in whatever she could at the last moment under duress. Anyone inspecting the bag wouldn't be the least bit suspicious of its contents.

The essentials were all there, starting with her passport and a small coin purse. There was also a toothbrush, toothpaste, hairbrush, extra pairs of panties and socks, a couple of mashed candy bars, and other sundries.

She'd also tossed in the e-reader tablet, earbuds and charger, pencil case and sharpener, and a spiral planning calendar filled with appointments, names, and phone numbers.

It was these latter items Linlin removed first, beginning with the spiral calendar. The German A4-size calendar was close to the American eight-and-a-half-by-eleven format. The daily/monthly calendar had plastic covers and sheets on the front and back.

She then pulled out the other items and began assembling her device.

Detaching the blade from the pencil sharpener, she carefully cut away the rear plastic "Holidays" page in her calendar. The half-millimeter page was actually a flexible polymer computer motherboard laminated between sheets of Gorilla Glass. That motherboard was a system-on-chip with a multicore CPU and an integrated graphics processor. Eight gigabytes of processing memory was built into it along with basic firmware and a minimal operating system.

The next thing Linlin did was to snap open the pencil sharpener's bottom revealing a high-density lithium-polymer battery providing four hours of stable power.

She then pulled out a ballpoint pen from the pencil case. She removed the pen's clip, which was actually an antenna gain filament. She attached it to the motherboard. The antenna gain boosted her wireless range significantly, and would easily receive and transmit through the ship's bulkheads.

Next, Linlin selected four different pens and laid them out in a line. Despite their different shapes, they all connected together to form a single eight-inch-long module.

The first pen was a large permanent marker. This unit was an additional system-on-chip board that doubled her CPU capacity, accelerating her encryption cracking and intrusion scripts.

The second unit, a stainless steel mechanical pencil, was a one-terabyte solid-state storage device. This could be used to store large data dumps of files and caches of live closed-circuit video feeds.

The purple gel pen she pulled out next was another lithium-polymer battery extending her operational time another two hours.

The fourth, a fountain pen, was a retractable high-grade fiber-optic probe tip. This could be used for interfacing with maintenance ports or direct network links, though neither existed in her cabin.

Linlin next fetched her two earbuds from their charging case and gently snapped them onto magnetic connectors located on the barrel of the stainless steel mechanical pencil. Each earbud contained a microprocessor cluster, two gigabytes of additional memory, and a micro battery.

She then opened up the small coin purse and removed three specialized hardware accelerators disguised as subway tokens. She attached them to an edge-embedded ribbon connector on the motherboard. The first token was dedicated to encryption and decryption, the second was a memory cache expander, and the third provided additional interface logic to reduce redundancy and stabilize network connections.

Finally, she Bluetoothed her touchscreen e-reader to the motherboard, providing her with a discreet, low-power control terminal and visual monitor.

Linlin checked her watch. She had assembled the entire cyberdeck in just under six minutes, a full thirty seconds faster than she had ever achieved during her training session. She was pleased. If necessary, she could disassemble it in half the time.

Now the fun could begin.

40

Linlin tapped the e-reader screen to scan for the ship's Wi-Fi. Her newly assembled covert cyberdeck cracked the system's encryption in just two minutes. Once inside the system, she proceeded to the mainframe and ran into her first firewall.

She instantly recognized Murphy's idiosyncratic coding signature—a brilliant, organized chaos deploying unorthodox yet ingenious solutions. One of their profs at MIT described Murphy's coding style as "Jackson Pollock writing haiku." Hacking Murphy's code would be as easy as hacking his heart. Within moments, his firewall was breached and she was navigating the ship's mainframe.

What she found stunned her.

Her first surprise was the discovery that the unremarkable cargo ship possessed a Cray supercomputer, one of the most advanced machines on the planet. Why?

She could hardly believe it. Every fiber of her being told her everything she was looking for would be found aboard the *Agua Linda*.

She was suddenly flooded with pure elation—a near euphoria. She took several deep breaths to calm herself.

Best to start with small steps.

She did a quick inventory of the ship's primary systems including navigation, power plant, and . . . weapons? Interesting.

But there was so much more. She skimmed past folders marked *Personnel Files . . . Regulatory Compliance . . . Maintenance*

Schedules . . . Port Operations . . . Logs and Records. She opened up
a few of them and found more granular subfolders like *Kitchen Supplies, W-2 Forms,* and *Berthing Invoices.* But that wasn't what she was
looking for.

And according to internal memoranda, the ship's true name was
Oregon, not *Agua Linda.*

She kept rooting around until she bumped into another unexpected
firewall—also typical of Murph. It took her a few moments to punch
through, but there it was.

The *Oregon*'s security system.

Linlin dove in and accessed the onboard closed-circuit TV cameras.
A single, multi-view screen generated small thumbnail images and
sound from nearly every location on the ship. Fortunately for her, each
of the nearly two hundred cameras was clearly identified.

She opened up the list of cameras and scrolled down until she found
Mark Murphy's cabin and activated its single camera.

She had a hard time believing what she was seeing. She rotated the
camera around. It hardly looked like a cabin on board a cargo ship—
or any other ship for that matter.

But then again, this was turning out to be a very unusual vessel. She
finally figured out what she was looking at.

"Of course," Linlin whispered to herself. "*The Matrix.*"

Murph's darkly lit cabin was modeled after the cockpit of the hovercraft featured in the movie. The exposed metal beams, hanging cables, and grungy steel walls contrasted with the glowing green Matrix
code scrolling across several oversize, high-end gaming monitors attached to reclining gaming chairs. This is where the uber nerd totally
nerded out, she told herself. But the more she explored it, the more she
began to admire it.

Actually, it was kind of cool.

She was tempted to keep investigating to find some piece of in-
criminating information, but it wasn't necessary. Her fingers were
tightly interlaced with his childish heartstrings—the slightest tug
could get her whatever she needed.

Linlin backed out of Murphy's cabin and reexamined the camera list. One name stood out. Her instincts told her it would prove to be an audio and visual gold mine.

The op center.

And she was right.

★

Cabrillo had already put in his laps in the *Oregon*'s Olympic-size pool and now was settling into his evening routine to wind down from the long day. He propped himself into a period-accurate overstuffed chair sipping from a grand snifter of fine sherry and reading one of his favorite Alan Furst novels.

He was looking forward to crawling under his silken sheets. Tomorrow's meeting with President Olmedo was inconvenient to say the least, but he was eager to meet the man touted to be the future of Latin American politics.

"Chairman, Linc on line four," the comms said overhead.

"Thanks." Juan crossed over to his mahogany desk and yanked the receiver off his Bakelite rotary phone.

"Brother Lincoln, Max was getting worried about you guys. All good on your end?"

"Not Bora-Bora-luxury-villa good, but good enough."

"Are you calling for a cab?"

"Not yet. Just reporting in. I know what a nervous Nellie you are."

"Yeah, I'm clutching my pearls even as we speak. What's your status?"

"We found a group of Farsi speakers. They broke away from the main group several hours ago and we followed them at a distance. We assumed they were heading for the base camp . . ."

"And?"

"And . . . we lost them."

"So what's the plan?"

"We'll keep searching. They can't be too far away. I just wanted you to know we'll be out here longer than we planned."

"How can we assist?"

"Just tell Gomez to keep the engine running. I've got a feeling things will get hot fast if we make contact."

"You and Raven keep your heads on a swivel, okay?"

Linc chuckled. "No worries, boss. We got this."

41

Juan, MacD, and Linda Ross had been ushered into the sumptuous dining room inside of President Olmedo's private residence. The soaring floor-to-ceiling windows offered stunning views of a terrace overlooking a neatly trimmed lawn lined with flowering bougainvillea, delicate white ginger lily, star-shaped plumeria and, most dramatically, Izalco, El Salvador's iconic volcano.

White-jacketed servers stood behind covered rolling carts by one of the grand windows as a barman prepared his service in a far corner. A round table set with china and crystal and bedecked with colorful flowers stood on the terrace. Three armed guards dressed in casual linen clothes stood watch on the deck. Another guard stood outside the interior doorway leading into the dining room.

The sprawling Spanish colonial–style mansion featured terra-cotta-tiled roofs, wrought-iron balconies, and arched windows. The hillside residence was nestled in a secluded valley at the base of Cerro Verde National Park, surrounded by fifty acres of dense tropical forest that provided complete privacy.

"Doc and Eddie are gonna wish they'd seen this place," MacD said. The two *Oregon* crew members were confined to their cabins, both stricken with the mosquito-borne Zika virus and unable to attend today's festivities.

"I saw motion sensors, security cameras, and a few guards," Linda said. "Not much in the way of executive security."

"I've read President Olmedo has an eighty-five percent approval rating," MacD said. "Who's there to be afraid of?"

"It's actually ninety percent in the latest poll," a voice said from the doorway.

The three *Oregon* operators turned in unison.

President Olmedo slipped into the dining room, his iconic beard split by a flashing thousand-watt smile. Tall and athletically built, the forty-something was dressed like a typical millennial soccer dad—jeans, Nikes, ball cap, and a pair of aviator sunglasses tucked into the collar of his light blue polo shirt. He approached Juan with his hand extended.

"You must be Señor Cabrillo. *Mucho gusto.*"

They shook hands.

"*Igualmente, Señor Presidente.*" Juan made the rest of the introductions, pleasant and informal.

Olmedo waved a hand at his attire. "Forgive me for not appearing more presidential, but my daughters had a tennis match and we only just returned."

"And your lovely wife?" Linda asked. "Dr. Olmedo?"

"She's on ER duty at the hospital. She'll be jealous of our time together. Perhaps you'll do us the honor of returning in the future?"

"We're honored to be invited into your home," Juan said. "It's a very generous gesture."

"The honor is mine. Perhaps a refreshment or two before we eat? My daughters will be delayed just a few more minutes. They very much want to meet the American heroes they've already heard so much about."

"Just doing our job, sir," Cabrillo said. "But I will take that drink."

The smiling barman served up champagne cocktails to order and Olmedo steered them toward their seats on the sunlit terrace.

★

The terrace of the president's mansion offered an unparalleled view of Izalco looming in the distance, its peak veiled by a wisp of fog. The

air was rich with the fragrant scent of honeysuckle, jasmine, and cit-
rus. White *palomas* cooed in the distance and iridescent humming-
birds hovered over the hibiscus.

"It's like heaven out here," Linda said, inhaling a deep breath of the
tropical aromas.

"This view would never get old," MacD remarked, admiring the
forested slope and the volcano beyond. His gaze scanned the horizon
before subtly shifting down to the lawn below and the armed guards
lazily patrolling the perimeter near the forest edge.

"Central America certainly has its charms," Linda agreed.

The president chuckled. "We don't always get credit for the beauty
and promise of our country."

Cabrillo took subtle note of the three armed guards in civilian dress
on the terrace. They seemed relaxed, almost bored. They wore holstered pistols and carried short-barreled SIG MPX 9-millimeter carbines slung across their chests. Olmedo's security team clearly wasn't
any more concerned about his safety than the president himself.

Olmedo signaled to one of the servers and drinks were refreshed.
As soon as the bubbles settled, the president lifted his glass in a toast.

"My nation owes the three of you a great debt. Because of what you
did, I will be announcing to the nation tomorrow night our decade-
long arrangement with the Chinese will finally come to an end."

"To El Salvador's bright future," Juan said before they sipped their
drinks.

Just then, Olmedo's twin eleven-year-old girls stepped bashfully
through the French doors and onto the terrace.

Olmedo stood, his face beaming with fatherly pride. MacD and
Juan stood as well.

"My daughters, Sofía and Yesenia," the president said.

★

Twenty minutes later, the group was seated around the table and enjoying an incredible meal of simple but delectable local dishes including a variety of sweet and savory pupusas, tamales, empanadas, and

pasteles. The twin girls also indulged in *atoles de elote*, traditional sweet drinks made from corn, milk, cinnamon, and sugar.

The conversation stayed clear of politics after the girls arrived. In faultless English, the two confident youngsters politely peppered the *Oregon* operators with questions about the United States and places they had seen. They were particularly fascinated with Linda Ross and the idea she could pilot a large vessel and also knew how to handle weapons.

Cabrillo couldn't help note how natural Linda was with the girls, and how obviously proud their father was. A momentary sadness washed over him. After the death of his wife, he never really considered getting married again, and in so doing, denied himself the possibility of raising a family.

The *Oregon* crew was his family now, and that was good enough.

But then again . . . Abraham was ninety-nine years old when Isaac was born, wasn't he? Cabrillo chuckled as he popped another pupusa stuffed with loroco into his mouth. The delicate flavor of the edible flower delighted him.

He glanced over at MacD, who was relishing the conversation with the Olmedo twins as well. Cabrillo made a mental note to give the big Cajun extra time off this year to spend with his young daughter back in Louisiana. MacD's long periods of separation from her must have been harder on the former U.S. Army Ranger than he let on.

Juan finally began to relax, utterly charmed by the springlike weather, the delightful conversation, and delectable repast. He cast his gaze upon the idyllic view beyond the terrace. The slight breeze stirred against the bougainvillea and rustled the palm leaves, suddenly quieting the birds.

It was a perfect morning.

Until the machine gun opened fire.

42

Two of the three presidential guards down by the tree line doubled over, their chests and bellies crimsoned by the short bursts of automatic gunfire. The third guard raised his weapon and sprayed wildly into the trees before he, too, was cut in half.

"Down!" Juan's command cut through the sudden chaos of gunfire and screams as he flipped the heavy teak table sideways, crashing plates and glasses across the terrace.

MacD hit the deck as Linda pulled Olmedo and his daughters behind the flipped table.

The three terrace guards pulled their rifles and began shouting orders to evacuate the president, but the nearest guard was flung backward by a heavy round to the chest. The farthest guard managed half a turn before a second shot caught him in the throat, and the last guard dove for cover behind a stone planter. He raised his carbine to fire, but a bullet in his brainpan put him down in a spray of pinkish mist.

MacD dashed toward the corpse of the nearest guard and wrestled the SIG carbine from his hands, then yanked the Glock 19 from the man's holster. He shot a glance at the grounds.

"Five tangos advancing," MacD called out as bullets shattered the big glass behind him. He tossed the Glock to Cabrillo.

"We move, now!" Juan shouted, leading the way.

MacD stood and ripped a couple of short bursts. Two of the tangos spun and dropped. The remaining three continued advancing with practiced precision.

Juan and the others dashed in a low crouch toward the open French doors leading back into the dining room, the twin girls shielded by Linda and Olmedo. Bullets whizzed past them, smashing stucco, tiles, and glass.

Inside, another presidential guard raced into the dining room from the kitchen door, his carbine at high ready, breathing hard, his face red with anger. Gunshots rang out in the rest of the house.

"*Qué está pasando?*"

Juan shouted at him in Spanish. "We're under attack. Get the president and his children out of here."

As if on cue, three armed men burst through the doorway Olmedo had first appeared in. The guard fired without hesitation, putting rounds into the lead attacker. Juan fired his Glock and dropped the other two, then darted to the fallen killers and snatched up two suppressed rifles—AK-74s.

Sporadic gunfire echoed around the grounds. Some of the guards were still putting up a fight—and losing.

Cabrillo shoved one of the rifles into Linda's waiting hands, then asked the guard, "Is there a secure route out of here?"

"The service corridor. It leads to the rear of the property and a safe house. Follow me."

"Let's move."

Cabrillo led the way behind the guard with Olmedo hustling his girls along, his arms sheltering them.

Linda followed just behind, gun up, with MacD covering the rear. He ripped off a couple of short bursts before retreating after them.

The desperate parade raced through the big gourmet kitchen and into a butler's pantry, where a steel door with a keypad stood. The guard keyed in the passcode and flung the door open.

A spray of bullets stitched up his torso and into his face, killing him instantly.

Cabrillo reached his gun around one-handed and emptied the mag outside the door, then pulled his Glock. He glanced around the corner. The guard's killer clutched his throat, drowning in his own blood.

Juan dropped the empty AK, reached down, and grabbed the fallen guard's loaded SIG, took another look outside, then turned around.

"How far to the safe house?"

"A kilometer, slightly less," Olmedo said.

"Wait for my signal."

"Aye," Linda said as Cabrillo made his way out into the yard.

"Where are the rest of my guards?" Olmedo asked. "They should be here." More shots echoed around the estate.

"Dead or dying."

A second later, a sharp whistle rang out.

Linda took point—and dashed out the door. She saw Juan in a line of trees some twenty yards away, on a small dirt path no wider than a footstep leading up to it. The others followed behind her.

They all crossed into the trees, their faces scratched by the low branches crowding the narrow trail. No one cared. The dense foliage was providing them cover. Juan stayed behind, protecting the rear, and ordered MacD to push on through.

Cabrillo trained his weapon on the open door and the dead guard still blocking it open. No one came.

Satisfied, he turned and raced away.

They all ran as fast as they could along the crooked trail. Seven minutes later, they arrived at a small stone building.

"Door code?" Linda asked, her fingers hovering above the digital door lock.

"Eleven, twenty-eight, thirteen," Olmedo said. "My daughters' birthday."

The twin girls managed a smile.

"Mac?"

"With ya." The two of them bunched up at the door, then raced inside.

Cabrillo covered the path behind them as the two operators swept the building.

"Clear!" Linda called out.

"Clear!" MacD repeated.

"Let's go," Juan said, motioning the president and his daughters inside.

Juan caught another glimpse of the volcano looming in the distance just before he slammed the steel door shut and locked it.

"The sofa," Cabrillo said. He and MacD shoved the heavy overstuffed leather behemoth against the door. It wouldn't stop an RPG, but it was better than nothing.

"Guns? Ammo? Anything?" Juan asked his team.

"No weapons or ammo. Just two bedrooms, a bath, a small kitchen, and this living room. Only one door—that one," Linda said, pointing at the locked steel. "And you're standing near the only window."

"Not sure if it's a safe house or a lobster trap," MacD said.

Juan took up position in front of the living room window as Linda disappeared into the small kitchen.

"Any chance this is bulletproof glass?" he asked.

"As a matter of fact, it is," Olmedo said as he steered his daughters into two overstuffed chairs far from the window.

"We need to figure out who these guys are and how they breached your security," Juan said. "Assuming we get the chance. You have your phone?"

Olmedo's face fell. "I left it on the table."

"There's a landline in back," MacD said.

"*Claro!* Of course!" Olmedo said. "I'll call for reinforcements." He turned to the girls. "Wait here, I'll be right back."

The girls nodded dutifully as he dashed for one of the back bedrooms.

"You are both so brave," MacD said.

"I'm not brave," Yesenia said. "I was scared."

"Me too," Sofía said.

"You can't be brave if you're not scared, now can you?" MacD said. "It's what you do while you're scared that counts. And by my reckoning, you two were champs."

The twins exchanged a glance—and almost smiled. "We never thought of that," Sofía said.

Linda appeared with two frosty cold bottles of water.

"Drink up, ladies. You must be thirsty."

"Thank you so much," they said in unison as they guzzled their waters.

Linda approached Juan by the window. "Those men were coordinated, well-armed, and knew exactly when to strike."

MacD crossed his arms. "They never tried to kill the president."

"Or his daughters," Juan said. "They were all sitting ducks."

"Kidnap?" Linda asked.

"Feels like it."

"Are they going to come after us again?" Yesenia asked.

Linda turned to the girls. "We're going to make sure that doesn't happen."

Olmedo reappeared and checked his watch. "I've alerted San Salvador. Two platoons of our rapid-reaction force have been dispatched. They'll be here within twenty minutes."

Juan and MacD exchanged a look. Twenty minutes was a lifetime. The president's security team had been wiped out in just under ten.

"We'll sit tight until then, and stay vigilant," Juan said. "Best if you and your girls went to one of the bedrooms." He nodded at Linda. She reached out her hands to the twins and guided them to the back of the house.

"Once again, I owe all of you a great debt," Olmedo said before he turned to leave. "You saved my family."

"We're not out of the woods yet," Juan said. "Whoever orchestrated this attack is still out there."

"Not all of 'em," MacD said. "We dropped six."

Juan pulled a magazine from the SIG carbine and checked the bullet count. Seven shots left, one still in the chamber. He slammed the magazine back home.

"Whoever shows up, we'll be ready."

43

COLOMBIA

Amador Fierro spiraled full throttle out of the clouds, his hands gripping the yoke of his ScaleWings Mustang, the SW-51.

Flying was his passion. Nearly all of his former women, from Brazilian bathing suit models to gold medal Olympic gymnasts, agreed he'd rather be in the clouds than with them.

And they were right. Up here, he was a god.

Fierro's eyes locked on the target drone inside the "donut of death" reticle on his heads-up display. The drone's evasive maneuvering program thrashed it around in the air, but Fierro's stick and rudder control was impervious to its defense.

Still at full throttle, he closed the distance quickly, waiting for the drone to fill his reticle before mashing the trigger. His carbon-fiber plane shuddered as the .50-caliber machine gun spat out shells, disintegrating the drone in seconds. But his high rate of speed was now a fatal problem as he rocketed toward the dangerous debris littering the flight path directly in front of his fragile aircraft.

Fierro snapped into a sudden roll, slipping his wings to near vertical as he yanked back on the stick, throwing the SW-51 into a gut-crushing turn, narrowly missing the spiraling metal shards slicing through the air. In seconds, he was clear of danger.

Fierro's heart raced with joy, not fear. He wasn't afraid of death so much as failing to live. A close call like that only affirmed his love of life. And shooting down drones was a great distraction from the problems at hand, including Narcisco Tamacas, who was still a threat.

What kept Fierro up nights, however, was Project Q's ticking clock. For years, it had been an exciting possibility, a grand vision to be realized. The thrill of the chase energized him. But now that he was so close to achieving it, anxiety gripped his heart like a vise. He agonized at the thought of failing so close to the finish line. On the ground, Fierro's sanity was hanging by the thinnest of threads, but up here he could breathe.

Just as he was about to order the launch of another target drone, a call patched through to his comms digital readout. Only three people had this number. Fierro yanked the yoke hard, punching the SW-51 through the clouds and into a bright azure sky.

"Dr. Bose, I trust you're calling with good news about Project Q," Fierro said as he leveled off.

"Actually, sir, I have a bit of good news and bad. There's a problem."

"And what might that be?"

"Our main computer has been breached."

Fierro's grip jerked on his yoke. The plane yawed sharply, but he corrected it instantly. "A breach? How? When?"

"We only just discovered it minutes ago. I called you as soon as I could perform a forensic analysis and damage assessment."

"How is this possible? Explain yourself."

"Technically, our operating systems weren't entirely breached. But some of the more complex coding we've been working on was stolen before the computer itself detected the break-in and stopped it. The good news is the project itself wasn't damaged or destroyed, and we're still on schedule."

Fierro exhaled with relief, his breath heavy in his headphones.

"What's the bad news you're not telling me?"

"The stolen piece of code reveals exactly what it is that we're working on. And worse, I suspect there's a possibility they might have discovered our location."

Fierro's teeth clenched, choking down a primal scream. He calmed himself. "Who's behind this? The Americans? The Chinese?"

"I think not. The Americans and Chinese use brute-force instrumentalities. This attack was subtle, like a thin dagger between the vertebrae. Quite admirable, actually. If I had to guess, it's a supremely talented individual or an independent hacker collective."

"Curb your admiration, dear Doctor. This attack poses quite a threat to us. The information they now possess is priceless. No doubt they plan on selling it to the highest bidder. They need to be stopped immediately, if it's not already too late."

"Agreed."

"Any ideas about how to find them?"

"That's the other good news. Once we identified the attack vector, we dissected their digital footprint and reconstructed their path through the system. By analyzing packet flows and correlating time stamps, we unraveled both the exploit and pinpointed the origin of the intrusion."

"Meaning?"

"The attack came from a region of Panama known as the Darién Gap."

Fierro pumped a fist in the air. "Excellent. I have assets in the region. Send me the exact coordinates. I'll send a snatch team in immediately. We'll find out what they've done and deal with them accordingly."

"I'm sending the coordinates to you now," Bose said. A moment later, Fierro's comms dinged.

"Got it. Thank you for the call, Dr. Bose. I don't need to tell you that pushing forward with Project Q at all possible speed is of the utmost importance."

"I can't change the laws of physics. It takes whatever time it takes."

"Four days is an eternity at this juncture."

"Patience, Mr. Fierro. In just four days, you will be king of the world."

44

EL SALVADOR

Eleven bloody corpses were laid out in an uneven row on the manicured lawn below the terrace of the president's private home. Here, in the land of the violent Mayans, Cabrillo imagined them to be a grotesque offering to their insatiable gods of chaos. The sweet aroma of the local flora had given way to the coppery smell of exsanguination, the birdsong to buzzing flies.

Juan knelt down next to the nearest corpse. He pulled up a sleeve, revealing a familiar tattoo. "This one's SAS."

"This boy was Wagner," MacD said, standing at the far end of the macabre line. The former Ranger was using his phone to collect fingerprints and snap photos of each of the killers for later ID.

Juan stood, his eyes scanning the carnage as his mind briefly replayed the events of the last hour.

One of the unfortunate by-products of the global war on terror was the endless supply of men trained to kill but with no more wars to fight. Too many of them succumbed to the temptation of big money in exchange for their lethal skills.

"How many in total?" President Olmedo asked his tough young sergeant. The rapid-reaction force soldier was one of sixty men who arrived on scene just fourteen minutes after Olmedo's call for backup. The RRF came prepared for pitched battle. Armed helicopters still circled the compound, their blades hammering the air above them.

"Only these eleven, sir," the sergeant said. "It's unclear how many might have escaped."

"And how many did we lose?" Olmedo asked grimly.

"Thirteen members from your security team were killed. Five wounded."

"How many security people did you have here?" Linda asked.

"Twenty," Olmedo said. "That means two are missing. I wonder if they were compromised?"

It wasn't really a question. He turned to Cabrillo. "I don't blame them. My enemies, though few, are wealthy, and our people are poor. The temptation is often too great."

"We'll keep searching for them, sir," the sergeant said. "If they're on the run, we'll find them."

"Thank you."

The sergeant turned to Cabrillo and pointed at the bodies. "These *pendejo* mercenaries were highly trained, and their attack well planned. If you had not been here, my president and his family might have been captured or killed."

"We were just doing our job."

The sergeant's fierce eyes narrowed as he threw a sharp salute. He held it until Juan threw a lazy John Wayne back at him. The soldier nodded and raced away.

Olmedo glanced back at the bodies, and then at his home. His face was grim but determined.

"Any idea who was behind all of this?" Cabrillo asked.

The president shrugged. "I have many enemies. Some political, some criminal. I would guess it's one of the big gangs, MS-13 or Barrio 18."

"You don't sound convinced."

Olmedo nodded at the corpses. "Those are professional soldiers. Some of them are even Tier One. That's expensive talent."

"I've heard of rumors of an organization called La Liga. Do you know it?"

Olmedo raised an eyebrow. "You are well-informed, my friend. My intel services tell me it's a consortium of the largest Latin American drug cartels. Their sources say its leader is a Colombian named Amador Fierro. Supposedly, he modeled it after Sparta's Peloponnesian League—the one that defeated Athens."

"A drug lord and a history buff. Quite a combo."

"Fierro is a highly intelligent man, and very gifted." Olmedo waved a hand at the corpses. "My understanding is that he is more cerebral than visceral."

"Even a cuddly panda will tear your face off if cornered."

"We have no proof he's behind this. I would prefer not to make him an even greater enemy with a false accusation."

"Fair enough. I'll have my people try and ID these mercs. Maybe that will tell us who ordered the attack."

"Thank you. I'm sure you have access to greater resources than we do."

"Is there anything else we can do for you, Mr. President?" Juan asked.

"Haven't you done enough? You've saved my family, and saved my life. It's kind of you to offer."

"It's not an idle gesture, sir. If you need anything, don't hesitate to ask."

Olmedo tugged at the back of his neck. "Actually, I do have a bit of a problem. Tomorrow morning I'm attending the opening of a rural hospital for Indigenous people."

He turned to Linda. "Built with confiscated drug money, by the way, Ms. Ross."

"I can't imagine a better use for it."

Olmedo turned back to Juan. "El Salvador has a long and ugly history with its Indian population. At best, past governments have made promises they haven't kept. That's why I can't disappoint them. Would it be possible for you and your team to attend with me? As you know, I have no personal security team now."

"What about the Army?"

"The Indigenous people are especially skeptical of the military. I can't show up surrounded by armed soldiers. Not only will it frighten them, it will make me look like another hated tinhorn Latin American dictator."

"If I were the head of your security, I'd tell you to reschedule the event. There's no way to guarantee your safety, and your children need you now."

"A reasonable suggestion, Mr. Cabrillo. But canceling is not an option. My country has just emerged from decades of such violence, and my people are still traumatized by haunting memories of this kind of terror inflicted on their families. My family is no more important than theirs. The whole nation will hear of this attack soon, and perhaps already have. If I retreat back into my *castillo*"—Olmedo gestured at his mansion—"behind a wall of armed guards, what message am I sending? If the wolves scare away the shepherd, the sheep will be slaughtered."

Juan nodded with admiration, but said nothing. He was weighing his options.

"If you can't come with me, I'll understand," Olmedo said. "You've already done more than enough." The president flashed his winning smile. "But you did say, 'Don't hesitate to ask.'"

"Yes I did, didn't I? Excuse me for a moment, sir."

"Of course."

Cabrillo pulled MacD and Linda aside and lowered his voice.

"No word from Linc or Raven?"

Linda shook her head. "Not yet."

"What's your opinion, Mac?"

"I'd assault the gates of hell for that guy."

Juan smiled. He felt the same way. If there was ever a servant leader, this was him.

Overholt was clear about Olmedo's strategic importance to the United States and the rest of Latin America. Several other presidents were planning on following Olmedo's criminal reforms in their respective countries. The region was shackled by violence and corruption preventing healthy economic development, which, in turn, fueled the immigration crisis streaming across America's borders. If Olmedo were suddenly killed by his enemies, those other presidents would likely waver and Central America would remain locked in poverty and violence.

Juan knew if he asked Langston's opinion he'd tell him to provide security until other arrangements could be made. The risk was relatively minimal. It was highly unlikely the opposition could put together another attack plan on such short notice.

But Cabrillo was first and foremost the captain of the *Oregon*. His primary responsibility was to his ship and his crew. He wouldn't jeopardize them without just cause. Overholt had been shooting them from mission to mission like a steel ball in a pachinko machine. Their luck was due to run out sooner rather than later, and that meant somebody getting hurt—or worse.

But what could be a more just cause than covering the six of a man like Olmedo?

Cabrillo turned back to the president and stuck out his hand.

"We'd be honored to join you, sir. We'll need to get back to our ship and make arrangements."

"Please text me the number of the event coordinator," Linda said. "There's about a million details we'll have to figure out."

"I'll text you a list of contact numbers as soon as I get back to my home office," Olmedo promised. "Thank you all again."

45

COLOMBIA

Rafael Vargas, La Liga's senior enforcer, hovered over a large computer monitor studying the split-screen image of a man in two different poses.

His boss, Amador Fierro, stepped into the darkened room. "Any news of the operation?"

"Unfortunately, I must report that Operation Arrow Heart was a failure."

"How? I thought your men had everything under control."

"They made excellent preparations, and key members of Olmedo's security team were compromised with cash and drugs. The breach was properly executed, and the operators well-trained."

"And?"

"They encountered an unexpected problem."

"Which was?"

Vargas pointed at the twin images on the monitor.

"This man."

The images weren't clear. One was a grainy screenshot from one of the cameras at the Port of Acajutla. The entire tape had been forwarded to Fierro from Peng De's office. The MSS chief was furious about the loss of the fentanyl shipment and was desperate to find the culprits. The Chinese had determined that some kind of jamming device had been temporarily deployed, knocking out warehouse security systems. But one camera hadn't been entirely disabled, and managed to pick up a short burst of damaged imagery.

The second picture came from the digital camera carried by the mercenary team lead, a long-distance shot of the terrace at President Olmedo's private residence. The camera had been focused on Olmedo's twin daughters—the kidnapping targets of Arrow Heart—but several other figures appeared in the footage as well, including the second partial image of what appeared to be the same man.

In both cases, Vargas had enlarged, enhanced, and cropped the images to pull in as much detail on the man's face as possible. He then ran the pictures through his facial recognition software, but came up empty.

"And who is this man?" Fierro asked.

"No idea. But somehow, I feel as if I know him."

"What about your friend in Colombian intelligence? Surely he has access to more databases."

"He drew a blank as well."

The Colombian friend Fierro was referring to was the current chief of field operations for the DNI—Colombia's National Intelligence Directorate. Technically, he was Vargas's handler.

Vargas had been working for him for over twenty years as a counterintelligence asset. Captured as a FARC revolutionary in his youth, Vargas bargained his way out of a prison cell by becoming an agent for the Colombian government.

After FARC was defeated, the Colombians turned their attention to the drug wars. They deployed Vargas as an undercover operative against the Colombian cartel networks and specifically Jerónimo Fierro, Amador's father.

But Vargas and Jerónimo formed an immediate friendship and Vargas secretly flipped his allegiance. For decades, Vargas fed only carefully curated information to the Colombian intelligence organization to take out Fierro's political and criminal rivals—and all without his Colombian handlers ever realizing it. In fact, Vargas was still considered their most valuable intelligence asset.

But neither the Colombians nor the Fierros understood the true reason why the psychopathic hit man was playing his duplicitous games nor his vengeful reasons for doing so.

"What do we do now?" Fierro asked. "Another kidnapping attempt?"

"The question answers itself." Vargas had warned his skittish boss previously that kidnapping operations were among the most difficult to carry out, as Arrow Heart proved.

Unlike his bloodthirsty father, Amador avoided killing whenever possible. Assassinations were always easier, and for Vargas, infinitely more satisfying. Now it would be nearly impossible to do either, since Olmedo and his security people would be on high alert for it.

Fierro sighed. "Then we must escalate."

Vargas nodded. "You need to go for Olmedo's jugular before Tamacas decides to tear your throat out."

"Killing presidents isn't like killing mice. It draws a lot of attention."

"You have several politicians on your payroll, including the president of the legislative assembly. Aren't you paying these people for exactly this kind of situation?"

Fierro scratched his beard, thinking. "According to the Salvadoran constitution, Olmedo can't run for a third term. In a perfect world, we could wait his term out and not spill any blood, but Narciso's impatience won't permit it."

"Agreed."

"The president of the legislative assembly has expressed his strong desire to become the next president."

"He won't mind becoming president sooner, will he?"

Fierro laughed. "Are you kidding? He's already designing his own presidential sword and sash."

Vargas laid a cold hand on the younger Fierro's shoulder.

"You must be decisive, and act swiftly."

"As my father would do."

"*Exactamente.*"

Fierro tapped the larger man's chest with his finger.

"I want you to handle it personally. I don't trust mercenaries. I only trust you."

"I am honored."

"But no failures this time. Understood?"

"Perfectly. And after this, *patrón*, I think I shall retire."

Fierro smiled broadly. "You've earned it, my old friend. You've served my family faithfully for many years. Kill Olmedo, and I'll hand you a king's treasure. You'll be able to retire anywhere in the world in royal luxury." He lowered his voice. "Maybe it's even time for you to get a woman."

Vargas darkened at that last suggestion.

"I'll make my preparations."

46

MCLEAN, VIRGINIA

Langston Overholt IV sat in his basement, stripped to his waist and lightly sweating inside his new infrared sauna. It was the latest addition to his elegant Tudor Revival estate located in proximity to both the Potomac River and CIA headquarters.

His preferred evening regimen of late had been a large balloon glass filled with two ounces of Monkey 47 gin and four ounces of Fever-Tree Mediterranean tonic—lightly stirred—poured over an ice sphere and garnished with a sprig of fresh rosemary.

Unfortunately, both his long-suffering wife and his general practitioner had insisted he trade the delectable discipline of gin and tonic for a bout of nightly infrared therapy. His primary consolation was the view through the sauna glass set directly across from one of the finest wine cellars in the area.

The other feature of the sauna making it slightly less unbearable was the excellent Bluetooth sound system. Overholt's eyes were shut, his soul embracing Joep Beving's hauntingly transcendent album *Solipsism*.

"I'm a great fan of the Dutchman," a voice said over the sound system. "Though I prefer his *Prehension* album."

Overholt's eyes snapped open, as if waking from a sharp dream. Instinctively, he gripped the towel around his waist, and deeply regretted the absence of a weapon in his sauna.

"I once saw him play in a private home in Stockholm," Overholt said. "He's even more impressive in person."

The voice continued. "I understand he's quite tall."

"Very."

"You seem rather relaxed. I'm sorry to have disturbed you."

Overholt glanced around the four-person sauna. He knew there were no cameras in there. His eyes turned to the window glass. Ah, yes. By the wine cellar. A CCTV camera. He lifted one hand and threw a jaunty wave.

"I would wave back at you but you wouldn't be able to see me."

"A pity, I'm sure," Overholt sniffed.

"Do please accept my heartfelt apologies. I am extremely protective regarding my own privacy and consider it almost a religious tenet to never violate the personal privacy of others."

"What, pray tell, has driven you to this self-proclaimed act of heresy?" Overholt wiped away a bead of sweat from the end of his nose.

"Time, unfortunately. I'm out of it."

"In what regard?"

"In twenty-four hours, I'll be dead."

"And how is that my concern, dear fellow?" Overholt tried to place the man's accent. His English was excellent, but clearly not his mother tongue. There were hints of clipped German consonants and rounded Slavic vowels. Moravian? Upper Danube? Pannonia Plain? It was impossible to tell exactly.

"In exchange for your services, I will hand you the greatest intelligence coup of the twenty-first century."

"That's quite an offer, depending of course on what services you require. Care to tell me the nature of that intelligence?"

"All I can tell you for now is that the world as you have known it for the last fifty years is about to be radically changed, and not for the better—unless you can stop it."

"That's not much of a clue. Sounds more like the plot of a dime novel."

"Your reputation precedes you, Mr. Overholt. Despite your slightly glistening skin, you are one cool customer. You know, I could have contacted your counterparts in Moscow, Beijing, or even Tehran. They would eagerly pay enormous sums of money for the information I can provide."

"Then why don't you contact them?"

"Because I rather like America, and I would hate to see her destroyed."

"You have my attention Mr., eh, what shall I call you?"

"You may call me Eidolon."

47

Cabrillo was in the armory loading semi-auto magazines for tomorrow's security mission with President Olmedo when Eddie Seng burst into the room, his skin still pale from his recent bout with Zika.

"Got a sec?"

Cabrillo ripped another line of 9-millimeter slugs into place with his ETS speedloader.

"Shouldn't you be in bed?"

"Dr. Huxley cleared me for duty."

"Somehow I doubt that. What's up?"

"You asked me to check out Murphy's girlfriend."

"Let's have it."

"Just got a text from one of my mainland sources. Linlin's story checks out . . . mostly."

"What do you mean, 'mostly'?"

"The firm she said she worked for? Zephyron Dynamics? She was right, it is secretly owned, at least in part by the CCP. What she didn't say was that the CCP had a controlling interest in it."

"Sounds like an illegal tech transfer operation. We need to notify the DOJ and Europol."

"Already have."

"But that's not your main concern." Juan rammed home another string of bullets.

"What if Zephyron Dynamics is actually a full-blown Chicom intelligence operation?"

"You think Linlin's deeper into it than she let on?"

"It crossed my mind. She was a project manager for her company's AGI program."

"Murph told us that."

"Did Murph know she got the job because her boyfriend-boss went fins up in a diving accident in Aruba?"

"He didn't mention it."

"Or that she was with him when it happened?"

"What are you suggesting?"

"I don't know. I just found it interesting."

"Anything else?"

"Her parents."

"What about them?"

"According to Murph, they both got sick when she was still in the U.S. She left Murph to go back to China to take care of them."

"But they've since died."

"They died all right," Eddie said, "but not in a hospital. They were both in a high-security prison for crimes against the state when they passed."

"So the question is, did the Chinese turn her into an anti-government crusader for killing her parents . . . or was she a superpatriot that ratted out her own blood to the Chicoms?"

"Either makes sense. I've got another feeler out there. I hope to hear back within the next twenty-four hours. I don't want to start pointing fingers until then, if you're okay with it."

"Which way are you leaning?"

Eddie pawed at the back of his neck, thinking.

"She's a little hottie for sure. Way out of Murph's league. I kinda don't get it."

"You know what they say. 'The heart has reasons of which reason knows nothing.'"

"Let me guess, the Smiths?"

"Nope."

"Radiohead?"

"Not even close."

"Selena Gomez?"

"Weirdly close. But no, Blaise Pascal."

"I couldn't shake the feeling she was x-raying me with those innocent eyes of hers. She's at least as smart as Murph, and that concerns me."

"If she's in trouble, I want to help her out. But if she is trouble, we'll
have to deal with it. Good work." Cabrillo checked his watch. "Team
room in twenty, right?"

"See you then." Eddie sped out of the room.

Juan pulled his magazine carrier and began stuffing mags into the
pouches when his phone buzzed. Another call from Overholt. He'd
already briefed him on the day's events and the mission tomorrow.
Why was he calling back?

"Problem, Lang?"

"More like an opportunity. I know you're tied up with President
Olmedo tomorrow but Linc and Raven are still in Panama if I'm not
mistaken."

"Correct. Why?"

"I just received a disturbing contact from a hacker identifying himself as 'Eidolon.' He claims to know where there is an AGI computer
that is about to be launched any day now."

"You think he's legit?"

"He displayed incredible skill breaking through my own security
systems. How he found me is beyond comprehension. It's not like I'm
listed in the Yellow Pages."

"Sounds like a scam to me. He's either a Nigerian prince or a
thirteen-year-old Romanian girl. Nobody's close to achieving AGI
anytime soon."

"Apparently someone is."

"And you believe him?"

"If it was a scam he would have asked for money."

"Then what does he want?"

"He needs to be rescued from his current location in the Darién Gap. Immediately."

"Who else knows about this?"

"Only the people Eidolon stole the information from. He believes they're dispatching a snatch team to get him even as we speak. Your people are nearly right on top of his location. They're his best chance of getting out of there alive."

Overholt was right. The terrain was too rugged to parachute into or drop in by helicopter. The only way to reach the heart of the Darién was by foot.

"I'm sending you the coordinates now. Pass them along to your people."

"Doesn't sound like you're asking."

"Do I need to? You fully understand the implications of AGI falling into the wrong hands."

Cabrillo hesitated. It would be a cataclysmic disaster if the Chinese or the Russians acquired AGI first.

But he'd already put Raven and Linc through the ringer. No telling what condition they were really in, and what kind of oppo they might encounter on this snatch and grab.

But Linc and Raven were pros. They knew the risks that came with the job, and they'd understand the stakes. They'd also realize they were this guy's best chance to survive—and likely his only one.

"I'll issue the order. Tell your hacker friend Eidolon my people are on the way."

"Excellent. Keep me posted."

48

Linlin couldn't believe her eyes. The *Oregon* had all of the accoutrements of an actual cargo ship. But her exploration of each camera deployed in nearly every cabin, compartment, and storage space peeled away the clever veneer.

The *Oregon* was actually a highly sophisticated intelligence-gathering operation—perhaps the greatest one ever assembled. Peng De would be jealous beyond imagination, she thought.

In addition to advanced electronic surveillance systems, she discovered a moon pool in the belly of the ship, perfect for operations with the three submersible vehicles suspended above it.

Shore operations would be supported by an incredible collection of vehicles including rigid inflatables, Jet Skis, and what appeared to be a version of an armored Mercedes-Benz Unimog.

But if all of that wasn't remarkable enough, she also discovered the vessel deployed an array of weapons worthy of a science fiction novel. She was well aware of her government's most advanced military research projects. None of them had yet reached this level of sophistication. When she stumbled upon the laser cannon, she suddenly realized why brilliant Mark Murphy was on board the vessel. There were rumors from former classmates that he had joined a top secret weapons development program after MIT, but she could never confirm it. The *Oregon* was now all the confirmation she needed that his advanced computer programming and engineering skills were indeed fully utilized.

Perhaps she had underestimated the boy.

But high-tech weapons weren't the prize. She was on the hunt for an organoid computer with AGI capabilities, and Murphy was the clue that had brought her here. Were the Americans working on a weaponized version of AGI? The thought terrified her—spurring her on to even greater effort.

Her espionage software had sifted through the labyrinth of directories on the mainframe, but found nothing directly related to organoid computing. The closest she got was finding Murph's one article on organoid software interfaces—the one she had already read and reread.

Having exhausted the databases, Linlin returned to searching the vessel via cameras for any additional clues. She switched over to the room on the list labeled *Armory*. Inside she saw Chairman Cabrillo. He was speaking out loud with someone over the ship's intercom. She caught the tail end of the conversation.

"I'll issue the order. Tell your hacker friend Eidolon my people are on the way."

"Excellent. Keep me posted."

Linlin gasped. She breathed the name. *Eidolon . . .*

The name evoked an almost divine reverence among her peers. Eidolon was truly the ghost in the machine, haunting the digital universe with godlike impunity—the Platonic ideal of the perfect hacker. His capture would be nearly as valuable as the AGI.

Why should she be surprised that a mystical presence like Eidolon would suddenly appear at such a critical juncture in human history?

More important, was it possible Eidolon was connected to her objective?

It was time to dig in deeper. Perhaps there was information on Eidolon on the Cray computer she had missed. Her fingers brushed the keys when her cabin door rattled with a couple of heavy thuds.

"Linlin! It's me, Murph!"

Linlin rolled her eyes. *Not now!* she wanted to scream.

But she didn't dare drop her legend of the sad, frightened girl waiting to be rescued. She'd brush him off quickly with some excuse and get back to work.

"Coming!"

She closed her search program with a couple of quick keystrokes, then swept the mini hacking rig into the mouth of her backpack before bouncing over to the door and flinging it open.

The scruffy genius beamed with pride as he showed her his prize. Murphy held a wide pizza pan aloft in one hand and a six-pack of Guinness in the other. He'd used the steel toe of his combat boot to knock on the door.

"Hawaiian pizza. Still your fav, I hope."

Linlin forced a wide smile. "Oh, yes. Awesome."

Murph pushed his way in past her and set everything down on her table.

"Hope you're hungry."

"Well, actually I—" But Linlin saw the disappointment that began welling up in his eyes and she caught herself. "I feel kinda grungy. Let me go wash my hands first."

"Hurry, before the pizza gets cold and the beer gets warm. We'll eat and hang out. I know how bored you get down here. I've got four hours before my next shift."

"Four hours?"

"Yeah."

"Awesome." Linlin swallowed her aggravation behind a gleaming smile. She headed to the bathroom to wash her hands and face and stifle a silent scream. Her Eidolon search would just have to wait. She couldn't blow it now.

Besides, who knew what Murphy might accidentally give up after a few beers? The lovelorn fool had always been such a lightweight on the liquor.

49

It was a bright, clear morning in the mountain highlands where the Lenca people lived.

The newly constructed rural hospital stood like a small glass jewel on the flat, emerald plain nestled beneath the forested hills above.

A crowd of over six hundred Indigenous local people dressed in colorful native garb had gathered in front of the elevated dais for the morning's festivities. Two dozen local officials were also there, along with the hospital's staff of white-coated doctors and uniformed nurses.

President Olmedo had just finished his speech commemorating the Peace and Unity Hospital and how it proved his government's war on corruption and violence was paving the way toward a future of prosperity and peace for all.

Ever the showman, Olmedo saved his best rhetorical flourish for the finale. He spoke his last words in the Lenca tongue, promising continued unity, health, and peace for all of El Salvador, "especially her first sons and daughters, the Lenca people, gathered here today." The audience exploded with grateful cheers and applause.

Cabrillo stood in the midst of the cheering audience still clapping and shouting. To blend in, he dressed in a traditional linen huipil shirt and slacks. He also wore a red bandana to hide his short-cut blond hair and a comms earpiece.

"Quite a stem-winder, from what I could tell," MacD whispered in Cabrillo's comms. "*He's got the magic.*"

"Magic doesn't make him bulletproof. We still clear?"

"Clear," Linda Ross reported. A half dozen other operators reported clear as well.

"Wepps?"

Murph was at his weapons station on the *Oregon* running the surveillance drone. "A couple of parrots and a toucan—just like on the cereal box."

Juan glanced around the compound. His operators were well hidden and out of sight, as per Olmedo's wishes. A half dozen of his crew and operators with Murph remotely operating a surveillance drone was hardly adequate for the president's security detail, but the president was insistent on a very low profile.

Cabrillo and his team arrived on-site early and conducted a sweep of the grounds and facilities for explosive devices and other weapons of mass destruction but found nothing. Cabrillo reluctantly gave the president the go-ahead to begin the celebration.

With Olmedo's speech ended and the applause still ringing, a signal was given and the musicians began to play a combination of traditional and local instruments, beginning with the deeply resonant beat of great wooden drums. Marimbas, guitars, and rattles followed suit.

The drumbeat signaled the sixty costumed dancers to form a circle. The *Danza de la Unidad*, the Dance of Unity, was a riot of color and texture. The men and women both wore huipils and long, flowing skirts called *faldas*. The men's shirts bore bold geometric patterns in deep reds, blues, and greens, while the women's blouses were vibrant florals in bright yellows, reds, and blues. All were adorned with various bracelets, mirrors, feathers, and metal ornaments. Most important, the dancers all wore carved wooden masks symbolizing deities, animals, and mythological creatures.

The dancers turned rhythmically in synchronized steps, twisting their bodies and raising their hands and arms in ancient, symbolic gestures. After the first turn, the circle separated and re-formed into three concentric circles moving in unison, the second circle turning in the opposite direction of the inner and outer ones, like an ever-shifting kaleidoscope.

Olmedo smiled and clapped along with the audience as the dance progressed.

A small girl in native garb approached him on the dais and held out her tiny hand. Utterly charmed, Olmedo took it and was led down the few steps and into the center of the dancing circles.

The audience cheered and clapped as Olmedo entered the innermost center. An old woman, a tribal elder, hobbled up to the president, took one of his hands, and began showing him a few simple dance steps. Her bright, toothless smile and twisting skirt encouraged the president to mimic her movements. He raised his hands, swayed his hips, and imitated the simple box step his guide provided. The audience cheered and laughed.

At that moment, the old Lenca chief approached the president. He carried an unusually heavy ceremonial mask exquisitely carved from black mahogany. Cabrillo wasn't overly concerned. His team had closely examined the oval mask before the festivities began. But Juan suddenly wondered if they could have possibly missed something. He needed to get closer to the president.

A translator had explained to Juan that the mask's exaggerated, almond-shaped blue eyes represented vigilance, and the soft red, slightly open mouth symbolized peace and honesty. Most striking was the prominent golden sun in the center of the mask representing the president's ability to safeguard the Lenca community and guarantee a prosperous future.

Olmedo could not have been more pleased and promised that the deeply symbolic mask would hang in a place of honor in his presidential office.

The chief held up the mask and Olmedo accepted it with humble gratitude. The chief gestured for him to put it on. The audience went wild again—they were nearly frenzied.

Cabrillo began to wonder if some of them were high on something other than enthusiasm. President Olmedo was definitely scoring a home run with these folks, Cabrillo told himself, and rightly so. The president seemed to genuinely enjoy being with his people, and they obviously relished his presence.

Once his mask was secured, Olmedo resumed his dance steps inside the turning circles.

★

Vargas stood on the hilltop above the hospital, hidden beneath a canopy of trees, his eyes fixed on Olmedo and the mask just attached to the president's face.

Without looking away from his binoculars, Vargas growled at the technician by his feet, a remote-control unit firmly in the man's grasp.

"Arm the unit."

"Yes, sir."

The tech's left thumb clicked off the safety as his other thumb hovered over the red firing switch.

★

Juan scanned the audience now also shuffling and dancing to the native music. They were pressing in close like sardines in a crowded tin.

Cabrillo turned his eyes back toward the president. One by one, the Unity dancers came forward from the inner circle and approached Olmedo, and improvised a smaller dance with him in the ever tightening Unity circle. Each dancer spun a few moves, then placed a thin beaded Unity necklace around his neck, then returned to the larger, moving circle.

Juan felt the pressure of shuffling bodies surge forward behind and in front of him as the Unity circle pressed in closer and closer. He wasn't surprised because the point of the dance was to demonstrate the closeness and unity of the people to its leader. But the press of bodies only added to Cabrillo's growing sense of urgency to get closer to Olmedo, and he began inching his way forward against a wall of resistance.

Juan watched the next male dancer drape another beaded necklace around Olmedo's neck and withdraw. Cabrillo scanned the other dancers. He wished he could see their faces, and especially their eyes, but their masks prevented it. Even cold-blooded killers had facial tells that betrayed their intentions, especially in the moment just before they struck their victims. All Juan saw were the weaponless hands and rhythmic bodies of the well-choreographed dancers as they moved in synch to the swelling music.

Cabrillo's eyes fell on the next female dancer waiting in line to approach Olmedo. She seemed the least talented of the group—almost staggering rather than dancing. Her movements were so awkward even the other dancers next to her held her hands trying to steady her. As soon as it was her turn to approach the president, she let go of their hands and danced forward in a stumbling gait.

An adrenaline rush hit Juan and he pushed his way ahead. Standing nearly a head taller gave him an advantage over the locals as he wedged himself between bodies, ignoring the angry looks thrown his way. He was under strict orders from President Olmedo not to cause a disturbance or frighten the Indians. The last thing Olmedo wanted to do was poison relationships with the Indigenous communities that he'd worked very hard to reconcile with.

But Juan's primary concern at this moment was protecting the president's life. The woman's jerky movements raised an alarm. If she was truly a dancer, she was a terrible one, or she was drunk, which seemed odd.

Cabrillo saw no weapons in her hands or on her person. He pressed in closer, and stood just a couple of rows away from the outer circle of dancers. The music was swelling toward a crescendo and roared in his ears.

As the woman got closer to Olmedo, Juan's eyes focused on her ornamental mask. His eye caught the slightest detail. On the fringe of the mask stood a nearly imperceptible piece of wire standing tall amid a clump of feathers.

It had to be an antenna.

The woman was four feet away from the president, staggering toward him slowly. Juan surged forward, but the bodies in front resisted his urgency and blocked his path. The woman stepped closer.

Three feet away.
Two feet away.

★

"Any second now," Vargas said to his technician. "Remember: on my mark."

"Yes, sir."

★

The woman stepped even closer.

Juan strained to burst through the crowd, but the wall of flesh wouldn't budge. He reached for the pistol beneath his shirt as he shouted into his comms—

"Jammers! Jammers! Jammers!"

But nobody answered.

★

"On my mark. Fire," Vargas said.

The tech stabbed the firing toggle.

★

The dancing girl came right up to Olmedo and took his offered hand.

Olmedo began his dance with her, but she suddenly stopped, clutched her stomach . . .

. . . and vomited.

Stomach juices burst from beneath her mask as her knees buckled and dropped her to the ground.

Olmedo pulled off his mask and fell to his knees next to the girl, ripping off her mask.

"Somebody call a doctor!"

★

"I said fire the weapon! Fire it now!" Vargas demanded.

"I'm hitting the button, sir!"

"Hit it again."

The tech hit it again. And again. And again. Nothing.

Vargas raised the glasses back to his eyes. He saw Olmedo hovering over the girl as doctors and nurses pushed their way toward them.

But what caught Vargas's attention was the tall man in the red bandana who suddenly turned and scanned the tree line. Their eyes locked somehow. It was as if the man were staring right at him.

Vargas's mil-spec binoculars saw the clear blue eyes as clearly as if the man were standing two feet in front of him.

"I know him—"

"Sir?"

"We need to leave. *Now.*"

★

ABOARD THE *OREGON*

"We've got a squirter, Chairman," Murphy said. "Heading southeast."

He had a clear, drone's-eye view of two men leaping into an SUV. The 4K image showed both had pistols on their hips. The one carrying some kind of controller yanked the driver's door open and jumped in. The other hesitated at the passenger door and glanced up, giving Murphy a full-faced view of the man. He was already running video, but he snapped a screenshot anyway. Seconds later, the SUV's engine roared to life and the vehicle launched down the rutted dirt path.

Murph's drone stayed hot on his tail.

"*Can you stop him?*" Juan asked over the comms.

"I can try."

Murph mashed the throttle and pushed the drone over a hundred miles an hour. It soared over the bucking SUV, slowed by the crappy road. Murph took up a position two hundred yards ahead at the mouth of a mountain tunnel. He couldn't follow the truck inside for fear of losing his signal. He only had five minutes of fuel left.

Murph's quadcopter drone carried a mini Gatling gun slung beneath its fuselage. It hovered menacingly five feet above the road. Murph watched the SUV barrel toward him in his monitor, refusing to slow down.

"He's not stopping," Murph said. "And we're going to lose him."

"Then take him out."

Murph hit the firing switch. A dozen rounds of 5.56 armor-piercing ammo burped from the mini gun, punching through the hood, spidering the glass, and shredding the roof as the SUV raced beneath the quadcopter's skids and plunged into the tunnel.

Murph spun the bird on its axis and emptied the rest of the drone's magazine. The rear window shattered and the tailgate puckered beneath the fury of lead, but the vehicle roared ahead and disappeared into the dark.

★

EL SALVADOR

In the front seat, Vargas clutched at his chest wounds as blood spilled over his lower lip like an overtopping dam.

"Get me . . . to . . . a hospital," Vargas said in a gargle of blood. His panicked eyes shut as he doubled over onto the floor.

"Jefe!" The tech shook him hard by the shoulder.

Too late.

The tech mashed the throttle to the floorboard and rocketed through the dark. He was fearful of his boss, whether he lived or died.

He would obey his last order no matter what.

50

Eric Stone was at his helm station when his earpiece buzzed with Hali Kasim's voice.

"I'm patching the Chairman through to you, Eric."

"Thanks, Hali."

"Stoney, you read me?" Cabrillo's voice barely cut through the shrill whine of the tilt-rotor's turbines and its thundering blade wash. "We're heading back to the barn now." Cabrillo and his crew had just lifted off from the assassination site.

"I read you five by five, Chairman."

"I just saw your text. You're confirming Amador Fierro?"

"Yes, sir. Those pics and prints of the dead mercs MacD recorded at President Olmedo's were matched to a third-party shell company operating out of Colombia. It took some digging but we found a direct connection to Fierro. He's our guy."

"Outstanding. Need something else from you. Murph grabbed a screenshot of the shooter he nailed with his drone this morning. I need you to ID him. I'm betting he's a Fierro stooge."

"On it. Anything else?"

"Oh yeah, that was the easy part. I need you to find out where Fierro's holed up, pronto."

"That won't be easy—"

"I'm tired of playing defense. Fierro's desperate and he's escalating.

If he's willing to take out President Olmedo, what else has he got planned?"

"With his resources he could be anywhere."

"I've known a few Colombians. For them, it isn't just a home—it's heart and soul. They hate to leave and they always go back as soon as they can. So start there."

"Will do."

"That's only half of it."

"Sir?"

"I want him located before my skids hit the landing pad. We need to work up an extraction package."

"He's going to have a heck of a defense set up."

"I don't care. He's either going to stand down or we're going to put him down."

"Well, sir, not to state the obvious, but if he really is a Colombian national, doesn't it make sense to let the Colombian government handle him?"

"The Colombian government is run by Marxists and as anti-American as you can get. There's no telling how much La Liga dinero fills the pockets of their security people. We call them, someone will pick up the phone, and Fierro's in the wind."

"But invading a foreign country and seizing a sovereign citizen is a crime."

"He's fair game. He's a terrorist who kills a lot of innocent people with drugs and guns. He's no different than Osama bin Laden or Carlos the Jackal. Our only other option is to sit on our hands and hope he decides to play nice from now on. Does that sound like a good bet to you, Stoney?"

"No, sir. It's always better to ask forgiveness than permission."

"Attaboy. Now go find this creep."

"We're on it."

51

PANAMA

Raven and Linc stood on the bank of the raging river in the suffocating dark.

Scudding clouds strobed the thin moonlight over the boulders arrayed like staggered stairsteps across the wide expanse. Heavy logs and branches swept through the roiling waters, thudding like rubber hammers against the rocks.

"Whaddya think?" Raven asked. They'd already trekked three miles off their trail. So far, this was the narrowest ford. Cabrillo only gave them twenty-four hours to reach Eidolon.

"We should've already been there. But if we get taken out by that river we're not gonna make it anyway."

"We can look for a better crossing, but no telling how long it will take to find one."

"So we risk drowning now or waste time and lose our target."

"Not much of a choice, is it?"

"Mission comes first."

"Always." A heavy cloud suddenly shadowed the moon, dumping a torrent of hammering rain. Raven wiped the hair out of her face. "I guess the only easy day was never."

Linc tightened the strap on his stolen AK rifle beneath his jacket. Raven secured her weapon as well.

"Follow me." Linc leaped to the first flat rock just beyond the muddy bank. He landed like a cat, but his boots slipped on the algae-slicked surface. His flailing arms barely kept him upright.

"No style points for you, big boy," Raven teased before launching herself. She landed next to him, steadied by his grip.

The cloud passed, stopping the rain as quickly as it had started. The moon bathed the churning waters in faint light.

"Two feet down. A hundred to go."

Linc picked his next target, waited for a tangle of broken tree limbs to race by, and jumped. He landed safely on the small rocky platform, but the rushing river swept over his ankles, gently tugging him toward the edge. There wasn't any room for Raven to join him.

"All good?" Raven called out.

"Just make sure you stick the landing."

For the next several minutes, the two *Oregon* operators navigated the treacherous crossing. Linc was two-thirds across when he thudded onto a rock, but it gave way and he plunged into the rushing water.

Raven watched him get swept away, his big arms windmilling in the water. A massive log just a few feet behind him threatened to crush him at any moment.

She considered jumping in after him, but knew she couldn't help. Instead, she focused on the far bank, picked her path of rocks, muttered a quick prayer, and vaulted.

She stuck the next landing, and the one after it, adrenaline narrowing her vision to the rocks ahead of her—not to Linc. Losing focus could get her killed.

Raven leaped again, but the rock wavered under her feet. She pinwheeled her arms to keep her balance, and only barely kept from falling in.

She glanced over and saw Linc fifty yards downstream, struggling to cling to a low branch of a tree on the far bank. His desperation put more fire in her belly.

Raven picked her last three rocks and bolted across each one, her eyes carefully calculating the debris surging down the river between each jump.

With a grunt she made the final leap onto the muddy far bank. She sprinted over to Linc as he hauled himself hand over hand against the swiftly moving current, grimacing with each strike of thick debris crashing into him.

Raven waded out into the river as far as she could, keeping a steady grip on the branch until she was close enough to reach out. Linc grabbed her small hand in his massive paw and she yanked with all of her might. It was slow, hard work, but ten minutes later she grunted with her last ounce of strength and pulled with everything she had. The two of them fell onto the muddy bank, safe but hardly dry, gasping for air, their muscles trembling.

"Well, that was fun," Raven offered when she finally caught her breath.

Linc stood, and made a feeble effort to brush away the mud from his jacket. He checked his weapon, still strapped to his chest.

"I always hated swimming."

Raven stood. "You were a SEAL. Don't SEALs do water?"

"Sure do. But only so we can get to dry land and get to work. Ready?"

"Yeah. I just hope we're not too late."

52

Eidolon paced the floor, ready to go.

Where were they?

Overholt had promised two American operatives would pick him up before the kill squad arrived. The Americans would escort him out of the Darién Gap to safety, where transportation would be arranged for his evacuation to the States—all in exchange for information on Project Q.

Kaarel Varik was the Estonian savant known as the infamous Eidolon. In the hacker world he was a god—an omnipotent, omnipresent, and omniscient force in the infosphere. His reputation evoked reverential awe among his lesser peers and existential dread from his many victims.

But in person, the shy but brilliant Estonian made little physical impression. Slightly built and standing just five foot one as a grown adult, he endured endless humiliations including being forced to purchase his men's clothing in the youth department. His physical deficiencies and poor personal hygiene attracted no women and his naturally abrasive and impatient personality prevented the possibility of any kind of male friendship. The resulting psychic rage only intensified through the lens of his mind like a laser, wreaking havoc on the unjust world tormenting him.

But even a man as brilliant as Varik had his resource limitations, and in recent years his enemies had nearly captured him. His retreat into the perilous Darién to his self-sustaining survivalist compound had saved his life, the jungle and its remoteness shielding him from scrutiny. More important, his encrypted satellite uplinks allowed him to continue his reign of vengeful terror on the internet. But now the noose had finally found his neck and he could feel the scratchy rope cutting into his throat. He was trading his greatest secret to save his life—but only if his rescuers arrived in time.

He checked his watch again. It was late in the evening. They should have been there two hours ago.

Suddenly, one of his security cameras alarmed. He dashed over to the monitor. He saw two hooded figures with rifles trudging out of the rainforest and heading straight for his shack.

Thank the gods . . .

But the flood of relief that surged through Eidolon's body turned to ice water in his veins when he saw three more men follow suit.

Overholt said he was only sending two.

Varik's heart raced. He spun his head around. His laptop and hard drives were packed up and ready to go—all of it destined for the Americans. But these were no doubt La Liga men—or mercs hired by them. There was no question they were there to kill him. He had no doubt they would add excruciating torture to the penalty for his theft of Project Q.

What to do?

Fight? Hide? Run? None were possible now. He could have fled earlier if he had known the Americans would fail him, though in truth he hardly had the strength or skill to navigate the long journey through the hazardous jungle. He only managed to arrive at his compound three years ago thanks to a highly paid escort of mercenaries and native porters.

Besides, where would he go? Nearly every intelligence agency on the planet was hunting for him. The Darién was his final refuge.

The promise of money he could offer them wouldn't dissuade men like these. Neither would his threats, which would lack all credibility given the circumstance. And certainly not begging—not that Varik would resort to that. What could he bargain with? What could he offer in exchange for his life?

Perhaps there was a way.

Varik snatched up his laptop and hard drives and tossed them into the giant microwave oven in his kitchen, his only means of cooking. He stabbed the full-power button and the microwave roared to life. The oven's magnetron poured out its electromagnetic radiation as he raced around the room, the superheating metallic casings already popping and pinging. A high-pitched whine erupted as delicate wiring vaporized, followed by the violent snap of rupturing lithium-ion batteries and cracking glass. Varik coughed as the acrid tang of burnt plastic filled the air.

Heavy boots shattered his front door and three La Liga thugs stormed in. The hawk-faced squad leader sniffed the air and his eyes fell on the humming microwave spitting out sparks and belching oily black plastic smoke.

Varik threw up his hands in surrender.

The squad leader charged over to the microwave and yanked on the handle. More smoke poured out, choking the room. He turned on his boot heel and slapped the smaller man hard across the face, knocking him to the ground.

"*Qué demonios hiciste?*" What the hell did you do?

"Sorry, my Spanish terrible," Varik replied in Russian. Of course, that was a lie. Varik spoke twelve languages, including Spanish. He recognized the singsong tone and elongated vowels of the man's Mexico City accent.

Another steel-toed boot crashed into Varik's ribs.

"You're no Russian," the Cuban hissed in the same Slavic tongue.

Varik balled up in pain. "No, I'm not," he said in English through gritted teeth.

"So why did you burn it all up?" the squad leader asked. Both he and the Cuban had served in their respective militaries.

"To save my life."

"That's not going to happen."

Varik rolled onto his back, his face pinched with pain.

"Your boss will be angry with you if he finds out the stupid thing you did."

"If I don't carry out my orders, he will kill me worse than I plan on killing you." The squad leader pulled his rifle and pressed the barrel against Varik's crotch. "Tell me why I shouldn't ruin you now."

Varik fought back a smile. The man's hesitation meant he'd found a toehold. Now to make the climb.

"Do you have any idea what was on those hard drives? That laptop?"

"Do I look like a computer scientist to you?"

"What I know is worth billions. Offshore bank accounts, gold vaults, even Bitcoin wallets—to name just a few. More important, I can provide all the information your boss needs to destroy his enemies . . . locations, secret crimes, betrayals, perversions, government snitches. I've got it all. But if you kill me now"—Varik touched the side of his head—"it all dies with me. What would your boss say about that?"

The squad leader smiled. "How will he know what you've just told me? Like you said, your secrets die with you." He raised the barrel of the gun and placed the muzzle on Varik's forehead. But Varik didn't flinch.

"True, but what do you think that kind of information is worth to him? And more important, how greatly will he reward you if you bring me to him—alive, and full of all of this valuable information? Isn't that what a good soldier does? Improvise? Adapt? Every boss is looking for that kind of initiative."

"You can't memorize all of that stuff."

"I didn't have to. I only needed to memorize one passcode that gives me access to a remote server that contains all of that information—and more."

"You're right. I should take the initiative. Maybe I'll cut off your eyelids, or better yet, dip your face in a vat of acid until you give me your passcode and anything else I'll need."

"Of course you can. Do whatever horrible thing you need to. And when I'm in abject pain and screaming in agony, I'll give you that passcode, no doubt. The only problem is this: if I'm wrong about just one number or letter or symbol . . . or even if I just get one of them out of order, the server will automatically erase itself and you'll get nothing. What will your boss think of that?"

"Maybe he'll never know."

The Mexican grinned as his finger tightened on the trigger.

Varik closed his eyes and drew in his final breath, his gambit failed.

The squad leader laughed as he pulled his weapon aside and turned to the Cuban. "Tie him up." He turned to the other man, a squat Guatemalan. "Find what you can, and grab it—fast. We leave in ten minutes."

"*Jefe*, it's been a long march," the Cuban said. "What's the hurry? Can't we spend the night here and head out first thing?"

The squad leader squared up. He wasn't used to anyone challenging his commands. But the Cuban was a good fighter and had earned his respect.

"Our orders are clear. In and out as quickly as possible."

"At least let me grab whatever food and water this *pendejo* has. The men are exhausted." They had broken camp with little preparation under orders to proceed immediately.

"Ten minutes. Then we go."

"Yes, sir." The Cuban reached down, grabbed Varik by the collar, and yanked him to his feet.

"You may have bought yourself some time, *pridurok*. But I wouldn't trade places with you for all the money in the world."

Varik nodded weakly, fighting back tears, but glad to still be breathing.

Where are the Americans?

53

COLOMBIA

Amador Fierro poured another glass of Yamazaki single malt whisky and handed it to Narcisco Tamacas, his third drink in the last five minutes. The fiery El Salvadoran gangster downed it in a single throw. Fierro wanted to tell him that the one-ounce toss disappearing down his throat would cost three hundred dollars in any fine restaurant in Medellín or Bogotá. But there was no point. It was a small price to pay to calm the man down—unless he got drunk, and then he might lose all control.

"Let me call down to my chef. He can prepare a couple of fresh steaks and *patacones* for us."

"I'm only hungry for blood, Amador. You promised me my father—or Olmedo's head on a stick." He threw his whisky glass into the fireplace, spattering glass across the hearth. "And I have neither!"

Fierro saw the man's nostrils flare, like a bull ready to charge. He and Narcisco were childhood friends. He never feared the man would assault him personally, at least until now. Tamacas was relentless, like a dog with a bone. He wouldn't stop attacking a thing until he cracked it open and got to the marrow. In the past, Fierro could always talk him off the ledge and reason with him. But tonight Narcisco was beyond reason—truly mad-dog kind of stuff.

Fierro's efforts to calm him down were clearly failing. Maybe the whisky wasn't such a good idea after all.

He wished Vargas was there to back him up.

"I understand your frustration, Narcisco. Your father is like a father to me."

"Liar! You could never stand the man."

"Not true. My father respected your father, and taught me to respect him as well. Sure, he operated differently than I do, but so did my father."

Fierro's own temper rose with the volume of his voice. He marched over to the smaller Narcisco and jabbed a finger into his thick chest. "Do you think I didn't respect my own father, *cabrón*?"

Narcisco crossed himself sloppily and kissed his finger. "I'm sorry your father is dead, God bless him. But my father is alive, and I intend to keep him that way."

"My sources inside the prison say he's safe."

"For how long? And can you guarantee his life?"

"I've sent orders to protect him at all costs."

Narcisco pressed in closer, nose to nose.

"The same orders that failed the kidnapping? That failed the assassination? What good are your orders, Amador?"

Fierro refused to look away, a sign of weakness. But his peripheral vision caught Narcisco's hand slipping toward the gold-plated pistol in his shoulder holster.

"'Patience in war is a virtue,' old friend."

"Stop lecturing me with your idiot philosophies. Action is all that matters."

"Action? Action? What the hell do you think I've been doing? And you think you can do any better, you stupid cowboy? Go ahead and pull your pistol—and see what happens. And then what? You'll round up a dozen of your men and assault the world's toughest prison with a couple of *cuernos de chivo* and blast your way in?"

Fierro felt more than saw Narcisco's hand carefully grip the pistol, but the Salvadoran's rage had blinded him to the fact Amador had slipped a razor-sharp blade into his own hand. The taller Colombian tensed to strike when the lights suddenly snapped off.

Tamacas froze. He was notoriously scared of the dark.

"What's happening?"

"The backup generator should be kicking on any second now."

Just then, the generator's big diesel engine fired up. Room lights flickered on for the span of a breath before crashing out again, dying with the generator outside.

Moments later, a sharp explosion erupted in the distance. Lights flashed like a strobe through the big picture window.

Fierro and Tamacas ran over to it, scanning the compound.

More flashing explosions erupted, rattling the bulletproof window glass.

Fierro froze with indecision. *Who was it?* It couldn't be the Colombian Army. They were in his pocket, and even if they weren't, he had spies who would have warned him in advance. Another cartel? Mercs?

Narcisco flashed a golden grin as he pulled out his big Desert Eagle pistol. "Let's go hunting!"

Fierro saw the jagged orange lightning of a machine gun firing into the air, and heard helicopter blades faintly thrumming in the distance.

"Forget it. Come with me!" Fierro grabbed Narcisco by the shoulder holster and dragged him toward a secret door.

"Where to?"

"To live—and fight another day!"

54

The *Oregon*'s tilt-rotor approached Fierro's mountain estate with Gomez on the stick and Cabrillo in the copilot's seat. Both men wore white phosphor goggles to eliminate visible light in the cockpit and avoid being seen from the ground or in the air, no matter how marginal the possibility.

Murphy and Stone wore the same, sitting at their respective stations behind the cockpit and eager to begin their phase of the operation.

Eddie Seng, MacD, and Linda Ross were farther back, each kitted out for the ground mission. Ross wasn't an official Gundog, but she was a trusted backup when the team needed an extra pair of boots on the ground.

"Thirty seconds," Juan whispered in the onboard comms.

The *Oregon* had raced to the west coast of Panama to get as near to Colombia as they could. Passing through the Panama Canal to get close to Fierro's place was out of the question. Under the best of circumstances it would have taken at least eight hours to traverse the canal in one direction and only if they had made prior arrangements.

Stone had made quick work figuring out where Fierro was based. He accessed old DEA files on Fierro's father, Colombian property records, purchase orders, and even delivery schedules from high-end gourmet food and beverage vendors. They all pointed to Amador Fierro's current location. Further scouring local open-source intelligence confirmed the head of La Liga was ensconced on the compound at this very moment, but there was no telling how long he would stay on the property. They needed to get there, fast.

The AW tilt-rotor had a thousand-mile range with external fuel tanks. That was the calculated distance for the round trip from the *Oregon*'s deck to Fierro's villa in the mountains of the Sierra Nevada de Santa Marta. Cabrillo checked the fuel gauges. They'd be touching back down on the *Oregon*'s decks on fumes instead of fuel, but that would be Gomez's problem, not his.

Assuming they all survived this half of the mission.

Juan and his team put together an assault plan based on Fierro's location. The lightly guarded, remote mountain estate was set in the middle of a working coffee plantation. That meant in addition to the armed guards there were also innocent civilian farmers in the area who didn't deserve to get caught in the cross fire. If their mission went as planned, there shouldn't be any civilian casualties. But what mission ever went according to plan?

Fierro's defenses were light because his place was surrounded by a deep moat of abject fear and high walls of bribe money. Local police, national army units, and even the Colombian government itself would provide sufficient defense should either of those fail. So far, they had proven to be enough.

Tonight's objective was the big man himself. Cabrillo didn't believe in the ladder of escalation or tit-for-tat exchanges. Juan's formula for tactical victory was simple: surprise, speed, and violence of action. And the best way to win a war was to cut off the head of the snake— and in this case, drag it back to the *Oregon*. Tonight's mission was designed with both in mind. Whatever happened to Fierro after tonight was still up in the air, but no matter the outcome, La Liga would get the message: nobody in their organization was safe from capture.

Cabrillo admitted to his team he was coloring way outside the lines. But since no government would or could deal with La Liga, it was up to the *Oregon* to do something about it. Otherwise, Olmedo's ticket would eventually get punched. Cabrillo didn't bother asking for permission from Overholt. If the old man told him he couldn't do it, he'd do it anyway. And if the old man approved the mission and it failed, Overholt would get the blame for it and no doubt be punished for Cabrillo's mistakes.

"We're in position," Gomez said.

The tilt-rotor hovered in high-altitude darkness a mile from the target like a predatory night bird, its noise-reducing rotors thrumming the air. Downrange, Fierro's sprawling compound was bathed in the faint glow of security floodlights.

"Stand by," Gomez said over the intercom.

He engaged the AW's advanced sensor suite and began sweeping the compound with a forward-looking infrared (FLIR) camera, synthetic aperture radar, and low-light optics. The resulting images flashed on the cockpit's panoramic heads-up display, the station monitors, and the wristband displays each of the operators carried. The team saw the scattered heat signatures of human bodies, the bright white-phosphor outlines of the main house, outbuildings, parked vehicles, and even the bright flare of lit cigarettes.

"I count two tangos north of the main house, four in the tree line to the east, three outside the guard shack, and four inside," Gomez said.

"They've got beaucoup security cameras, which means motion sensors, too," Murphy added.

"So we confirm nine tangos in the open, four inside the shack. That it?" Cabrillo asked.

"Confirmed," Eddie said.

"Those security cameras and motion detectors won't do us any favors. Nuke 'em."

"On it," Eric said as his fingers touched the EMP cannon controls. A moment later, a silent river of electromagnetic waves washed over the area. In an instant, the compound was thrown into utter darkness as floodlights snapped off, and every other light-emitting diode, LED and incandescent bulb was snuffed out of existence.

For just a second, Fierro's emergency backup diesel generator roared to life, but just as quickly died when hit by a surging wave pulse. Stone swept the compound with electromagnetic pulse radiation for another thirty seconds. Anything not wrapped in a Faraday cage or otherwise hard-shielded was dead.

The outside guards bolted from their positions as they snatched up dead radios, phones, and flashlights, trying to figure out what was going on. Unless they were complete idiots, it wouldn't take them long to determine what had just happened. The *Oregon* team needed to move fast.

"I think we're good to go, Chairman."

"Wepps, your turn at bat."

Murphy grinned ear to ear. "Launching recon drones."

A hatch in the tilt-rotor's belly released four fast-moving quadcopters optimized for silent running. Each surveillance drone deployed infrared sensors, low-light optics, and directional acoustic microphones.

Within moments, thermal and optical imagery tagged and auto-tracked each guard.

"Launching attack drones," Murph said.

A second compartment on the AW released thirteen smaller drones, each carrying a large but nonlethal flash-bang canister. Onboard AI-guidance processed the recon drones' real-time data, assigning attack drones to cover all of the guards. The thirteen kamikaze attack drones raced low just above the treetops, each pursuing their assigned targets.

The first flash-bangs erupted in the trees, their brief flashes of blistering light whiting out the infrared screens. The microphones on the recon drones broadcast the noise of the blasts, as well as the panicked shouts and curses of the remaining guards, now alerted to the surprise attack from out of the sky. Seconds later, the other perimeter guards were splayed on the ground, their unconscious forms gray and still on the tilt-rotor's displays.

One of the shack guards raised his CZ Scorpion submachine gun skyward and ripped off a mag at one of the drones zipping past. The staccato light from his weapon flared on the AW monitors.

"Good luck with that," Stone said, chuckling. "Dipwad."

Four more flash-bang kamikazes crashed into the guard shack—one straight through the front door. The windows shattered. Three limp bodies smashed hard into the concrete walls before tumbling to the floor. The fourth guard staggered a few steps outside, clutching his head and screaming before he face-planted into the dirt.

"Get that man an Excedrin," Stone said.

"All clear," Murph said. "Perimeter secure."

"Good work, Wepps," Cabrillo said. He checked the digital count-down clock. The guards had been neutralized in just eight seconds. But all of that commotion must have alerted Fierro and whoever else was inside the main house. Cabrillo unbuckled himself to head back into the cabin, clapping Gomez on the shoulder and telling him, "Time to get our groove on, boyo."

"Yup." Gomez eased the controls forward and mashed the throttle. The tilt-rotor raced toward the compound. Moments later the tilt-rotor slowed as it descended to the landing zone, but Juan and the three operators in back bolted out of the AW before it touched the ground. They dashed in a crouch toward the front door of the estate.

Gomez lofted away to a safe distance nearby, activating the tilt-rotor's remote-controlled overwatch machine gun while Murph and Eddie retrieved the recon drones.

All four operators stacked up at the front entrance. Eddie breached the heavy door with shaped charges along the hinges, blasting it inward. The Gundogs dashed in with their night vision goggles down and weapons up, clearing rooms as they went. They had trained this way together for years, practicing for countless hours in the *Oregon's* onboard shoot house. More important, they had executed dozens of live-fire missions with faultless success.

Ten minutes later, the vast house was secured. A terrified live-in housekeeper and a bearded, bare-chested chef were the only people they encountered. Since neither offered any resistance they were handled gently, though their hands were flex-cuffed behind their backs and mouths gagged for security. The unconscious guards outside would wake up within the hour and could free them when they came to.

"No Fierro, boss. Now what?" MacD asked.

"We'll spread out and pick up whatever intel looks interesting—

calendars, laptops, thumb drives, you name it. But time's a-wastin'. No telling who might have called this in, so put some scoot in your boot."

"Aye," Eddie said. The operators split up.

"You catch that, Gomez?" Cabrillo asked.

"Your cab will be waiting at the curb in ten, hoss."

"Perfecto."

Ten minutes later, the team scrambled on board the tilt-rotor and Gomez lofted the bird into the starry sky, and headed for home.

55

We need to move," the Mexican squad leader said to his mercs. "Saddle up, and let's go."

The other two men shouldered their packs and picked up their weapons as the Mexican grabbed Varik by the collar and dragged him to his feet. Eidolon's hands were already flex-cuffed in front of him.

"Hope you're ready for a hike, little cockroach," the Mexican said. "We've got a long way to go."

"I don't know if I can make it," Eidolon said. "My health isn't so good."

"If you slow us down, you won't like it. After all, you don't need your fingers to remember a passcode, do you?"

Varik swallowed hard. "I'll do my best."

The squad leader pulled him close. "And if you're lying to me about this passcode?" He ripped off a string of epithets that would make a Danish sailor blush.

Varik could smell his cigarette-stale breath. He wanted to gag.

"If I'm lying to you, then your boss will kill me."

"It's not you I'm worried about, *cucaracha*."

"But if I'm telling the truth, he'll thank us both—and make you a very rich man."

The Mexican squad leader nodded to the Guatemalan, who flung the door open. The Mexican shoved Varik onto the wide porch and followed him out with one hand gripped on his collar. The Cuban came next, trailed by the Guatemalan, who didn't bother shutting the door behind him.

Five steps out onto the front porch the Mexican stopped and looked around. The thick clouds heavy with rain shadowed the moonlight. It was nearly pitch-black. He scanned the area for his two men standing guard outside, but didn't see them.

"Paco! Ramiro!" He looked around. It was deathly quiet. Even the insects were silent. The Mexican's neck tingled as his eyes made out a shadowed lump on the ground several yards away.

"Quick, back into the shack!"

Too late.

Bang! The Cuban's head split open like an overripe melon as the heavy AK round ripped through the side of his skull. Varik screamed as the hot gory mess splattered over him.

The Mexican dragged Varik behind him, close on the heels of the Guatemalan racing back inside the cabin.

Two sharp cracks of a 9-millimeter pistol echoed in the house, dropping the Guatemalan to the floor.

His ears ringing from the gun blasts and nearly blinded by the flashes, the Mexican pulled his weapon and fired in the direction of the pistol shots, but Raven had already ducked behind the cabinet in the kitchen.

The Mexican pulled Eidolon close just as heavy footsteps thundered through the front door. The Mexican whipped around firing point-blank, but the big African American judo-rolled to safety behind the nearest wall.

The Mexican wrapped an arm around Eidolon's throat and pulled him against his chest like a Kevlar vest, and pressed his back against the wall, using Eidolon as a human shield.

Link and Raven drew their weapons and put a bead on the Mexican from behind their respective covers.

"There's no way out. Give him up," Raven called out in Spanish.

The Mexican pointed his pistol at Raven's slim profile, then swung the barrel back over toward Linc in the opposite direction, trying to make himself as small as possible.

Both Raven's and Linc's weapons were pointed directly at him. There wasn't a clear shot. They couldn't take the chance of killing Eidolon.

The Mexican pressed his pistol against Varik's temple.

"You're right, there is no way out," he said in English.

"We can figure this out," Linc said.

"I already have, *yanqui*."

Bang! Eidolon's head jerked violently as blood geysered from the wound. Without hesitation, the Mexican put his pistol to his own temple and pulled the trigger. Both bodies hit the floor with a sickening thud.

Link and Raven rushed over to the pile of carnage.

"What was that?" wide-eyed Raven asked. "Why?"

Linc shouldered his weapon. "The man's job was to kill Eidolon, but somehow the little guy sweet-talked him into taking him out of here instead. But when we showed up, that guy must have remembered his mission was to kill Eidolon. If we had gotten to Eidolon instead, his boss would murder him in ways I don't even want to think about." Linc nodded at the Mexican's corpse. "He figured a bullet to the head was the easy way out."

"What do we do now?" Raven asked.

Linc sniffed the air. "Smells like someone had fried electronics for dinner. Let's take a look around." Linc spotted the microwave oven. He dashed over, yanked open the door, and looked inside.

"Yep, Eidolon must have had some sort of early warning and destroyed his equipment."

"But why? His value was in those machines and hard drives," Raven said. "Unless he had access to other hard drives through some secret account or something."

"It doesn't matter." Linc checked his battered Timex watch. "Let's see what we can find and then we need to vamoose."

They tore through the small cabin searching for anything of value, but after fifteen minutes of searching found nothing.

Linc crossed back over to Eidolon's corpse and rifled through his clothing, hoping he had a thumb drive or something else on his person. All he came up with was an old wallet with a Panamanian driver's license, a couple of Panamanian balboas, and a U.S. ten-dollar bill. The sleeves where the credit cards were usually stored were empty, but Linc pried them open anyway with his thick fingers.

"What's this?"

"What'd ya find?"

Linc held up his hand. Pinched between his thumb and index finger was an old-style memory card, smaller than a postage stamp.

"That's an old MicroSD card. For cameras. We used them back when I was in the military police." Raven looked around, then dashed over to where an old Canon point-and-shoot digital camera hung from a wall peg. She popped open the drive door. It was empty. She tried to power it on, but the battery was dead.

"Worthless. Probably just tourist photos anyway."

"Bring it, just in case," Linc said. He put the memory card back into the wallet and pocketed it. "Let's get out of here. We've got a hard march through rough country and the landing zone is at least eight hours away."

"One sec." Raven dashed over to the other La Liga man's body. His ruck was larger, in better condition, and mil-spec. More important, it was partially open and stuffed with water bottles, candy bars, and fruit. She dropped her own pathetic thrift-store pack, pulled the rucksack off the body, and shouldered it. Linc came up behind her, saw the Cuban's ruck was loaded as well, and swapped out his, too.

"No rest for the wicked," Linc said. "And the righteous don't need any."

Raven grinned despite her fatigue. That was one of Cabrillo's favorite sayings.

"Easy peasy," she said.

Linc laughed. That was his signature line.

The two of them marched off the porch and sped out into the night. They wanted to clear the area in case there were more thugs headed their way. They'd call Cabrillo at their first rest break with the bad news about Eidolon.

The two *Oregon* operators worked their way through the jungle, navigating by the stars when the canopy and clouds permitted it, and relying on the GPS inside Linc's phony Timex when things got sketchy. They mostly walked in silence, their hearts heavy with tonight's outcome, their minds reviewing what they could have done better. Delayed by the swollen river and muddy terrain, they had arrived late to Eidolon's compound, just at the moment when his captors had burst through the front door.

Linc, the more experienced operator, made the call to hold back and wait to see what developed while he formulated a plan. There was no chance of breaking Eidolon out of the cabin, since they were outnumbered five to two. Instead, the former SEAL operator made the hard call to take out the two outside guards first and wait for the others to appear. Raven dropped one guard with Linc's borrowed blade, while the big former SEAL slipped behind the other and snapped his neck with a quick twist of his massive hands.

Cabrillo had drilled into his team that killing was always the last resort. The truth of the matter was Linc and Raven were both beyond exhausted after the brutal cross-country march to the compound after several hard days and nights of trekking through the Darién. With their energy reserves utterly depleted, tracking the five bandits and Eidolon for another long distance over hard terrain would have proven impossible, let alone racing ahead of them to set up some sort of ambush, lethal or otherwise. Unfortunately, the shortest distance between them and Eidolon was a kill box, taking out the tangos as quickly and efficiently as possible—especially given the importance of the target. The improvised plan had worked to perfection—right up to the moment Eidolon had his brains splattered all over the cabin.

Failing a mission was never an option in the Chairman's mind, and he never failed to meet his own high standard. Raven and Linc both dreaded disappointing him. Worse, Eidolon's secret didn't exactly die with him—only their access to it. The infamous hacker had hinted at something very big and dangerous and that mysterious thing was still in the wind. Each ragged step toward the landing zone only added to their fear that failing to bring in Eidolon had put the United States in its fatal crosshairs.

56

THE CARIBBEAN SEA

Amador Fierro and Narcisco Tamacas made their way through the underground escape tunnel. They were far beyond the compound when Cabrillo and his team breached the front door. Twenty minutes later, the two La Liga bosses were in the air and racing toward Nicaragua, where Fierro had a special long-distance seaplane waiting for him at a private airfield.

The ShinMaywa US-2 was a short takeoff and landing aircraft that was as comfortable on the water as it was in the air. Fierro's love of aviation and all things Japanese only confirmed his decision to purchase the rare and expensive aircraft at considerable cost. Few aircraft could match its incredible range of twenty-three hundred nautical miles, and he'd need every inch of it for the trip out to the *Baktun*.

Fierro had already made previous arrangements for the flight to the Nicaraguan airfield that evening. The Sikorsky S-92 helicopter was fully fueled and a pilot standing by, along with a hulking security guard. Fierro was preparing to leave for Nicaragua via a refueling stop in Panama when Narcisco barged into his home. The mad dog was temporarily tamed by the surprise attack, and even grateful for Fierro's escape plans.

Tamacas's gratitude diminished considerably in mid-flight when Fierro nodded to his guard, who promptly dispatched the Salvadoran gangster with a hard crack across the back of his skull with his heavy metal SIG P229 Legion pistol.

Tamacas slumped unconscious. Fierro instructed his guard to zip-tie his childhood friend, and ordered the pilot to hover in place some five hundred feet above the moonlit sea. The cabin door was flung open and Fierro himself tossed Narcisco into the night sky, cowboy boots and all. The unfettered legs of the lifeless body fluttered in the wind, making Tamacas look like he was running toward the sea. Fierro couldn't help but grin at the absurdly tragic image.

Narcisco's body diminished into a silvery splash erupting far below, its noise masked by the Sikorsky's hovering turbines. His friend's death was an unfortunate necessity, Fierro seeing no other way to resolve the issue. There was no reasoning with Narcisco's atavistic impulses nor blunting his reckless behavior. Vargas had always been right. Killing Narcisco was an inevitability he shouldn't have tried to avoid. He took no pleasure in his friend's death, but a terrible burden was now lifted from his shoulders.

Fierro shut the cabin door and ordered the pilot to resume his flight plan, his spirits soaring. Project Q would be launching any day now, and the world would never be the same.

★

PANAMA

Raven and Linc finally took a break about an hour from Eidolon's camp. Raven called Juan via the emergency radio and filled him in on the details, including the death of their target.

"At least he didn't fall into anybody else's hands," Cabrillo said over the roar of the tilt-rotor engines still heading for the *Oregon.* "Thank God you guys are okay. When will you make the LZ?"

"Six a.m. local, if all goes according to plan."

"Does it ever?" Juan asked.

"Looking forward to seeing the AW. Getting pretty tired of the walking tour down here."

"Won't be in the AW. Gomez just informed me there's a problem with the hydraulics. Looks like you two will be hitching a ride on the Joby. You'll just be in range." The Joby was capable of traveling over five hundred miles with its hydrogen-electric battery system.

"Looking forward to it."

"If anything changes, let us know. Otherwise, I'll put a pot of coffee on the burner for you two in the morning. Godspeed."

"You too, Chairman. I hope you know that Linc and I—"

"Forget it, Rave. I know you two left it all on the mat. That's all any of us can do. We leave the rest to fate."

"We never did find that Quds Force camp, either."

"Are you hearing me, little sister? You get back to the ship safe and sound and I'll be one happy camper. Got it?"

"Got it."

"Cabrillo out."

57

Amador Fierro piloted the large seaplane onto a splashy landing in the choppy Pacific some hundred yards away from the *Baktun*. It was a skillful maneuver even for an experienced pilot, and though Fierro was an excellent aviator he hadn't put much time in behind the yoke of his most recently purchased airplane.

A low, heavy cloud layer hung above the ship like a lingering umbrella of cabin smoke in a cold mountain valley. Fierro feathered the four Rolls-Royce turboprops to a standstill before pulling off his headset and turning the controls over to the plane's regular pilot, who immediately began his preflight checklist. The plane was still well within its certified range of twenty-nine hundred miles and the fuel tanks were just over half full. A refueling from the *Baktun* was possible, but neither desirable nor necessary in the suboptimal conditions.

An inflatable from the *Baktun* pulled alongside the fuselage cargo door just as Fierro's supersized bodyguard yanked it open. The two men leaped into the bobbing boat and the helmsman rocketed away. Moments later, the inflatable pulled up next to the pilot's boarding door near the waterline. Despite his sleepless exhaustion, Fierro grabbed the interior handles and easily pulled himself up, brushing away the assistance offered by the two burly crewmen nearby. His gunman followed suit.

"Welcome aboard, sir," the Brazilian first officer said. "I hope the boat ride wasn't too unpleasant."

"Where's Stokes?"

"The captain is waiting for you in the CIC."

Fierro grunted his disapproval. It wasn't as if Fierro were a mere passenger. Did Stokes forget who owned this boat?

"Take me to him."

"Yes, sir. Follow me."

The Brazilian led Fierro and his bodyguard to an armored compartment located one deck below the amidships superstructure. Stokes and Bose were inside amid the glowing LCD monitors and flashing electronics. The techs in the darkly chilled room were all former military, but no one shouted, *Attention on deck!* or snapped to attention when Fierro, a civilian, entered. They all turned around to catch a glimpse of the man with the inexhaustible bankroll who paid their lavish salaries. The few women in the room were instantly attracted to his smoldering good looks. The men envied his wealth and power.

"You can all return to your duties," Fierro said. The techs turned back around to their monitors, keyboards, and joysticks.

Stokes flashed a pleasant smile and extended his hand, noting the drug lord's grim and tired face. He avoided the soul-snatching stare of Fierro's muscular goon, scanning the room for threats against his *patrón*.

"Welcome aboard, Mr. Fierro. I'm glad you made it safely."

Fierro ignored the handshake. "I almost flew past you beneath that cloud cover. Why didn't you answer my radio call?"

"As I informed you before, we're on complete radio and electromagnetic silence."

Fierro pointed at the techs and their stations. "Then what are they doing?"

"Passive sensors only. Optical and electromagnetic invisibility is our best protection. Nobody can shoot at us if they can't find us."

"And the artificial cloud cover?"

"We've been dispersing micron-size metallic nanoparticles to obscure high-altitude satellite imagery, along with a thermal-blocking silica-based aerogel mist that disrupts infrared sensors."

Fierro gave a begrudging nod to the ingenuity.

"Lucky for you I'm an excellent pilot. Otherwise, you might have missed your next paycheck."

"You pay me to keep the *Baktun* safe, Mr. Fierro, not run a taxi service."

"How was your flight, Mr. Fierro? Uneventful, I trust?" Bose asked as she approached. She smiled pleasantly, trying to smooth the turbulent waters threatening to overwhelm the two alpha males.

"It was a very long and very loud helicopter ride from Colombia to Nicaragua with a refueling stop in Panama," Fierro said. "And an equally long flight from Nicaragua to here."

"You mentioned in your radio message that you had been attacked?"

"By the Americans, I'm sure of it."

"How did they find you?" Stokes asked.

"A leak in Colombian intelligence most likely."

"Terrible," Bose offered.

"And how can you be sure they don't know you're here?" Stokes asked.

"I took precautions, if that's what you're suggesting," Fierro said.

Stokes frowned. "You may have put us all in the crosshairs."

"That's also what I pay you for." Fierro turned to Bose. "Where are we on the AGI launch? Still on time?"

Bose turned to a newly installed digital countdown clock.

"Forty-seven hours and twenty-one minutes from now, we will change history."

"And if I recall, that means we can't fire up the engines for forty-seven hours and . . . twenty-two minutes. Is that correct?"

Bose nodded. "Correct."

"Unless the Americans show up," Stokes said. "We may need to evade or maneuver."

"Do that and you'll destroy the AGI," Bose protested.

"We won't move a millimeter until Project Q has launched," Fierro said. "Our lives depend on it."

"Sir?" Bose asked.

"My La Liga colleagues will murder us most cruelly if we fail this mission. I've spent billions of La Liga dollars to make this happen." He turned to Stokes. "That's why we won't engage the engines until the AGI comes online."

"If we're sunk, the AGI will never come online."

"If we're sunk, then it doesn't matter anyway."

"It matters to me," Bose said.

"Then make sure it launches on time." Fierro pointed at the clock. "And not one second longer." He turned back to Stokes. "Once that clock hits zero, the engines are all yours. But if Project Q fails to launch, you better find us a place where La Liga can never find us—and on this side of hell, I don't know where that is."

"It will be online and on time," Bose said. "You have my word."

"If La Liga isn't bad enough, the Americans are hunting me now as well. With AGI online, we'll seize the American energy grid, and drive them to their knees."

Stokes nodded. "Pride cometh before a fall, and the damned Yanks are long due for one."

"And did I mention that both of you will receive five percent of Project Q profits once it launches?"

Stokes and Bose exchanged a surprised glance.

Fierro smiled for the first time. "You'll both be richer than gods." He glanced down at his flight suit and sniffed the air. "I need a shower. I'm heading to my stateroom. Is it ready?"

"It hasn't been touched since you were here last," Stokes said. "Silk sheets and sweet-smelling soaps fit for a king, I'm told."

"I'll be back in an hour. Have coffee sent to my suite. Food, too. And contact me immediately if anything changes."

"Yes, sir."

Fierro turned on his heel and sped out of the compartment. His gunman scanned the room one more time, then laid his eyes on Stokes. The old English war fighter didn't flinch, but he breathed a sigh of relief when the killer left the room.

Stokes waited a few moments, then motioned to Bose. "Come with me."

★

Stokes shut the door to his spartan cabin and motioned Bose into a chair. His cramped little room was only slightly larger than the Indian doctor's own quarters.

"Five percent, and richer than gods? That's a bit of a twist, isn't it?" Stokes asked.

"A ridiculous attempt to cement our loyalties. He must be concerned."

"He should be. He's obviously losing control, and the forces around him are closing in."

"That makes him especially dangerous."

"Indeed, it does. To you and me most of all. He'll blame us for his own incompetence."

"His thug terrifies me. What happened to his man Vargas?"

"No idea."

"What are your thoughts on our situation?"

"I think that Colombian idiot will lead the Americans to us. Unfortunately, we're blind and deaf out here on electromagnetic silence."

"Can't you turn on the radar for just a brief moment to catch a glimpse of things? Get an early warning? And then shut it down?"

"I could, but even a momentary burst of energy can be detected and triangulated. It's not worth the risk for what little information we may or may not get. Though truthfully, there's nothing I relish more than a chance to sink the *Agua Linda*."

"Don't let your vanity endanger the project."

Stokes laid a hand on her shoulder. They had become intimate in the last few days, surrendering themselves to their smoldering desires. If any of the crew suspected the mating of the two lonely scorpions, they wisely hid their views.

"Of course not. I know how important Project Q is to you."

"And to the world."

"Once you bring the AGI online, Fierro will become the most powerful man in the world."

"Then we need to stay in his good graces."

Stokes nodded thoughtfully. "In his good graces, most assuredly. But we must also survive."

"We're all counting on you, my sweet. You are our chosen warrior."

"A warrior with one arm tied behind his back, and his best shield left hanging on the wall."

"You will find a way to prevail against the Americans—or anyone else who threatens us."

"Threats come in many forms."

"What are you suggesting?"

"Sometimes fate makes the wrong man king."

Bose smiled. "I've thought the same thing myself. It occurs to me that at this moment, Fierro needs us more than we need him."

"I promise to do everything in my power to see this thing through."

"I know you will."

They both turned their heads toward the sound of the seaplane's big turboprops suddenly roaring to life beyond the ship's hull as it raced along the surface of the sea for takeoff. Fierro's copilot had strict orders to keep his GPS beacon turned off until he reached the coast of Nicaragua.

Stokes straightened his posture, reasserting his military bearing.

"I need to get back to the CIC. I can't have Fierro mucking about unattended."

58

A ship-wide alert sounded as the Joby approached the *Oregon* with Linc and Raven safely on board. They were arriving two hours later than planned, but for good reason.

On their way to the landing zone, the two Gundogs accidentally stumbled onto the Quds Force base they had been originally assigned to locate. Practically sleepwalking in their fatigue, they almost bumped into an Iranian guard patrolling the perimeter of the training camp. They ducked out of sight in the nick of time, but were forced to make a long, circuitous detour around the Iranians before heading back toward the landing zone. Linc recorded the GPS location on his fake Timex before they left the area, allowing them to finally complete their mission.

Stone and Murphy were there to greet them on the hangar deck along with Cabrillo, Max, and Dr. Huxley.

Raven and Linc were utterly exhausted, dehydrated, and stricken with a combination of swollen mosquito bites, fungal infections, and heat rashes. Huxley ordered the two of them immediately to sick bay for hot showers, saline IVs, antibiotics, and observation for the next twenty-four hours.

"I was hoping for breakfast in bed and a foot massage," Raven joked.

"Breakfast I can arrange," Huxley said, adding with a wink, "and

I can think of a half dozen young crewmen that would eagerly volunteer their toe-rubbing services."

"Breakfast will be fine," Raven said as Linc handed over his pack to Stone.

"Got this from Eidolon's place," Linc said.

Eric opened it and pulled out a grimy leather wallet and a beat-up Canon point-and-shoot digital camera. He held it up. "Quite an antique."

"Check out the wallet," Linc said as he unbuckled his Timex and handed it to Cabrillo. "There's some cash and probably a fake ID. But there's also a memory card in there. I think it goes with the camera. Didn't know if you needed the camera to read it or not."

"We'll check it out. Could be interesting."

"Hope so," Raven said.

Juan saw the guilt in her eyes. Failing to capture Eidolon alive was still eating her up. He understood the sentiment. He'd feel the same way. If Overholt was right, Eidolon's intel could have prevented a catastrophe.

Cabrillo hoped whatever baton they had managed to pass along to his brainiac researchers could take them to the finish line, but he didn't see how that was possible.

Not by a long shot.

★

Eric Stone and Mark Murphy were perched in front of a large computer monitor in the research lab. Though using the same computer, they each had their own wireless keyboards for input.

They had already pored over Eidolon's measly "pocket litter" Linc had recovered. The Panamanian driver's license was easily dismissed as a fake, just as Linc had suspected. They also examined the dead man's money under a microscope in search of microdots, hidden text, or numerical codes. They even looked for nano-fabricated data threads woven in with the paper fibers, but they came up short. If there was any kind of code or message embedded in any of those bills, they couldn't find it.

That left the old-school digital memory card.

They pulled the Canon ELPH to see what was on the SD card. They wanted to use the camera to view the photos on the disk to protect the *Oregon*'s mainframe computer from any kind of virus attack that might be hidden in it. They scrounged around and found a Li-ion battery for it, but when they went to power it up they discovered a chunk of bullet shrapnel had smashed the processor—a lucky break for Raven, but a terminal outcome for the Canon.

Now that the camera wasn't an option, they took other precautions to view the card.

The first thing Murphy did was create a virtual machine on the mainframe. This guaranteed complete isolation of whatever nasty bugs might be on the MicroSD card from infecting the rest of the *Oregon*'s systems.

"I don't think that's enough," Eric said. "Eidolon's the devil. We need to chain him down in computer hell."

"Go for it."

Stone's fingers danced across his keyboard as he pulled down a sandbox tool, adding an additional, isolated layer of protection for the virtual machine's own operating system.

"That's locking him in a steel box inside of an iron cage," Murph said.

"Can't take any chances with a trickster god like him."

"Shall we proceed?"

"Indubitably."

Murphy connected a card reader to the computer and Eric inserted the camera's memory card into it.

"Whaddya think?" Murphy asked. "Time to upload?"

"I'd feel better if we sprinkled some holy water on it."

"Yeah, me too, but it might start swearing at us in Babylonian. Will you do the honors?"

"My pleasure." Eric launched his favorite antivirus software to scan the memory card directly while it was still mounted in the reader before uploading the picture files.

While it was running, Murph downloaded image analysis software into the sandbox.

Twelve minutes later, the antivirus software signaled the disk was virus free.

"Looks like we're good to go," Eric said. "Your honors."

Murph uploaded the picture files into the image analysis program. Within moments, one hundred forty-seven thumbnail images appeared on-screen.

Both men held their breath, expecting a system crash or an alarm warning of a viral infection that somehow escaped both the box and the cage they had constructed. But neither happened.

"You thinking what I'm thinking?"

"Better safe than stupid."

"Hit it again."

Eric ran the antivirus program one more time—just in case there was embedded malware somehow hidden from the first scan.

"All good," Eric said with a sigh of relief. "Now what?"

"Let's just do a visual and see what we can see."

Murphy enlarged the first photo in the lineup, a bright red flower with a prominent stamen.

"That's it? The big secret? A bunch of nature photos?" Eric said.

"Moving on." Murph sped through the next one hundred forty-six photos—all flowers in a variety of colors. Stone didn't know any more about flower species than Murphy did, so he ran them all through a botanical identification program. Eidolon had apparently assembled a collection of bromeliads, heliconias, rainforest daisies, violets, hibiscus, passion flowers, wild ginger, and orchids.

"I don't get it," Eric said. "Why all the flowers?"

Murphy sat back in his chair, his elbows on the rests and his hands tented as if in prayer.

"Huh."

"What?"

"All these pics? They're all different." Murph pointed at the screen. "Except for these three. He took the same picture of an orchid three times. Why?"

"I dunno. An orchid fetish?"

"Same orchid. Same picture." Murph leaned forward, squinting. "I mean, the exact same picture. Same angle, same size, same everything." He tapped a few keystrokes, pulling up the metadata of the three pictures. "See?"

Now Eric leaned forward. "Exact same picture, reproduced three times. Huh."

"Yeah, 'huh.' You thinking what I'm thinking?"

"Steganography."

"Bingo." Murph's eyes lit up as he rubbed his hands together. "Time to open the pod bay doors and step through the looking glass."

"Mixed metaphor alert," Eric mumbled as Murphy deleted one hundred forty-four images, leaving only the three identical orchid photos.

He then uploaded them into a digital image forensics tool that began a detailed analysis of the three photos, some sixty million pixels in all. The program's greatest strength was pixel analysis. When it finally finished, it generated a comprehensive forensics report.

The two techs scanned it and both drew the same conclusion. The first and third photos were identical in their entirety. Yet the second photo contained extremely small but numerous changes.

"There's LSB encoding in the second picture," Stone said.

"No doubt about it."

LSB, or Least Significant Bit, encoding was a method of hiding digital data within an image. Digital cameras didn't capture photos directly—they stored numbers. Each pixel in a digital image, representing red, green, or blue, was rendered as an eight-digit binary number. The final digit—the least significant bit—represented the smallest value. Changing that digit wouldn't produce any differences in the picture noticeable to the human eye. But those tiny modifications could represent a secret code.

Unfortunately, the forensic program couldn't reveal the actual contents of the embedded code. It basically handed them an unsolved Rubik's Cube of jumbled colors.

"Steganography. Man, that's old-school spycraft for sure," Murph said. "Shoulda guessed it with that steampunk camera of his."

"Okay, let's pull down Steghide and see what we've got."

The Steghide program would align the jumbled colors of the unsolved Rubik's Cube and solve it perfectly, and finally reveal the code.

Eric ran the keyboard, typing in the command:

```
steghide extract -sf orchid.jpg
```

Steghide prompted back: "Passkey? _ _ _ _ _ _ _ _ _"

Both men looked at each other, completely flummoxed.

Eidolon had protected his file.

"Now what?" Murph asked.

Eric rechecked Steghide's prompt and counted the number of underscores—nine, as it turned out. He grinned, and snatched up Eidolon's phony driver's license.

The Panamanian license featured several pieces of personal data including Eidolon's nine-digit *e-cédula* national identity number. He handed it to Murphy.

"Read that to me."

As Murphy read out the numbers, Stone keyboarded: "316825265."

Steghide instantly extracted the LSB data and generated a file:

```
saladus.message.txt
```

Murphy opened up the text file. All it showed was a long string of 1's and 0's. It reminded Murph of his exchange with Linlin earlier.

"Gotta be an ASCII code."

"This takes Russian nesting dolls to a whole new level," Stone said.

"I'll script something in Python." Murphy banged out several lines of programming code to convert the binary numbers into human-readable words.

Moments later, Eidolon's message appeared in plain English.

The two *Oregon* computer whiz kids stared open-mouthed at the screen like a couple of dorky gargoyles. Murph was the first to break the trance.

"We need to call the Chairman. *Now.*"

59

Juan dashed into the research lab, where he was greeted by his two enthusiastic techno-wonders standing by the oversize computer monitor. They insisted he come down to the lab rather than give him the results over the phone.

"We got it, Chairman," Eric said, grinning like the Cheshire Cat.

"How?"

"Steganography!" Murph blurted out. "Dang clever. Embedding LSBs into a matrix of—"

Cabrillo raised his palm to Murphy like a traffic cop, cutting him off mid-sentence.

"Forget the sizzle. Just give me the steak."

For years Juan tried to discipline his young techno-turks to cut to the chase in their briefs. He understood their youthful enthusiasm helped fuel their intense and relentless curiosities, which, in turn, produced actionable results. But there wasn't time for any of their nonsense today.

Eric held up the camera's memory card.

"Bottom line, Eidolon embedded his coded message on this. We're sure it's what he wanted to trade Overholt for his life."

"And what is that message?"

Eric and Murph stepped aside, revealing the computer monitor. They had enlarged the text for easy reading. Juan stepped closer to it, leaning on the desk.

> The Baktun is a civilian oceanic research vessel
> operating as an advanced software and
> hardware research lab for an AGI-powered
> organoid computer known as Project Q. This
> secret project is funded by the billionaire cartel
> boss Amador Fierro and headed up by Dr. Anima
> Bose. Fierro plans on using AGI to seize control
> of the U.S. energy grid and to expand his criminal
> empire. Project Q is scheduled to launch at
> 11:00:00 three days from today.

Juan's mind reeled with the horrifying possibilities.

"If Fierro seizes the energy grid, he could knock it down completely whenever he wanted to. That would disable ninety percent of the U.S. population within days."

"It's worse than that," Stone said.

"How?"

"For starters," Murphy began, "the Fierro organization will be able to completely secure their communications. That means no more signals intelligence, no more tapping phones or email or texts."

"And if they maintain AGI supremacy," Eric said, "they'll soon disrupt, corrupt, or exploit all law enforcement surveillance programs, local and national intelligence, and personnel files, counterinsurgency ops—you name it. AGI will afford them nearly perfect offensive and defensive capabilities."

Cabrillo stood erect. "It's a world-class disaster. We can't allow La Liga to acquire this technology."

"Or anybody else," Murph added. "Criminal, political, or military."

"We've got to capture it for ourselves," Eric added. "Think of the advantages that would give to our country. Our economy would dominate the planet. Our military would be invincible."

"Did Eidolon's file indicate the *Baktun*'s location?"

"No, sir. He said it was an oceanic research vessel," Murph said.

"That makes it a deepwater ship, which, come to think of it, makes a lot of sense. The 'vasty deep' is a pretty good place to hide from the rest of the world."

"It said three days from now. When was that text recorded?"

"Yesterday. So two days from today."

"That's not much time to search the world's oceans for an unidentified boat," Eric said.

"But we know it's Fierro's boat," Cabrillo said. "He's not going to tell anybody where it is. But I'd bet credits to navy beans he's heading out to it now. He'd want to be there when Project Q launches. And that explains why he wasn't at his place in Colombia." He turned to Eric. "You said he was there, right?"

"No question about it."

"We must have spooked him when we showed up. He'll need an airplane to get to his boat if he's in a hurry."

"Maybe he had one hidden somewhere close by," the *Oregon*'s helmsman said.

Murph nodded. "We could hack into regional air traffic control. Find any airplanes traveling from his location around that time last night."

Eric shook his head. "That's a lot of airspace to cover. And no telling what he's flying."

"He'll need something with a lot of range," Juan said. "Either he left Colombia with that kind of aircraft or he's flying to a location where there is one."

"Still doesn't narrow things down," Eric said.

Cabrillo headed for the door.

"I'm confident you two can handle it. I'll notify Overholt, then brief Max and Linda."

"We're on it," Murphy said.

"See you boys in an hour."

"It might take longer than that," Eric said.

Juan turned around. "If it does, Fierro wins—and the world is doomed."

★

Eric and Murphy were seated again at their joint computer terminal. The long minute hand on the analog wall clock had already devoured three minutes.

"How much energy do you think it would take to power up a boat like the *Baktun*?" Eric asked. "Especially for the kind of research work they're doing."

Murph scratched his wispy beard. "Depends on exactly what they're doing, but my guess would be a lot. Just training large-model AI requires megawatts of electricity—enough to power a small town. That's why Microsoft recently signed a deal to resurrect the nuclear reactors at Three Mile Island. And the *Baktun*'s energy source would have to be both continuous and stable, especially for the organoid components."

Eric snapped his fingers. "That boat we tangled with—the demon ship? I bet it was gobbling up a ton of power. AI-powered weapons, multiple platforms, cloaked . . . probably high speed, too."

"If I were building the world's first AGI computer on a ship-based platform, I'd do everything I could to protect it. And I'd put it out in the middle of nowhere. So, yeah. It makes perfect sense. The *Baktun* is our demon ship."

"That means we need to focus our radar search for an aircraft headed into the Pacific," Eric said. "And not just the Pacific, but that dead zone in the east where we had our gunfight."

"How far out?"

"At least a thousand nautical miles. Could be farther out, or maybe the *Baktun* will come in closer for the rendezvous, depending on the range of the airplane or helicopter Fierro's using."

"We might find a few ships out there, but I doubt we'll find any private aircraft. I mean, except for someone highly motivated to go out there."

"You mean motivated like Fierro?"

"Why don't we just call the Navy?" Murph asked.

"And tell them what? 'Please deploy your scarce resources in search of an unidentified boat we think might be in the Pacific and board or sink her for no legal reason?' And all based on a criminal hacker's photograph of an orchid? The Navy would never go for it. Neither would POTUS, especially on such short notice."

"I guess that just leaves us," Murph said. "Even though most of what you said applies to us, too."

Eric nodded. "You know what Cabrillo always says. Our mandate is to color outside the lines, especially when our country is under threat."

"Better grab our crayons, then."

★

Murph and Stone got to work, brainstorming a plan of attack to find the *Baktun*.

The earliest Fierro could have taken off from a field near his mansion was twelve hours ago. That was enough time to fly either directly to the *Baktun* or to an airport along Central America's Pacific coast to refuel or acquire a different airplane. Unless Fierro planned to parachute onto the ship, it had to be a long-range seaplane.

Now what?

"Trust the Cray," Murphy said. The *Oregon*'s Cray supercomputer was one of the fastest pre-quantum machines on the planet, loaded up with every imaginable kind of software. It was the perfect tool for brute-force data acquisition and processing.

Eric hacked into regional air traffic control databases and downloaded twelve hours of radar and satellite tracking logs. These logs provided details like call signs, aircraft IDs, positions, altitudes, speeds, and headings. He and Murph then searched for seaplanes and found several in flight.

But one had lifted off from a private Nicaraguan airfield. The Shin-Maywa US-2 was heading due west toward the dead zone, where the *Oregon* had once battled the *Baktun*.

The two researchers then tracked the US-2's progress on the radar log. About two hundred fifty miles off Nicaragua, its radar signature vanished as it left radar range. Satellite tracking picked it up until about nine hundred thirty nautical miles, when its signal suddenly disappeared.

"What happened to it?" Murph asked. It wasn't possible for the satellite to lose the signal. There weren't any obstructions between the aircraft and low-earth orbit.

"He killed his transponder."

"Why now?"

"Maybe because he landed."

Murph dropped a virtual pin at the GPS location where the transponder shut off, and then drew a fifty-mile radius around it just as Cabrillo reappeared in the doorway.

"Time's up, gents. What do you have for me?"

Remembering the steak and forgetting the sizzle, Eric pointed at the map pin and the fifty-mile-radius marker.

"We have Fierro's type of aircraft and the approximate location of the *Baktun*."

"That data is about two hours old," Murph said. "Can't guarantee he'll stay put or that he's even still there."

"Let's assume he is." Cabrillo studied the map. "He's out in the middle of nowhere—just about where we ran into the pirate vessel."

He looked at the boys. "You think the *Baktun* is one and the same?"

"We do." Both techs nodded, like telepathic twins.

"And I take it no other radar or other signals in the area?"

They both shook their heads. "No, sir."

Juan gave an approving dip of the chin. "That's outstanding work, gentlemen." He threw a thumb over his shoulder at the analog clock behind him. "And with seven minutes to spare."

Both men beamed with pride.

"You've busted your tails. Take a break and head to the galley and fill 'er up. I'm going to need you both shipshape and in Bristol fashion when we get underway."

"Aye, sir." They both stood to leave.

The two techs turned to go, but Cabrillo snagged Murphy by the elbow and pulled him aside.

"One more thing."

"Sir?"

"We're most likely headed for a gunfight. I need you to get your girlfriend off this boat for her sake, and yours. I need your head in the game."

Murph nodded grimly. "Yeah, you're right."

"Get her packed and put her on the Joby immediately. I want her in San Salvador within the hour. I'll have Linda make the travel arrangements. Any idea where she wants to go?"

"She told me she has an aunt in Toronto. But I'm not sure."

"Then we'll get her an open ticket. She can fly anywhere she wants. Tell her to bill us later for any expenses."

"Thank you."

Juan laid a hand on Murph's slumping shoulder.

"Don't look so glum, kiddo. You can catch up with her when this is all over and play all the kissy-face you want."

Murph blushed. "It's not quite like that."

Juan winked. "Yet."

Murph grinned hopefully.

"I'll head up to her cabin right now."

60

Still trapped in her claustrophobic cabin, Linlin Zhang was grateful for the CCTV cameras deployed in the *Oregon*'s research lab. Those four cameras afforded her a perfect view of everything, including the big screens on the computers Murph and Stone had used to crack Eidolon's code and locate the *Baktun*.

Even though she had access to all of the *Oregon*'s two-hundred-plus CCTV cameras, she had decided to only follow Murphy wherever he went rather than randomly investigate the other crew members and departments. Her instincts had proven right. Murphy had been the key to finding the AGI system Peng was so desperate to locate.

And because she had tracked with Murph, she had not only seen but heard and recorded both Eidolon's coded message and the probable location of the *Baktun*.

Now she had to transmit all of that information without getting caught. But with Murphy on his way up to take her to the waiting tiltrotor, she had very little time to accomplish her task.

The main obstacle she faced was avoiding the *Oregon*'s advanced Sniffer electronics suite. It could easily detect her unauthorized radio or satellite/cell transmission and blow her cover.

But she had already put together a plan. She would avoid detection by hiding her secret transmission within an authorized *Oregon* transmission.

Because she had already broken into the *Oregon*'s mainframe, she had access to every aspect of the ship's operations. One of the things she had discovered was the *Oregon*, like many other legitimate commercial cargo ships, automatically uploaded navigational updates every ten seconds to a commercial satellite system. Each update included longitude, latitude, speed, and time.

Linlin took a cue from the brilliant Eidolon. She exchanged decimal numbers from the navigational updates with her own encoded message.

She then set up a program that automatically uploaded those altered navigational updates. Unless someone had a reason to check every decimal number, there was little chance the ruse would be noticed. In fact, navigation systems tolerated minor rounding or fluctuations in such numbers.

But that wasn't enough. After navigational updates were uploaded to a satellite they were then directed to a server on the other end for use by third parties. In this case, she noticed the *Oregon* was connected to a cargo service. But Linlin's Guardian contact didn't have access to it.

To solve that problem, she accessed the *Oregon*'s satellite system on the mainframe and added a secondary IP address—just like adding a "cc" to an email. Now the adulterated navigational update containing her encoded information about Project Q would be delivered to an untraceable dark web Guardian server.

As soon as Eidolon's message about the *Baktun* was deciphered by Murphy and Stone, she encoded her message and then sliced it up into smaller fragments, feeding each one into one of the ten-second satellite updates. In less than three minutes, the first part of the message was delivered to the dark web server.

She had to wait another fifty-three minutes before Murph and Eric cracked the location problem. Once that was solved, she coded, sliced, and uploaded the second part of her message in just fifty seconds.

The more time-consuming task was to erase all of the logs that showed her accessing the *Oregon*'s Cray computer. She also needed to delete all of the other digital breadcrumbs she'd left behind as she traipsed through the mainframe, including the security camera and navigational systems.

She was so utterly focused with her task she lost track of time.

When Murphy knocked on her door it rang like a shotgun blast, sending a shock wave through her system.

"Coming," she said as she frantically shoved her makeshift computer into her backpack with a sweep of her hand and tossed it onto her bed as she crossed over to the door.

"Murph! So glad you stopped by." She waved him inside. "Come in." She saw the hangdog look in his eyes, pretending not to know what was behind it. "Something wrong?"

Murphy shrugged. "No, actually it's good news. The Chairman is arranging for you to fly wherever you need to go and he'll pay your hotel expenses and stuff, too."

"Really? Wow. That's very kind of him. When will this all be happening?"

Murphy ran a hand through his mop of hair.

"Uh . . . now, I guess. You need to get packed right away."

"Oh. So soon?" She pretended to be upset. In fact, she was thrilled to get off the boat and as far away as possible before the *Oregon* techs figured out what she had done.

"Any idea where you want to go?"

"I'm still not sure. I think my aunt in Toronto is my safest bet. She hates the Communists."

Lying was as easy as breathing for the Chinese spy. She had no intention of letting Murph or anyone else know where she was going. She glanced around the room. "I'll need a few minutes to get packed up and ready. Do I have time to take a shower?"

"Sure. Do you need any help?"

"In the shower?"

Murph blushed. "No, I meant packing."

Linlin smiled at his discomfiture. "Give me fifteen minutes and then come get me, okay?"

"Okay."

She gave him a gentle shove out the door and shut it, desperately trying not to shout with joy.

Her plan had worked perfectly, and Eidolon's stolen secret was safely on its way.

61

MONGOLIA

The base camp was located in the Baga Oigor Valley, famous for its twelve-thousand-year-old petroglyphs and other archaeological treasures. The camp was organized around a series of ancient Scythian burial mounds known as kurgans. Like many other scientific expeditions in the region, this camp was comprised of temporary but comfortable housing, satellite dishes, computers, radios, and a steady supply of food and other necessities to service the five-person team of scientists.

Located in the far western reaches of Mongolia near the borders of Russia, China, and Kazakhstan, the remote high-altitude valley hidden deep in the Altai Mountains was about as far away from civilization as one could get. The UNESCO World Heritage Site was also protected by international treaty obligations and was totally off-limits to national military and police intrusions.

In short, it was the perfect place for the Guardian leadership to both hide and operate. "Leadership" was too strong a term for the small band of committed techno-warriors who referred to themselves as the Nexus. Their primary tasks were gathering and synthesizing intelligence, communications, setting objectives, and coordinating attacks.

The "first among equals" within the Nexus was a Scottish national by the name of D'Arcy Falconer, who taught himself Latin at the age of five in order to read Newton's *Principia Mathematica* in the original. The mathematical prodigy mastered the intricacies of computer programming before he could grow the voluminous red beard he now wore like a Pictish berserker.

Falconer was recruited into the Guardians by one of its founding members, a Japanese national named Takai. Falconer then arranged his own mysterious death in a supposed mountaineering accident in the Andes, his body never recovered from the fall into the deep crevasse. His technical knowledge combined with his preternatural tactical and strategic acumen catapulted him into the nomadic Nexus in short order.

The Guardians were a vast international network of crusader scientists animated and unified around the singular idea that artificial intelligence was an extinction-level threat to the entire human race. Their devotion to this idea generated a self-sacrificial loyalty both to the cause and to each other, though the scope of that human loyalty extended only to the small three-person cells in which they were each contained. Replicating like superintelligent bacteria, the Guardians exponentially increased their power and effectiveness through the swarm-like coordination of the Nexus.

The Nexus had provided timely and effective guidance to the rest of the Guardians, all organized within the tightly contained cell structures. The lack of communications between each cell protected the larger organization from disruption. It also minimized the strategic effectiveness of any individual cell.

The Nexus was necessary for coordinated action, but it was also the organization's weakest link. Each member of the Nexus could communicate with every cell in the Guardian body, though that communication was all top-down. If an enemy ever captured one or more of the Nexi (as they called themselves) the entire organization would be put at risk. This was the reason they maintained a nomadic lifestyle in the farthest reaches of the planet. It was also the reason why they had tooth implants loaded with four nanograms of botulinum toxin type A—more than enough for a near-instantaneous death.

Falconer sat at his laptop inside of his tent, the walls whipping in the frigid high winds sweeping the valley.

"You sent for me?" the woman said. Her cheeks were red with cold. The sixty-year-old ethnic Russian was in better health than women half her age. She climbed these rugged mountains with the agility of a Siberian ibex and was the only trained archaeologist on the Nexus team.

Falconer handed her the printout, his face lacking all emotion.

She scanned it, her jaw dropping farther with each word. *Baktun. AGI. Organoid computing. Fierro. Bose.*

"You think it's really possible?" She handed the paper back to him.

Falconer struck a match and lit the corner of the flash paper. It disintegrated into ash in seconds.

"We can't afford to take a chance it isn't."

"But we thought this was still years away."

"Singularities in science are notoriously unpredictable," Falconer said. "The Indian report seems to confirm it. Looks like Bose will cross the finish line before everyone else and in very short order."

"Not if we can stop her."

"My thoughts exactly."

The Russian fell into a camp chair. "What if that message is a trap? Some kind of lure?"

"Highly unlikely. My source is impeccable."

"Who?"

"Our Swiss friend."

The Russian nodded. "He's never failed us yet. Did he say where he got it from?"

"No. But that's the point, isn't it?"

The Russian bolted out of her chair. "If the information is correct, we haven't much time. We've got to find a way to destroy that ship."

Falconer tilted his head, fingering his thick beard. He'd long feared this moment. Humanity now stood on the edge of the abyss. The Russian was right.

The *Baktun* had to be sunk, no matter the sacrifice—even if it meant starting World War III.

62

He had slept like the dead, dreamless and void.

He didn't realize he'd been asleep until he became vaguely aware of consciousness, his mind still on the edge of oblivion. But the fact he was aware that he was aware woke him up a bit more, driving his reluctant mind toward the rippling surface of lucidity.

He didn't want to make that journey, and kept his eyes tightly shut hoping he could fall back into the peaceful abyss of nothingness.

But such was not his fate. His chest ached as if struck by a sledgehammer, the dull pain shallowing his breaths and fueling the raging headache inside of his skull.

A nearby machine issued gentle puffing sounds, and a soft electronic beep tapped out a simple rhythm. He focused on the beep and noticed that, as he did so, it increased in tempo.

"I think he's waking up."

It was an unfamiliar voice speaking. A woman's voice. In Spanish. But a strange Spanish. An accent. German? Italian?

Even these few thoughts hurt his head.

Where was he?

He opened his eyes with difficulty, his lids fluttering against the bright lights. His vision was blurred. He could hardly see through the gauzy film clouding his eyes.

"Yes, he is awake," the woman's voice said.

"It's a miracle," another voice said. Also a woman, though younger.

Nurses, he told himself. He lifted heavy hands and rubbed his eyes until his vision cleared. He took a closer look at the two voices. His heart sank.

Nuns.

"Where am I?"

"You're in the mission hospital on Isla de San Alejo," the older nun said. "We are the Sisters of Divine Mercy." Like the other nun, she wore a nurse's uniform. "You're fortunate to be alive."

The younger nun smiled beatifically. "God must have a special purpose for you."

"How are you called?" the other nurse asked.

The man frowned for a moment, genuinely confused. He wasn't sure. He'd had many names. What was the last one?

The old nun frowned. "Don't you know your own name?"

The man looked down at his aching chest. Thick bandages covered the place where it hurt the most. IV and blood bag lines were taped to the backs of his hands. He touched the cannula under his nose as his eyes caught sight of the oxygen regulator puffing away by his bedside.

"You were shot," the old nurse said, hoping to jar his memory.

"And you lost a lot of blood. A friend brought you here, just in time."

"It's a miracle we had your blood type here. Very rare."

The man noticed the younger nun had a bandage on her forearm, exactly where a blood-draw needle would be placed.

"*Gracias*," he whispered hoarsely. He was irreligious, but not an ingrate.

The young nurse blushed as if caught in a sin, her bandage a kind of immodesty.

"Your name?" the older one repeated, as if he were a stupid child. "Do you remember your name?"

He nodded. He remembered now. It all came back. The attack. Olmedo. The tall man in the red bandana.

He knew that man.

He clenched his teeth, raging.

The heart monitor alarmed as his blood pressure surged.

The young nurse's eyes widened. "What's happening to him?"

The old nun grabbed a hypodermic needle, filled it with sedative, and fed it into his IV tube.

Moments later, the man's eyes got heavy. He felt the darkness falling over his mind like a heavy blanket, fading his headache. His eyes closed against his will. He heard a distant voice, almost like an echo.

"What is your name?" the old nun asked.

He saw the man's face again. He hated him. The woman's voice was fading.

"Your name? Tell me your name."

He whispered his name. The last one he'd used. Not his real name. Never his real name.

"V . . . Var . . . Vargas."

"Your first name, my son?"

He didn't answer.

His mind searched for the name of the man in the red bandana. He clutched to his image like a drowning sailor at sea clinging to a piece of drifting flotsam, hoping for rescue. Hoping for his name.

But still Vargas couldn't find it. He held on for as long as he could until his mind finally let go, swallowed by the fathomless dark.

63

Emily Nighswonger's eyes fluttered open. She had no idea where she was, but noticed the IV tube inserted into one of her heavily tattooed arms. She lay rock-still in her bed, unable to move despite the lack of restraints, though she managed to roll her head to one side. She caught a glimpse of pine-studded mountains shrouded in fog framed in a large picture window. A serene Chopin nocturne played softly overhead.

Her face clouded with confusion as the room's only door silently swung open.

Peng De pushed a steel cart in front of him, its tray covered with a white cloth. He wore surgical scrubs like a medical professional, though his face was unmasked. He wheeled the cart next to her bed.

"Doctor . . . where . . . am I?" she said in flawless Mandarin.

"You're in a special clinic. You were in an accident, remember?" Peng responded in British-accented English with a low, soothing voice. He noticed the small spot of blood on her head bandage.

"No, I don't." Nighswonger took a deep breath. "What happened exactly?"

"You were nearly killed."

She struggled to move, but neither her torso nor limbs responded. She blanched with fear.

"I'm paralyzed."

"Yes, but only temporarily." Peng nodded at the IV. "I've administered a small dose of a neuromuscular blocking agent."

"Why?"

"To restrain you, of course. It was that or chain you to the bed. This seemed a more pleasant alternative."

Nighswonger's eyes narrowed.

"You're not my doctor."

"No, but I am your savior, if you cooperate."

The door opened again. Square-jawed Agent Tu entered the room. He had arranged for Nighswonger's transport from the hospital to this secret facility. He took up a position in the corner, his large-caliber pistol barely concealed beneath his ill-fitted suit coat.

"You're MSS."

"Very perceptive."

"I have nothing to say to you."

"I have a few questions for you. Please answer them truthfully and I can make you comfortable."

"Go to hell."

"You are already there."

Peng smiled as the woman's face flooded with panic.

Peng pulled back the cloth on the steel cart, revealing three syringes on the stainless steel tray. He let her study the needles.

"Now do you remember the car wreck?" Peng asked.

Nighswonger turned her head aside, and stared stone-faced at the ceiling. A single tear fell from the corner of her bloodshot eye.

"Yes, of course you do. It's all coming back now, isn't it?" Peng lifted one of the syringes, and plunged its needle into the IV access port.

"I have just administered a newly developed drug, Zhenqing-7. It's a biochemical compound ten times more effective than Pentothal, otherwise known as a truth serum. In a moment, the compound will take effect and I will ask you a series of questions. You will answer those questions truthfully because the drug will make you answer them, and there is nothing you can do to resist telling me the truth. Understood?"

A few moments later, the brain-altering compound took effect. Emily's hardened features softened as her eyes dulled and her mouth fell open.

Peng sat on her bed and took her hand in his, patting it like a father comforting a frightened daughter.

"What is your real name?"

"Emily," she whispered in a raspy voice.

"Nighswonger?"

"Yes."

"Excellent. And you were formerly a biomedical researcher at the Lawrence Livermore National Lab?"

"Yes."

"But now you are a member of the Guardian organization, correct?"

"Yes."

"You were with a man named Aidan Scally. Was he a Guardian as well?"

"Yes."

"He's dead, by the way."

Nighswonger's breath held for a moment, then she whispered a pathetic "Oh."

"Let's talk about the Guardians. How large is your organization?"

"Three people."

"Only three? That's not possible."

"Only three people . . . in my cell."

"So the Guardians are organized into cells?"

"Yes. Each cell, three people."

Peng nodded. "As I've long suspected. You organized that way so that no one of you can betray all the other members of the organization, correct?"

"Yes."

"How many Guardians are there in total?"

"Don't know. No one does. The cell organization prevents it."

"Then give me an estimate. Surely you have thought about it. Fifty? One hundred?"

"Five hundred."

"People?"

"Cells." Through sheer force of will she managed a small smile. "And growing."

Peng frowned, hiding his surprise. He glanced over at Agent Tu. The normally stoic operative couldn't conceal his shock.

"What foreign governments do you work for?" Peng asked, his even voice still calm and comforting.

"None."

"Are you mercenaries?"

"No."

"Political terrorists?"

"No."

"Then why do you kill and destroy?"

"Ideology."

"And what is your ideology?"

"AGI is evil. Must destroy it . . . before it destroys humanity."

"You said you operated in small cells. But your attacks are coordinated and effective. How are you contacted?"

"Encrypted text. Burner phones. One-way comms."

"From whom?"

"The Nexus."

"Nexus? What is the Nexus?"

"Leaders."

"How many are in the Nexus? Who belongs to it? Where are they located?"

"Don't know."

"If you don't know who the leadership is, how do you know it's not a CIA operation? Or FSB?"

"We attack . . . everyone."

"Can you tell me all of the attacks you have participated in? Places, dates, objectives?"

"Yes."

Peng glanced over at Tu. The agent pulled a Sony digital voice recorder from his pocket and handed it to Peng.

"Please proceed."

Nighswonger spent the next ten minutes providing specific mission details from her past operations.

Peng fought the urge to strike the helpless woman as she confessed to over a dozen attacks that resulted in the loss of millions of dollars of state property and valuable Chinese lives.

"And that's all you can remember?"

"Yes."

Peng held up the voice recorder and Tu pocketed it for later transcription and dissemination.

"Any other names you can think of? Any Guardians you haven't already mentioned? Friends? Allies of your organization?"

Emily blinked hard, trying to fight against the serum that was beginning to wear off. Her teeth clenched.

Peng stroked her forearm, and cooed soothingly. "Emily, don't fight this. If I'm forced to give you another dose, you *will* talk. But the risk to your sanity would be very grave. I don't want that. Neither do you. Just give me the name, and then you can rest."

Nighswonger's clenched jaw softened, and her lips parted.

"Only saw her . . . once."

"Go on."

"We call her the Huli Jing."

"The Fox Spirit. A shape-shifter. A spirit of deception."

Nighswonger smiled fondly. "Yes."

"Tell me about her."

"Beautiful. Brilliant. With special knowledge. A true believer."

"What is her nationality?"

"Chinese."

Peng lifted an eyebrow, surprised and curious.

"What is this 'special knowledge' that Fox Spirit possesses?"

"She works for you."

"The Chinese government?"

"Yes."

"Which branch?"

"MSS."

Peng was stunned. He glanced over to Agent Tu.

"How did you meet her?"

"Computer science conference."

"Where and when was this computer science conference?"

"Frankfurt. Three years ago."

"Did she have a name then? Other than Fox Spirit?"

"Yes."

"What was her name?"

Nighswonger took a deep breath and held it, as if willing herself to die. Despite the gossamer web of altered brain chemistry clouding her mind, something deep inside of her knew she must not utter the name.

Peng marveled. He'd never seen such resistance against his mind-altering drug. He didn't want to give her another dose. That would only induce hallucinations at this juncture. What he needed was the truth.

"Her name, my sweet? You've been so helpful. You must tell me her name. Please." He squeezed her hand gently.

Nighswonger coughed, unable to hold her breath any longer. The drug had won.

"The name, Emily?"

Her eyes welled with tears.

"Zhang."

"Zhang? Zhang is a common name. Zhang what?"

"Linlin Zhang."

★

Peng fought with every ounce of his strength to control the sudden surge of rage and shame electrifying his entire body. The woman he had recruited, trained, nurtured and, yes, longed for had betrayed him.

Perhaps the serum had worn off. Perhaps this vile creature was using Linlin's name to destroy her.

"You are certain of this name, Emily? We wouldn't want to punish the wrong person, would we?"

"Yes. I'm sure. Linlin Zhang."

"I say that's impossible. What proof do you have?"

"Zephyron . . . Dynamics."

Linlin's German employer, Peng reminded himself. The front company that arranged for the ASML lithography machine transfer that was destroyed.

"A plane was destroyed. Was she involved?"

Nighswonger nodded.

"How? Did she tell you about the transfer of the equipment?"

"Yes."

Peng still couldn't believe it. His best operative? A traitor?

"What does Linlin Zhang look like?"

"Young. Striking. Serious."

Peng's eyes narrowed. He knew in his soul she was describing Linlin.

His desire for Zhang had blinded him. The emotions welling up now threatened to overwhelm him. He tamped it all back down through the sheer force of his considerable will, his mind already plotting the next steps.

"Anything else you can tell me about this Zhang woman? The Guardians?"

Nighswonger shook her head. "No. Nothing."

"Are you certain?"

She nodded. "I'm so . . . tired." She closed her eyes.

"Of course. You have done well. Let me give you a sedative."

Peng stood as he reached for the hypodermic containing a lethal dose of fentanyl. He planned a quick and humane death for the terrorist. He was not a cruel man, and rejected the violent methods of his predecessors.

But that was before she had confessed to a list of murderous crimes against his people.

Instead, Peng picked up the empty hypodermic he had already used. He pulled back the plunger and filled the void entirely with air. He then inserted the needle into Nighswonger's IV port and smoothly depressed the plunger under his thumb, forcing the deadly bubble into her bloodstream with cold precision.

Moments later, the air embolus did its work.

Emily's eyes snapped open as her body jerked involuntarily, her mouth pried open by a horrified grimace. Her chest heaved with short, shallow breaths that could gather no air, and her numbed fingers twitched as they tried to claw the sheets. Sweat beaded across her paling face even as her lips blued. Her panicked eyes fell on Peng's smiling face, his arms crossed as he stood triumphantly above her.

Nighswonger's breathing shallowed into ragged gasps, her sightless eyes darting wildly across the ceiling. The fabric of her gown rippled with each thud of her hammering heart until she took one last, final draw of empty breath from her gaping mouth.

Peng savored the image of the dead Guardian's corpse. He hoped her death was as painful and terrifying as it appeared to be.

He turned to Agent Tu.

"Colonel Shi is in San Salvador. Get him on a secured line immediately."

Tu nodded curtly and sped from the room to fetch a satellite phone.

Peng pulled the sheet over Nighswonger's face as he made his final plans for his beautiful traitor Linlin Zhang.

64

The Joby's six propellers were spinning up, no louder than a human conversation. Gomez sat in the pilot's seat, his eyes avoiding the touching scene unfolding beyond his windscreen. A swiftly setting sun threw long shadows over the deck as the eastward sky darkened into deeper blues.

Murphy towered over Linlin, his eyes wet with emotion, his smile forced.

"I can't thank you enough for everything you did for me," Linlin said.

"Anytime you need me, you know I'll be there." He handed back her phone. Cabrillo had confiscated it when she boarded. "I charged it up for you."

"Thanks." She slipped it into her backpack. "I'm sorry we didn't have more time together. Perhaps you can get some time off from your work and come visit me in Toronto."

"I'd like that a lot." He fished a card out of his pocket. "There's a private email where you can reach me. Untraceable. Just be careful where you send it from."

"Yes, of course." She took it and slipped it into her pants pocket. "I'll contact you as soon as I get settled and can set up some sort of security arrangement."

"Can't wait. I wish I could ride with you to San Salvador, but I've got—"

She touched a finger to his lips. "I understand." She leaned into Murph's chest, his long arms enveloping her small frame. She pulled him tight for a long hug, then released him.

"I guess this is goodbye," she said, glancing up into his face.

Murph leaned down and kissed her gently on the mouth.

Linlin pretended to swoon, then ended the kiss.

She grabbed her backpack and scampered into the copilot seat next to Gomez. She waved meekly at Murph as Gomez threw him a half salute before engaging the controls and lofting the Joby into the air. The electric vertical takeoff craft sped toward the coast, its carbon-fiber skin licked by the last rays of fading sunlight.

Murph's heart sank as the Joby vanished into the deepening twilight, afraid he'd never see Linlin again.

★

EL SALVADOR

The Joby was back in the air and already hurtling over the coast as Linlin approached the private-jet terminal. She didn't bother going inside. Linda Ross had already made her a hotel reservation in the city and handed her a fully flexible airline ticket so she could make her own flight arrangements the next day. All she needed to do was hail an Uber and get to her hotel.

She stood in front of the terminal doorway, pulled out her phone, and activated her Uber app, typing in the address of the hotel. There was only one Uber ride nearby. She was glad it was there and hailed it. According to the app it would arrive in just two minutes.

In the rush to pack, shower, and leave, the MSS spy had little time to consider when she would contact Peng or what she would tell him. She couldn't inform him about the *Baktun* or its precious cargo or else he would attempt to seize it. Considering China's vast naval resources he might be able to grab it before the Guardians could destroy it.

As far as the Guardians were concerned, China acquiring AGI was the worst possible outcome imaginable. To hold Peng off, she simply needed to report that the Mark Murphy lead was a dead end. In order to maintain her cover, she needed to communicate to him her great disappointment and her zealous desire to immediately find the next target of inquiry. She also had to be careful not to draw his unwanted attentions. Despite his promise to the contrary, the man's ego was only matched by his libido. With any luck, both would soon overwhelm him.

Linlin had been playing this dangerous game of double agent for quite some time now. She never felt comfortable in that role, but it was that discomfort that kept her from getting caught. She also had the feeling her time was running out as a double agent and she considered how she might be of use to the Guardians if she abandoned her post with China's state security apparatus.

She brushed these thoughts aside as the Uber approached. She double-checked her app, confirming the car make and model, license plate, and driver photograph as it came to a halt. She wasn't one to take chances. She jumped into the back seat of the Toyota compact and buckled herself in.

Because she ordered the Uber on the app, the address was already posted on the driver's phone. There was no need to tell him where to go or even attempt to engage in polite conversation through the unexpected plexiglass security window separating the two of them. Six minutes outside of the airport the Uber fed into the flow of speeding traffic on the way to the Hilton.

She buried her nose in her phone and scrolled through her emails and texts searching for confirmation that her delivery to the anonymous internet dead drop had been picked up, something she hadn't been able to do while on board the *Oregon*. There was no indication it had been received, but her Guardian contact might have been overly cautious and covered his tracks.

Linlin pulled up her search engine, trying to plot out her next moves, careful to leave a trail of breadcrumbs that, if intercepted by Peng, would indicate she was actively searching for other AGI leads. She occasionally flipped to her Uber app live map to verify the driver was on track, but twenty minutes into her trip she failed to notice the first turn off the prescribed route. But the second unexpected turn caught her attention. They were now in an industrial district.

"Driver? Where are we going? Why aren't we on our route?"

"*No hablo inglés*," the driver muttered.

Linlin flipped to Google Translate, spoke into the app, and held the phone against the plexiglass as she played the Spanish translation for him.

The man shrugged and kept driving.

"Stop the car. *Alto! Alto!*" She pulled on the door handle, but the door was locked. The driver punched the gas as she screamed and pounded on the plexiglass security window.

A minute later, the Toyota slammed to a stop at the loading dock of China Biopharma, a pharmaceutical warehouse, far from prying eyes.

Linlin glanced through her window just as Colonel Shi Chang stepped out of the shadows and into the harsh light of the dock's sodium lamps. The door locks clicked open, a sign for her to get out.

She wasn't sure what was going on. Chang's stoic features betrayed no emotion. There was no way the MSS operative could possibly know what she had done—or did he? This detour wasn't part of the plan. And how could he have known she had left the *Oregon*?

Her heart raced. The longer she sat there, the guiltier she looked. She swallowed hard. She had long ago made her peace with this moment. She knew it could come some day. Why not today?

But she wasn't doomed yet. She had bluffed her way out of tighter spots than this one.

She flashed a big smile, shoved the door open, grabbed her pack, and stepped outside, slamming the door shut behind her. The Uber's tires screeched as it rocketed away, filling the air with the acrid stench of burnt rubber.

Her father taught her that courage was better armor than steel, she reminded herself, as Chang's vicious mouth bent with an oily smile.

65

Unlike his boss, Peng De, Colonel Chang had no patience for truth serums. A chemically altered mind would indeed answer specific questions, but that presupposed the interrogator knew exactly what questions to ask—like a fine needle searching for a thin vein.

In Chang's experience, abject terror in anticipation of insufferable agony was a far more effective device for getting the whole truth, and actual pain doubly so. Just as the single slice of a surgeon's scalpel could open up the belly, panic's razor-sharp blade forced the victim unwittingly to "spill their guts" both literally and figuratively. Unfortunately, he wasn't authorized to use physical force—at least not yet.

To her credit, Zhang didn't flinch when he told her a captured Guardian had named her as a co-conspirator. Nor did she balk when he laid out the instruments of torture he would soon be using on her—even if she did cooperate.

Chang peppered her with a dozen questions over and over. Her answers were always slightly different, a possible sign she was telling the truth. Perfectly memorized answers always meant the response was rehearsed. As hard as he tried, he couldn't get her to admit any guilt. The video camera recorded everything. He would forward the digital files to Peng in Shanghai for an advanced computer analysis, searching for micro movements in her face and eyes for any other indicators she was lying.

He was due for Peng's conference call soon. There was no point in questioning her further.

"Peng has ordered a traitor's death for you. How quickly and how painlessly it comes depends on you."

"I can prove my innocence," was all she offered, neither panicked nor pleading, knowing full well Chang's promise of Peng's tender mercies in exchange for her cooperation was a lie. But she was quick to add, "I know you're only obeying orders, but I suggest you step very carefully."

Chang considered her words, but he had heard Nighswonger's confession with his own ears. He was certain Linlin was a traitor. And yet, she had planted a seed of doubt, or at the very least, caution. Had the Guardian managed to lie even under the influence of Zhenqing-7?

Chang was surprised a highly trained operative like Zhang had been so careless. He was certain the appearance of only a single Uber car would have alerted her that something was amiss, though his technician assured him the ruse would work. GPS spoofing made sure that only Chang's compromised Uber would appear on Linlin's Uber app. A connection error attack blocked all other Uber drivers nearby from seeing Zhang's ride request, and a geofence around the private-jet terminal guaranteed the La Liga Uber driver Chang had hired would be the only car assigned to her.

Of course, what Linlin also didn't realize was Peng had fitted her covert cyberdeck computer with his own secret tracking device. Nor could she be aware of the confession he had milked out of the red-headed Guardian in Taiwan.

Linlin Zhang's arms and legs were zip-tied to the chair. Her pouty lower lip had stopped bleeding after Chang had slapped away the arrogant smile from her pretty doll's face.

Most victims would have offered him a generous bribe by now, and women, the treasures of their pearly flesh. He considered harming the traitor more severely, and taking advantage of her lithe and compliant body. But Chang knew she was the object of Peng's lust and vengeance, so he would indulge neither.

Chang checked his watch. Twenty minutes until the Peng call. He nodded to his tech in the far corner working on Zhang's computer.

"Any luck?"

"Not yet."

★

Linlin Zhang felt the fool. A still, small voice had told her the single Uber car on her ride request was problematic. She should have listened to it. Too late for regrets, and ridiculous to think she would ever get the chance to take advantage of the lesson learned. She took a small satisfaction in the momentary fear she saw in Chang's eyes when she threatened him though bound to the chair. Men were so weak, the violent ones especially.

Her only concern now was surviving this ordeal without betraying the Guardians or the message she had sent.

All she could see were two options. Lie convincingly about her innocence or lie about the information Peng so desperately wanted.

Neither might work.

She considered confessing her role as a Guardian and accepting her fate. But the sight of the torture instruments Chang had gleefully revealed on the surgical tray had robbed her of her father's courage. She strained every sinew of her soul to keep from crying out and begging for mercy. Only the sure knowledge that no mercy would come kept her mouth tightly shut.

Linlin also worried that Chang's tech would crack into her computer, but that was highly unlikely. She had designed the security system herself. Still, there was a chance he would figure it out. There was only one way to prevent that. She considered her options.

Chang's fear was the key. Or at least a thread she could tug on, however carefully.

"I must relieve myself, comrade," she said to Chang.

"What do I care?"

"Please respect my basic needs. I very much need to use the restroom."

"Shut up and hold it."

"You're in charge. You have all the power. You therefore have the ability to respect my dignity."

"Why should I care for the dignity of a traitor?"

"Because respect earns compliance. Isn't that what Peng wants from me?"

Chang's eyes narrowed, thinking.

Linlin lowered her head, and whispered.

The colonel knelt down to hear what she was saying.

"Do you remember what I said about stepping very carefully?" she said in a cold, soft voice that sent chills through Chang's steely spine.

Chang stood and pointed at one of his female operatives standing in the corner.

"Take her to the *máofáng*. And hurry."

★

The female guard cut Linlin's bonds with a Spyderco tactical knife. She pocketed the blade and grabbed Linlin roughly by the elbow, pushing her in front of her and toward the steel door into the women's bathroom.

"Privacy?" Linlin asked.

The scowling guard yanked the door open, shoved her inside, stepped in behind her, and shut the door. She pointed at one of the three stalls.

"Privacy. There. Hurry."

Linlin smiled as she rubbed her aching wrists, her hands just in front of her mouth.

"Thank you for your kindness, comrade. Men are such beasts. Only another woman understands a woman's needs, don't you agree?"

"Hurry."

"Which stall do you want me to use?"

The guard shifted her eyes to the stalls to point one out.

That nanosecond of distraction was just enough time for Linlin to thrust the rigid fingers of her right hand into the woman's throat, shattering her larynx, cutting off both her wind and voice. The woman's hands unconsciously grasped at her ruined throat as Linlin cracked the side of her skull with her elbow, striking the mandibular nerve behind the jaw and knocking her out instantly.

Linlin caught the guard's body before it could hit the ground. She set her gently down on the filthy tile floor knowing she would die of asphyxiation before she regained consciousness. Such was her service to the Party.

Zhang pressed the door lock shut, and rifled through the guard's pockets until she found the razor-sharp knife and snapped it open.

It would have to do.

She glanced over at the large mirror over the sink. She saw her father standing behind her, his rough farmer's hands resting on her shoulders. He smiled proudly and whispered in her ear.

"Be brave, daughter."

66

Peng paced the vast videoconference room at MSS headquarters, his blood pressure soaring. The big screen on the wall was black and flashed giant red sinograms that read "No connection" on the other end of the broadcast.

Colonel Chang was twenty-seven minutes late on his video call—something was clearly wrong. He supposed it was a technical issue, but his intuition feared something far worse.

The last message Peng got from Chang was a cell phone call informing him the traitorous wench Zhang was in the colonel's custody. They also set up an appointed time for the conference call. The colonel was conducting a preliminary interview with her, softening her up psychologically for Peng's interrogation over the internet. No matter what answers Zhang gave—true or false—he would then release Chang to do his worst to her short of death. Chang would then escort her back to China, where Peng would personally mete out her agonizing execution. With any luck, she would have already divulged all of the information he needed to assault the Guardian organization directly. More important, he wanted to know how long she had been disloyal to him and to the state.

Suddenly, the videoconference screen beeped and the red sinograms flipped to green, reading "Connection secure." The screen went from black to live action. Colonel Chang fell down into a chair in front of his laptop, his clothes slathered in drying blood.

Peng gasped.

"Colonel Chang! Are you wounded? What happened?"

The colonel fought back his emotions.

"I'm fine, comrade. The traitor Zhang killed one of my guards . . . and then killed herself."

"How?"

"She slit her throat with the guard's knife."

"Foolish guard."

Chang motioned at his ruined clothes. It was clear he had wiped blood off of his face as well. "I tried to stop Zhang's bleeding, but it was too late by the time we broke through the door."

Peng swore violently, something he hadn't done in years. Self-control was a matter of both pride and decorum, especially in front of his lessers. But Zhang's final act of betrayal was to rob him of the pleasure of torturing her to death for her many disloyalties.

"Please tell me you learned something about the Guardians before she took the coward's way out."

"Unfortunately, I can't. She protested her innocence and said she could prove it."

"It is impossible for me to express in any of the several languages I speak how desperately disappointed I am in your handling of this affair, Colonel Chang."

The colonel sat up a little straighter.

"But there is some good news, sir."

"How could there be?"

"While I was interrogating the traitor, my tech was attempting to break into Zhang's computer. Unfortunately, it was biometrically password-protected—by voice command, actually."

"That explains why she slit her throat," Peng said. Had the biometrics been fingerprints or retinas, the colonel could have easily amputated the correct fingers or removed the eyes and applied them.

Peng nodded thoughtfully, secretly admiring Linlin's tactical brilliance.

"By silencing her own voice, she robbed us of whatever valuable information she was trying to hide. Worse, she was demonstrating self-sacrificing loyalty to the bandit Guardians she was in thrall to. Colonel, I don't have to tell you how important it is for you to personally return that computer to my office. Perhaps one of our scientists can find a way to—"

"That won't be necessary," Chang interrupted Peng with a raised hand. "We found a way to break through."

"How?"

"My tech took a sample of her voice from my video interrogation, ran it through an AI program, and manipulated it. He was then able to answer Zhang's password prompts in her own voice and break into her computer."

"Outstanding!" Peng beamed, unable to hide his excitement. "What have you learned?"

"Agent Zhang did, in fact, discover the AGI program you were searching for, along with an organoid computer to sustain it. The computer and program are known as Project Q."

Peng's elation turned to panic.

"Where is it located?"

"It's located on board the research vessel *Baktun* in the far eastern Pacific. I'll send you the coordinates, though they are only speculative."

"Is it already online?"

"No, sir. According to her message, it launches in approximately forty-eight hours."

Peng's heart raced. There was still time to avoid total catastrophe—but just barely.

"Are you confident this information is correct, Colonel? Could it be a ruse? A magician's diversion to hide something else?"

"She sent the message to a dead drop server address on the dark web. It is highly unlikely this was a trick, since Zhang never would have expected us to acquire her computer, let alone crack into it."

Peng marched over to a desk phone and yanked up the receiver to make a call, still interrogating Chang. "Who owns this vessel? Who's behind all of this? The Americans?"

"No, sir. It's your Colombian contact, Amador Fierro. It's his project entirely."

Peng stopped dialing. "Are you sure?"

"According to the message Zhang sent."

Peng nearly crushed the phone in his hand. It was yet another deception—and betrayal—by someone he thought was an ally.

"I'll deal with Fierro myself," Peng hissed. "Tell your tech he is a hero of the state and will be rewarded for it. You as well, Colonel. In fact, your entire team."

"Thank you, sir. We are privileged to serve under—"

Peng snapped off the transmission, and punched the number for his secretary. His PLA Navy liaison was on emergency standby for just such an event, as were the corresponding officers of the Air Force and Army. The Central Military Commission had already granted Peng and any other ranking department head carte blanche for any operation regarding AGI.

Peng suddenly realized if he could capture the AGI he might well realize his lifelong ambition to achieve the Politburo Standing Committee and—dare he hope?—the chairmanship of the Party itself. China's future, as well as his own, depended on capturing that ship.

"Get me Admiral Qian—top priority."

67

It was late, but Murphy couldn't sleep and, worse, couldn't game. He was heartsick. It had been four hours since Linlin had left the ship and they were now far from shore. The five-hundred-ninety-foot *Oregon* was well underway, flying at over sixty knots across the water like a cigarette boat, the air blowing across her decks like a windstorm.

Murphy wished he had told Linlin exactly how he felt about her. He also worried for her safety. The Chicoms were superlative spy hunters, and he couldn't protect her now that she was out of his reach. She might not be safe in Toronto. She might not even make it there.

He asked Linda Ross for permission to call her at the hotel, but his request was denied for operational security reasons, which he completely understood. He thought he might be able to tell her over the phone what he couldn't in person, but in truth he was kind of relieved when he wasn't allowed to make the call. He didn't want to scare her away or take advantage of the fact she trusted him enough to reach out to him for protection.

But he still missed her terribly. He decided to console himself by going back to her cabin. They had created a few great memories there. Maybe those could be a down payment on even better ones in the future.

At least a guy could hope.

Her cabin door was unlocked. Murph stepped inside, flipped the light on, and looked around. He took a deep breath through his nose just to catch a whiff of her familiar scent before the room got nuked with industrial-strength Pine-Sol by the cleaning crew tomorrow. The small bed was still neatly made, and the tiny desk cleared. They'd spent a lot of hours there, catching up on the good times they shared and remembering the hard professors and tough classes they suffered through together at MIT.

Murph turned to leave, but a silvery flash in the corner of the floor caught his eye. He crossed over to the far bulkhead and picked up a curved piece of thin silver-plated metal about two inches long. It looked just like the pocket clip of a ballpoint pen.

Probably fell off some fancy pen she had, Murph told himself. He started to toss it into the empty wastepaper basket by the desk, but something stopped him. He pulled the clip close to his eyes and examined it with closer scrutiny. He saw a tiny circular contact point at the base of the clip. He'd never seen anything like that before. Or had he?

He took it over to the steel desk and set it down, putting the contact point down first.

Click.

The pen clip was now magnetically attached to the desk.

Murph's confusion turned to worry as the subroutines of his computerlike brain began running emergency scripts. Something told him this was bad.

Really bad.

He dashed out the door and headed to his lab to figure out what it was.

★

Thirty minutes later, Cabrillo, Max, and Linda stood in Murphy's research lab. Cabrillo was in a set of silk pajamas and deerskin slippers, while Max wore a ratty old terry-cloth robe over a faded SEAL T-shirt and flip-flops, scratching his large belly and yawning like a hippo. Linda in her duty uniform was the night watch officer on deck.

"What's the emergency?" Juan asked, clearly agitated.

Murphy pointed to the pen clip on the desktop, stripped down to its component parts. The three officers leaned over to examine it.

"You want to show us some trash you found?" Max asked. "I'm heading back to my rack."

Murphy pointed at the curved strip of silver. "This is a high-gain antenna filament." He then pointed at the miniature magnet, now removed. "And this little speck is a magnetic contact point, used to attach to a micro transmitter."

"Transmitter?" Linda asked. "Like for a radio?"

"A radio, or a computer."

"Where'd you find this, son?" Juan asked.

"Linlin's cabin, about half an hour ago. I brought it down here to examine it. I'm positive it's for some kind of device she must have smuggled on board."

"We checked her things," Linda said. "All she had in that bag was a few personal items, an e-reader, and a bunch of pens. And of course, we had her phone until we gave it back to her today."

Murphy shrugged. "If she's with the MSS, they might have figured out a way to hide the component parts in ordinary things like pens. And I sure didn't examine that e-reader. No telling what kind of motherboard or CPU it was hiding."

"What could she do with a computer?" Max asked. "Isn't our mainframe protected from all of that?"

"I already contacted Stoney. He's checking computer logs now. If it was anybody else, I'd say she couldn't have hacked our system. But Linlin Zhang is top drawer, and if she's working for the Chicoms, she's got the best in the business backing her up."

"What are the chances she erased her logs to cover her tracks?" Linda asked.

"About one hundred percent," Murphy admitted.

"So your little China doll is a spy," Max said. He turned to Linda. "We should call the American embassy in San Salvador and have them pick her up."

"I'll call the Hilton first," Linda said. "If she didn't check in, we'll know she's flown the coop. If she's still there, then we'll have the CIA station chief pay her a little visit."

"She's the least of our problems right now," Cabrillo said. "We have to assume she did hack the system, if she's half as good as lover boy here thinks she is."

"That means she knows what we know," Max said.

Linda frowned. "And so do the Chinese."

Murph shook his head. "I'm such an idiot. She played me."

"Played you? That girl Jimi Hendrix'd your Stratocaster, son," Max said. "With prejudice."

Murphy turned toward Juan, his voice cracking with emotion. "I'm so sorry."

"Your poor judgment has put our mission and our ship at risk."

Max glowered at Murphy. "Too bad we never built a brig."

"Never thought we needed one," Linda said.

Cabrillo laid a hand on one of Murphy's slumping shoulders.

"I'm confining you to quarters until I can figure out what to do with you."

"But, sir, I'm your best gunner. We're heading into battle—you said so yourself."

"I know. And that's on you, too. When you screw up, it doesn't just affect you."

Murphy reddened with shame. "So I've put the *Oregon* in double jeopardy?"

"When this is all over," Max said, "you and me are gonna have a little talk about the birds and the bees and the Chinese double agents, capisce?"

Murphy nodded.

"Aye, sir."

68

Murphy confined himself to his cabin while the rest of the crew made preparations for the mission ahead. The *Baktun* had proven itself a worthy opponent, deploying weapons they had never seen before. They had barely survived the last encounter. There was no telling what other techno-tricks the mystery ship had up its sleeve.

He had no interaction with the crew save for the knock on his cabin door preceding meal deliveries. Clearly nobody wanted to talk to him. And who could blame them? No doubt the scuttlebutt about him had flown fast and furiously. If he hadn't been so stupid, they wouldn't have anything to gossip about. Juan, Max, and Linda were his ranking officers, but also faithful friends. Though they would never say anything to damage his reputation he still felt overwhelmed with shame for having been played by Linlin and guilt for letting his friends down.

The only genuine kindness shown him so far came from Maurice, the ancient ship's steward. When he delivered Murphy's evening meal, he whispered with a knowing smile, "This, too, shall pass, m'lad" before departing.

Murphy's aching fear was the very real possibility Cabrillo would fire him when the mission was over. He loved his work on the *Oregon*, but the thought of losing his incredible friends was eating him alive. Worse, he couldn't be at the weapons station deploying his unmatched skills to protect his friends. If any of them were killed in the upcoming combat, that would be on him, too.

Like many other high-IQ individuals, Murphy was plagued with an inability to stay still. Some people called it attention deficit disorder. One school counselor informed his mother that her gifted son was "on the spectrum." All Murph knew was that his intense curiosity couldn't rest without trying to solve the next puzzle his brilliant mind was always searching for.

And now that he had time on his hands, he decided to pick at the splinter that had been festering in his mind ever since he and Eric had cracked Eidolon's code. He just couldn't shake the idea that a premium hacker like Eidolon with his trickster-god reputation would be content with burying a simple ASCII-coded message inside of a mundane steganography matrix.

Murphy's nagging intuition told him that there must be another code-within-the-code and he was determined to find it.

69

Senior Captain Zhao Meili stood on the bridge of her ship heaving beneath the heavy swells. She held the binoculars tightly to her eyes, scanning the windy skies until—*there!*—a chute fluttered open and the man beneath its canopy began his hazardous descent.

Zhao was the first woman in the People's Liberation Army Navy to achieve full command of a surface combat vessel. The Dalian Naval Academy graduate was awarded not only the command of a combat vessel but also the distinction of conducting a round-the-world cruise with the newly commissioned *Fuzhou*, the latest and most powerful version of China's Type 055 destroyer. Like her crew and contingent of fire-breathing Marines, she wore her Navy's iconic digital blue-gray naval combat uniform with cap, shoulder boards, and gold-trimmed insignia displaying her hard-won rank.

The *Fuzhou*'s last port of call was the remote Pacific island nation of Vanuatu and now she was steaming across the vast Pacific toward the Panama Canal. The passage of the Chinese warship through the canal would prove a symbolic repudiation of America's outdated Monroe Doctrine. It would also demonstrate the strategic threat China's blue-water Navy posed to the Western Hemisphere.

Zhao had been selected for this assignment because of her distinguished service record, her aggressive instincts and preternatural skill in tactical warfare. No one was better suited for this mission.

But now that mission had been interrupted by Admiral Qian's urgent call ordering her to a new location on a matter of utmost national security. He told her in no uncertain terms that China's future was at stake. To prove his point, he gave her permission to destroy any opposition to her mission, even if that meant taking on the Americans.

Nothing could have pleased her more.

Zhao's star was swiftly rising, but even she could scarcely believe Qian's promise of an early promotion to rear admiral upon successful completion of the emergency reassignment. He described this mission as the most important of her career, and perhaps in all of China's history.

Zhao turned her binoculars to the *Fuzhou*'s inflatable racing toward the landing zone. Spray blasted beneath its rigid hull with every strike of the rough sea's high-rolling waves. Under the best of circumstances, a parachute jump like this was problematic. But in today's weather conditions, the foolhardy decision could prove fatal to the man beneath the swinging canopy. Zhao had to admit the man had guts. It also spoke to his desperation to get to her ship.

Admiral Qian's instructions were clear. The man coming out to her vessel would oversee the operation. She was to grant him every privilege as well as unwavering obedience to his every instruction. Zhao noted the underlying anxiety in her superior's voice.

Of course she readily agreed despite deeply resenting the need for any kind of supervision. But she knew the interests of the Ministry of State Security took precedence over all else, including the plans of the proud and mighty Chinese Navy.

Zhao turned her glass back to the parachutist. She watched in horror as his chute thrashed in the high winds, hurling the man in all directions as he plummeted toward the ocean. He hit the water with a thunderous cannonball splash several hundred yards from the proposed landing zone.

The inflatable turned sharply and headed for the tangle of chute scabbing the surface. The captain panicked.

The man was nowhere to be seen.

★

The inflatable cut sharply as the seaman turned the wheel and slammed down the throttles, landing the boat just inches from the black chute floating on the surface like an oil stain.

The chief petty officer in charge leaned over the bucking hull, holding on tight with one hand against the rising swells that threatened to throw him off. The chutist fought desperately against the tangle of cords and canopy wrapped around him, sputtering and coughing seawater like a man near to drowning.

The chief petty officer grasped one of the chutist's hands and pulled him with a thunderous grunt halfway up onto the hull. The seaman driver charged over and grabbed two fistfuls of the chutist's black tactical jumpsuit in his thick hands. A moment later, the two sailors managed to haul the half-drowned security man into the bottom of the boat, still snarled up in cords. The seaman pulled a razor-sharp knife and cut the cords away as the petty officer lifted his walkie-talkie to his mouth. He had to shout over the whistling wind and crashing waves.

"Captain Zhao! We have him!"

"What is his condition?" Zhao asked over the crackling speaker.

The sailor glanced over at the man, now smiling as he pulled off his chutist's goggles and flashed two thumbs up.

"Director Peng is alive and well. We're heading back now."

70

The *Oregon* was well underway at top speed, and El Salvador far behind in her rearview mirror.

Juan and his senior leadership team were gathered in the conference room for a pre-mission briefing. Only Murphy was missing, still confined to his cabin.

Modeled after the White House Situation Room, the conference room featured a large mahogany desk ringed with high-backed leather executive chairs, banks of large LCD monitors on the walls, and videoconferencing stations at each position. Eric Stone had a laptop open in front of him.

"What are we looking at exactly, Stoney?" Max Hanley asked. He nodded at one of the monitors displaying a map of the Pacific Ocean. A gray-shaded fifty-mile-radius circle marked the map's center, contrasting with the deep blue background. A small red triangle representing the *Baktun* sat at its core. The circle's eastern edge lay nine hundred thirty nautical miles west of Nicaragua, the exact point where the seaplane's last ADS-B signal vanished. A bright yellow line traced the seaplane's path from a Nicaraguan airfield to the red triangle.

"That's our target area," Eric said, "and our best guess as to the probable location of the *Baktun*, based on the radar and signal logs we recovered and the flight-range specs of the ShinMaywa US-2."

"Unless he was carrying spare fuel tanks or planning to refuel at the *Baktun*," Linda noted. "Then the range could be much farther."

Eric shrugged in agreement. "In that case, he could be almost anywhere in the world."

"I'm confident this is the target area," Juan said. "Let's continue."

"Why don't we have a pinpoint location?" Max asked. "Why the fifty-mile circle?"

"Because we don't know if Fierro shut off his satellite signal the moment he landed or before. And that circle represents the maximum distance the seaplane could have traveled and returned safely to its base in Nicaragua on a single tank of JP-5."

"Given the initial ships' traffic we've encountered and the sea state conditions farther ahead, we'll be lucky to maintain an average speed of fifty-five knots," Linda said.

"That will put us at the outer edge of that circle in just over sixteen hours." Juan checked his watch. "That puts our ETA at approximately 1030 hours tomorrow."

"Eidolon's text said Project Q will launch at precisely 1100 hours," Linda reminded everyone.

Max frowned. "That's cutting it pretty close. If Eric's estimate is off even just a fraction, we're going to be late to our own funeral."

"And that's assuming they don't accelerate the timeline," Eric added.

"Was Mr. Overholt able to get a reconnaissance satellite tasked over the area?" Linda asked. The spy satellites possessed Hubble Space Telescope capabilities—only, these cameras were pointed at Earth, not outer space.

Cabrillo shook his head. "He checked into it. There currently aren't any birds on a near-pass trajectory over the target zone. The soonest he can get one is four days from now. He might be able to get us a Lacrosse/Onyx radar satellite in twenty-four hours but no guarantees. That's too late anyway."

"Doesn't matter," Eric said. "That boat was darn near invisible and we were within spitting range of it when it hit us. The *Baktun* must deploy some kind of suite of cloaking technologies. I doubt either optical or radar sats would have done us any good."

Cabrillo leaned forward. "Let's assume we know where the *Baktun* is. What else do we know about her?"

"In our prior engagement we encountered holographic drones . . . surveillance drones . . . swarming drone mini torpedoes . . . and a full-size carbon-fiber-hulled torpedo," Linda said.

"We fired the Melara seventy-six-millimeter at her," Eric said. "Airburst munitions. No damage we could ascertain. We assumed that meant she was capable of high-speed maneuvers to be able to clear the shrapnel area that quickly."

"In short, that bucket is dangerous as all get-out," Max said. "But nothing we can't handle."

"Don't be so sure," Cabrillo said. "We don't know what she was holding back. We surprised her with our little charade. We might have won the battle, but my gut tells me she withdrew for other reasons. Next time we might not be so lucky."

"My money's on the *Oregon*," Max said. "Though I am a bit prejudiced, since I helped design her."

"Well, add this to your calculation, old friend." Cabrillo leaned on the desk, folding his hands to emphasize the point he was about to make. "Overholt has stated in no uncertain terms we are to acquire Project Q and its underlying AGI technology."

"In other words, we can't sink her," Linda said. "We have to capture her."

Max rolled his eyes. "That means we're heading into a gunfight with a Nerf bat. Might as well try to put a saddle on a great white shark while we're at it."

"It's a challenge, no doubt," Cabrillo said. "And we know the Chinese will get in on the action."

"We've tangled with Chinese gunboats before," Max said. "So far, it's *Oregon*, one; Chicoms, bupkes." Hanley was referring to the *Oregon*'s sinking of the Chinese destroyer *Chengdu* years before. The gun battle resulted in the partial loss of Cabrillo's right leg.

Juan propped his prosthetic limb up on the conference table and pulled back the pant leg revealing Nixon's handiwork of lifelike skin and fine blond hair. "C'mon, Max. You gotta give the Chinese at least a half point."

Everyone around the table laughed, lowering the emotional temperature a few degrees.

But Eric Stone had worked long enough with Cabrillo to know his humor was masking something else.

"What aren't you telling us, boss?"

Ross sighed. "Oh, Lord. Don't tell me Overholt didn't forbid us to fire on the Chinese, too?"

Cabrillo pulled his leg off the table and rolled his pant leg back down.

"I would love to tell you that, Ms. Ross, but like my mama used to say, lying is a sin, even if it's for a good cause."

"Why the order?"

"The Pentagon's afraid of starting a shooting war with the Chinese. Taiwan is a tinderbox and we can't be the match."

Max's eyes widened. "Are you kidding me? How are we supposed to fight both the *Baktun* and the Chinese without being able to sink either of them?"

"You remember that old kids' game Operation?" Juan asked. "We just have to be very, very careful."

"Yeah, except if we're not careful, it's more than our big red noses that will get lit up."

Juan leaned back in his chair.

"And there's one more thing."

Everybody leaned forward.

"And that would be?" Max asked.

"Overholt said we can't let the Chinese get that technology, no matter what."

"So that puts even more pressure on us to succeed," Eric said.

"But you just said we can't fire any weapons at them," Max said.

"All that means is we need to get to the *Baktun* first and grab that tech before the Chinese show up," Linda said.

"I've been thinking a lot about the *Baktun*," Eric said, almost as if talking to himself. "It's a high-tech vessel, which means they've got passive electromagnetic detection systems, most likely mil-spec. If we go in hot with radio and radar blazing, we'll spook them and we'll never find them again."

Max threw up his calloused hands. "So besides tying one hand behind our backs, dropping our guns, and picking up a Nerf bat, now we have to go in deaf, dumb, and blind?"

"Stoney's right," Juan said. "We don't have a choice."

"Said the one-legged man taking tap-dancing lessons." Max waved a hand at Cabrillo. "No offense, chief."

"None taken. I do a mean Watusi, by the way. Eric, given what you just said, how do you want to approach the *Baktun*?"

Eric tapped a few more keys on his laptop. Another window opened up on the LCD monitor displaying the past-reported "demon" attacks by the *Baktun*. He'd pulled those calculations together when they were first trying to find the mystery ship.

"The *Baktun* was probably on some level of radio silence when we encountered her. But it was still able to detect these ships it previously attacked, including the *Oregon*."

"My guess would be with a drone screen," Juan said.

"Exactly. You see where these ships previously attacked by the *Baktun* are located? We used the relative distances between them to determine the *Baktun*'s general operating area when we first set out to find them. But as you can see by the additional information I've laid over this map, I've been able to calculate the approximate distance between the victim ships and the *Baktun*. The average is thirty kilometers—about eighteen miles."

"And that's how far her drone screens extend," Linda said. "That's about the limits of tripod-mounted optics."

"We know he's hiding from electromagnetic detection. But he can't escape the human eye if a ship gets close enough. That boat really does want to stay invisible," Max said.

"That's good work, Stoney," Linda said.

"So we park ourselves out at twenty miles. Then what?" Max asked.

"I'd make it twenty-five miles, just to be safe," Eric said.

"I've got a few ideas about what to do next," Juan said. "But first, we need to call in Eddie and his Gundogs and get them up to speed. They'll need to work up a mission plan for a boarding party if it comes to that."

"Let's break for coffee," Linda said. "I'll call brother Seng and we'll meet them in the team room in thirty."

"Agreed," Juan said. "And after that briefing, I want a meeting with all of the department heads. I want every station, every motor, every weapon, every battery, every ammo mag, push broom, mop bucket, and electric toothbrush battle ready by 0500 tomorrow. No surprises. Anything else to add?"

"I've got a weird question," Linda said. "It's been bugging me a lot."

"Shoot."

"What does the name *Baktun* mean anyway?"

"Could mean a lot of things," Eric said. "But a *bak'tun* is a unit of time in the Mayan long calendar. It represents one hundred forty-four thousand days. The end of a *bak'tun* signals the end of an era, and the dawn of a new one."

Everyone in the room stared at Stone like he was an alien life-form.

Max finally broke the silence. "Remind me never to play Scrabble with you, son."

"Almost like the AI singularity," Juan said. "Or should I say, AGI singularity?"

Eric shook his head. "No, sir. More like the end of the world."

71

Captain Stokes stood bleary-eyed in the combat information center, a cup of his favorite Royal Navy tea gripped in one hand. He and Bose both had a fitful sleep, and Fierro was no better off. Being so close to ultimate success meant every moment was an existential agony as they waited for Project Q to finally launch. The countdown clock on the wall read 02:29:42.

"Sir, there's an incoming message," the comms tech said, touching his earpiece. He turned in his chair to face Stokes.

"Who is it, man?"

"It's the Chinese warship *Fuzhou*. He wants to speak with Mr. Fierro."

Fierro frowned furiously. "With me?"

Stokes marched over to the comms station. "I'll take it."

"What about maintaining radio silence?" Bose asked.

"The Chinese are bouncing a very narrow low-frequency beam off the troposphere," the comms tech said. "We'll respond in kind. No one will find us this way."

"Patch the call over the speakers," Stokes ordered.

"Aye, sir." He turned back to his monitor and spoke into his headset microphone. "*Fuzhou*, I'm putting you through to Captain Stokes." He punched a button.

Stokes heard the familiar click of an open line.

"This is Captain Stokes. Who am I speaking with?"

"My name doesn't matter, Captain. I need to speak with Amador Fierro. I imagine he's on your vessel—even standing next to you."

Fierro recognized Peng De's voice. His face flushed with heat even as his blood ran cold.

Stokes pointed a finger at the comms tech to mute the call. As soon as it was muted, he turned to Fierro.

"I can see by the look on your face you know this man."

Fierro nodded. "He's Chinese intelligence."

"What in the blazes does he want?"

Fierro gathered himself. "Let's find out." He nodded at the tech to resume the call. The tech glanced at Stokes, who nodded his permission. The call resumed.

"It's good to hear your voice, Mr. Peng. I confess, I'm somewhat surprised by your call. May I ask how you found us?"

"Why ask me? Ask Dr. Bose. I'm sure she's there with you."

Fierro wheeled on Bose, startling her.

"You said the breach was inconsequential."

"It was," she said, gathering her wits. "He only stole a few lines of code before we shut him down."

"Not true, Dr. Bose," Peng said. "The hacker-thief was named Eidolon, now dead. He provided details about Project Q, your ship, and your location. He even knew your AGI program will be launching just two hours and twenty-seven minutes from now."

The countdown clock now read exactly: 02:27:00.

Fierro, Stokes, and Bose were stunned.

"I should add that the Americans know this as well," Peng said. "A ship known as the *Oregon* will be arriving at your location in less than two hours. One hour and forty-eight minutes, to be exact. You need to evacuate the area immediately to avoid capture."

"That's not possible," Bose blurted out. "The AGI will be disabled and perhaps even destroyed if the engines are powered up."

"Where are you?" Fierro asked.

"The *Fuzhou* is approximately two hours away, due west."

Stokes signaled to comms to mute the call, then swept his pointed finger around the CIC like a clock's second hand, singling out each station in rapid succession.

"Where is this brigand Chinese? Anybody?" Stokes demanded, his tactical senses on high alert.

All heads shook no.

"The Americans?"

Nobody saw a thing.

"They both must be on transmission silence as well," the comms tech offered. "Invisible on the electromagnetic spectrum, just like us."

"Put the Mandarin back on."

"Sir."

Stokes began to speak, but Fierro shut him down with the flip of his hand.

"What do you want us to do about the Americans, since we can't move?" Fierro asked.

"We'll bloody fight them," Stokes said.

"Your ship is worthless to me if the AGI is harmed," Peng said. "Do not fight the Americans. Do not move. Instead, stall them."

"How?" Fierro asked.

"With a bluff. A promise. A ruse. You are expert in such things, Amador. I should know."

"I never lied to you, Peng."

"Withholding the truth is the same as a lie. You have no doubt spent billions building out your AGI because you know exactly what it can do. And yet you said nothing about it to me. I must assume your intentions are hostile."

"I will only use it against the Americans, I assure you."

"You will use it against anyone you consider a threat, including us."

"Your nation has always befriended us. We've worked together for years against the Americans. I would never deploy it against you."

"Since we're friends, you should be happy to share it with us, yes?"

"Of course. We'll discuss it when you arrive."

"Until we do, maintain electromagnetic silence. With any luck, the Americans have miscalculated your position. But if they do appear, as I suspect they will, stall them."

"And then?"

"The mighty *Fuzhou* will sweep the *Oregon* off the face of the sea."

★

ABOARD THE *FUZHOU*

Peng turned to Captain Zhao. She and the rest of the bridge crew had heard the entire exchange with Fierro.

Zhao's reputation as an iron-willed and duty-bound commander had been further cemented in Peng's mind ever since he boarded her ship. Her outstanding leadership and superlative command presence had inspired fanatical loyalty in the sailors under her authority.

But Peng noted with delight that the flinty-eyed captain allowed herself the slightest smile when he told Fierro, "*The* Fuzhou *will sweep the Americans off the face of the sea.*" The officers and enlisted crew around the bridge stiffened with pride as well, each face eager for the promise of combat against the hated Americans.

"Captain Zhao, I've committed this ship to battle. Are you surprised?"

"No, sir. Admiral Qian suggested the possibility in his briefing before your arrival."

"Once we are closer to the *Baktun*, I give you permission to drive the Americans from the area—or blow them apart."

Zhao nodded curtly, barely able to contain her excitement at the prospect of tangling with an American warship.

"The *Fuzhou* stands ready, sir."

72

SUNAN AIRPORT, NORTH KOREA

The Hwasong-17 ICBM loomed like a deadly obelisk on its mobile platform, its cone pointed at the cloud-shrouded, predawn sky. Heavy rain pummeled the launch site, pinging against the missile's aluminum-alloy skin.

Rain-geared military personnel scrambled for cover as final checks were called out by launch operators inside the underground command and control bunker.

The mission control officer, an Army general, gave the terse command to initiate the countdown, and thirty seconds later the Fire Star's massive engines roared to life with a fiery flash.

The thundering shock waves above echoed inside the bunker, trembling the ground beneath their feet. Tracking cameras flared with refractive bloom against the white-hot corona of flaming gases trailing the missile on its long flight to its distant target range in the far Pacific.

A faint smile and satisfied nod from the general ignited a round of wild cheers and applause inside the bunker. It was another successful launch, and a clear signal to the hated Americans that North Korea held a nuclear knife to their naked capitalist throats.

★

SEA OF JAPAN

The hundred-thousand-watt halogen lamps of a South Korean squid-jigging boat blazed across the surface of the dark, rain-roiled sea. The bright lights lured the deep-diving Japanese flying squid to the surface, where fishermen tricked the squid into seizing the jigged fluorescent lures flickering like darting shrimp.

The high-tech squid boat deployed a seasoned and highly patriotic crew. They happily shielded the secretive work of the two men and one woman, who identified themselves as South Korean National Intelligence Service operatives. Their mission was to monitor the early-morning North Korean missile launch.

Squid boats were common in these waters, and always operated at night. North Korean patrol boats wouldn't suspect anything nor even bother them this far beyond the Communists' economic zone.

The squid-jigging crew knew not to interfere with the intelligence work, pry into their activities, or gawk at their incredibly sophisticated equipment. Not even the captain dared to closely inspect or verify their credentials.

Despite the nearly daylight-bright halogen glow surrounding their vessel, the North Korean rocket trail was clearly visible almost from the moment it launched, its fiery plume muting behind the thick rain clouds as it punched through the storm.

Within moments, the Guardians had accomplished their first task of the mission.

73

Eric Stone idled the *Oregon*'s engines and rotated its thrusters, keeping the big ship in place like a swimmer treading water. He had just put the *Oregon* twenty-five miles due east from the *Baktun*. If his estimates were correct, that put them safely beyond the range of its tripod-mounted optics and, hopefully, well outside the estimated perimeter of the *Baktun*'s sensor drones. They hadn't picked up any active radar or sonar activity from the mystery ship, nor had the Sniffer detected any radio, satellite, or laser communications.

Like the *Baktun*, the *Oregon* was also maintaining complete electromagnetic silence, careful not to send any kind of signal that would trigger the *Baktun*'s electronic spiderweb of passive sensors and send her scurrying away. But without active sensors, they still needed a way to confirm the *Baktun*'s location.

"Madyar's ready to launch, Chairman," Gomez said. He was the *Oregon*'s senior drone pilot when he wasn't flying either the AW609 tilt-rotor or the Joby.

"This will be the first time we've deployed the Madyar in combat conditions," Linda Ross said. She had replaced Murphy at the weapons station since he had been relieved of duty.

"She tested in her sea trials well enough," Cabrillo said.

Max huffed. "That's like shooting paper targets at the range."

"But it's not the first time these Ukrainian drones have been around the block," Ross protested. "They've flown against Russian defenses without much of a hitch."

"The Russkies don't hold a candle to what these *Baktun* boys have, at least in the technology department."

"We're about to find out what the *Baktun* can really do," Cabrillo said.

Juan wasn't completely confident. The whole point of the Madyar drone was to avoid any kind of detection or destruction by enemy electronics. They named the drone Madyar after its inventors, the "Madyar's Birds," otherwise known as Ukraine's 414th Drone Strike Regiment.

Of course, Max, Murph, and Eric couldn't help but tinker with the battle-proven drone when they first got their hands on it a month ago. They extended both its range and optics, and modified its carbon-fiber airframe to *Oregon* specs. The Madyar was relatively small—no bigger than the deck of a push mower—which aided in its stealth capabilities.

Cabrillo nodded at Gomez, seated at his command station. "Launch the Madyar."

"Roger that."

Gomez pulled on his first-person view goggles and flipped a couple of toggles on his desktop. His first-person view was now displayed on one of the op center's giant bulkhead LCD monitors. He worked a traditional pilot's joystick affixed to the station.

The drone's camera displayed black until the launch tube door popped off, revealing a cloudy gray sky above a wine-dark sea spattered with small whitecaps marching off into the distance.

The drone shot out of its pod with a mighty whoosh of air. Its spring-loaded quadcopter limbs deployed and its four motors instantly powered up. Their high-pitched whining rattled the overhead speakers until Hali Kasim nudged the sound level down.

Unlike most drones, the Madyar wasn't controlled by wireless RF signals. There was no question wireless drones carrying small-explosive payloads had changed the face of modern war. But defensive technologies were beginning to swing the pendulum in the other direction. Ukrainian, Russian, Chinese, Iranian, British, Turkish, European, and American drone operators were discovering that electronic countermeasures, especially jamming of RF signals, were increasingly successful knocking drones out of the sky. Interrupting the signal between the operator and drone was responsible for seventy-five percent of drone losses in the Ukraine-Russia war.

Worse, jamming tech was becoming ubiquitous. Besides the large and expensive theater-wide systems being deployed, smaller devices like "backpack jammers" and even narrow-beamed radio wave "rifles" were suddenly flooding the field.

But wartime engineers were nothing if not inventive, and it wasn't long before the drone fighters discovered the virtue of wire-guided drone flights. Drones were now carrying specially wound spools of fiber slung beneath their airframes like fishing reels, providing a direct, high-bandwidth data link between the operator and the drone. That physical connection meant radio interference was impossible. Better still, the drones themselves now emitted no radio waves that could locate either the drone or the operator by electronic detection. The ultimate bonus: the quality of video imagery of the "flyby fiber" technology was exponentially higher than traditional RF systems.

The *Oregon*'s modified Madyar carried over thirty miles of fine filament, strong enough that the drone could even fly backward or turn in circles without breaking the line or having it tangle in the rotors.

In place of munitions, the *Oregon* team mounted a 10x camera and gimbal, extending the Madyar's optical range far beyond its thirty-mile cable limit. Gomez flew the bird at twenty-five feet above the ocean at radar-avoiding "sea-skimming" levels. The slight chop in the water added to the sea clutter, making radar detection and targeting of the Madyar even more unlikely. At that low height, and with the current weather conditions, the drone should be able to spot a ship the size of the *Baktun* around thirteen miles away.

The Madyar gave the *Oregon* the best possible shot at stealthy, long-range optical reconnaissance. With any luck, they'd find the *Baktun* without the *Oregon* ever being detected, its electromagnetic systems in a state of complete silence.

What happened after that would be anything but quiet.

Cabrillo glanced at the countdown clock on one of the bulkhead monitors. Only twenty-nine minutes until Project Q launched.

Max was right. Despite charging across the Pacific at full tilt, they had cut it close getting here. Maybe too close. That countdown clock was only an estimate based on Eidolon's stolen code.

And if that estimate was wrong, they might even be too late.

★

"What's that?" Max asked, pointing at the big video display. In the far distance, a jagged speck appeared on the choppy water. The Madyar had flown just over six miles since leaving the *Oregon*.

"I'm pretty sure it's not a duck," Cabrillo said. He stood near the wall monitor, his thick arms crossed against his wide swimmer's chest.

"It's some kind of a ship, but I can't quite make it out," Ross said. All eyes in the op center were glued to the image playing on the wall-size LCD screen. Several minutes later, the jagged speck morphed into the unmistakable outline of a large oceangoing vessel.

"She matches the *Baktun*'s description," Eric said as he threw a stock photo of the vessel up onto an adjacent screen. Eidolon's coded message didn't include either a picture or a description of the mystery ship. But scouring the maritime databases for a vessel of the same name finally turned up the *Baktun*, a global research vessel registered to a nonprofit environmentalist organization.

One of the *Oregon*'s research team, Russ Kefauver, deployed his forensic accounting skills to uncover a carefully hidden and legally tenuous connection between the nonprofit organization and a sizable Fierro offshore bank account.

With each passing second, the *Baktun* came into clearer relief.

"That high foredeck definitely looks like the *Baktun*'s helipad," Ross said. "I'd say we have confirmation."

"No visible weapons," Gomez said.

"She looks dead in the water to me, and quiet as the grave," Max said. "I wonder if she's playing opossum."

"What do you want me to do, skip?" Gomez asked. "I've got plenty of rope left on the saddle. And by the looks of things, we haven't rattled any cans down there."

"Push on a bit, and let's gain some altitude. I want to see if she's hiding any surprises."

"You got it." Gomez eased the stick back and raised the Madyar to over a hundred feet.

Every jaw in the op center dropped when a second vessel appeared a short distance beyond.

"What the heck is that?" Max asked as Eric's fingers raced across his keyboard. The former weapons designer pulled up a recently posted Pentagon image and threw it on the screen. It was a perfect match.

"That's the *Fuzhou*," Stone announced. "China's latest version of the Type 055 destroyer."

What caught everyone's attention wasn't the photo so much as the list of weapons on the spec screen. The top of that long list showed the carrier-killer kitted out with hypersonic anti-ship missiles, torpedoes, two helicopters, and even an experimental rail gun. Despite its label as a destroyer, it was more of a cruiser given its size and armaments.

Max whistled. "She's a monster, all right. And a quiet one at that."

The *Oregon*'s electro-optical display estimated the *Fuzhou* was steaming at less than ten knots toward the *Baktun*, some three miles distant, and due west of the slightly smaller ship. At that speed and with its noise-reduction engineering, it was impossible for the anchored *Oregon* to pick up her screw noise this far away.

"They beat us here—but how?" Linda said. "And why didn't our passive systems pick her up?"

"The hydrodynamic-flow noise from our engines at max speed interfered with our passive hull sonar," Juan explained. "The good news is that the *Fuzhou* couldn't hear us, either."

One of the many advantages of the *Oregon*'s revolutionary propless propulsion system was that it didn't produce the acoustic signatures detected by passive sonar systems. Without active pinging by the Chinese, the *Oregon* was functionally invisible to them.

"Interesting," Linda said. "So now we have three ships, including ours, all running silent."

"That means whoever farts in church first is gonna have to pay the preacher," Max said.

Eric stifled a snorting laugh.

"Doesn't matter how she got here," Juan said, falling back into the Kirk Chair. "We knew they'd show up some time."

"At least they don't know we're here," Max said.

"No radar, no sonar, no weapons activated," Linda said, checking her instruments. "What are the Chinese up to?"

Cabrillo leaned forward, studying the screen. "A rendezvous. Either they're going to escort the *Baktun* back to a home base or they're going to transfer tech and personnel right here."

"Skip . . ." Gomez said.

All eyes turned back to the wall monitor. The Madyar's automated optics put a red square around a distant object lifting off the rear helo deck.

"That's one of the *Fuzhou*'s choppers," Max said.

Cabrillo stood, his eyes fixed on the Chinese helo lofting high into the air, his voice calm and measured.

"Hali, sound battle stations. We're blown."

74

Peng and Captain Zhao leaned over the shoulders of the tactical data link operator, observing the live video feed from the *Fuzhou*'s Z-20F helicopter.

The seasoned chief petty officer optimized the digital image, sharpening the pixelation and smoothing the motion blur from the chopper's shaky 30x telephoto camera. The officer zoomed in on the ship's hull and pulled up the name, *Oregon*.

"A cargo ship?" Zhao asked. "Impossible."

"It's the American spy ship, certainly," Peng said. "We were expecting them."

"But a cargo ship? Not a combat vessel?" Zhao asked.

"It matches the description my former agent provided. Though how it reached this location in such a short amount of time is a true mystery."

"It must be a stealth ship of some unknown type."

Peng turned to Zhao. "And for the record, why didn't your sonar sensors pick up its arrival?"

Captain Zhao straightened to her full height.

"We'll get the answer as soon as I slap the *Oregon*'s captain in irons."

"No need for dramatics just yet, Captain. After all, 'the supreme art of war is to subdue the enemy without fighting,' is it not?"

Peng marched over to the comms station and snatched up the microphone. He flashed an arrogant smile at Zhao.

"Let me show you how it's done."

★

ABOARD THE *OREGON*

"Chairman, the *Fuzhou* is hailing us," Hali said. Like the rest of the op center team, he was harnessed to his station chair, ready for anything.

"All of *Fuzhou*'s systems are hot now," Linda said. "She's not hiding anymore."

"Put her on the overheads," Juan said. "This oughta be good."

Hali nodded. "*Fuzhou*, this is *Oregon*. Proceed with transmission."

"Cargo ship *Oregon*, this is PLA Navy Destroyer *Fuzhou*-120. You are violating a temporary maritime security zone of the People's Republic of China. You are instructed to leave these waters immediately. If you do not comply, you will be held responsible for any consequences."

"Destroyer *Fuzhou*," Juan began, "we do not recognize your authority to declare a temporary maritime security zone, nor are we able to comply with your suggestion we leave the area. We are currently experiencing engine difficulties."

An alarm sounded. "That chopper has weapons lock," Linda said. She checked her monitor. The *Oregon*'s combat computer automatically put up the helicopter weapons specs on a wall monitor, but Linda read it aloud, as per protocols.

"Data profile indicates carrying two TL-2 anti-ship supersonic. Missiles with a range of eighteen miles. Fifty-kilogram warhead. Millimeter-wave targeting radar."

"We got your message, *Fuzhou*," Cabrillo said. "Stand down. We need thirty minutes to repair, and then we'll depart the area."

"*Fuzhou* just opened two vertical launch system doors, Chairman." Ross was referring to the coverings over anti-ship missile wells. "Likely firing YJ-21 Eagle Strikes. Hypersonics—Mach 10–plus."

"Somebody got up on the wrong side of the futon," Max said.

"Duly noted," Cabrillo said to his number two. He then shouted to the overhead speakers, "*Fuzhou*, we need at least twenty minutes—"

Linda shouted, "TL-2s fired! Twenty seconds to impact!"

Alarms blared across the ship as battle station lights flashed red.

On the big port-side wall monitor, the two TL-2 supersonic missiles raced toward them like burning stars.

"Helm, full starboard yaw, forty-degree vector—execute now!"

Stoney slammed the throttles and thrusters, banking the ship hard like a fighter jet. Anyone or anything not secured was thrown across the deck or slammed into bulkheads as the op center crew strained against their harnesses.

As Stoney executed the breakneck turn, the ship's AI defensive systems kicked in. Jamming signals were automatically pumped into the atmosphere as chaff rockets fired, throwing up a wide-area radar interference cloud of carbon-coated fiberglass strips.

Linda at the weapons station called out the automated plays like a football color commentator, her fingers hovering over switches and toggles in case of computer failure.

"Chaff and jamming no effect. EMP cannons firing," Ross said as the two weapons surged with power high above decks. The invisible electromagnetic wave pulses rippled the ocean water like a stiff breeze on the incoming-missile monitor.

Suddenly, one of the TL-2s yawed violently, then spun out of control before splashing into the sea in an explosion of spray and shrapnel.

"Missile number two still on course—ten seconds to impact," Linda called out. "Laser-point defense engaging."

A white-hot invisible beam seared the air, lancing across the missile's fuselage and slicing off a tail fin, its track now wavering and erratic, but still coming on fast.

The bank of three starboard Vulcan close-in weapons system Gatling guns opened up in a hellish crescendo that rang through the hull. The Chinese missile plowed into a wall of 20-millimeter armor-piercing rounds, breaking it apart. But the remaining wreckage lashed forward at supersonic speed.

Linda called out, "Three seconds to impact. All hands brace."

The Melara 76-millimeter auto cannons opened up just then, firing airburst proximity shells, throwing a cloud of shrapnel in front of the runaway train of missile debris. The shrapnel cloud stripped away the worst of the red-hot wreckage like a coffee filter straining grounds. But a fiery chunk of fuselage shot through and hit the *Oregon*'s superstructure with a hard glancing blow, punching a gaping hole through the corner of the third-story deck.

The debris strike rang like a hammer blow throughout the ship.

"Damage report," Juan called out.

"No casualties, minor damage," Max replied from his station.

"Wepps?"

"No radar locks, no missiles, chopper retreating," Linda said. "All clear."

"We're playing rope-a-dope again," Max said. "I know we could sink that tin can if you'd let us."

"Orders are orders," Juan said. "Even the ones that suck lemons."

"You want to splash that helo, send a message?" Linda asked.

"Don't even put a surface-to-air lock on it. Let the Chicoms think we're playing nice."

The forward bulkhead monitor showed open sea and sky, and the high prancing bow of the *Oregon* arcing across the horizon.

"How far do you want me to take her, Chairman?" Eric asked.

Cabrillo saw the radar track. The *Oregon* was now twenty-eight miles from the *Baktun* and the *Fuzhou*, now closing on her.

"Put the *Baktun* between us and the *Fuzhou*, then hove to."

Eric grinned. "To block the *Fuzhou*'s line of sight. Aye."

"Think the grumpy neighbor has stopped shouting at us?" Hali asked.

"He's gonna yell a lot louder if we charge back onto his lawn." Cabrillo was thinking about the carrier-killing hypersonic Eagle Strikes the *Fuzhou* deployed. There was no way the *Oregon* could outrun them, let alone survive a single hit. And according to the specs Eric posted, the Chinese destroyer carried at least twelve of them.

Cabrillo glanced at the Project Q countdown clock.

Just ten minutes to go. He had to do something.

But what?

75

Stokes and Fierro stood in the CIC. The La Liga crime lord waited anxiously for news from Dr. Bose down in her lab. She promised the organoid AGI would launch precisely ten minutes from now.

But Stokes was straining the leash, salivating at the prospect of combat. The old war dog had watched the supremely fast and violent exchange between the *Fuzhou* and the American ship—no doubt the one he had fought with before. It deployed the same weapons and speed that had defeated his attacks earlier. And now it had a new name. *Oregon.*

His eyes glanced at the countdown clock. In less than ten minutes the AGI would launch and he could power up his engines without fear of harming the project and earning Fierro's wrath. But after Project Q was stood up on its own two feet, he'd retake control of his ship, and give battle to the *Oregon* no matter what Fierro said. He'd waited his entire adult life for a moment like this—and he'd fire on the Chinese, too, if it came to that.

"Mr. Fierro, Director Peng is calling for you," the comms tech said.

Fierro stepped over to the comms station.

"We saw your skirmish, Peng. Well done."

"Never mind that," Peng said. "I'm coming over to your ship. I want to personally witness the historic moment when Project Q comes to life."

Fierro swallowed his irritation. "Of course. I look forward to finally meeting you in person."

"We'll make all the necessary preparations for your arrival," Stokes said, enjoying Fierro's discomfiture. "The helo deck is already cleared for you."

"Thank you, Captain Stokes. We'll be lifting off shortly."

★

ABOARD THE *FUZHOU*

Peng turned to Captain Zhao, her face still a welter of confusion after the *Oregon*'s incredible performance. She'd never seen anything like it. *Lasers on a cargo ship?*

Peng read her mind, and shared her concerns.

"America may be a dying empire, but she still has a few dangerous tricks up her sleeve."

"I wonder what kind of propulsion she has," Zhao said, almost to herself.

"I'm sure our engineers will figure it out soon enough. Be sure to forward all your combat data to my office, Captain."

"And to Admiral Qian as well."

"Of course. Prepare your other helicopter. I want a squad of your best Marines armed and ready for battle to accompany me. I don't trust these shameless parasites. Once the AGI comes online, I will seize control."

Zhao turned toward the senior Marine commander standing nearby, and barked her orders as Peng checked his watch.

"There are only minutes to spare, Captain. I want you to close to five hundred yards, and prepare to train your deck guns on the bridge. We don't want to sink her, but killing half the crew won't keep us from towing her back to port if it comes to that."

"I will carry out your orders to the letter. Anything else?"

"I'll need a pistol and body armor just in case Fierro has a change of heart."

"They will be waiting for you on the helicopter. Good luck, comrade."

Peng nodded his thanks, and dashed for the *Fuzhou*'s deck hangar.

76

ABOARD THE *OREGON*

The *Fuzhou*'s vertical launch doors remained open, but the Chinese vessel hadn't fired off any more weapons. Instead, the big destroyer had inched closer to the *Baktun* and was now just five hundred yards away.

"Helo lifting off," Linda called out from the weapons station.

"Got it," Gomez said. Cabrillo had ordered him to loft a specialized observation drone six hundred feet above the *Oregon*, tethered to a graphene power cable copied after the *Spook Fish*. That gave the 50x digital-optical camera on board the drone enough reach and bandwidth to observe the *Fuzhou* and its helicopter in 8K despite its distance. Gomez threw his image up onto the port-side bulkhead monitor so the entire op center could see it.

"It's keeping a low altitude," Max said. "They're headed for the *Baktun*."

Juan's grip tightened on the Kirk Chair. *Not good.*

"Looks like the Chicoms want to get in on the party," Linda said.

"That's not a party. That's a shotgun wedding, and the *Baktun* is the reluctant bride," Juan said, nodding at the Chinese destroyer.

"What do you want to do, Chairman?" Max asked.

"Our orders are clear. We can't fire on the *Baktun* without risking the AGI, and we can't fire on the Chinese for fear of starting World War Three."

"I don't think the Chicoms got that note," Max said. "Those weren't exactly spitballs they threw at us."

"Doesn't matter. We get our paychecks from Uncle Sam, not the Bank of China." Juan checked the clock again. "Boys and girls, we only have five minutes to stop the apocalypse. I'm open to suggestions."

★

ABOARD THE *BAKTUN*

Dr. Bose stood at the observation window, her eyes fixed on the Neural Reef crowded inside the holding tank. The biometric readouts indicated perfect metabolic stats across the board. Every node of the structure was now fully illuminated and no longer pulsating.

According to the clock, there were still five minutes to go.

What did that mean? Was something wrong?

A dozen anxious faces stared up at her from the laboratory floor.

Bose could scarcely breathe.

A digital panel suspended above the tank flashed on. Single letters forming Hindi words in elegantly structured Devanagari script began appearing.

Tears flowed from the Indian's handsome face as she whispered the words aloud.

"Namaste, Dr. Bose."

★

INSIDE THE *BAKTUN'S* COMBAT INFORMATION CENTER

"Director Peng's helicopter will be landing in three minutes, Captain," the radar officer reported.

"Thank you." Stokes dreaded Peng's arrival. The Chinese were never part of his deal with Fierro.

"Sir, Dr. Bose on line one for you," the comms tech said.

Fierro frowned anxiously. "Is there a problem?"

"How should I know?" Stokes turned to the comms tech. "Put her through." Stokes pulled an intercom receiver and held it to his ear.

Fierro strained to hear the conversation on the other end of the line. He marched over to Stokes just as he hung up the phone.

"What did she say?"

"Congratulations, Mr. Fierro. Project Q is alive and well."

Fierro clasped Stokes's shoulders in his hands and shook him with a near-maniacal laugh.

"*Fantastico!*"

The CIC crew cheered.

Even the stoic captain couldn't help but smile. But he wasn't happy for Fierro. His mind was already forming a battle plan to take on the Americans. He told his helmsman, "Prepare the plasma wave engine immediately."

"Aye, sir."

"And I want all systems online, including weapons."

His crew acknowledged his commands and got to work.

"Our Chinese partners will be pleased," Fierro said.

Fierro's words darkened Stokes's weathered face. "And that's acceptable to you?"

"Don't be so glum, Stokes. No need to worry about Peng. Our arrangement still stands. I can still take down the American energy grid, and you'll still be a rich man."

"What makes you think he'll allow you to keep the AGI?"

"Do you think I'm an idiot? He won't have a choice." Fierro pointed at an Indian engineer sitting at the satellite console. "Prepare for the uplink."

"With a program that large, it will take several minutes," the Indian said.

"Then get after it, man." Fierro was anxious to put the AGI to work as soon as possible. He turned to the comms tech. "Tell Dr. Bose I need her in the CIC immediately."

"Yes, sir."

Fierro was worried. With the American ship prowling around there was no telling how much time he had left before they might seek to capture or kill him. Despite Peng's impressive show of violence, Fierro wasn't convinced the Chinese destroyer was equal to the *Oregon* and its incredible power.

Once the uplink was established, Fierro would have Dr. Bose transfer a copy of the AGI program to a server located in a secured compound he had built in New Zealand. After that, he'd unleash AGI on the American vessel and destroy it.

"Are you sure you want the Chinese to have access to it as well?" Stokes asked. The distant beat of helicopter blades signaled Peng was on his way.

"At this juncture, I don't have much of a choice, do I? Besides, the Chinese hate the Americans as much as I do, and Peng has been a good business partner over the years. It's not my preferred arrangement, but I can live with it." He turned back to the comms tech. "Where's Bose?"

"She hasn't responded."

Stokes stepped closer. "A private word with you, in my cabin, if I may?"

Fierro frowned, annoyed. "What? Now?"

"It's about Bose. It's urgent."

★

ABOARD THE *OREGON*

Murphy had tapped into the *Oregon*'s comms ever since they arrived on station. Like a retired fire horse hearing a clanging alarm bell, everything in him wanted to run up to the weapons station once the fireworks began. Of course, he couldn't. Cabrillo had locked him in his stall for the duration.

He didn't care about all of that now. A hardwired compulsion within his brain told him the key to everything was finding and solving Eidolon's code-within-a-code. Like a paleographer deploying AI-powered X-ray imaging to decipher ancient text from burnt papyrus scrolls, Murphy managed to pull minuscule shreds of data from Eidolon's code, one bit at a time. After many sleepless hours he finally extracted the last digital bits—just as Stoney began throwing the *Oregon* around in a slalom run across the Pacific. By the time the *Oregon* hove to, he'd uploaded the data into a software program originally designed to predict the complex folding patterns of DNA protein structures.

Bleary-eyed and jacked up on energy drinks, he was staring at his monitor as it suddenly began spitting out the decrypted digital chaos: Eidolon's code-within-a-code.

Murphy shouted like a babysitter in a slasher film.

In a good way.

★

"Chairman, the *Baktun*'s satellite mast just lit up," Hali Kasim said.

"What? Why now?" Cabrillo asked. "Is it comms?"

"Not according to the Sniffer. The signal indicates major bandwidth."

"That means AGI is online," Eric said. "They need to upload it in order to be able to deploy it properly."

"But there's still five minutes to go," Max said.

"It must have completed early," Stone said.

"Wepps," Cabrillo called out. "Deploy the Melara and take out that mast. Fire at will."

"Aye, sir!"

Linda engaged the auto-targeting program for the Melara 127 auto cannon. *Bull's-eye at twenty-eight miles? No problem,* she joked to herself as she painted the *Baktun*'s distant satellite mast. Juan would have deployed the high-powered laser because of its inherent precision, but it only had an effective range of six miles.

Linda selected the Melara's Vulcano round as the computer locked onto its swaying target, automatically loading the first fin-stabilized, laser-guided 127-millimeter shell into the breech.

The difficulty of such a long-range hit was complicated beyond human measure as both the *Oregon* and *Baktun* bobbed in the running swells. The physical, atmospheric, and tactical challenges in the highly dynamic environment made targeting nearly impossible.

The AI-powered targeting program overcame all of it by integrating the suites of sensors, gyros, electromechanical mounts, and radar-tracking controlling the automated deck gun. They all could hear the clank of the weapon's steel container as it fell away high up on the deck, and the faint whirring and clicking of servos, gimbals, and hydraulics snapping the auto cannon into place.

Boom! The big gun sent a single shell downrange. Traveling at nearly five thousand feet per second, it would take twenty-five seconds for it to reach the target twenty-eight miles away.

The high-explosive fragmentation round would act like a shotgun blast. The fragments covered a wider range of destruction than a precision armor-piercing round, making a hit on the fragile mast far more likely and at the same time eliminating the risk of sinking the *Baktun*.

Three seconds later, Linda fired a second shell—in case the first one missed.

"Chairman, Murph online for you," Hali called out. "He says it's an emergency."

"Put him through."

"Chairman, I did it. I broke the code."

"Kinda busy right now, kid—"

Boom! A third shell erupted from the cannon.

"You don't understand. Eidolon hid another code inside of his code. I just broke it open. He left a back door open on *Baktun*'s mainframe. I can access it from here."

All eyes turned toward Cabrillo.

He leaned forward in his chair, grinning.

He knew exactly what to do.

77

I told you before I don't trust the Chinese—and you know I hate them," Stokes said as he waved Fierro toward his cabin. "The filthy vermin cost me my career."

"It is what it is, my friend," the tall Colombian said as he stepped through the door.

"We now have the world's most powerful weapon, Fierro. Let's use it. Don't give it to the enemy."

"You forget your place, *Capitán*. It's my weapon, not yours. And I'll do with it as I please."

Stokes shut the door behind him. Bose's Sikh bodyguard stepped out from behind a curtain before Fierro could turn around. The Sikh's powerful hands gripped the side of Fierro's head and squeezed it like a vise. The squirming Colombian clawed at the larger man's powerful hands, but couldn't move. The big bodyguard spun Fierro around to face Stokes.

"What is the meaning of this, Stokes?" Fierro howled.

Stokes stepped close enough to smell the panicked Colombian's souring breath.

"You may have financed Project Q, Fierro, but you clearly don't appreciate the magnitude of my sweet orchid's invention. Perhaps you should relinquish it to someone who does."

"And I suppose that's you?" Fierro hissed as the Sikh's hands pressed harder.

"Who else, old boy? I'm a warrior, born for battle. Not a foppish dilettante with delusions of grandeur."

Fierro's eyes flared with rage.

"I will have you—"

Snap!

Fierro's neck cracked like a dry twig inside the fatal torque of the Sikh's twisting hands. He relaxed his grip, dropping the Colombian to the steel deck with a dull thud.

"Nicely done," Stokes said.

The silent Sikh nodded curtly to the captain.

Stokes and Bose both previously agreed they had no need for Fierro, and every need to control Project Q.

And now they did.

Stokes felt a sudden surge of power. And control.

But both evaporated with the first explosion high in the rigging—and sent Stokes running for the CIC.

The second explosion cracked overhead seconds later as he raced along the corridor. He was breathless by the time he reached the combat center.

"Status!"

★

ABOARD PENG'S HELICOPTER

Peng was strapped into the copilot's seat for the short hop from the *Fuzhou* to the *Baktun*. He wore body armor over his civilian clothes and a semi-auto 9-millimeter pistol on his hip.

The helo's actual copilot was strapped in the back along with a dozen burly Marines kitted out in body armor and QBZ-191 bullpup rifles.

Peng's eyes were fixed on the *Baktun*'s helo deck when suddenly the air cracked with a blistering light high up near the *Baktun*'s satellite mast. The cockpit shuddered with the shock wave.

"Hang on," the pilot shouted. "Diving low."

The pilot shoved the cyclic forward and stomped his anti-torque pedals, rolling a hard left while shoving the collective down, dropping the airframe below the roiling shrapnel cloud.

"Dumping flares."

Peng's face was bathed in a sheen of sweat when the pilot called out, "Jinking," yanking the cyclic left and right, weaving the aircraft violently, trying to avoid any kind of radar lock. Peng felt his body strain against the harness when another shell cracked over the *Baktun*, rocking the sky with shock waves and shrapnel.

Peng's vision narrowed as the pilot continued his high-g maneuvers. He reached for the mic to call Zhao and issue an attack order, but he couldn't reach it.

★

ABOARD THE *OREGON*

As soon as Cabrillo gave Murphy his marching orders, he turned to Stoney.

"Helm, set a course for the *Baktun*—midships. Flank speed."

"Sir?"

"Run it right down his throat."

Max could hardly contain his glee.

"Everybody hold on." Eric slammed the throttles and whipped the joystick. Moments later, the *Oregon* stepped into a sharp turn, then rocketed at full speed toward the *Baktun*.

"What's the play?" Linda asked. "You really going to ram her?"

"Our orders were we couldn't sink the *Baktun*. Doesn't mean we can't ruffle her skirts."

Linda scowled with confusion as the first explosion ripped above the *Baktun*.

"Haven't had this much fun since wakeboarding on the Mekong," Max said, recalling his days as a swift boat captain.

"They're establishing a satellite uplink," Hali said.

"First shot's a miss," Linda said.

The op center held its collective breath. Seconds later, the second round exploded. Everyone saw the *Baktun*'s satellite mast torn apart like bird shot through a sheet of tinfoil.

"Satellite signal dead." Hali smiled.

The op center cheered.

"Great shot, Wepps," Juan said.

"Chairman," Linda shouted. "Missile launch!"

★

ABOARD THE *FUZHOU*

Captain Zhao heard the first airburst over the *Baktun* and watched her pilot's swift evasive response to the explosion. Her initial reaction was that the Americans had elected to fire at her ship, but she quickly dismissed the idea. The Americans would have used much more powerful ordinance against her mighty vessel.

The second explosion two seconds later infuriated her. The dogs were trying to damage or sink the *Baktun*, no doubt to capture or destroy the AGI program.

Zhao didn't radio Peng for instructions. He had already given her permission to destroy the American ship if they threatened the *Fuzhou* or the AGI program.

Zhao shouted orders as a third round passed harmlessly overhead.

"Helm, flank speed."

"Aye."

"Weapons station, launch Eagle Strike."

78

What is that madman up to?"

Stokes studied the radar screen, watching the *Oregon* plowing directly toward him from some distance away. Now that Fierro was dead, he had to protect Bose's AGI at all costs, keeping it from both the Chinese and the Yanks.

A thundering roar erupted beyond the bulkheads.

"*Fuzhou* launching missile," the Brazilian first officer said, calm as a clam.

"Chinese turbines spinning up," the sonarman said. "She's engaging the American."

Stokes nodded, admiring the American captain. He now understood what he was doing. The American wasn't charging at the *Baktun*—he was only closing the distance to the *Fuzhou*.

For a split second, Stokes considered the tempting option of firing his weapons at the distracted Chinese, their attention focused on the Americans.

But the *Fuzhou* was a stout ship, and close-quarters battle with a heavily armed gunboat was risky at best, and most likely fatal.

He also thought about joining the *Fuzhou* in combat against the *Oregon*. But it was too late to join the battle. The sudden launch of the Chinese hypersonic meant the Americans had less than twelve seconds to live.

His other course of action was clear, now that he had full access to the ship's fusion reactor.

"Helm—pulse wave engine status?"

"One hundred percent."

"Set a course for heading oh-one-oh. Flank speed."

"Aye, sir. Engaging engines."

"Comms, notify the crew to brace."

The supercavitating zone created by his high-tech propulsion system would drive the *Baktun* to sixty knots, nearly double the *Fuzhou*'s top-rated speed. The Chinese could never catch him, and surely Peng had orders not to destroy the *Baktun* after the Americans were annihilated.

"Helm, why aren't we underway? Engage!"

Stokes turned to his man, who was furiously punching switches on his board.

"Engines don't respond."

Stokes charged over. "What's happening?"

"No idea. We're dead in the water."

Stokes made a quick calculation. Unable to flee the Chinese, there was only one logical course of action to protect Project Q.

★

ABOARD THE *FUZHOU*

The Chinese Eagle Strike hypersonic missile vaulted out of its vertical launch tube with a loud hiss of high-pressure nitrogen in a white cloud of condensed vapor. Two seconds above the deck, the engines fired up and the missile began its fiery climb to space altitude, where it would transition to glide phase, then race back to its target at over Mach 10. Its sophisticated guidance and maneuvering system ensured a fatal strike against the bulky American cargo ship despite the *Oregon*'s unbelievable rate of speed.

"Captain, *Baktun* weapons spinning up. Radar target lock!"

"Why are they attacking the Americans?" Zhao demanded.

"They're not. They're targeting us."

★

ABOARD THE *BAKTUN*

Captain Stokes stood in the *Baktun*'s combat information center, his clear gray eyes fixed on the monitor. The *Fuzhou* filled his screen, its bridge and hull suddenly painted with dozens of targeting reticles. At only five hundred yards distance, the Chinese Type 055 destroyer was a sitting duck.

Calmly, firmly, Stokes uttered his command.

"Fire."

The entirety of the *Baktun*'s lethal arsenal unleashed with sudden fury.

The *Baktun*'s 30-millimeter GAU-8 Avenger Gatling gun opened up first, spitting fire and lead in a deafening roar, unleashing seventy armor-piercing rounds per second. The storm of tungsten projectiles shredded the *Fuzhou*'s bridge instantly, obliterating radar antennas, sensors, and communication arrays, and tearing through armored glass and steel bulkheads like wet rice paper.

Simultaneously, the *Baktun*'s two big naval auto cannons joined the fury, smashing the *Fuzhou*'s thin-hulled superstructure in relentless, pinpoint volleys of explosive fragmentation shells.

★

ABOARD THE *FUZHOU*

Captain Zhao barely registered the *Baktun*'s first muzzle flashes before a blinding storm of destruction erupted around her. The bridge vanished instantly in an explosion of glass, fire, and twisted metal. Zhao and her crew were torn apart in the maelstrom before realizing the battle had even begun.

Belowdecks, sailors screamed in horror and confusion as explosive shells punched effortlessly through the hull, detonating deep within the vessel's core. Internal bulkheads collapsed under the blasts as fire surged through passageways, filling compartments with choking black smoke and suffocating darkness.

Miraculously, a dying weapons officer deep in the combat center managed to smash his mangled hand against a firing button. This single act of dying vengeance unleashed a short burst of 130-millimeter cannon blasts before he was torn apart by an explosive shell slicing through the armored bulkhead.

Below the waterline, the *Fuzhou* shuddered violently as dozens of swarming mini torpedoes found their marks. Several simultaneous detonations ripped massive breaches through the ship's hull, flooding the engine room and other critical compartments almost instantly. The few surviving sailors scrambled for ladders and escape hatches as seawater surged into their dying ship.

Chaos reigned as the *Baktun*'s Gatling guns continued raking the upper decks, chainsawing bodies in their wake, slicing the steel beneath their feet in gore. Secondary explosions hurtled sailors against the bulkheads like rag dolls, splattering crimson brushstrokes on the buckling walls.

Within seconds, the *Fuzhou*'s comms, propulsion, and fire-control systems were completely obliterated.

★

ABOARD THE *OREGON*

"Looks like the *Baktun*'s in trouble," Cabrillo said.

Like the rest of the op center team, Cabrillo was stunned at the near instantaneous destruction of the *Fuzhou*. But it appeared the Chinese had gotten a few shots off as well, punching holes in the *Baktun* just below the waterline underneath the bow.

If the *Baktun* sank, Cabrillo couldn't capture the AGI Overholt so desperately wanted.

The *Oregon* was already running at full tilt, its massive engines pulsing astronomical power. Even at her current high rate of speed it would take his ship a full twenty-four minutes to get to the *Baktun* and board her to secure Project Q—if she stayed afloat that long.

But the *Oregon* might not survive the next few seconds. The *Fu-*

zhou's deadly hypersonic missile was still streaking toward them at over Mach 10. There was no way to outrun it.

The *Fuzhou*'s "dead hand" missile strike was about to kill them all.

★

ABOARD PENG'S HELICOPTER

Hovering just twenty-five feet above the sea a half mile away, Zhao watched in stomach-churning horror as the great Chinese warship suffered crushing blow after crushing blow. The *Fuzhou* barely had a chance to respond. Its single deck gun got off a few shots just seconds before succumbing to the *Baktun*'s relentless cannonades. It appeared to be sinking.

The pilot checked his fuel gauge. Only thirty minutes of flight time was left and there was no other Chinese ship or base anywhere near. It was only supposed to be a short flight to the *Baktun*, so he hadn't ordered a refueling.

The pilot turned in his seat and glanced at the anxious Marines in back and saw their young faces ghosted white with terror.

"Will the *Baktun* let us land, comrade?" the pilot asked. "If not, we'll all drown out here."

Peng mopped away the flop sweat from his eyes.

"We'll have to try. All they can do is kill us quicker."

79

Eagle Strike descending," Eric called out.

The *Oregon*'s radar had tracked the ship-killing hypersonic missile through its entire trajectory and now it was racing down toward them at over ten times the speed of sound.

"There's no way to outrun it," Eric said. "Brace for impact."

"No need to," Cabrillo said without looking at him.

"Sir?"

"Because it has a minimum range of twenty-five miles," Murphy said with a grin, standing in the op center doorway. "And by charging toward the *Fuzhou*, you got inside that range."

All eyes turned toward the monitors. The streaking missile roared overhead in a blaze of blinding light—and overshot the *Oregon*. Before anyone could exhale, the Eagle Strike exploded harmlessly in the distance in a massive wall of water.

★

ABOARD THE *BAKTUN*

Stokes bolted from his command chair, raging at his startled CIC crew as the first salvos from his guns fired at the *Fuzhou*, demanding to know who authorized the attack without his permission.

But his voice was lost in the din of roaring gunfire, blaring alarms, and the shouts of his men calling out the attacks as they unfolded. Stokes stopped raging as he caught sight of the *Fuzhou*'s bridge exploding, knowing full well no one could survive that kind of blast. Had the *Fuzhou* been in battle stations, the captain and her team would have secured themselves in their armored CIC belowdecks.

Stokes's shock and rage gave way to sudden elation as he watched his ship rip the Chinese battle cruiser to shreds. But when the *Fuzhou*'s deck gun opened up and punched fatal wounds into the *Baktun*'s hull, he knew the game was over. He turned toward his second-in-command and gave his final order to the stalwart Brazilian.

"Sound the alarm, Rodrigo. Abandon ship."

The taciturn officer nodded. "Aye, Captain."

The automated voice, light, and signal alarms lit up as Stokes raced out of the CIC and headed for the lab.

★

ABOARD THE *OREGON*

"*Fuzhou* listing hard," Gomez called out from his drone station. "*Baktun* going slowly down by the bow."

"Goose it harder, Max—emergency power," Juan said. "We gotta get there before we lose that AGI."

Cabrillo was running a brutal interior monologue, railing against his too-smart-by-half decision to use the *Baktun* to take out the *Fuzhou* to keep the Chinese from capturing Project Q.

Overholt said the *Oregon* couldn't fire on the Chinese vessel, but didn't say anything about the *Baktun* doing the dirty deed. In a court martial, a judge and jury would call that a distinction without a difference and likely keelhaul him. But as far as Cabrillo was concerned, he had held to both the letter of the law and the spirit of the mission.

What Juan hadn't counted on was the *Fuzhou* striking back. Murph had cut loose with every weapons system on board the *Baktun* simultaneously, but some dying Chinese gunner put enough well-placed rounds downrange to seal the *Baktun*'s impending fate.

With any luck, the *Oregon* would arrive in time to insert a boarding party, snatch up any Project Q hard drives, organoid material, and personnel they could lay their hands on, and get off with enough technology to advance America's own AGI program.

Cabrillo prayed that Dr. Bose was still alive. She would be the key to unlocking everything and piecing it all back together. But there was no telling if she had survived the *Fuzhou*'s fatal hits. Cabrillo consoled himself with the knowledge that even if he didn't get there in time, at least the Chinese wouldn't get their hands on Project Q, either.

"Missile detected!" Murphy called out from the weapons station. Linda had gladly given up her seat to him when Juan waved him back over to it.

"Hypersonic speed—Mach 10.3!" Stone called out.

"Another Eagle Strike?" Cabrillo asked. "How did we miss it?"

"Negative," Stone said as he rechecked his readings. "Wrong trajectory."

"Then what is it?"

"It's that Nork Fire Star ICBM they launched earlier this morning."

The *Oregon*'s top secret status and Overholt's pull gave the spy ship automatic access to all of the nation's highly sensitive intelligence including the alert posted that morning by a U.S. Space Force satellite. It had detected and identified the Hwasong-17 Fire Star's unique infrared engine signature moments after it had launched.

"Where's the Fire Star designated impact area?" Cabrillo asked.

"It was supposed to be eighteen hundred miles from here," Eric said.

"And now?"

"It's heading in our direction."

Cabrillo knew the Fire Star was a highly maneuverable, precision-guided missile capable of hitting a target even as small as the five-hundred-ninety-foot *Oregon*.

"Talk to me, Wepps."

Murphy's fingers sped across his keyboard.

"By my calculations, it looks like it's targeting . . . the *Baktun*."

Cabrillo could hardly hide his shock.

"Why would the Norks want to sink the *Baktun*?"

"Maybe it's not the Norks," Eric said.

"You mean someone's hijacked it?"

"Could be."

"Who? Why?" Linda asked.

"Someone who doesn't want anyone else to have Project Q," Cabrillo said as he turned in his chair.

"Comms—hail the *Baktun*."

★

ABOARD THE *BAKTUN*

The last of the Project Q techs, a young Thai national, thundered up the steel staircase in a mad dash for the lifeboats. Her backpack brushed roughly against Stokes without apology as he scrambled down into the bowels of the dying ship and the lab within.

The flashing red lights cast a hellish strobe effect across the darkened expanse, the nightmare phenomenon amplified by the shrieking alarms and automated voice commands still ringing overhead.

Stokes knew exactly where Bose would be. He dashed over to her side standing at the base of the great containment tank holding her precious creation.

"We've got to go. Now," Stokes said, tugging on her arm.

She shook him off, tears streaming from her eyes. "I can't leave."

"Don't be so dramatic. It's not a child, it's a machine . . . a robot."

Bose wheeled around and slapped him hard across the face.

"How dare you."

Stokes saw the wounded fury in her eyes. He began to mount an argument about how she could start over again, build a new Neural Reef somewhere else, and earn her fame in due time. But before he could draw another breath he knew that would be as calloused as a soul-numbed preacher telling a grieving graveside mother she should just get pregnant again.

In truth, he understood her pain. He even felt it. The *Baktun* was his pride and joy, an extension of his own storm-tossed soul. Stokes smiled to himself. His ship had performed magnificently today, killing a mighty Chinese warship and most of its crew in mere seconds. It was the most satisfying moment of his life and he knew he would never get such an opportunity again.

"My apologies," he told her as he gathered her up in his arms. She sobbed deeply into his chest.

The radio on his hip squawked. Cabrillo's voice screeched over its tiny speaker, barely audible above the alarms.

"*Baktun! Baktun!* This is *Oregon*. Do you read me?"

Stokes kept one arm wrapped around Bose as he keyed his radio.

"This is Captain Stokes. What do you want?"

"Incoming missile headed your way. Ten minutes to impact. What's your status?"

"I suspect you know, old boy. You hijacked my weapons and engines. Well played, I must say. We're dead in the water, literally and figuratively."

"I've released your engines. Clear away from the area immediately. We'll cover you with air defense as best we can and rendezvous to take on any of your crew. My medical team is on standby."

"A beau geste, Captain. But too late, I'm afraid."

"Is Dr. Bose still with you?"

"She is, indeed."

Stokes hurled the radio against the nearest bulkhead, smashing it to bits, then gathered Bose back into his bosom.

"I'll not abandon you, my precious orchid, nor my beloved ship."

★

ABOARD PENG'S HELICOPTER
Peng had already briefed the Marines before the flight took off. He told them to expect resistance and to kill anybody who opposed them. But their primary mission was finding Fierro, Bose, and any equipment related to Project Q.

"Hardware. Thumb drives. Documentation. Anything."

Peng had no idea how long the *Baktun* had before it sank beneath the waves. The Navy helicopter pilot estimated twenty minutes at most. The pilot demanded one of the privates help him locate the aviation fuel and resupply the helicopter if at all possible. Peng reluctantly agreed, since acquiring Project Q personnel or materials would be irrelevant if they all crashed back into the sea.

As the helicopter approached the helipad, Peng issued orders to the Marine major in charge. "We leave in fifteen minutes, no exceptions."

"My men won't fail you, sir."

The twelve Chinese Marines leaped out of the helicopter before the skids hit the angled deck located on the elevated bow, scattering in pairs in all directions. One Marine stayed with the pilot, and a burly sergeant stood by Peng's side.

Peng's instincts told him the machine would be belowdecks. He pulled his pistol, nodded to the sergeant, and dashed for the ladder.

★

ABOARD A LIFEBOAT

The *Baktun* was a registered, oceangoing vessel subject to periodic safety inspections. Accordingly, it maintained a full array of well-kept emergency escape equipment, including a contingent of enclosed fiberglass lifeboats.

One of those lifeboats puttered away on its electric motor, piloted by one of the deckhands, a grizzly Swede who willed the bobbing craft as far away from the two sinking hulks as possible, praying they could escape the downward pull that could easily suck them to their doom. Slowing his progress were the five survivors clinging to two ropes trailing the overcrowded lifeboat. They held on for dear life as the lifeboat inched its way through the chop.

Packed with over a dozen terrified techs and piloted by the Swede, the big orange lozenge had managed to put a mile between itself and the *Baktun* in the ten minutes since the abandon ship alarms had sounded. The Swede's pale gray eyes were fixed on the *Baktun*'s high, proud bow as it knelt down toward the unforgiving sea.

The sudden flash startled the old mariner like a gunshot in the dark. The explosion emitted a supersonic shock wave that rippled across the water, nearly capsizing the lifeboat. The confusion and horror of the moment amplified the terrified screams echoing inside the claustrophobic bubble. White-hot shrapnel whistled through the air, punching a dozen jagged holes through the fiberglass-reinforced hull. Arterial blood spattered a half dozen faces as another agonizing scream rang out above all the others.

The Swede pulled out the emergency medical kit and tossed it to the man seated nearest the screaming woman, clearly bleeding out.

"Do what you can," was all he said. He was neither a doctor nor a priest.

He glanced out the tiny portal of the lifeboat to check on the people holding on to the trailing ropes. Two floated face down and spread-eagled in the water far behind the boat, no doubt killed by the blast.

Two others still held on, their determined faces white-knuckling the rope saving their lives.

The fifth floated upright in the water, her backpack bunched up around her shoulders. Her stunned eyes beneath her bleeding scalp were fixed on the rope now hopelessly beyond her reach and pulling away. The young Thai woman had waited too long to exit the lab. In her mad dash up the staircase she'd even bumped into the captain before reaching the top deck and hurling herself into the sea.

The Swede's heart went out to the young woman, but his boat was already overcrowded and meagerly provisioned for however many days and nights might lay ahead. By his reckoning she wasn't long for this world anyway, so he motored on. He turned away from the pitying sight.

The old Swede hadn't prayed in years.

Now seemed to be a good time to start.

80

The Thai neurobiologist wasn't a great swimmer, but she knew it wasn't about swimming at this point, just surviving. When the lifeboat abandoned her, she removed her waterproof pack from her back and turned it around, put her arms through the straps, and pulled it close to her chest, using the pack like a float.

Her spirit sank when the lifeboat left her behind, but it was the blood loss and shock from the shrapnel wound to her scalp that shut her eyes. She fell asleep, gently rocked by the rolling waves, her head half submerged in the cool water.

She had the vague sense of floating in her dream state, but the sound of high-pitched mosquitoes whined in her ears. If the sound would just go away, she could go to sleep forever . . .

A hard bump against her leg jolted her awake. Her bulging eyes caught sight of the speeding shark fin racing past, spiking her heart rate to the edge of ventricular fibrillation.

She quickly spun around, roiling the water like a wounded fish. Something told her that was a dumb move. Her ears were clogged with water and her mind was fogged, but she could see she was in big trouble now.

The sight of three more shark fins confirmed it.

She tasted the blood in her mouth. She touched the scalp wound that hadn't stopped bleeding. In fact, she'd left a trail of blood in the water—no doubt drawing the hungry sharks to her. Her peripheral vision caught sight of another shark fin racing toward her in the distance, but the back of her neck tingled like a burglar alarm as the distant whining grew louder. She refused to take her eyes off the charging shark—

The ear-splitting whine of a big four-stroke motor exploded behind her. She cried out in confused terror as she felt herself yanked out of the water at speed and tossed onto the long hard seat of a big Yamaha WaveRunner that had barely slowed.

"Hold on tight, missy," Cabrillo said as he gunned the throttle, racing away from the circling sharks and back toward the *Oregon*.

The girl could barely wrap her thin arms around the muscled torso of the man driving the Jet Ski. She felt the backpack pressed against her chest, forgetting she even had it. She breathed a sigh of relief.

The hard drives with all of the core Neural Reef algorithms were safely tucked inside, along with living tissue samples suspended in neuroplasm. She hoped Bose had survived, but doubted it after that huge explosion. At least the doctor's creation would live on.

She closed her eyes again, and laid her forehead against the man's broad back.

She was safe.

81

COLOMBIA, 1997

Vladimir Suárez was cuffed to a steel chair beside a battered desk inside the dank cell. A single naked bulb burned with a sallow light high and out of reach. Anguished cries echoed in the corridors beyond the steel door.

Two weeks earlier, the American spy had delivered him bound and gagged to the fascist Colombian Army, who dropped him into this secret prison. His body bore the evidence of their interrogations. His left eye was now swollen shut, his unshaven face was caked with dried blood, and his flesh was covered in deep bruises from the brutal punches and truncheon blows of the sadistic inquisitors.

He didn't care.

In fact, he wished they'd finish the job. Just beat him to death and get it over with. Anything to quiet the agonizing screams of his wife burning to death every night in his fitful dreams.

A set of keys jangled in the lock and the steel door swung open.

A lean, clean-shaven man stepped inside. He wore a pair of Levi's 501s, a loose collared cotton shirt, Saucony running shoes, a thick mustache, and an easy smile. He also carried a worn canvas messenger bag. The soulless prison guard shut the door behind him.

Suárez feigned indifference, but he sized up the man with his one good eye, catching him in his peripheral vision. As near as he could tell, the man was unarmed.

"So you're the new torturer?" Suárez asked.

"I don't believe in it."

The man pulled out a pack of Marlboros and a lighter from his shirt pocket, lit one up, and put it in Suárez's mouth. The Colombian killer took a long drag as the man pulled a key and unlocked his cuffs, then tossed them with a noisy clang onto the table.

Suárez rubbed the blood back into his wrists as the man lit a smoke for himself. He then pulled the other steel chair around from the back of the table, dragged its scraping feet across the tiled floor next to Suárez, and fell into it.

The two Colombians smoked for a minute in silence, like two old friends on a park bench. Suárez inhaled deep lungfuls of nicotine as if it were pure oxygen. The small room clouded with blue smoke.

Suárez dragged the last bit of cigarette to its filter and then flicked it away.

"If you want information," Suárez finally said, breaking the silence, "it will take more than a cigarette."

The man held up the pack. Suárez took another, snatched up the lighter, and took a long drag. "And it will take more than two."

The man chuckled.

Suárez closed his eyes, and let the tendrils of smoke escape his nostrils like a brooding dragon. He didn't open them when the peep slot on the steel door slid open and the guard looked in to see what was going on.

The easygoing interrogator threw a look at the guard that made him nearly soil himself. He slammed the peep slot shut and didn't come back.

The man returned his attention to Suárez, his face a mask of unrelenting grief—impervious to any physical pain anyone could ever level against him.

"I'm sorry about Nadia," the man began softly.

Suárez opened his eyes. They flickered with simmering rage.

The man continued. "I once watched a man burn to death. It was the worst thing I ever saw."

Suárez shut his eyes tightly as if he could drive his wife's screams out of his mind.

"They roughed you up pretty badly. Those Army guys are real *pendejos*. They shouldn't have done that to you."

"My *abuela* hits harder than that major of yours."

The man squinted. "Looks like he knocked out a couple of teeth. We can fix that. What did you do to make him so angry?"

"The pig said my people killed his father and brother."

"Did they?"

Suárez shrugged. "Does it matter who or when or why? We're all in the same charnel house. Nobody gets out of here alive."

The man leaned back. "So you're a philosopher."

"And you're Colombian intelligence."

"Emilio Cabral."

"Is that what your mother calls you?"

Cabral shook his head with a grin. He was dealing with a real pro. And fearless.

"My mother calls me a lot of things."

"What is it you want from me, Señor Cabral?"

Cabral dropped his smoldering cigarette to the floor and crushed it beneath his shoe.

"You know the drill. Names. Places. Dates. These FARC cockroaches you worked with need to be exterminated."

"Those 'cockroaches' are my comrades."

Cabral laughed. "Comrades? You? A rich college kid? With an IQ off the charts? I don't think so. You're only playing revolutionary hero so you have permission to kill."

Suárez leaned forward. "I believe in the revolution."

"You don't believe in anything. I've read your dossier. You're godless. Soulless. Like a wolf. You've tasted blood. Lots of blood. All you want is more. That's all."

"Go to hell."

"You misunderstand, Vladimir. I admire you. I can use you."

Suárez raised an eyebrow, confused.

"I can get you out. Put you back in the hunt."

"What do you mean?"

"You have a talent in high demand. I can take advantage of that. Discreetly, of course. I'll put you in deep with one of the cartels. You'll help us break the back of those animals from the inside."

"But only if I give you the names of my FARC comrades first."

"They threaten the government."

"I don't care about the government."

"I don't blame you. But only the government can set you free. Don't you want to be free?"

Suárez shut his eyes again. Only, this time he could see the CIA man who killed his wife. See his own hands wrapped around the CIA man's throat, feel his larynx crushing beneath his grip, his blue eyes bulging out of their sockets.

"I want it badly."

"So tell me. Names and places."

"Who is the CIA man?"

"I've made an inquiry. He's a ghost. I'll help you find him, but you'll have to be patient. A man like that will always be in the shadows somewhere. And that's where you'll be, too. You're bound to meet him eventually."

"And all I have to do is give you what you want, and I'm free?"

"Totally free. But you'll report to me, though rarely, and carefully. And if you ever betray me? Well, you can imagine how that will go. What do you say?"

Suárez lit another cigarette. He took a long pull, thinking. He held the cigarette between his fingers, twisting it, turning the smoke into tight little curls that rose like climbing grapevines toward the ceiling light.

"How will it work, exactly?"

"You'll need a new identity, of course." Cabral reached into his canvas bag and tossed a Colombian passport onto the table.

The assassin picked it up and read his new name aloud, "Rafael Vargas." His practiced eye scanned the rest of the document. Faded entry stamps, coffee-stained pages, and the like.

"Pretty good work."

"Better than CIA. You'll receive advanced training in weapons, comms, and tradecraft before we send you out. You'll need some plastic surgery, too. I'll make all the arrangements."

"When do I start?"

Cabral reached back into his messenger bag. He tossed a yellow pad and a couple of pens onto the desk.

"Names, places, dates. You know the drill."

Suárez picked up a pen and wrote the name "Rafael Vargas."

"What's that?"

"Wanted to see how it felt." Vargas scratched it off and wrote down his first FARC name.

"Hungry?" Cabral asked.

"Starving." He didn't look up from the pad.

Cabral stood. "I'll grab some hot food and a couple of cold *cervezas*."

"I'll be here, *jefe*."

"We'll make a good team, you and me."

82

A month after the sinking of the *Fuzhou* and the *Baktun*, the *Oregon* crew finally got its hard-earned vacation at their private island in the eastern Caribbean.

It had been touch-and-go for a moment. Juan's strict orders were to not fire on the Chinese nor sink the *Baktun*, and Cabrillo's explanation that he had technically done neither didn't sit well with Overholt or the director of national intelligence.

But the few surviving Chinese sailors rescued by the *Oregon* all confirmed their ship was sunk by the bandit ship *Baktun* in an unprovoked attack and not by the Americans. In fact, they even praised the Americans' heroic rescue efforts, superlative medical care, and respectful treatment. Their testimonies completely exonerated the *Oregon* in the eyes of the Chinese authorities. If the *Fuzhou* had been recording the events of that day, they never got the data files transferred.

The death of Dr. Bose and the loss of the *Baktun* kept AGI out of China's hands, which was to Cabrillo's credit. The denial of the same to the American AGI program was counted against him. But Cabrillo's rescue of the young Thai neurobiologist and her treasure trove of Project Q materials, along with dozens of other surviving techs, ultimately put him in good stead with both Overholt and the federal government.

What still perplexed everyone was the question of the Hwasong-17. Who had hijacked the Korean ICBM and, more important, used it to destroy the *Baktun*? The Russians? The Iranians? The American intelligence community was in a lather. It was a problem Cabrillo couldn't be bothered with.

Besides Project Q, the *Oregon* had completed all of her other assignments.

First, thanks to Linc and Raven's indomitable efforts to find the base, the Quds Force threat had been eliminated by a combined American-Israeli off-the-books operation. The predawn raid by a mixed unit of Delta Force and Sayeret Matkal operators began with jamming the Iranians' comms. As they approached the camp by foot, snipers took out sentries with suppressed, subsonic rounds before the rest of the team swarmed in silently, tossing grenades into the command tent and cutting loose with automatic fire on the rest of the compound. Within minutes, the entire Quds Force had been either captured or killed, the survivors frog-marched out of the jungle and into waiting Black Hawk helicopters several miles away.

The elimination of the Quds Force unit was a real coup. An active Iranian special forces outfit would have given the ayatollahs an important strategic foothold in Latin America. Besides the fact they could have been used to cross over into the U.S. to engage in terrorist acts, the Quds Force would have bolstered anti-American regimes like Nicaragua, Cuba, and Venezuela. The Iranians could have also joined forces with Hezbollah or other terrorist organizations operating in the region. All of those ambitions died with the destruction of the smoldering Quds Force camp.

Next, the demon ship mystery had concluded with the sinking of the *Baktun*. And finally, President Olmedo was not only alive but had formally broken ties with the Chinese government and was now counted as America's most important ally in Central America.

"Just another day on the job," Juan told Overholt. "All that's left to do is cash your checks."

Overholt gladly transferred Cabrillo's customary fees along with a hefty reimbursement for a long list of itemized expenses. The windfall profits would be divided proportionately among the crew as active shareholders in the Corporation.

The vacation island arrival was uneventful and the weather was heaven-sent. By the third day, the crew had feasted, played, and partied like well-mannered pirates. The tightly bonded ship grew even closer under the sunny Caribbean sky and the windy, starlit nights. The crew all worked hard, fought valiantly, and served selflessly. Cabrillo believed they deserved every sun-kissed moment of rest and relaxation.

He didn't mind putting his own toes in the sand, either.

★

It was late morning on the fourth day of their vacation island sojourn. Cabrillo rocked gently in a hammock strung between two palm trees rereading one of his favorite Louis L'Amour novels, *The Walking Drum*. Unlike L'Amour's classic Westerns, this was the swashbuckling epic of an adventurous warrior-scholar set in the turbulent worlds of the twelfth century. In other words, right up Juan's alley.

Cabrillo was making the last stand with Kerbouchard against the Petchenegs in the novel when his phone vibrated. He grunted, irritated by the interruption of a great read. He'd told the rest of his crew to stay off the electronic stuff unless absolutely necessary. The whole point of a private island, he'd told them, was privacy. Social media only invited a world of troubles into their idyllic island paradise.

But with a crew as large as the *Oregon*'s, Juan knew he needed to be available to them, especially when he wasn't on board the ship. He picked up the phone. The caller ID read "Unknown," which was odd. He thought about dismissing it, but chances were that some federal agency yahoo working a government desk needed to follow up with him about recent events.

"Cabrillo here."

There was silence on the other end. Then a *ding* as a video file popped onto his text messenger. He opened it.

His heart sank.

Two nuns dressed in habits were handcuffed by their wrists and ankles to a large crucifix inside a brightly lit cave. They were obviously alive but in great discomfort.

A young nun faced the camera, struggling to keep her composure. Cabrillo couldn't see the other nun's face. She was chained on the opposite side facing the back wall of the cave.

The video read "Live" in the left-hand corner of his smartphone window. Juan leaped out of his hammock.

A large man limped into the camera frame, holding a flamethrower in his hands and carrying a napalm pack on his back. He was clearly struggling as if he had been injured.

The nuns squirmed, but didn't cry out. Cabrillo saw the young nun's faith in her stoic demeanor.

The man turned and approached the camera until his face filled the frame.

"Recognize me, Cabrillo?"

"You're the puke that tried to kill President Olmedo."

The man darkened. "Olmedo got lucky."

"So did you, apparently. My drone operator put a couple of bullets in you. You should be dead."

"You can't kill a ghost."

"I'm happy to try again."

"We met before once, Cabrillo. Many years ago."

Murph had grabbed a screenshot of the guy, but Eric never could ID him. Still, he seemed somehow familiar. He couldn't pull up a name.

"I see you're struggling. I had plastic surgery, though I had the same problem recognizing you, at first."

"What's wrong? Did I forget to sign your high school yearbook? Steal your girlfriend?"

"You were flippant that night, too." The man spat on the ground.

"What's this about? And who in the hell are you?"

"Do you remember the name Nadia?"

A cold shot of pure terror seized Cabrillo. The memory of the woman flooded back over him like a waking nightmare. It was the Colombian snatch-and-grab mission that had gone sideways. Nadia's screams had cried out to him over the years.

"I can see by the look on your face you do remember my beautiful Nadia. I think maybe you even dream about her as I do."

Cabrillo watched the man's face twist into a maudlin grimace even as his eyes flared with rage.

"She suffered terribly. So will you."

While Suárez spoke, Juan secretly sent a link of the live video to Linda, who was officer of the day, standing watch in the op center.

"It wasn't intentional, Suárez. I told you that a long time ago. I thought she was dead or I never would have left her there."

"And yet you did—and she burned alive. Can you imagine a worse death? She was such a beauty. It was as if you set fire to the Louvre that night. Humanity can never forgive you for her loss, nor can I forgive you for her suffering."

Suárez turned around and approached the two bound women, holding up his fiery weapon. His gloved hand turned the ignition valve and a thin blue cone of flame like from a welding torch arced to life at the tip of the pilot assembly. He stepped closer to the young nun.

Juan tensed, fearing the worst was about to happen.

"Suárez! Don't!"

Suárez raised the old Soviet-era flamethrower to the young nun's face. She cringed as the scorching blue flame licked her skin. She refused to cry out, but finally fainted with a shuddering whimper as a huge red blister bloomed on her cheek.

Suárez pulled the flamethrower away and killed the pilot light, ignoring the other nun's fervent prayers.

Suárez turned back to the camera, unaware that Ross had just sent Juan a text.

Crew notified. Recording video. Horrible. Please
advise.

"So what do you want, Suárez?"

"Do I really have to spell it out for the CIA man?"

"What are your terms?"

Suárez unshouldered the heavy pack with great difficulty, his face pinched with pain. The Colombian assassin approached his smartphone perched on a tripod broadcasting the horror show.

"Terms? Here are my terms. You have exactly ninety minutes to turn yourself over to my custody. You will trade your life for the lives of these two Sisters of Divine Mercy. I will release them upon your arrival. You will come to the cave alone. I'll send the GPS coordinates as soon as I end the call and that's when your countdown begins."

"You know I'll be there."

"Of course you will. And you'll try to bring in your operatives, and free the women and kill me. Well, let me save you the trouble. I don't care if I die. In fact, I would consider it a favor." Suárez hacked with a phlegmy cough. He pulled his ungloved hand away from his mouth. It was bloody. He showed it to the camera. "You see? I haven't much longer to live anyway." He wiped his hand on his pants.

"You also need to know I have cameras located all over this little island. If you jam them, these women will be burned alive. If anyone approaches the cave other than you, the women will be burned alive. Do anything other than what I tell you, and these nuns will be soaked in napalm gel and lit up like Nero's torches. Am I completely understood?"

"Understood."

"I will be broadcasting this event live for your crew. I want them to see your suffering. I want your screams lodged in their brains for the rest of their lives. *Hasta luego, cabrón*."

Suárez killed the call.

Cabrillo was already sprinting toward the *Oregon* when the GPS coordinates arrived on his phone five seconds later.

★

Cabrillo was shocked to find two dozen crew crowded into the op center, where Linda had played the live feed and then replayed the recording when the others arrived. Every face was tense with either fear or anger or both, none more so than Juan's.

"So this mook, Suárez, blames you for his wife's death?" Linda asked. "What happened?"

"No time to explain."

No one paid attention to Eric tapping furiously on his computer keyboard, searching for whatever intel he could find on Suárez and his wife.

"I've already loaded the coordinates into the AW's nav computer," Gomez said. "We need to get going."

"Roger that." Juan turned to Max. "You have the helm until I get back."

Max could hardly speak. "Copy that."

"We're not going to let this guy get away with this are we?" Eddie Seng said. He and his Gundogs were ready to pounce.

"You heard the man. He's got this thing wired shut."

"There's gotta be another option," Linda said.

"Maybe there is but we don't have the time to come up with it. Right now, this is my only play."

The other crew began to protest, some even began to weep.

But Juan threw up his hands and said, "I need to get to my cabin to take care of some things. If you're the praying type, I can use it— and so can those nuns. Otherwise, I'll see you on the flip side."

★

Cabrillo dashed into his cabin and ran straight to his biometric safe. He placed his hand on the lock and it popped open. He pulled out a manila envelope. Tucked inside was a newly drafted but unsigned will along with specific instructions. He'd been putting off signing it for weeks. If he really was going to die, the last thing he wanted to do was leave the Corporation in a state of legal and financial limbo.

Cabrillo pulled out the papers and grabbed a pen. Standing at his desk, he flipped pages as fast as he could, signing where he needed to. His door popped open. He glanced up.

"Kinda busy right now, Kevin."

Nixon stood in the doorway, his hand gripping a canvas utility bag. "Chairman—"

"Save your breath. You're not stopping me and you're not going with me. But I appreciate the gesture."

"I just . . ."

Cabrillo signed the last page and tossed the pen aside.

"Do you remember what I told you when you joined the crew?"

"Yeah, I sure do. 'We do what's right, no matter the cost.'"

Cabrillo nodded. "That's right. It'll all work out. You watch."

Kevin smiled. "You're right. It will."

★

Cabrillo sent a text from his cabin and ordered the crew to remain belowdecks. He didn't want to make any kind of a scene.

The crew remained assembled in the op center or crowded into the conference room. They all watched Juan on the monitors scrambling into the AW tilt-rotor, his face grimly set on the task at hand. He wore a ball cap, loose fitting slacks, and a breezy cotton shirt instead of the cargo shorts and tank top he'd been in earlier. Cabrillo threw a jaunty salute at the deck camera as he shut the door and the AW roared off the deck.

And just like that, Juan Cabrillo was gone.

83

ISLA DE SAN ALEJO

Gomez landed the AW right on time. Juan followed Suárez's texted instructions and easily found the cave on the far end of the island, jogging the whole way to make sure he reached it in time.

Suárez stood inside the cave, the flamethrower tanks strapped once again to his shoulders. The pilot light burned brightly, and the pressurized relief valve on the tanks hissed.

Cabrillo noticed blood spotting through the man's shirt.

Suárez checked his watch. "And two minutes to spare." He glanced up with a phlegmy cough, and wiped his hand again on his filthy pants.

"Why so glum, Cabrillo? I've given you a great gift. A chance to give your life as a ransom for others—they'll be making movies about you one day, no doubt." He pointed at the tripod providing the live feed. "They're watching your great sacrifice right now. Hollywood will want to use the footage, I'm sure."

"Just get on with it."

"As you wish. First, my end of the bargain." Suárez raised the flamethrower and pointed it at Juan as two gunmen stepped out of the shadows. One cut loose the older nun, then zip-tied her hands behind her back. She offered no resistance, like a sheep to the slaughter.

"No tricks, Cabrillo. Make one move and I'll fry you right here—and them next."

Juan remained frozen in place as the second nun was cut free and zip-tied by the other man.

"Sir, you don't have to do this for us," the young nun said. "We're prepared to die."

"I know. That's why you need to live."

"How noble, Cabrillo." Suárez laughed, then spat.

"We will pray for you, señor."

The younger of the two gunmen pulled a pistol, pointed at the cave exit, and followed the two nuns out. It was hardly necessary. The nuns were eager to leave the scene of horror about to unfold, both feeling guilty but relieved they were spared the impending cruelty.

As soon as the two women left the cave, Cabrillo asked, "I have your word of honor those women will be spared?"

"As soon as I give the signal that your end of the bargain has been consummated. I harbor no ill will toward them. In fact, they saved my life. I'm relieved you had the *cojones* to show up here. Killing them would have troubled me greatly."

"What are we waiting for?"

"The camera's rolling, hero. Step on over."

Cabrillo marched over to the crucifix and let the other man cuff him to the cross, wrists first, then ankles. No way for him to move his legs.

"You can go," Suárez said. The other gunman bolted out of the cave, happy to escape the madman.

"Any last words, hero?"

Cabrillo faced the camera.

"Serving with all of you on the *Oregon* has been the greatest honor of my life. Carry on."

"That's it? How droll."

"I have an idea."

"Enlighten me."

"How about you and I play a game of Russian roulette with that flamethrower? You go first."

"Ha! That's more like it. Brave words, like an action hero."

Suárez turned toward the camera.

"This pig murdered my wife by fire. Today, I am getting justice for my Nadia, and for me. Say goodbye, Juan Cabrillo."

"Suárez," Linda called out over the tinny phone speaker. "I have something you need to see."

Suárez scowled. "No time for games."

"No games. I have a video of Nadia."

"Nadia? Impossible."

"We found it in an old CIA file. Watch it before you do anything you might regret."

The swarthy Colombian frowned with confusion. He turned toward Cabrillo, his finger on the trigger, ready to pull it. But curiosity got the better of him and he lowered the weapon and marched over to the phone.

Linda's face was in a tiny picture-in-picture window on the screen. Suddenly her face was replaced by a grainy black-and-white thumbnail captured from old surveillance footage of a young and beautiful teenage Nadia when she was a student at the Sorbonne in Paris. The burn-in across the top left read in tiny block letters: 123 RUE SAINT-JACQUES | 30 APRIL 1983 | 16:59.

Suárez nearly gasped at the haunting image, but choked down his emotions.

"Worthless. It's just an old photo." He turned to unleash a fiery hell onto Cabrillo.

"You're wrong. It's . . . a video. A classified video I'm sure you've never seen."

Suárez's eyes rounded like dinner plates as he let the flamethrower lance fall to his side. He snatched the phone off of its perch and pulled it close to his face.

"Activate the thumbnail to play it," Linda said.

Suárez didn't wait for her direction. He instantly clicked on the thumbnail and opened up the video. The undercover surveillance video Eric had managed to find and steal from the CIA archives played like an old home movie. It was obviously shot from a parked vehicle across the street from Nadia. She was sitting at a narrow iron café table in front of stone-fronted café flanked with worn shutters. A striking African woman about the same age sat across from her. They were both laughing as they chatted and smoked oily Gauloises cigarettes, with plates of croissants and demis of beer parked between them. A whining Vespa scooter throttled past them as a distant church bell rang in the background, but Suárez couldn't hear what Nadia was saying.

The brutal Colombian mashed the volume button as he pulled the phone closer to his face, his nose practically touching the screen. His eyes blurred with tears at seeing his wife so young and beautiful. He wiped his eyes with one hand.

"Make it bigger."

"We can't. The file is too small. But keep watching. There's something you really need to see. It's coming right up."

★

ABOARD THE *OREGON*

Hali Kasim sat at his comms station, with Linda hovering over his shoulder. Max was in the Kirk Chair, with Eric at helm, and Murph on weapons. Hanley had ordered everyone else to clear the op center.

Suárez's tear-streaked face loomed large and fish-eyed on the live video feed playing on the wall monitor.

Hali's fingers hovered over the engage button.

Linda squeezed his shoulder. "Now."

★

ISLA DE SAN ALEJO

Suárez was so focused on the video he didn't register the high-pitched whine milliseconds before the blinding white-hot flash detonated the phone battery. Razor-sharp fragments of glass and molten battery shrapnel shredded his eyes. He tumbled backward into the dirt, clutching at his ruined faced, blood streaming through his fingers.

Juan couldn't believe what had just happened. Somehow the *Oregon* had put the phone in thermal overload—turning the lithium-ion battery into a miniature grenade.

"Cabrillo!" Suárez raged as he clutched blindly for the flame-thrower lance. His hand finally found purchase, and he gripped the weapon in his bloody palm. He rolled over and raised the flame-thrower in the direction he thought Cabrillo was chained.

Juan swallowed hard. The nozzle was pointed directly at him.

"Burn in hell!" Suárez shouted as his finger began to mash the trigger.

But a burst of gunfire from Eddie Seng's MP5 put three slugs into the Colombian's skull before Suárez could unleash a torrent of flaming napalm. The wiry *Oregon* operator stormed over to the corpse with MacD hot on his heels. Seng disabled the flamethrower as MacD fished around in Suárez's pockets for the handcuff keys.

"We'll get you outta here in a jiffy, boss," MacD said.

"The nuns?" Cabrillo asked.

Pistol shots rang in the cave as bullets spanged the rock walls. Cabrillo screamed as a jacketed hollow-point bullet ripped through the palm of his right hand in a spray of blood.

Eddie and Mac wheeled on their toes and opened fire as Suárez's two gun thugs charged into the cave. The pistoleros spilled into the dirt, nearly cut in half by the wall of lead. They both tumbled, dead before they hit the ground.

Eddie ripped a bandage from his kit as Mac unshackled Cabrillo from the cross.

"Eddie! Mac! Report!" Linda shouted in their comms.

★

ABOARD THE *OREGON*

Max, Linda, and the rest of the op center team breathed a sigh of relief as Eddie Seng reported in on a live camera feed from the AW cabin. The thrumming rotors nearly drowned out his voice. Cabrillo lay in a webbed cot on the cabin floor.

"Chairman's stable," Seng said over his comms. "But he's lost some blood."

"Doc Huxley has the surgical team prepped and ready," Linda

said. "She has two O-negative donors heading for transfusion. She's searching records for the Chairman's blood type now."

"It's O-positive." The familiar voice came from the back of the op center.

Linda turned and nearly screamed as she faced the doorway.

Hali, Eric, and Mark whipped around in their chairs, mouths agape in utter confusion.

Juan Cabrillo stood in the op center rubbing the back of his neck, his face pinched with a throbbing headache.

"What the—?" Max did a comical double take of one Cabrillo in the doorway and the other Cabrillo on the big screen.

Juan smiled. "Tell Hux she's prepping for Kevin Nixon."

84

While Kevin was under the knife, Cabrillo took Linda down to his cabin to show her what had happened.

He pointed at the tranq gun Kevin tossed to the ground after he shot Cabrillo with it. He then took her to his marble-tiled bathroom, where silicone spray, squeeze tubes, and other makeup items lay scattered on the bathroom counter. Nixon's empty canvas bag was tossed on the marble tile floor along with the pair of Bermuda shorts and yellow T-shirt he had worn earlier. The bag was big enough to hold everything on the counter along with the change of clothes and the tranq gun.

Linda reached inside Nixon's bag and pulled out a silicone storage pouch labeled "JC." It was the kind of pouch that Nixon used to carry the hyper-accurate 3D printed masks he had perfected over the years—lifelike masks that put the CIA to shame, and fooled everyone.

Cabrillo showed her a contact lens case marked "JC/blue" and the charging case used to carry a voice synthesizer, also labeled "JC." They'd both seen Kevin put one of the clear Band-Aid–like devices on Juan's throat plenty of times when he outfitted Cabrillo for one of his undercover missions.

"He's just about your size and weight, too," Linda noted. "Makes sense, now that I see it all here. But I never would have guessed he would do something like this."

"He's the best in the business." Cabrillo checked his watch. "Let's head back to the sick bay. Kevin should be coming around soon."

As they made their way back up to the sick bay, Cabrillo asked, "So how did you manage to pull off the phone attack on Suárez?"

"We were grasping at straws and got lucky. It all came together just at the right time."

"How so?"

"Hali's Sniffer dissected Suárez's cell signal as soon as he called you on the beach. That gave Hali the phone's unique electronic signature along with the exact make, model, and software version he was using. Murphy used that intel to find an exploit in the phone and built a malware program. Meanwhile, Eric was searching CIA files for any information he could get on Suárez and just happened to come across old footage of his wife, Nadia. It was Eric's idea to embed Murph's malware into the video."

"Something he knew Suárez couldn't resist."

"Murph's malware bypassed the phone's safety measures and overloaded the lithium-ion battery with rapid charge and discharge cycles."

"Inducing a thermal runaway. No wonder the airlines hate lithium batteries."

"It was a Hail Mary play for sure."

"And all that in forty-five minutes?" Cabrillo asked. "Those two young geniuses never fail to impress."

"It was our only shot. We were just too far away to use shipboard weapons."

"And how did you sneak Eddie and MacD onto the island?"

"As soon as Gomez lifted off in the AW, the Joby slipped in behind him, using the AW as a screen. The side of the island where you—I mean, Kevin—were held was on top of a cliff."

"If Gomez flew the AW, then Arnie Davis must have flown the Joby." Cabrillo's decision to hire the temp contractor pilot had paid off handsomely.

"He was aces. No surprise there. He's former Air Force Spec Ops."

"I'm guessing Arnie held the Joby just beneath the cliff to stay out of sight and waited for your signal to infil after Suárez released the nuns?"

"Bingo."

"What's their condition?"

"No physical harm. Just a little shook up. But they're a pair of troopers, for sure. Arnie's flying them back to their convent as per their request."

The two *Oregon* executives arrived at the sick bay. Juan pulled open the door and ushered Linda inside.

★

Kevin Nixon lay in an *Oregon* hospital bed, propped up with pillows. A thick bandage was wrapped around his right hand. He had just polished off a tall cup of ice water when Cabrillo marched into the room with Linda in tow. Kevin flashed an awkward smile. Diminutive Dr. Huxley stood by his bed updating his digital chart.

"You look good, Kev," Linda said. "How are you feeling?"

Nixon held up his hand. "Reminds me of *The Mummy* remake I worked on a few years back." He examined the bandage more closely. "Not exactly period accurate, but Dr. Huxley did a good job."

"What's the prognosis, Doc?" Cabrillo asked.

Huxley shot Kevin a glance. Technically, patient confidentiality rules forbade her to answer, but Kevin gave her a wink. The *Oregon* crew were like family.

"The bullet passed clean through, but that hollow-point slug did quite a bit of damage—bones, muscle, tendons, nerves. I put things back together as best I could and stopped the bleeding. But he needs a level of care I can't provide on this ship and he needs it right away. James Heiskell is the best orthopedic hand surgeon in the world. His clinic is in San Diego. I've already reached out to him."

"How soon can we move Kevin?"

"Jimmy's rearranging his schedule so we can get him on his table tomorrow afternoon."

Juan turned to Linda. "Make the travel arrangements with Max and Gomez, pronto."

"On it." Linda sped for the door.

"What's my long-term outlook, Dr. Huxley?" Kevin asked.

Huxley forced a smile. "You probably won't lose the hand."

"But I won't get it fully back, either, will I?"

Huxley laid a hand on Kevin's shoulder. "If anyone can work a miracle, it's Jimmy." She turned to Cabrillo. "I need to forward Kevin's complete medical records to him. I'll be back shortly."

Huxley's departure left just Cabrillo and Nixon in the room.

"Need anything?" Juan asked.

"I'm guessing forgiveness."

"I'm not sure if I should keelhaul you or kiss you for what you did."

"Kinda nutso, I know. But I just figured one broken-down makeup artist wasn't as important as the captain of the *Oregon*."

"I couldn't disagree more. That was a heck of a thing you did. I'm more grateful than you know."

"Seemed like the right thing to do."

"You could've gotten yourself killed."

Kevin chuckled. "For a moment there, I thought I was a goner. Just glad I didn't soil my skivvies." Nixon laid his head back down on his pillow and closed his eyes. He was still groggy from the anesthesia. In just moments, he fell back to sleep.

Cabrillo slipped away, not wanting to disturb him. But he stopped in the doorway, remembering the last time he'd visited Kevin's private quarters. A framed photo of Nixon's beloved sister stood on the nightstand by his bed. Juan had picked it up and studied it closely. They were fraternal twins, and according to Kevin, very close. Etched into the frame was his sister's favorite saying:

There is no greater way to love than to give your life for your friends.

Cabrillo thought that fit Kevin to a T.

And the rest of his crew, too.